Because there was no other answer he could make, Robert drew her into his arms. He felt her breath shudder through her. For a long time they stood together in the still warmth of the late afternoon, sharing a comfort that neither dared put into words.

But the moment could not last. Not when her shoulder brushed the naked skin at the open neck of his shirt. Not when the fragrance of her skin assaulted his senses. With weary disgust, Robert felt his body hardening against her own. He could not even offer her simple comfort without sparking the flame of lust. He drew back, knowing he had to put her from him.

But Emma would not let him go.

He could deny himself, but not her. With an impatience born of denial, he tugged at the ribbons on her hat. It fell to the floor. He slid his fingers into her hair, sending a hail of pins after the hat. Her lips parted. Unable to contain himself any longer, he lowered his head to her own.

The world receded until nothing was left but the magic that was Emma. He was drowning in it and knew himself willingly lost.

Eyes shut, arms close around her, he brushed his lips against the corner of her mouth, her temple, the hair curling back from her forehead.

"Robert." Her arm tightened around his neck. Her voice held a note of desperation. "Don't stop. Don't let me go."

Dell Books by Tracy Grant

SHADOWS OF THE HEART
SHORES OF DESIRE

Shores
of Desire

Tracy Grant

A Dell Book

Published by
Dell Publishing
a division of
Bantam Doubleday Dell Publishing Group, Inc.
1540 Broadway
New York, New York 10036

The trademark Dell® is registered in the U.S. Patent and Trademark Office.

ISBN: 0-440-22168-4

Printed in the United States of America

Published simultaneously in Canada

November 1997

10 9 8 7 6 5 4 3 2 1

OPM

*For Kyle, who will appreciate the good
sportsmanship,
Ross, who will appreciate the battles,
And Devlin, who will appreciate everything else*

ACKNOWLEDGMENTS

I would like to thank a number of people who helped me along the way in the writing of *Shores of Desire:* my editor, Laura Cifelli, for her support and encouragement and for helping make the book inestimably better; my agent, Ruth Cohen, for always being there for me; Pamela Collins, Madeleine Mills, Kate Moore, Joanne Pence, Monica Sevy, and Barbara Truax, for invaluable feedback and advice; my friends Jim and Penny, for always being ready to listen; my father, Doug, for putting up with my preoccupation and frequent panic and generally taking care of me; my late mother, Joan, whose spirit is definitely in this book; and finally Gemma, Fiona, Alessa, Midnight, and Lescaut, for being wonderful distractions.

Prologue

It was a fool's errand. Robert Lescaut drew his cloak more tightly around himself and walked toward the lights at the end of the dark, rain-drenched street. This was the fourth inn he had entered in his search for his errant wife.

A chilling gust of wind blew back the hood of his cloak, bringing with it the salt smell of the sea. Robert pushed open the door and entered the warm, smoky interior of the inn. He stripped off his sodden cloak and let his eyes adjust to the sudden light.

The room was long, with a low, blackened ceiling. At one side a stairway rose to the floor above. A dozen or so men and three or four women sat drinking at the tables. A noisy quarrel at the far end of the room stopped abruptly at his entrance. The men eyed him with the wary curiosity accorded strangers. The women looked at him with unfeigned interest, their attention apparently caught by his uniform. One of them, no longer young, rose from the table at which she had been sitting and came toward him. Robert shook his head, and she returned to her table, tossing her head in annoyance.

He did not think it likely he would find Lucie in such a place, although his wife had frequently surprised him. After seven years of marriage he knew her little better than he had on their wedding day.

The proprietor threaded his way through the tables and stopped before him. What, he wanted to know, was the gentleman's pleasure.

"I'm looking for a woman."

The proprietor, a fleshy-faced man with a greasy black moustache, raised his brows and gestured to the room behind him.

"A particular woman," Robert said. "She came to meet someone. She would have asked for a room. Young, well dressed. Dark hair, deep blue eyes. She's very beautiful. You would remember her."

The proprietor eyed the insignia that showed Robert was an officer in the Imperial French Army. "A friend, Captain?"

"A wife. I've come to take her home."

"Ah, in that case . . ." The proprietor nodded in understanding. "Come this way. She has a room above."

"Is she alone?"

"That I cannot say. People come and go. I don't keep track of them all. But yes, she had a visitor earlier this evening. I didn't see his face and I didn't see him go. Do you want me to inquire?"

"I'll come with you."

The proprietor shrugged his shoulders as though to say it was all the same to him, but he hoped the gentleman would not be violent.

Robert followed him up the narrow stairs, thinking of Paul's warning. "She's gone to Ostend," his cousin had told him. "I don't know why. She knew you were coming home on leave."

"Philippe?" Robert had asked. It made no sense. Lucie had no need to leave Paris to see the soft, handsome young aristo who by all reports had been her lover the past year.

"He's dead, Robert. Knifed and robbed and left to die in the streets less than two months ago. Lucie's been distraught."

Not Philippe, then. Yet she must have come to meet someone. Another lover? No, not so soon. Lucie was fickle and unpredictable, but her passions, though fleeting, ran deep. Something was wrong, Paul had said, his eyes dark with worry. Paul did not worry without cause. Robert left at once for Ostend.

A half-dozen doors opened off the corridor at the head of the stairs. The proprietor led him to one set a little apart. "The lady wanted privacy," he said with a knowing smirk.

The proprietor stank of wine and tobacco and garlic and seemed to notice nothing amiss as they reached the door. Robert, used to life in the field, recognized it at once, the faint but unmistakable smell of blood. He pushed past the proprietor and threw open the door.

She was lying on the floor near the bed, her white dress slashed and bloody. Robert flung himself down beside her and took her in his arms. She was alive. He gave thanks to a God he did not believe in and gathered her closer. "Lucie. Lucie."

Her eyes, glazed with pain and shock, widened in recognition. Robert turned his head toward the proprietor, who was standing transfixed in the doorway. "Get a doctor." He probed the wound gently, trying to ascertain its extent. There was more than one. The man, whoever he was, had stabbed her in the chest repeatedly.

He stroked her face, leaving trails of blood on her hair and cheek. "Who did this, Lucie? Who?"

She struggled to speak. Blood bubbled from her lips and spilled out the corner of her mouth. Her hand, with infinite slowness, moved to a blue velvet ribbon she wore around her throat. Robert pulled it from the neck of her dress. On the ribbon was a ring, the silver ring too large for her to wear that he had seen among her possessions shortly after their marriage. She had told him it was her father's and refused to say any more. He had believed her then. Now he was sure of nothing she had told him—that she was a Scotswoman, that she had fled her family, that her name was Lucie Sorel.

Robert looked at the ring, wondering what had induced her to wear it this day. Then he suddenly knew why she had come to this lonely inn. The man she met must have come by boat, most likely from Scotland. He held the ring before her face. "Is this who attacked you? Tell me, Lucie. Give me a sign."

She tried once more to speak. The blood frothed again from her mouth. She lifted her hand. Robert gave her the ring and closed her fingers around it. She made a slight movement of her head, her eyes never leaving his face. How strange that now, in extremity, she could look at him with perfect trust.

He thought to move her to the bed but feared the wounds would bleed afresh. It was too late for Lucie. He knew it by the tears streaming down his face. He held her gently, scarce daring to breathe, until the life fled from her eyes.

For a moment he was suspended in time, feeling nothing at all. Then he was engulfed by a flood of remorse and guilt and a growing, terrible anger. He had trapped her into a marriage she did not want. At the least he had owed her his protection. "Lucie," he whispered, and made a silent vow.

I'll avenge you, my wife.
For the sake of our son.
For the sake of what might have been between us.
I swear it.

"Charlie Lauder, may your soul rot in everlasting hell. What are you doing with Blair cattle?" Emma Blair picked up the folds of her cloak and ran down the streambank to the gully where Charlie lay sprawled, half hidden by a stand of scarlet-berried rowan.

"Don't yell at him, Mama. I think he's hurt." Emma's daughter Kirsty scrambled beside her, boots crackling over gorse and bracken.

"I didn't take them, Emma love." Charlie's voice came from the rowan. "I was trying to bring them in. You want them back, don't you?"

"We didn't want them out in the first place." Emma reached the rocky streambed and stopped short as she saw the cause of Charlie's distress. He was pinned beneath a fallen rowan tree. "Wretched boy." She dropped to her knees beside him and wiped his sweating face with a handkerchief. "Are you badly hurt?"

Charlie began to shake his head then stopped as though the movement pained him. "It's my shoulder. My arm's gone numb."

"That's all right." Kirsty was kneeling opposite Emma. "Mama's good at fixing people who are hurt."

For a sensible child of seven, Kirsty had rather too much faith in her mother's abilities. Emma summoned up a smile. "First things first. We have to get you out from under this tree." She tested the weight of the rowan. The bark chafed her hands through the York tan of her gloves. The tree wouldn't budge. "I'll have to go for help. Fortunately the Blair men are all out on the estate. Looking for our cattle."

Charlie grimaced. "I told Matt and Archie not to cut the hedge, but they wouldn't listen. After they left I slipped out to see if there was aught I could do. These were all the cattle I found." He indicated the dozen or so cows standing on the opposite bank, their gentle lowing the only sign of their agitation. "Then I saw the calf there and came down to get it out."

For the first time, Emma noticed the half-grown calf standing just beyond the bend in the stream, its legs trapped among the loose rocks of the streambed. "That's how you fell?"

"More the fool am I. The rocks were slippery and then the bloody tree came down on top of me."

Emma pushed his unruly dark hair back from his forehead. "You're a better man than your brothers, Charlie Lauder."

A flurry of powdery snowflakes blew against them, carried by the biting north wind. Emma glanced about. Even with luck on her side, it could be over an hour before she found help and returned to Charlie. She should try to build a fire before she left. And even then—

"Someone's coming, Mama." Kirsty was looking up the bank.

Emma followed her daughter's gaze. Then she heard it too. Footsteps on the hard, frozen ground. Thank God. Some of the other searchers had found them.

Shores of Desire

A moment later two figures appeared on the streambank. Emma shaded her eyes with her hand, squinting against the wintry afternoon light. A tall man wrapped in a cloak and a shorter, slighter figure who looked more like a boy. Neither was from Blair House. Still, she would take what help she could get. "There's an injured man here," she called.

"We'll be right there." The man had a pleasant, flexible voice and his accent was unmistakably English. There was a thud of booted feet and a swift blur of movement and he and the boy were kneeling beside them.

The man grasped hold of the rowan. "We'll have you out of here in a moment. David, give me a hand."

The man and boy braced their legs and lifted the end of the rowan to the man's shoulder. The man motioned the boy aside, straightened up slowly, raised the tree until it was upright, and sent it crashing into the stream, rather in the manner of a Scotsman tossing the caber at Highland games.

Charlie grunted and tried to get up.

"Don't move." Emma pushed him back on the ground. "Take a breath. Is it painful?"

Charlie nodded.

"I'd venture you've a couple of cracked ribs." She opened Charlie's coat and waistcoat and explored his shoulder. Charlie yelped. "It's out of joint." Emma looked at the man. "Can you reset it?"

"Here now," Charlie said. "It's my shoulder."

"And you should want it reset as much as anyone." Emma continued to look at the man. "Can you?"

"Yes." He looked down at Charlie. "But it's going to hurt."

Charlie gave a weak grin. "Looks as if there aren't any alternatives. Fire away."

The man turned back to Emma. "We'll need to remove his coat so I can see what I'm doing."

This process caused Charlie to curse and cry out in pain. Emma leaned on his chest while the man grasped his arm, held it upright, and pulled. There was a satisfying crack accompanied by a gasp from Charlie. His face broke out in fresh sweat and he began to shiver. "All done," the man said. "You'll be right as a fiddle in no time. But don't put strain on it for a few days or you'll have it out again."

Emma eased Charlie into a sitting position. "His ribs should be bound."

"Use my cravat." The man stripped off the length of muslin and helped her wind it tightly around Charlie's chest.

Emma sat back on her heels. "I'll see to the calf." But she turned to see Kirsty ankle-deep in the stream, leading the freed calf to the opposite bank. The boy, David, a thin, dark-haired lad, pushed the calf from behind.

"Your daughter?" the man asked.

Emma nodded. "Kirsty. Your son?"

"Yes. David." He held out his hand. "My name's Melton. Robert Melton."

"I'm Emma Blair." Emma clasped his hand. His fingers closed around her own in a strong, firm grip. She had a brief impression of chestnut hair, gray eyes and sturdy, blunt features. Then he gave a quick, easy smile that transformed his face as if candles had flared to life in a darkened room.

He released her hand, yet she could still feel the imprint of his fingers on her own. She reached up to smooth her hair, then let her hand fall to her side. "This is Charlie Lauder."

"I'm in disgrace," Charlie said. "It was my brothers who cut the hedge and let the cattle out."

"It's a long story," Emma said in response to the question in Robert Melton's eyes. "Kirsty," she called, "is the calf injured?"

"She's all right. How's Charlie?"

"He'll do. Take the animals up the bank and keep them there." Emma turned to Charlie. "Can you stand if we help you?"

"I've been trying to stand for the last quarter hour." With Emma on one side and Robert Melton on the other, Charlie managed to clamber to his feet. At last he stood leaning against the trunk of a rowan tree, his pale skin paler than usual, his tousled hair sable dark in contrast. His teeth were chattering with cold and the effects of pain. Melton drew off his cloak and wrapped it around the boy. "Bad day to be without a warm cloak."

"Left mine on my horse. Didn't want it to get in the way." Charlie lurched and might have fallen had Melton not put out an arm to restrain him.

"Can you walk?"

"Of course. I can ride too." Charlie's voice held a note of disdain. Then he looked up and gave Melton a shy grin. "I'm all right, truly. Thanks. For everything." He looked at Emma. "I haven't thanked you, either, have I? You know I do."

They moved slowly up the stream and climbed the bank to where Kirsty and David waited with the animals. The errant calf was now nuzzling her mother. David and Kirsty had also retrieved the horses, including a gray mare Emma recognized as Charlie's.

Charlie mounted with Melton's assistance, swayed in the saddle, then with obvious effort, pulled himself erect and grasped the reins. "I'm fit," he insisted, his blue eyes defiant. "Fit enough to help you take the cattle in."

Emma bit back an instinctive retort. "I'll be glad of your help. Ride up front with Kirsty and David. I'll ride in the rear with Mr. Melton." She turned to Robert Melton. "You'll come back to Blair House with us, I trust. It's the least we can do after you rendered us such help."

"Thank you, Mrs. Blair. We'd—" He hesitated as though perhaps about to say more. "We'd be honored."

The cows moved unhurriedly, their udders full, their great weight cracking the frozen grass. The air had turned colder, and the folds of the Pentland Hills shimmered blue in the distance. Robert Melton said nothing until the cows had lengthened their line, and he and Emma were out of earshot. Then he turned to her with a smile. "You're a trusting woman, Mrs. Blair. No questions about why David and I are wandering around on Blair land?"

Emma laughed and felt the tension rush from her body. "I've been too busy being grateful for your appearance. Did you lose your way in the storm?"

"More or less. The landlord at the inn in the village told us about a shortcut off the main road. David was asking me if we were lost when we heard voices from the streambed."

"Where were you bound?"

His smile deepened, showing an unexpected dimple. "Blair House."

She should have guessed, but visitors were rare at Blair House. Especially interesting visitors. A charge went through her that was part surprise, part delight. "You were coming to see us?"

His face grew serious. "To pay my respects to your family. I knew Allan Blair in Spain. Unless there are two Emma Blairs, I think he must have been your husband."

"Yes." Emma tightened her grip on the reins.

"I'm sorry." Melton's eyes warmed with sympathy. "I wish there was more I could say. But if there are words that ease such a grief, I have yet to discover them."

Emma forced a smile to her lips. "I've had more than two years to come to terms with Allan's death. It's the way of war, Mr. Melton. My father was killed fighting in India. My brother Jamie and my cousin Will fought in the

Peninsula along with Allan. Blair men have been soldiers
for centuries. Blair women are expected to accept it with
good Scots fortitude. Somehow I never mastered the
knack."

"I should confess that I'm a soldier myself. Captain
Melton of the 52nd."

"Oh, dear." She managed to make her voice light.
"And here I thought you were a man of sense."

"All I can say in my defense is that I joined up when I
was very young."

He was smiling again. His eyes shifted from gray to
blue with the changing light. Emma glanced away and
tugged at the hood of her cloak. She was being a fool. He
had a son, riding up ahead with Kirsty. And a wife no
doubt. Mrs. Melton, wherever she was, was a lucky
woman. "You've come a long way to pay your respects,
Captain Melton. You're not a Scotsman, are you?"

"No, I'm from Devon. But David and I were visiting
friends in Durham over the holidays. With the war, we've
had little time together. We thought we'd see something
of Scotland."

"Your wife is a generous woman to spare you."

The smile left his eyes. "My wife died three years ago."

"I'm sorry." Emma bit her lip. "And here I've been
sounding mawkish about Allan. How very self-indulgent
of me."

"On the contrary. My wife would have understood exactly how you feel."

Emma stared down at her hands. There were shards of
bark on her gloves. She brushed them off. She was sorry
about his wife, truly. Yet she could not deny that suddenly the snow seemed whiter, the air crisper and
cleaner, the scent of the pine trees sharper. And all because she was alone with an eligible man, an attractive
man, for the first time in more months than she cared to
count.

An eligible, attractive man who had come to Blair House because he knew her husband. "The 52nd wasn't Allan's regiment," she said, her gaze still on her hands. "Where did you meet?"

"In a village near Ciudad Rodrigo in '12. We shared a supper of stale bread and moldy cheese and some quite tolerable wine the villagers had managed to keep from the depredations of the French."

For a moment, her memory of Allan was so strong she could almost smell the cedar of his shaving soap. "If I know my husband, he was the one who found the wine."

Melton grinned. "As a matter of fact he was. We spent the better part of a week evading the French and traveling back to our battalions. Allan invited me to visit him if I was ever in Scotland." Melton paused, then added, "He told me he had a very beautiful wife whom he missed very much."

Emma looked him full in the face. "You're a liar, Captain Melton."

Melton raised his brows.

"I appreciate the sentiment," Emma said, "but I'm sure Allan never said anything of the kind."

Melton was silent for a moment. "If he didn't say it, he should have."

Their eyes met. There was an intensity in his gaze that made it impossible to look away, an intensity that came not from the color of his eyes but from something within them. Her breathing quickened. Her lips parted as though in anticipation of a kiss.

"Mama." Kirsty's voice was carried back on the wind. "Shall we go to the barns?"

Hot color flooded Emma's face. She hadn't even noticed that they'd reached the rise of ground above Blair House. "Yes," she called. Her body still felt warm from the pressure of Robert Melton's gaze. Her lips tingled as though she had been kissed. She was conscious of a strong wish that she had been.

"Blair House?" Melton asked.

His voice was neutral, polite. She risked a glance at him, but he was looking at the house below. Perhaps the moment had meant nothing to him. Oh, the devil. She was behaving like a giddy schoolgirl, not a widow of seven-and-twenty.

She fixed her gaze on the familiar pile of the house, half hidden behind stands of beech and oak, their bare branches making a black tracery against the soft tawny color of the stones. "The corner tower dates back to the fourteenth century," she said, then wished she hadn't. Her attempt to smooth over the moment merely drew attention to its awkwardness. "You'll stay the night with us, Captain Melton." Worse and worse. She swallowed and forged on. "Sir Angus will want to talk to you. Allan's father."

Melton glanced ahead at Charlie Lauder, riding between Kirsty and David. "I fear we've come at an awkward time."

"No more than most." Emma turned her horse toward the barns, where Kirsty was leading them. "You've got to understand us, Captain Melton. Lauders and Blairs have been feuding and killing each other for nigh on four hundred years. But we're neighbors. The children grow up together, scrapping and fighting, and the women struggle for a bit of sanity, and the men nurse their grievances and issue their challenges and go to their deaths happily if they can provoke or mortify their neighbors in the process. God in heaven, I wish they'd grow up."

"Sir Angus?"

"As hot-tempered and unreasonable as the rest."

"A difficult family to marry into."

"I had the dubious fortune to be born into it. Sir

Angus is my uncle. He raised my brother and me after our parents died."

They were nearing the barns. The cattle, as though aware of approaching shelter, quickened their pace. The snow had dampened their coats to a deep glossy red, and their breath steamed in the frigid air. The children stayed in the lead, but Charlie pulled aside to let the cattle pass.

"They'll be safe enough now, Em," he said when she and Melton reached him. "I'll be on my way."

"You'll do nothing of the kind," Emma returned. "You'll come with us where we can keep an eye on you, or you're likely to fall from the saddle and we'll have your death on our hands. There's whisky and hot soup and a bed at Blair House. I'll send a message to your father. You'll stay the night."

"I can't do that." Charlie's finely chiseled features seemed sharper than usual, his nose more aquiline, his chin more stubborn. "Not after today."

"I'll take care of my uncle, if that's what you're thinking. Captain Melton, stay with him. If he dares make a move, knock him out and tie him behind your saddle."

Emma wheeled her horse and rode ahead to meet the cowherd who was not pleased to see a Lauder on Blair land. By the time she had calmed his anger and turned the cattle over to him, it was growing dark. When they finally rode into the courtyard of Blair House, the wind was blowing fiercely, driving the snow into their faces. Neither Kirsty nor David showed any sign of fatigue, but Charlie slid from his horse and would have fallen had Melton not steadied him.

Two stableboys appeared to lead the horses away. Charlie shrugged off Melton's supporting arm. Emma picked up her cloak and led the way to the house.

They had only gone a few steps when they heard the clatter of approaching hoofbeats. Emma bit back a curse as she turned to see her brother, Jamie, ride into the courtyard, accompanied by her cousins Will and Arabel.

There was no time for greetings or introductions. Jamie's gaze swept the group in the courtyard. "You thieving bastard." He swung down from his horse and hurled himself on Charlie.

2

Jamie's fist smashed into Charlie's chest. Charlie staggered back with a grunt of pain. Arabel screamed. Emma
ran forward. "Jamie, no, he's hurt."

Jamie drew back his arm to launch another blow. Melton seized him by the shoulders.

Jamie whirled in Melton's grasp, his hand raised. Melton caught his wrist in midair. "Easy. My name's not
Lauder."

"Take your bloody hands off my cousin." Will's booted
feet thudded against the ground as he swung down from
his horse.

Melton tightened his grip on Jamie. "Young Lauder
didn't cut the hedge. He helped rescue the cattle and got
a shoulder out of joint and a pair of cracked ribs for his
trouble."

Charlie drew a shuddering breath. "I can fight my own
battles, Melton."

"What happened?" Jamie turned to stare at Charlie.
"Decide this time you'd gone too far?"

Charlie flushed but did not look away. "I didn't cut the
hedge. I'd never do anything so stupid. But Matt and
Archie had cause. You dammed up the burn and flooded
our east meadow."

Angry color suffused Jamie's face. "Why you miserable—" He lunged forward. Melton pulled him back.

"Stay the hell out of this." Will grabbed Melton from behind. Jamie broke free.

"Stop it, all of you." Emma ran between Jamie and Charlie. The blow Jamie intended for Charlie caught her beneath the chin. She fell hard on the snow-covered flagstones.

"Uncle Jamie!" Kirsty ran to Emma. "You hurt Mama."

Arabel sprang down from her horse. "Jamie, you monster."

Melton pulled free of Will's grasp and knelt beside Emma. "Are you all right, Mrs. Blair?"

Emma nodded. Her jaw smarted, and the impact of her fall reverberated through her body. But the concern in Melton's eyes steadied her. She gave him her hands, and he took them in a warm clasp and helped her to her feet.

The others had gone very still. A gust of wind ripped through the courtyard, intensifying the flurry of snowflakes. "I'm sorry, Em," Jamie said. "But what the devil did you mean by getting in the way?"

"What the devil did you mean by raising your hand against an injured man?" Emma looked at Melton. "This scapegrace is my brother, Jamie. The man who grabbed you so unceremoniously is our cousin Will. The girl who looks as if she'd like to strangle him is his sister Arabel." She fixed her brother and cousin with a hard stare—lithe, auburn-haired Jamie and sturdy, red-blond Will, twins in their stubborn pigheadedness. "This is Captain Melton of the 52nd, a friend of Allan's. He and his son, David, were a great help this afternoon. They're staying the night. So is Charlie."

Jamie's brows snapped together. "See here, Em—"

"You'd best get your horses stabled," Emma said in a

voice that dared him to contradict her. "Charlie, let's get you in out of the cold."

"I'll help him, Em. You can see Captain Melton and David settled." Arabel went to Charlie's side, strands of fair hair escaping the hood of her cloak and swinging about her with defiance as she moved past Jamie and Will.

Arabel and Charlie started for the house. Jamie cast a look after them that was pure venom. Then, shoulders firmly set, he and Will led the horses toward the stable.

"Come on." Kirsty tugged at David's hand. "We'll show you the house."

Emma turned to Robert Melton. "I'd like to tell you that was an aberration, but I'm afraid we're every bit as wild as we seem. Welcome to Blair House, Captain Melton."

Emma pulled the door of her bedchamber closed behind her and leaned against the oak panels. Her legs ached from hours in the saddle, her temples throbbed, and her jaw smarted where Jamie had struck her. But there was a tingling in her nerve endings, a sense of expectation welling up in her chest. The image of laughing blue-gray eyes and a brilliant smile danced in her mind.

She turned to her dressing table mirror and grimaced. Her hair fell about her face in a tangled windblown mass, her gown was crumpled and streaked with dirt, her jaw marked by Jamie's fist. She stripped off her soiled dress and crumpled chemise, unlaced her sodden boots, peeled off her damp stockings. She put on a clean lavender-scented chemise and a pair of silk stockings that were mercifully free of snags, poured water into the pink flowered china basin and scrubbed her face. But when she went to the wardrobe and reached for a fresh gown, she hesitated. Her favorite blue merino looked unexpectedly sober tonight.

Emma returned the dress to the wardrobe and reached into the back for a brilliant green silk. The dress was cut simply, but the fabric felt delicious, and the color made her hair a richer auburn and her eyes a deeper green. The skirt was trimmed with a band of rich braid, the long sleeves ended in lavish falls of lace, and the neck was low enough to make her feel like a woman. When she'd ordered the gown three years ago, she'd been thinking of Allan, determined that when he returned home they would put the past behind them and get on with their lives. But Allan had not come home.

"Em?" Jamie's voice came from the corridor. He stepped into the room, still wearing his mud-spattered riding clothes. "I'm sorry."

Emma hunted in the bottom of the wardrobe for a pair of green silk slippers with ivory rosettes. "So you said."

"Damnation, Em, you know I'd never hurt you."

She put on the slippers, straightened up, and looked at her brother. "You did hurt me, Jamie. Quite a lot." She put her hand to the mark on her jaw and winced. "That's where this stupid feud leads."

"That's what happens when you insist on interfering in things you don't understand." He stared at her for a moment, his eyes narrowing. "You're very fine tonight. What's the occasion?"

"I felt like it." She sat at her dressing table and applied powder liberally over the red mark.

"Putting on fine feathers for our English guest?" Jamie flung himself into a high-backed chair. "How much do you know about this Melton fellow?"

"He knew Allan in the Peninsula." She added rouge for good measure, hoping to distract attention from the results of Jamie's blow.

"Did Allan write to you about him?"

"Allan never wrote me much about anything." Emma splashed on some scent and dragged a brush through her tangled hair.

The chair creaked as Jamie leaned back, probably soiling the upholstery with his muddy coat and breeches. "Don't you think it's odd?"

"Don't I think what is odd?" She twisted her hair up, leaving the ends free to fall to her shoulders.

"Melton showing up here like this."

"Why shouldn't he look up Allan's family?" She took a handful of hairpins from a silver box on her dressing table.

The door opened again. "Em—" Arabel stuck her head around the door. "Oh, it's you." She stopped at the sight of Jamie.

Jamie looked up at her. "What do you think of this Melton fellow, Bel?"

"He has an indecently attractive smile. Why can't you and Will invite friends like that to stay?" Arabel moved into the room. "Charlie's asleep, Em."

"That's another thing." Jamie sprang to his feet. "What the devil possessed you to bring that whelp into the house?"

"Kindness." Emma stuck a pin into her hair. "It seems to be in short supply in this family. Go and change, Jamie. You're not fit for the dining room."

Jamie stood over her, taut with anger. "Good God, Em, doesn't what the Lauders did bother you?"

"Bother me?" Emma swung around to look at him. "Of course it bothers me. We lost cattle. Our people could have been injured. Charlie could have died if we hadn't found him before nightfall. But if you hadn't dammed up the burn, Charlie's brothers wouldn't have cut the hedge. For God's sake, don't let it go any further."

Jamie tossed his head with bravado and reached for the door handle. "Don't worry, Em. Leave it to the men."

The door closed behind him. Emma looked at Arabel. "I can't imagine any words that would make me feel less confident."

Arabel grimaced. "Does Da know Charlie's in the house?"

"Not yet." Emma anchored her hair with a last pin and got to her feet. "Want to give me moral support while I tell him?"

"The way the Blair men are acting you don't need support, you need protection." Arabel paused in front of the glass to adjust the skirt of her gown. Her primrose sarcenet gown, Emma noticed, with melon sleeves, the gown Arabel had ordered specially for their uncle Gavin's party this last Hogmanay. It seemed like only yesterday Arabel had been playing tag with the stableboys and coming to Emma to bandage her scraped knees. Now she was twenty, taller than Emma, and with her riot of red-gold hair and brilliant blue eyes, more dazzling than Emma had ever hoped to be. And she, too, had noticed Robert Melton's smile. Emma put her hand to her face, feeling the dry skin around her eyes.

"Ready?" Arabel turned from the mirror.

"Ready." Emma gave herself a mental shake. Competing for men with Arabel. She'd be growing jealous of Kirsty next.

She and Arabel walked around the gallery and down the open-well staircase. Soft candlelight and a booming voice greeted them as they entered the sitting room. "I'll not have that devil's spawn in my house, d'ye hear me?"

Angus Blair's angry presence seemed to overflow the dark-paneled, low-ceilinged room. His fierce, bushy eyebrows were drawn low. His blue eyes were as hard as the leaded glass panes of the sitting room windows. Even his sandy hair seemed to stand on end.

Arabel strode toward him, hands on her hips. "You've

got no heart in you, Da. And no sense either. You're as bad as Will and Jamie."

Emma stepped between the combatants. "I wouldn't go that far, Bel. Uncle Angus, you don't really want Charlie to freeze to death."

"I never said I wished the lad harm." Angus's voice was gruff. "I just don't want him under my roof."

"Where else is he supposed to go?" Arabel demanded.

"Pipe down, Bel." Jamie strode into the room, Will at his side. "Do you think Lord Lauder would take Will or me in if we were hurt?"

"I'm sure he would," Emma said. "Just as I'm sure Uncle Angus wouldn't really throw Charlie out in the snow."

Angus opened his mouth as though to argue, then closed it. Emma couldn't believe her uncle had given in so easily. Then she realized Angus was looking beyond her. She turned to see Robert Melton standing in the doorway, Kirsty and David beside him.

Emma felt the oddest rush of relief. She had known Melton a scant few hours, yet she looked on him as an ally. She met his gaze and saw a glow in his eyes she would swear was admiration. A warmth spread through her that was part self-consciousness, part pleasure. "Don't mind the noise." She walked forward, enjoying the swirl of her skirts and the feel of her hair stirring against her neck. "We're always like this. Come and meet my uncle."

"Any friend of Allan's is welcome here for as long as he wants to stay." Angus cut short her introductions, shook Melton by the hand, and gave David a hearty buffet on the shoulder. "Fine young lad ye've got there."

Jamie moved away from the fireplace. "I understand you fought in Spain, Melton."

"Yes, with the 52nd. Allan told me you and your cousin"—Robert nodded at Will—"are both in the cavalry. I'm flattered you'll stoop to dine with an infantryman. You aren't worried the taint might rub off?"

Jamie gave a reluctant smile, then looked as if he was annoyed at having been tricked into doing so. "You're stationed in England now?"

"No, my battalion is part of the Army of Occupation in the Netherlands. But my colonel was good enough to give me leave to come home. I hadn't seen my son in over a year."

"Will and I are on leave, too. But we're stationed in England."

The two men faced each other, Jamie in a black coat and cream-colored breeches, Melton still in riding dress, though his boots had been brushed and the fresh cravat she had had sent in to him was neatly tied. Jamie looked as if he wanted to pick a fight and wasn't sure how. Melton returned his glare with an affable smile and a quizzical lift of his brows.

"The important thing is you're all safe home now." Angus waved Melton and David to seats by the fire. "And that monster Bonaparte is packed away on Elba where he belongs. By God, Wellington's a good general. Pity he's an Irishman and not a Scot."

"It's a pity he isn't here to keep the peace." Arabel perched on a footstool. "Jamie and Will don't know what to do with themselves without any Frenchmen to shoot. They have to shoot Lauders instead. Does someone have to be killed before you'll stop?"

"Don't be stupid, Bel." Will kicked a fallen log back into the fireplace, letting loose a shower of sparks. "Seems to me you've forgotten what your name is."

"I know what my name is. I don't want to see it dishonored."

Jamie brought his fist down on the mantel. "No one is going to dishonor the Blair name."

Arabel glared at him. "I suppose that means you'll go out and take your revenge for today."

Will stared into the fire. Jamie moved to a chair, sat down, and crossed his legs with deliberate unconcern.

Arabel turned to Emma. "Say something, Em, they're only going to make things worse."

Emma was sitting in a high-backed chair. Her fingers closed on the chair arms. She glanced at Robert Melton and was surprised to find that he was looking at her, not Arabel and Will and Jamie. What she saw in his eyes helped her moderate her voice. "I've already said a great deal."

Arabel turned to Angus. "Da?"

Angus leaned back in his chair. "I'm sure they won't let things get out of hand, lass."

"You mean you don't care what they do as long as you don't know about it."

Will looked up from the fire. "If you and Emma hadn't brought Charlie Lauder into the house—"

"Quiet, all of you." Angus's voice echoed through the room. "Young Lauder can stay in the house for the night. Don't push me further, Bel." He looked meaningfully at Jamie and Will. "No one will lay a hand on him while he's under our roof. For the rest, I trust to your judgment."

The door opened again, this time to admit one of the footmen. Emma got to her feet. "Dinner. How fortuitous. Your arm, Captain Melton?"

"It's not like I expected." David drew his feet up under the bedclothes and wrapped his arms around his knees. "I thought I'd hate them."

"Things are rarely so straightforward." Robert sat on the edge of the bed and smoothed the blue-and-red quilt. It was a boy's quilt, with geometric military shapes, slightly faded but still colorful. Emma Blair had been thoughtful in arranging David's room.

David plucked at a frayed thread on the quilt. "Kirsty seems friendly. So does Mrs. Blair." He looked up at Robert. "She reminds me of—"

"I know." Robert laid his hand over David's own. For a moment when he first looked at Emma Blair, he had thought he was looking at his dead wife. The long oval face, the pointed chin, the luminous eyes, the wild tumble of hair. A second glance had shown him where he was wrong. Emma Blair's nose was a shade longer than Lucie's, her mouth wider and fuller, her hair auburn not sable brown, her eyes gray-green not dark blue. "It was a shock to see her," Robert said. "You handled it well."

"So we must be right, mustn't we?" David's blue eyes—Lucie's eyes—were wide and candid. "Maman must have been a Blair."

"Yes." Robert's fingers tightened for a moment around David's own. "One way or another she must have been."

The wind howled outside the shuttered windows. The house creaked and sighed in response. David settled back against the pillows. "I know I don't like Jamie. Or Will. But Mrs. Blair and Kirsty— I got squirmy inside when we lied to them."

Robert looked down at their linked hands, his own sun-darkened and crisscrossed by a scar, David's softer, smoother, infinitely more fragile. "It's never pleasant telling lies. But sometimes it's justified."

A drop of wax fell from the candle on the bedside table and pooled in the base of the brass candlestick. David studied Robert in the flickering candlelight. "You talked just like you were an English soldier and you were glad that we lost the war and Napoleon was exiled. I almost believed you really knew Kirsty's father in Spain."

"The trick is not to say too much."

David continued to watch him. "You've pretended to

be an English officer a lot, haven't you? When you were a—when you worked in intelligence."

"When I was a spy." Robert smiled, but he could feel the cynicism in the curl of his mouth. "No sense in wrapping plain facts in clean linen."

David's level brows drew together. "Everyone has spies. There's nothing wrong with spying for your own side."

Robert could hear his own mother's voice in his son's words. Anne Lescaut, an Englishwoman by birth, had taught both Robert and David to speak the language without an accent. She had also filled her grandson's head with all manner of nonsense about his soldier father. It was as well that David began to learn the reality of the life his father had led. And so, against his better judgment, Robert had brought the boy with him to Scotland.

David folded his arms behind his head. "I did like you said at dinner. Asked questions but didn't make it look too obvious. Sir Angus has two more children besides Will and Arabel. There's a boy named Neil—he's the oldest—who has a sheep farm ten miles from here. And there's a girl named Jenny who's married to a lawyer in Edinburgh."

"You know more about the Blairs than I do."

"Kirsty told me. Sir Angus has a younger brother who lives in Edinburgh too. Kirsty has lots of uncles and aunts and cousins." David's eyes grew dark. "But none of it explains where Maman fits in, does it?"

Robert tucked the quilt around his son. "It's possible some of the Blairs didn't even know of your mother's existence."

"Sir Angus was beastly about Charlie. Do you think he really would have thrown him out?"

"I wouldn't care to bet on what Sir Angus might do when he's in a temper."

David sat up very straight. "You don't suppose—"

"I don't suppose anything yet. It's too soon." Robert gently pushed David back down in the bed.

"But—"

"We need facts, not speculation." He ruffled David's hair. "Sleep well. I'll be right next door."

In his own room, Robert dropped down on the edge of the bed and pulled off his boots. It was certainly too early to suppose anything. But David was right about Sir Angus. He reminded Robert of a colonel he had known in Spain, a bluff, good-humored man. He had written to his wife and children faithfully every week. And he had raped a fourteen-year-old Spanish girl after the sack of an unimportant village and shown no sign of remorse.

Robert reached into his coat pocket and pulled out the ring that was Lucie's last message to him. A wolf cub with a thistle between its teeth. After her death he had searched in vain for the ring's significance, but in the end he had had to return to the Peninsula.

And then the British had driven the French out of Spain and followed them across the Pyrenees. Napoleon Bonaparte, the last, tarnished remnant of the cause of liberty that had fired Robert's young soul, was exiled to the island of Elba, while a scion of the House of Bourbon once more sat on the throne of France.

The search for Lucie's killer had been all Robert had to hang on to, a lifeline that kept him from drowning in a sea of failure and disillusionment and self-disgust. *You can't live in the past, Robert,* his mother had told him, watching him with her usual sharp-eyed concern. His cousin Paul had been even more blunt: *The war's over. We made a hash of it and trampled on our ideals and then the British trampled on us. If you found Lucie's murderer ten times over it wouldn't change that.*

Robert hadn't listened to either of them. A drunken Scotsman in a Paris tavern had given him the name he sought. The Blairs, a Midlothian family. An English officer eager to swap war stories had provided the details he needed to make his acquaintance with Allan Blair believable.

Robert's hand clenched so that the metal of the ring cut into his palm. Paul was wrong. His quest was fueled by more than the need to escape the failure of his cause. He owed it to Lucie. He had made a vow. The mystery was so much more complicated than the reason for her death. Lucie had been his first love, but he had never really known her. He saw again his wife's face, the delicate, haunting features, the dark cloud of hair, the eyes that always seemed veiled, even in passion.

Then the image blurred and the eyes were green, not blue, the hair tinged with flame.

Robert rubbed his hand across his eyes. He hadn't meant to flirt with Emma Blair. But it was almost a reflex, using charm to obtain the information he wanted. The taint of self-disgust it brought to his throat should be as familiar by now as the smell of charred flesh on a battlefield.

He got to his feet, splashed icy water on his face, removed his clothes, and climbed beneath the welcome warmth of the quilt. The storm continued, sending scatterings of snow against the windowpanes and chilling the already chill air. He must have fallen asleep, because he woke suddenly, aware of a sound that had nothing to do with the storm. He reached for his pistol. Then he remembered where he was and realized the sound was someone banging on the door.

"Captain Melton?" It was Emma's voice, taut with fear.

Robert pushed back the quilt, wincing at the cold air. He pulled on his breeches and shirt and opened the door.

Emma stood outside, wrapped in a dark wool cloak, her hair tumbling about her shoulders, a candle in her hand. "I'm sorry to wake you," she said. "But I need your help."

3

Emma tightened her fingers on the candlestick, trying to hold it steady.

Understanding flashed in Robert Melton's eyes. "Is it your brother?"

"And Will."

Melton strode back into the room and struck a flint to light the lamp. "What will they do?" He sat on the edge of the bed and reached for his stockings and boots.

"I don't know. Last time they flooded the meadow. This time I'm afraid it will be worse." She set her candle down and moved into the room. "The sound of the horses woke me. By the time I got to the window, they were riding out of the yard."

Melton tugged on his second boot. "You didn't wake your uncle?"

"He'd only tell me to go back to bed."

"Men from the estate then?" He stood and shrugged on his coat.

"I don't want to involve the servants in our idiocy. Here." She lifted his cloak from the back of a chair.

For the first time since their exchange in the doorway, they looked at each other directly. Though he had put on his coat, he hadn't bothered with a waistcoat or cravat.

His shirt gaped open at the neck. The lamplight picked out glints of copper and gold in the hair on his chest.

Emma swallowed, her throat gone dry. She had come to his room because she needed help and there was no one else to whom she could turn. Until now she hadn't considered the implied intimacy of her actions. She was standing in his bedchamber in the middle of the night. She had watched him dress, for all the world as if he were one of her cousins. Or something even more intimate.

For a moment, the shared realization hung between them. Then Melton reached for the cloak. Emma snatched her hands back without touching him. "We'd best be off."

They descended the great staircase in silence, her candle casting pools of light on the well-worn oak treads. He kept far enough behind her to avoid accidental touching. She held her cloak tight about her and fixed her gaze straight ahead.

A shock of chill air greeted them when she opened the front door. But though a blanket of powdery white covered the courtyard, the sky had begun to clear. Moonlight shone brilliantly against the snow.

They saddled the horses and led them from the stable in silence. Melton held out his hands to help her into the saddle. A shock of heat went through her as his hands circled her waist to lift her onto the horse's back. And all because of a commonplace courtesy, one any man would have shown her, one he would have offered to any woman. Still conscious of the feel of his hands through the layers of her cloak and gown, Emma gathered up the reins and led the way out of the courtyard.

They galloped through an avenue of pine trees and over a stone bridge into the rolling snow-covered hills. The hoofprints of two horses were plain to see. She and Melton followed the trail through the hedged grazing land and the unenclosed land on the outskirts of the estate until at last they reached the stone wall, moss-covered and innocuous looking, which was an unmistakable boundary for any Blair or Lauder.

Emma reined in her horse. "The Lauders' land starts here."

They jumped the wall easily. As they started up the hill beyond, Emma's blood turned cold for reasons that had nothing to do with the weather. The quickening wind brought cool air and the scent of pines and an acrid smell that was sickeningly out of place. She glanced at Melton. With one accord, they urged their horses to the top of the rise.

White, snow-covered fields lay before them, broken by the dark of frosted hedges. And the ruddy glow of flames.

Emma knew the building at once, the south barn, used for storage and repairs. There would be no people or animals inside, thank God, but that did not diminish the horror of the blazing roof casting smoke and firelight over the snow-covered ground.

Nearer, beneath a stand of pines, two figures on horseback were visible. Emma touched her heels to her horse and galloped down the hill. "What the bloody hell do you think you're doing?"

Jamie glanced over at her. "What the devil are you doing here, Em?"

"Trying to save you from your own folly. I never dreamed you'd go this far."

"No one's in there, Emma." Will's breath frosted in the air.

Emma's gloved hands clenched on the reins. "And that makes it all right?"

Jamie's brows drew together. "Curse it, Em—"

"If you learned anything at all in Spain, gentlemen, you know a fire can quickly burn out of control." Melton spoke from behind her, his pleasant voice gone as hard and deadly as a steel blade. "Where's the nearest farm? We're going to need buckets and all the hands we can muster."

The flickering light of the fire caught the burst of anger in Jamie's eyes. "Why in God's name did you bring him?"

"Because the number of sane men in the house is distressingly small." Emma turned to Melton. "There's a farm to the west, this side of the next ridge of hills. I'll go for help."

"I'll see if anything can be salvaged inside." Melton regarded the Blair men through narrowed eyes. "Best go home if you haven't a mind to help. No sense in standing around in the cold."

Jamie's chin jutted out. "I'm not following your orders, Melton."

"Suit yourself." Melton swung down from his horse.

As Emma turned her horse westward, a terrified scream rose above the crackling of the flames.

"Christ." Melton raced toward the barn. Emma jumped from the saddle and ran after him. A large section of the roof crashed to the floor below. A moment later, a thin figure in white stumbled through the barn door, flames licking at her clothes and her long blond hair.

Melton knocked the woman to the ground and flung his cloak over her. The woman pushed herself to her knees. "Geordie! He's still i' there!"

She struggled to her feet. Melton hauled her back. "I'll get him. Don't let her move." He pushed the woman into Emma's arms.

Emma held tightly to the struggling woman. "Jamie! Will! Someone's trapped inside."

Her brother and cousin were already halfway to the barn. At least they were not wholly lost to decency.

"Geordie," the woman cried again.

"It will be all right." Emma smoothed the woman's hair. "Is he hurt?"

The woman looked up at Emma. She was a girl really, no more than sixteen or seventeen. Her thin, pretty face was blackened by smoke and her pale blond hair was scorched on one side where it had caught the flames. "He was right behind me, but he stumbled. Then the roof came down. He mun be trapped."

"They'll get him out." Emma drew Melton's cloak over the thin chemise that was the girl's only garment. Dear God, there was a burn mark on her shoulder. Mercifully, she seemed in too much shock to feel the pain.

"The flames woke us. If only we hadna fallen asleep." The girl clung to Emma, like Kirsty when she'd woken from a nightmare. "We shouldna ha' been there, but we thought no one would ken. It's so noisy at home wi' no-where to talk, let alone— Oh, Da's goin' to kill me. He doesna like Geordie as 'tis—" Another piece of the roof crashed in. "He's dead, I know he's dead. God is punishin' me."

"Hush," Emma said, her mouth dry. "None of this is your fault."

"But—"

"My name is Emma. What's yours?"

"Sally." The girl drew a shuddering breath. "Sally Drummond."

"Well then, Sally. You're being very brave. Geordie will be proud of you."

Melton and Jamie staggered through the barn doorway, a dark form slung between them. Will was close behind.

"Geordie!" Sally cried.

"By the pine trees." Melton jerked his head toward the stand of pine.

Sally ran after them and flung herself on her lover as Melton and Jamie laid him down in the snow. Emma pulled her back and laid her own cloak over the injured boy. Geordie looked little older than Sally, a handsome lad with light brown hair and a smattering of freckles. His eyes were closed, his shirt was charred, and there was a livid mark on his forehead.

"Geordie, wake up." Sally shook him by the shoulders.

"One of the beams collapsed and hit him on the head," Melton said. "He's had the sense knocked out of him, but he should come around in a bit."

Emma looked at Melton. His hair was disarranged, his face smeared with perspiration and soot. His eyes held a concern that belied his soothing voice. Emma understood. Geordie might come to in a few moments. Or not at all.

Jamie stared down, brows drawn, mouth truculent.

Will shifted his weight from one foot to the other. "We didn't know there was anyone in the barn."

"Shut up, Will." Emma put her arm around Sally. "The barn?" she asked Melton.

"Gone, I'm afraid."

The flames had reached the walls and were curling around the doorframe. Shards of burning wood fell and lay hissing on the snow.

Emma was still looking at the barn when she heard the echo of hooves against the hardening snow. Two cloaked riders were approaching from the north at a furious pace. A shaft of moonlight caught the familiar dark hair and fine-boned faces. Archie Lauder, the heir to the title and estate, and Matt Lauder, a soldier like Jamie and Will.

Jamie jerked his head at Will. "We'll meet them. Don't you dare interfere, Em."

"As far as I'm concerned you can all beat yourselves to a bloody pulp."

Jamie and Will strode across the snow toward the riders.

"Sally?" Geordie's eyes flickered open.

Emma drew a breath of relief and heard Melton do the same.

"I'm here, Geordie." Sally seized his hands in her own. "Are ye bad hurt?"

Melton crouched down beside him. "Can you move your legs? Your arms?"

"Aye. I think so." Geordie looked at Melton out of unfocused eyes, but he wriggled his feet and squeezed Sally's hands. "Aye."

Melton held his hand out, the first and second fingers raised. "How many?"

"Two."

"Good lad. You'll do."

"You filthy Blair cur!"

Emma turned to see Matt Lauder leap from his horse and fling himself on Jamie with a force that carried them both to the ground. Will seized hold of Matt's cloak and hauled him to his feet. Matt spun around and punched Will in the stomach. Jamie scrambled to his feet. Archie Lauder jumped off his horse to join the melee.

More riders were approaching from the north. "Lord Lauder." Emma recognized the lean, gray-haired man in the lead. The time of reckoning had come.

"Oh, no." Sally shrank closer to Geordie. "He'll tell my da for certain."

Emma squeezed the girl's arm. "I'll talk to him, Sally. He'll have other things on his mind."

Like wringing Blair necks. It was no more than Jamie and Will deserved, but she couldn't abandon them to Lauder's mercies. Emma looked at Melton. He helped her to her feet and they walked forward together.

Lord Lauder reined in his horse. "By thunder, is this a fire or a brawl?"

The four brawlers went still.

"A bit of both," Melton said. "Lord Lauder?"

"Yes. Who the devil are you?"

"Robert Melton," Emma said. "A friend of my late husband's."

Lauder stared at her, then swung around in the saddle to look at the barn. Only the skeleton of the structure remained, still engulfed by flames. "Dear Christ." He fixed Will and Jamie with a hard stare. The light from the fire fell across his face, emphasizing its harshness. "So flooding our meadow wasn't enough for you. And this time you had to drag your sister into your crimes. Damme, you're no longer boys. I've a mind to call the baillie."

Emma tensed. Behind Lauder, four of the estate servants had reined in their horses.

"In fairness," Melton said, "the cut hedge gave them provocation."

"Hedge?" Lauder asked.

Melton turned to Archie and Matt with a look of pleasant and quite chilling inquiry. "You didn't tell your father?"

"Tell me what?" Lauder's voice was dangerously quiet.

Archie glanced from one side to the other. "They flooded the meadow, sir. They had it coming."

"Then why not tell your father all about it?" Will took a step forward. "Tell him how half our cattle near froze to death. We're still missing thirty head."

Lauder's head snapped around in Emma's direction. "Is this true?"

"Our north hedge was cut," Emma said. "We barely managed to round up the cattle before the storm hit. Charlie helped us. That's how he injured himself."

"You lack-brained fools." Lauder turned back to his sons. "What were you about, putting animals at risk?"

Matt's face flushed with anger. "They dammed up the burn—"

"Never mind what they did. I'd hope any son of mine

would have the wit not to endanger good cattle." He turned back to Jamie and Will. "Not that it's any excuse for arson. Does your father know about this?"

"No," Emma said.

"Aye." Lauder snorted. "I daresay he made it a point *not* to know about it. I know Angus Blair." He glanced beyond her to the trees. "Who's there?"

"Two of your tenants," Emma said. "They were caught in the barn. The young man fell and hit his head, but mercifully it doesn't seem to be serious."

"There were people in the barn?" Lauder's voice cut as sharp as the wind.

Will looked at his boots. "We didn't know."

"They weren't supposed to be there," Jamie said.

"By God—"

"Oh, please, my lord." Sally ran forward. "We be all right. Only dinna tell my da."

She looked as fragile as a china doll standing barefoot in the snow, clutching Melton's cloak over her chemise, her blond hair tumbling about her shoulders. Lauder grimaced, swung down from the saddle, and strode over to Geordie. Emma put her arm around Sally and followed a little behind.

"Can you ride, lad?" Lauder crouched down beside Geordie.

Geordie nodded.

"Good." Lauder jerked his head at the four men he had brought with him. "See the injured boy and the girl home." He walked over to Sally. "I'll have a word with your father, lass."

Sally gave him a tremulous smile. "Thank ye, my lord."

Lauder laid a hand on her shoulder and caught sight of her burned skin. His lips tightened, but he said nothing. He and Melton helped Geordie onto one of the men's horses. Another of the men took up Sally.

When the riders had set off, Lauder turned his attention back to the Blairs. "Those children could have burned to death." His voice and eyes were colder than the snow. "I won't call the law in this time. It seems my sons have been culpable as well. But don't think I'll forget this."

Jamie and Will stalked to the trees where they had left their horses. Lauder walked over to Emma. "You can tell your uncle that I have no more control over my sons' actions than he has over his."

Emma rubbed her arms. She had left her cloak with Geordie. The wind cut through her gown. "This afternoon I begged Jamie not to take vengeance for the cut hedge. After tonight's work, I have no right to ask the same of you. But this has to end somewhere."

Lauder regarded her in silence. "You're a brave and warmhearted woman, Emma. But I wish you'd learn that you're best off staying out of this. I don't want to see any women hurt."

Emma's fingers tensed with cold and frustration. "I don't want to see *anyone* hurt."

Lauder turned away with a curt nod. Emma found she was trembling. Melton took her arm and steered her toward their horses. They mounted in silence. As they rode back toward Blair land, she turned to look at him. "Do you think women should simply leave men to their foolery?"

"I hate to think of the consequences if they did."

Emma found she was able to smile. "I seem to be forever thanking you. I'm not sure how I'd have survived today without you, Captain Melton."

An answering smile lit Melton's face. "I daresay you'd have thought of something, Mrs. Blair."

"Oh, very likely. Whether or not it would have worked is another matter." She glanced away, fingered the reins, then glanced back at him. "I meant it, Captain Melton. I don't know many men who'd be willing to do all you did today. My husband was fortunate to find so loyal a friend."

Something wavered in Melton's eyes. The teasing light was gone, leaving his gaze dark and unreadable. "For a sensible woman, you form judgments quickly, Mrs. Blair. After half a day's acquaintance, how can you know I'm loyal?"

"Because of what I've seen."

He smiled again, but this time there was a trace of bitterness in the smile. "You learn loyalty in the army. And deceit and betrayal."

His face had gone hard. Like Jamie and Will and Matt Lauder, he was a man of war. Emma thought of how he had been during the fire, stripped down to hard, unyielding determination. Against an enemy, she suspected he could be far more fierce and deadly than her brother and cousin. "I have no illusions about war, Captain Melton, any more than I have illusions about the feud."

The bitterness left his eyes. "It could have been a great deal worse tonight." His voice softened. She warmed to the sound of it, as she might to a longed-for caress.

She met his gaze. "So it could. But this isn't the end of it."

4

"Young scamps." Angus drained his coffee cup and returned it to the breakfast table with a thud. "And what were you about, my girl? You could have been hurt."

"You'd have preferred it if those two children had burned to death?" Emma turned from the sideboard. Breakfast had seemed like a good idea, but now that she was alone in the breakfast parlor with her uncle, the sight of the porridge and kippered herrings turned her stomach. She took a bannock from a warming dish and sat down opposite Angus.

Angus picked up his fork. "Jamie and Will would have got them out."

"I doubt they'd have been able to without Captain Melton."

"Yes, that's another thing." Angus speared his last piece of herring. "What the devil did you mean by dragging a stranger into our affairs?"

"I needed help." Emma took a sip of coffee and regarded her uncle over the primrose-flowered rim of the cup. "He was the only one in the house I could count on."

"By God, lass—" The breakfast parlor door opened. Angus coughed. "Ah, Melton. Good morning. It seems we're in your debt, sir."

Robert Melton closed the door behind him and advanced into the room at a leisurely pace. "I interfered in what was not my quarrel."

"As did I," Emma said.

Angus made a sound that was neither assent nor dissent. "Yes, well, Will and Jamie were upset. But it was a witless thing to do, not thinking to look that the barn was empty."

Melton moved to the table and pulled out a chair. "They came to young Geordie's aid when they saw that it was not. They acquitted themselves well."

Emma bit back an instinctive retort and forced some more coffee down her throat.

Angus's posture relaxed, though his eyes were still guarded. "Ye're a sensible man, Melton." He pushed back his chair with a decisive scrape and got to his feet. "I've much to attend to. I'll see you at dinner, Melton. Emma."

He strode from the room, covering the yellow-and-cream carpet as though it were a stretch of turf. Emma poured Melton a cup of coffee, but held her tongue until the door closed behind her uncle. "This is the second time you've rescued me from one of Uncle Angus's bursts of temper. You knew just what to say to him."

"I knew a colonel like him in Spain. He didn't like to be thwarted any more than your uncle does."

"Thwarted?" Emma handed him the coffee, shamelessly relishing the brief brush of his fingers against her own as he took it from her.

"Sir Angus has been thwarted on all sides. By the Lauders, who put him in the wrong, by Jamie and Will, who were responsible. And by you and me for drawing the whole episode to his attention."

Emma laughed. "That's it exactly."

Melton leaned back in his chair and took a sip of coffee. "This can't have been an easy morning for you."

"There've been better." She pushed a loose curl behind her ear and wished she'd taken more time to dress her hair. "At least Charlie's on the mend. He insists he's ready to ride home and I think he may actually be right." She broke off a piece of bannock. "I've sent one of the servants to the Thistle for your boxes. David told me that's where you were staying. He and Kirsty are exploring the attics."

"Ah, I wondered why he was so eager to be off this morning. I'm glad they've taken to each other. David spends too much time with adults."

"So does Kirsty." Emma spread marmalade on the bannock. "She plays with the tenant children, but there's always the manor between them. They know she's different and she hates it. She's been desperate for a friend where there's no question of bloody rank or privilege to get in the way." She looked up, her face growing warm. "I'm sorry. I sound like Jamie. It *has* been an awful twenty-four hours."

Melton pushed his chair back. "You need a change of scene. Arabel says you have a very handsome picture gallery. Would you show it to me?"

"Of course." The words were out of her mouth quickly, perhaps too quickly. "I should warn you the pictures aren't very interesting," she said as they climbed the stone turnpike stairs in the west wing. "A lot of Blair ancestors."

Melton paused, one hand on the rough whitewashed wall. "But it strikes me as the last place we're likely to encounter Jamie and Will."

His eyes glinted with humor and something more. A shock went through her as though she had touched a piece of metal too near the fire. "How very wise of you, Captain Melton. Are you chivalrously protecting me from their wrath or prudently avoiding battle on your own account?"

He grinned. "A bit of both. I must confess I quite

cravenly took myself off on a tramp about the estate this morning. I didn't see much point in coming to fisticuffs with Jamie across the breakfast things."

"Very wise. There's no one more pigheaded than a Blair in a quarrel." Emma gestured to the carved panel at the head of the stairs. "Our family badge. The Blair wolf cub with the royal thistle of Scotland between its teeth."

Melton cocked a brow at her. "To symbolize the family's loyalty to the crown?"

"That's one explanation. Another is that the Blair family will bow to nothing and no one, not even the king."

The picture gallery ran half the length of the first floor, a long room lit by banks of mullioned windows. The storm had cleared and cool sunlight was spilling across the oak floorboards as Emma opened the door.

"Do you like paintings?" she asked.

"I like people."

She looked down the ranks of her ancestors. "You're right, there's not much to be said of them as pictures, but as likenesses they do well enough."

"They're all Blairs?" Melton pushed the door closed.

"Most of them." Emma looked at his hand as it rested on the door panels. An old scar showed against his tanned skin, but his fingers had a supple grace. She found herself wondering how they would feel against her naked flesh. She drew a breath. "That's Andrew Blair, the oldest of the lot as you can tell by the fancy coat. Uncle Angus's great-great-grandfather."

"A strong-looking man."

"A stubborn one. They're stubborn, the Blair men. Stubborn and passionate and willful."

"And the Blair women?"

She met his questioning gaze. "They have to be to survive. Not all of them do. My mother died when Jamie was born. Our father was away fighting in India and she was living with Uncle Angus and his wife. It can't have been easy for her."

"How old were you?"

"Scarcely two. I don't remember her." Emma pulled her paisley shawl more closely around her. "My aunt Alice was strong. Uncle Angus's wife. The house lost its heart when she died."

"Leaving you to take her place."

The light from the windows fell across his face. He was looking at her with eyes that understood. Perhaps too much. She shook her head. "Hardly that. I've done my best, but Uncle Angus will never listen to me like he listened to her. Aunt Alice and Lady Lauder were friends. They kept the feud in check. Now that they're both gone it's flared to life stronger than ever."

An uncomfortable welter of feelings rose up in her chest. She didn't want to confront them now when she was enjoying being alone with Robert Melton. She pointed to a portrait of a man with a fleshy face and shrewd eyes. "My grandfather, Thomas Blair."

Melton accepted the turn in the conversation. "Sir Angus is his son?"

"His second son. The eldest was called Thomas too." She walked a few steps and indicated a portrait of a thin-featured young man with unfocused eyes and a soft mouth. "He died unmarried a few years before I was born."

"Another soldier?"

"No, he had an accident with a hunting rifle just after his father died. That's Uncle Angus, beside him. The man in the hussar's uniform is my father, James. And then my uncle Gavin, the youngest. He's an advocate. What you English call a barrister."

Melton paused to look at Gavin Blair. "He has a family?"

"A son at university and a daughter a few years older than Kirsty. They live in Edinburgh."

"You visit them often?"

"Not nearly often enough."

He looked at her, his gaze appraising. "You're fond of Edinburgh, then?"

She laughed. "You've guessed my secret, Captain Melton. When I read about the lectures and plays and concerts, I grow quite green with envy. Edinburgh's always seemed to me—oh, full of life and excitement and—"

"Everything you don't find at Blair House?"

She glanced across the gallery, out the windows that were as old as the portrait of Andrew Blair, into a snow-dusted countryside that was Blair land as far as the eye could see. "I love Blair House. But it's a confined world. Edinburgh seems—limitless."

Melton nodded. "It's a vibrant city. Sir Angus's elder daughter lives there as well, doesn't she?"

"My cousin Jenny." Emma took a step down the gallery. "Her husband Bram Martin is a lawyer, too—a writer to the signet—a solicitor in England." Her fingers curled inward. Speaking of Bram was never easy. The familiar guilt bit her in the throat. "Bram and Jenny are in Paris now. Bram's parents were French émigrés who came here during the Terror."

"He's gone to France to see if he can get their estates restored?"

"Yes." Emma looked back at Melton. "Have you been to Paris?"

"Briefly."

"I'd like to see Paris." She ran her fingers down the linenfold paneling between the paintings. "Allan and I used to visit Bram and Jenny in Edinburgh whenever we could, just to get away from Blair House. Bram can talk about all sorts of things besides farming and soldiering and feuding with the Lauders."

She paused, breathing in the damp that always invaded the house from November to May. She wasn't used to talking about herself. Words kept spilling out, leaving her giddy and uncertain.

"You're close to your cousin Jenny?"

"We grew up together." She spoke quickly, before the catch in her breath became obvious. "We're like sisters." The words sounded inadequate. But what else could she say? *Jenny's as lovely and fragile as gilded crystal and I always envied her for it.* Or, *She has a genius at getting people to take care of her, including me.* Or, damning and undeniable, *I fell in love with her husband.* Emma swallowed. "I don't suppose he ever mentioned it to you, but Allan once planned to read for the law too."

"I didn't realize. He struck me as very much a soldier."

"He was. But it took me years to realize it. When we were first married, I thought we wanted the same things from life. Perhaps he did too."

Melton took a step toward her. "If it hadn't been for the war—"

"The war was a convenient excuse." The words burst from her lips with a passion that surprised even her. She hadn't talked so freely about her marriage to anyone. Not Aunt Alice, who had died shortly before Allan, not Arabel, who had been a child at the time, certainly not Angus. How strange at last to be able to speak of it to her husband's soldier friend. "I wish you could have seen Allan's face the day he told me he was joining up. Like a little boy who's been offered some spectacular treat. I wasn't very understanding."

She put her hand to her jaw, where Jamie's blow had left a bruise. The pain brought a vivid memory of her quarrel with Allan. She could still feel the sharp contact of Allan's hand on her cheek and her own stunned surprise. She had known then that her husband's longing for battle was stronger than anything he could feel for her.

"Battlefield glory is a common dream of young men." Melton's voice was as soft as a brush of lamb's wool.

Emma's fingers twisted in the ends of her shawl. "In Allan's case the dream lasted. After two years he was sent home wounded, and I thought I had him back. But home held nothing for him, not his wife, not his child. He couldn't wait to return to his battalion."

"Emma—" Melton stretched out his hand, then let it fall to his side. "Young men can be fools."

"So can young women." She glanced down at the floorboards, then looked into his eyes. She wanted him to put out his hand again. She wanted to take hold of it.

The case clock at the end of the gallery broke the stillness, chiming the quarter hour. "Oh, poison." Reality came rushing in. "I promised to speak with Cook about dinner and I've got to send a message to the stable about Charlie's horse—"

"Don't mind me. I'll amuse myself with the paintings."

Emma nodded, swallowing a pang of regret. The trivialities of life returned. She felt foolish for having revealed so much, naked and exposed despite the sturdy brown poplin of her gown. And yet— As she reached the gallery door she turned back to him. "Captain Melton?"

He gave an inquiring smile. The look in his eyes was enough to banish any qualms about confiding in him.

Emma returned the smile. "Thank you for listening."

Robert watched the gallery door close behind Emma Blair. He had achieved his objective for the morning. She had supplied him with a wealth of details about the current and past generations of Blairs. But she had also confided in him about her marriage, her hopes, her disappointments—confidences he suspected she had made to few people. Emma Blair needed a friend every bit as much as her daughter did.

And so she had turned to him, a man who had betrayed her the moment he told her his name. Some might find it humorous, but he was not quite cynical enough to laugh.

He strode back to the paintings of Sir Angus and his brothers. Thomas, who had died young and unmarried. Sir Angus. James, Emma's father. Gavin, the advocate. All their legitimate offspring seemed to be accounted for. But if Lucie had been illegitimate, she could belong to any of them. She could even be the result of a love affair their father had indulged in late in life.

Robert studied the dates on the brass plates below the pictures. Both Sir Thomas Blair and his son Thomas had died in 1783, the year Lucie had been born. An interesting coincidence. Or perhaps more. Both men would have had time enough to leave a daughter on this earth before they left it.

Robert walked slowly along the gallery to the door. Lucie's parentage was only the first question. More important, he had to learn to whom she had been a danger, whom her existence might have threatened.

He pulled open the door to the stone turnpike staircase. The door opened without a sound. The wide stairs curved gracefully below him, lit by bands of light from the windows set high in the stone wall. The light fell on two figures standing at a bend in the stairs, their arms entwined, their bodies pressed close together. The woman's back was toward him, but he recognized Arabel's bright hair. The man was Charlie Lauder.

Before he could retreat, Charlie and Arabel broke apart with the quickness of conspirators discovered plotting.

"Sorry to intrude." Robert reached for the door handle. "I'll go around by the front stairs."

Arabel grinned. "You might as well come down. You've seen the worst."

Robert found himself grinning in return. "Speaking as one of your elders, I haven't found that staircases make the best trysting places."

"This one is usually deserted. And you mustn't blame Charlie. I cornered him and insisted he say a proper good-bye to me."

"Liar." Charlie was watching Robert with appraising eyes. "See here, Melton—"

"You won't tell anyone, will you?" Arabel said.

Robert stopped two steps above them. Their eyes were clear and shining, unshadowed by regret or disillusionment. It seemed impossible that he had ever been that young. But he had, of course. And he had been as ready to slay dragons for Lucie as Charlie now was for Arabel. A pity he had failed to discover where the dragons lurked. "I don't see that it's any business of mine how two people choose to say good-bye."

Arabel gave a bright, unforced smile. "I knew you were a good man."

Charlie met Robert's gaze. "Arabel and I consider ourselves betrothed. But—"

"But neither of our fathers would consent to the marriage, and without them neither of us has any money." Arabel clasped Charlie's hand. "I've told Charlie I don't care about money as long as we're together, but—"

"But I couldn't put her through that."

"You may have to. I won't give you any choice."

"Does Emma know?" Robert asked, and then realized he should have referred to her as Mrs. Blair.

Arabel shook her head. "I don't want to force her to lie to Da. This is my fight."

Something in the way Arabel lifted her chin reminded Robert of her cousin. He found himself wishing he had known Emma when she was that age. And when he had been as young as Charlie and as sure he could conquer the world. He spoke on impulse. "I'd like to see something of the estate before the bad weather returns. I could use a guide. And if we happen to encounter young Lauder while we're out, I don't see who should know of it."

Arabel's blue eyes lit with pure happiness. "I hope you were decorated in the war, Captain Melton. You're a hero."

"I can't tell you how much we'd appreciate it." Charlie suddenly reminded Robert of David. "Though I don't see any earthly reason why you'd feel obliged to help us."

"I have a weakness for star-crossed lovers."

And yet, Robert acknowledged as he continued down the stairs, leaving Charlie and Arabel to finish their good-byes in private, he could not say what had prompted him to make such a rash gesture. He had long since learned the perils of becoming involved in the lives of those one was deceiving.

He reached the ground floor and opened the door to the corridor. The truth was, he had let himself be moved by Charlie and Arabel's plight. Or perhaps by memories of his own youth. Or what he wished his youth had been. Lending his assistance to the two young lovers was less dangerous than looking into Emma Blair's eyes.

Robert closed the door behind him and started down the corridor. He was used to guarding against a knife attack in a dark alley, a rifleman's bullet from a hilltop, an enemy patrol stealing through the night. The dangers at Blair House were more subtle and insidious. And far more seductive.

5

"You can be sure those bastards are plotting something."

Jamie's voice came from the great hall below. Emma moved to the gallery railing. Her brother and Will were crossing the hall, their stride long and determined.

"We can't be taken unawares." Will opened the library door and the two men went inside, drowning out the rest of their conversation behind the heavy door.

Emma swore under her breath. This was only the second day since the fire. Yesterday Jamie and Will had been quiet, brooding over the bad turn their actions had taken. But this morning they were beginning to plan fresh devilry.

She started down the stairs. It was not yet noon and already her head was beginning to throb. A movement out the window caught her eye as she reached the half landing. Two riders were approaching the house. Emma's fingers clenched the window ledge. Despite the film of condensation on the glass, the riders were all too visible. Robert Melton was smiling, the smile that lit his face with humor and warmth and something else that made her body grow embarrassingly warm. But he was not smiling at her. He was smiling at Arabel, who was smiling back, laughter in her eyes, as he swung her down from her horse.

Emma released the window ledge and wrapped her arms around herself. Two nights ago when they rode to the fire, Melton's hands had circled her waist just as they now circled Arabel's. But she was not Arabel. Seven years separated them, years in which Emma had borne a child and buried a husband and become the lady of the house. Arabel was young and vital, long legged and distractingly pretty. Just the sort of girl to remind a man of all that was good in life.

Melton and Arabel had started for the house. They were not quite touching, but the intimacy between them was palpable. Melton's hair was disarranged and his cravat slightly askew. Arabel wore a deep blue riding habit, the color of her eyes, and tendrils of red-gold hair were visible beneath the filmy veil on her beaver hat.

Emma's stomach churned with jealousy and self-disgust. She and Melton had shared two adventures, but that had hardly been his choice. And that morning in the picture gallery, she was the one who had burdened him with her confidences. He had been pleasant and charming to her, but then he was pleasant and charming to everyone. Perhaps she had imagined that there was more in his eyes when he looked at her. This morning at breakfast it was Arabel with whom he had exchanged meaningful glances and Arabel with whom he had gone riding, clearly not desiring any other company. Emma knew she didn't have exclusive rights to him just because she had seen him first.

But when she heard the opening of the door and the sound of Arabel's light voice and Melton's deeper accents, Emma picked up her skirt and ran down the stairs to the great hall.

Arabel greeted her with a sunny smile. "It's a beautiful morning, Em. I can't believe spring is far away."

"Don't try to deceive Captain Melton. There's no softening the reality of a Scottish winter."

"Don't worry, Mrs. Blair, I don't deceive easily." Melton was pulling off his riding gloves. His tone was easy, but he turned away from her gaze and she could not read his expression.

Emma glanced at Arabel, who was staring dreamily at the bowl of dried flowers on the hall table, then took a step toward Melton. "I've decided to go to Edinburgh the day after tomorrow to visit my uncle Gavin. I'll stay for a day or two. I think I can persuade Jamie and Will to come with me. It will at least get them away from temptation for a bit." She looked Melton full in the face, her determination sweeping aside her guilt for so blatantly trying to claim his attention. "I'll take Kirsty with me, too, of course. I thought perhaps you and David would like to come as well."

Melton met her gaze. For a moment, it seemed there was a flicker of hesitation in his eyes. Then he smiled, making the breath stop in her throat. "I don't think David would forgive me if I let you take Kirsty off without him. We'd be delighted, Mrs. Blair."

Her spirits lightened as if she had drunk a glass of sherry too quickly.

Arabel turned from the table. "You're going to Edinburgh, Em? Good, I've been wanting to order a new riding habit. When do we leave?"

A sharp blast of wind from the north, out of place in the decorous environs of St. Andrew Square, blew into the carriage as the coachman opened the door. Emma reached up to adjust her bonnet, a new bonnet trimmed with ostrich feathers and rose-colored ribbons, which made her feel foolish and a good five years younger.

Kirsty and David jumped to the ground as soon as the steps were let down. Melton climbed from the carriage after them and turned to help the women. Emma gave him her hand, longing to see some spark in his eyes that was just for her, cursing herself for her idiocy. He smiled brilliantly at her, then turned to help Arabel with, she feared, just the same smile.

Jamie and Will, who had ridden beside the carriage, had already dismounted and were standing on the pavement. A shout came from the door of the gray freestone house. "You've been ages. I thought you'd never get here." Twelve-year-old Violet Blair came running down the steps, dark ringlets bouncing on her shoulders, white skirt bunched up in her hands, and flung herself on Emma and Kirsty.

"It's bad manners to suffocate guests upon their arrival, infant." Violet's brother Andy strolled down the steps, cravat expertly tied, tassels swinging from his glossy Hessian boots. "Emma, you look like a Paris fashion plate."

"Meaning this bonnet is too extravagant or too young for me or both." Emma leaned forward to accept Andy's kiss. At nineteen, he finally seemed to have stopped growing. He was a tall, slender lad who had inherited his mother's air of elegance along with her straight dark hair. Not at all a typical Blair.

Andy led them to the drawing room where his parents waited. Gavin, broad shoulders tamed by a well-cut coat of dark blue superfine, sandy hair smoothed back from his face, ushered them to seats by the fire. Eleanor, stylishly gowned in cherry-striped sarcenet, dark hair dressed with just the right degree of softness, poured tea from a chased silver pot.

Emma sank into a green damask armchair and smoothed her travel-creased skirt. As usual, everything about Gavin and Eleanor's house—from the discreet, pale green plaster walls to the Staffordshire figures on the mantel—seemed brighter, newer, smarter than Blair House.

Eleanor handed a gold-rimmed teacup to Melton. "It's nice to meet a fellow countryman. I'm an Englishwoman myself, you know. When I married Gavin, my parents were convinced I was being carried off to the wilderness."

"Andy went to school in England." Violet helped herself to a bannock. "At Eton. Uncle Angus said it was treason to send a Blair to a bloo—"

"Violet," Eleanor said in a quiet but firm voice.

Violet broke the bannock in half and spread strawberry jam on it. "The servant who brought Emma's letter said the Lauders had stolen Blair cattle."

"That's not the half of it." Jamie, who had been staring into the fire, snapped to attention. "We lost nearly thirty head."

"Thirty head?" Gavin stared at him. "By God, they should pay for that."

Jamie and Will were silent. Arabel set her cup down on a satinwood table with precision. "They have paid for it. Jamie and Will set fire to their barn."

Eleanor drew in her breath. Violet gave a gasp of delight.

"It was empty," Will said. "At least, we thought it was."

"Thought?" Andy asked.

"Yes, but the people got out. No one was hurt."

"On the contrary." Emma looked Will directly in the eye. "They were both burned. It will be some time before they recover."

"Good God," Andy said under his breath.

"You don't understand." Jamie's gaze clashed with his cousin's. "You never have."

"No, I'm afraid I'm not much of a Blair." Andy leaned back in his chair. "I've never seen bashing Lauder heads as my purpose in life."

"Don't be flippant, lad. It's no joking matter." Gavin's voice roughened, sounding more like Angus's.

"Captain Melton put out the fire." Arabel looked across the room at Melton with a proud smile.

"Oh?" Gavin ran his gaze over Melton as though taking his measure again. "You're a brave man, Melton. Or a reckless one. It's a risky thing to do, putting yourself in the midst of the feud."

Melton gave a smile at once sweet and dangerous. "At Blair House, it seems one has little choice, sir."

"Gavin Blair might be Maman's father." David perched on the windowseat in the bedchamber to which he and Robert had been shown. "That's why you wanted to come to Edinburgh, isn't it?"

"Partly." Robert pulled a chair close to the windowseat and sat facing his son. In the past days, David had seemed content to spend time with Kirsty and had asked few questions about the quest for Lucie's origins. But now that he had spoken, he deserved an accounting. "We know that there's no Blair daughter of your mother's age who's missing or presumed dead. So it seems likely that her parents weren't married."

David nodded. "That explains why no one talks about her. Or maybe even knows about her." He drummed his fingers against the blue-striped chintz of the windowseat. "So where did Maman live before she came to France?"

"A very good question. We know that someone taught her to speak French like a native."

David's eyes lit up. "There are a lot of French people in Edinburgh. But Kirsty says most of them came here during the Terror. Maman would have been born before that, wouldn't she?"

"Well before."

"There's more, isn't there?" David leaned forward. "You've learned something. Was it when you were talking to Gavin Blair's wife in the sitting room?"

"You're too clever for me, lad." Robert ruffled his son's hair. "Thank God I never had to match wits against you. Eleanor Blair mentioned a school, Mlle. Hébert's. It's been here since before the Revolution. Mrs. Blair says it's frequented mostly by future governesses and tradesmen's daughters."

"So Maman might have been sent there to keep her out of the Blairs' way."

David spoke matter-of-factly, but Robert's fingers curled inward. "Yes." He sat back in his chair. "I'll call at Mlle. Hébert's first thing in the morning."

"May I go with you?"

"Best not. Mlle. Hébert might be less willing to talk in front of a ten-year-old boy. Not everyone knows how precocious you are."

"But you'll tell me everything you find out?"

"Of course."

"Promise?"

"I promise." Robert got to his feet. "We should change for dinner."

David went to the bed where their valises were laid out. "The Blairs are having guests in after dinner. There's to be dancing." He cast a sidelong glance at his father. "Maybe you can dance with Emma."

Robert's fingers stilled on the latch of his valise. Since that morning in the picture gallery, he had deliberately avoided being alone with Emma. He looked at David. "I don't think that would be a good idea."

David looked back at him, eyes questioning. "You said yourself Emma and Kirsty probably don't even know about Maman."

In David's clear blue eyes, Robert could already see the beginnings of divided loyalties. "But they're Blairs," he said. "They love their family. They won't thank us for uncovering unpleasant things about the Blairs."

"Even if it's the truth?"

Robert pushed the lid of his valise open with a firm snap. "Especially if it's the truth."

"It's been an age since we've had dancing." Arabel dropped her apricot satin cloth gown over her head with a whoosh. "There never seem to be enough couples at Blair House."

"There never *are* enough couples at Blair House." Emma started to do up the tiny buttons on the back of her cousin's dress.

"I expect Captain Melton's a very good dancer." Arabel twisted her head around to look over her shoulder at Emma. "Perhaps you can waltz with him."

Emma kept her gaze fixed on the buttons. "Don't you want to waltz with him yourself?"

Arabel gave a full-throated laugh. "I wouldn't mind. But I doubt I'd be his first choice of partner."

"I don't." Emma fastened the last button.

Arabel turned around to face her. "Don't be daft, Em. He's old enough to be my uncle."

At that, Emma laughed herself, though it was a sort of hysterical release of tension. "Thank you, Bel. And I could be your aunt, I suppose."

"Oh, poison, that's not the way I meant it." Arabel dropped down on the bed. "I've seen the way he looks at you, Em, when he thinks no one else will notice."

Emma moved to the dressing table so Arabel wouldn't notice the self-conscious flush in her cheeks or the glimmer of hope in her eyes. "I've seen little of him in the past days. I think the poor man felt I monopolized him enough his first twenty-four hours at Blair House."

"Perhaps he needs a little encouragement." In the dressing table mirror, Emma saw Arabel pull on her satin slippers and tie the ribbons around her shapely ankles.

"Where did you learn such worldly wisdom cooped up

at Blair House?" Emma fingered the crystal stopper on her scent bottle. "Arabel, if Captain Melton does take an interest in you—you shouldn't worry about it—you should feel free to respond."

"He's not interested in me." Arabel got to her feet and took a pair of long white gloves from her dressing case. "Honestly, Em, anyone would think you were afraid to be happy."

"Don't be silly." Emma looked at the scent bottle a moment longer. Then she removed the stopper and splashed on her lily-of-the-valley scent, more lavishly than usual.

"I suppose it would be too much to hope you know how to dance a Scottish reel." Arabel appeared at Robert's side as the Axminster carpet was being rolled back for dancing.

"On the contrary," Robert said, grateful for his mother's instruction. "We aren't entirely backward in England."

"I'm relieved to hear it." Arabel glanced across the room to where Emma stood talking with Eleanor. "I suggest you ask Emma to dance."

Robert, who prided himself on rarely being taken by surprise, stared at her.

Arabel grinned. "You've been very kind to me, Captain Melton. I wouldn't want you to suffer for it."

Robert suppressed a groan. The Blair women were too damned perceptive. He let his gaze stray to Emma. The candlelight gleamed against the rich wine-colored velvet of her gown and made her pearl earrings shimmer, but she seemed lit with an inner radiance.

As if aware of his regard, she turned and looked at him and Arabel. The smile faded from her eyes. Robert had seen that look on her face more than once in the past two days, starting with the morning he had gone riding with Arabel. When he had understood the cause, he had been surprised, then amused, then frustrated. Now an unexpectedly savage curse rose in his throat. For Christ's sake, Arabel was closer in age to David than to himself. He was fond of her, but it was nothing like what he felt when he looked at Emma.

Robert started across the room. He was playing with fire and he knew it, but when had he been immune to the seduction of danger?

"May I hope you aren't claimed for this dance, Mrs. Blair?"

A light flared in her eyes and then was quickly banked. "Don't tell me you know how to dance the Scottish reel, Captain Melton. You continue to surprise me."

Robert offered her his arm. "I may not be your cousins' equal, but I think I can promise not to disgrace you."

It was many years since Robert had attempted a Scottish reel, but with the first notes of the music the steps came back to him, and he heard again his mother's cheerful voice explaining the dances she had known as a girl. The exuberance of the music kindled a spark within him. Or perhaps it was Emma who did that, her face flushed with color, her elegant gown swirling about her, her hair coming free of its pins and tumbling around her face.

Her hands were warm in his own. Her gown felt soft when he lifted her in the air, but he knew the body beneath was softer. He was forced to draw a breath, and not because of the exertions of the dance. Then he looked into her face, framed by the fall of her disordered hair. She was laughing with careless, unthinking joy. Emma could alway stir him, but with her face bright with laughter she was irresistible.

Even when the dance separated them and he took another partner by the hands, it was Emma who filled his senses. The music quickened, the blood pounded in his head, and there was no room for thought. By the time the dance came to an end, they were both laughing. His hands were still around her waist. She swayed toward him. The scent of lily of the valley and clean perspiration washed over him. Her lips, the color of ripe peaches, parted slightly. A lock of hair fell against her cheek where he would like to brush his fingers. The silk braiding at the neck of her gown stirred with her rapid breathing. One of her sleeves had slipped, revealing the creamy curve of her shoulder.

The air seemed heavy, the fire stifling, the lamplight unnaturally bright. Looking into Emma's gray-green eyes, as misty as the Scottish countryside, he felt a moment of naked vulnerability, as if a part of him he had kept locked away for years had been laid bare. In the clear depths of her eyes he saw that her defenses had been breached as effectively as his own.

"You dance almost as well as a Scotsman, Captain Melton." Emma's usually level voice was breathless.

"High praise indeed." Robert forced himself to release her. Another minute and he would have been kissing her, there, in front of her family.

Emma tugged her sleeve back into place as if the loss of physical contact had made her self-conscious. "I must go and take my turn at the piano." With a bewitching smile she added, "It's a long time since I've enjoyed a dance so much."

While Emma played the piano, accompanied by Andy on the tambourine, Robert danced with Arabel, and then with Eleanor Blair, and then with Kirsty. It was not the same as dancing with Emma, but he enjoyed himself. The high spirits and good humor of the company were infectious. Listening to the laughter and fragments of talk, watching the blur of movement and the flickering light of the fire, Robert was reminded of evenings at his parents' house. The free and easy mix of generations. The lack of formality. The dancing, though minuets and waltzes had predominated during his childhood. The snatches of political talk, though these had had a sharper urgency in those heady early days of the Revolution and in the bitter years that followed. His parents' circle had been less conventional than the Blairs', but the atmosphere had been much the same.

When Eleanor called a halt to the dancing and said supper was ready, talk was lively and informal around the damask-covered table. "I had a letter from Jack yesterday," Andy said, reaching for a plate of cold beef. "He's in Brussels now. It's full of English visitors because of all the British troops stationed there. It sounds as if our soldiers spend most of their time dancing."

"Andy." Arabel frowned at him. "Captain Melton is stationed in Brussels."

"That's all right," Robert said. "It's an apt description." At least it was from what he had heard about the British forces left to guard the Netherlands.

"Jack says Brussels is ten times more exciting than London. And here I am stuck in Edinburgh. It's like rubbing salt in the wound." Andy speared a piece of beef and transferred it to his mouth.

"Jack Sheriton's mother is a cousin of Aunt Eleanor's," Emma told Robert. "He and Andy have been friends since Eton."

"And then I persuaded him to go to university in the wilds of Scotland," Andy said. "Only Jack managed to get himself sent down before Christmas. So for his sins, his brother's taken him to the Continent. While I, having been on my best behavior—well, more or less—am rewarded by continuing to slave away at my books."

"Poor Andy." Arabel's voice was tinged with mockery. "Your life has been so very dull."

Andy made a face at her. Arabel threw her napkin at

him. Andy caught it in midair. "As if the rest isn't bad enough," he went on, "Jack wrote that they've seen the Durwards. Friends of his brother's. We met them when we were traveling together two years ago."

"What's that got to do with anything?" Arabel asked.

"If you'd seen Caroline Durward, you'd understand why I'm jealous."

Robert's fingers tightened around the stem of his wineglass. Apparently, Andy was acquainted with the only English people Robert could count as his friends. The irony was perfect. Adam Durward would appreciate it. "Good Lord." Robert decided it would be best to be open about the friendship. "Do you mean the Caroline Durward whose husband is an aide to the British ambassador?"

"I say, do you know Caroline and Adam?" Andy said. "Oh, of course. You must have met when Adam was stationed in Portugal."

"Yes." It was perfectly true, though it didn't begin to tell the story of Robert's friendship with Adam Durward.

Talk turned to a play currently being performed at the Theatre Royal. Robert sat back and listened. Thus he was the first to become aware of shouts and the protesting voice of one of the servants coming from the hall. He glanced at the door. Beside him, Emma stiffened. The talk and laughter continued, punctuated by the clink of silver and glasses.

Emma pushed back her chair. The paneled door burst open. The candlelight wavered. Matt Lauder stood framed in the doorway, dressed in rumpled riding clothes, hair on end, a pair of leather gloves clutched in his hand. His gaze went straight to Jamie. "I knew I'd find you here. Thought you could hide, did you?"

The table went suddenly still. Gavin rose from his chair. "See here, Lauder—"

Jamie was on his feet as well. "What the hell are you doing here?"

"Watch your tongue, Blair, there are ladies present." Matt made an elaborate bow in Eleanor's direction. "Your pardon for interrupting, Mrs. Blair. Jamie and I have some unfinished business to settle."

"You won't do it in my wife's dining room," Gavin said.

"No, Uncle." Jamie's eyes didn't leave Matt's face. "Let him say whatever he's come to say."

Matt strode down the room to confront Jamie. "Too many other people have been dragged into our business. It's time we settled this, just the two of us." He flung one of the gloves down at Jamie's feet. "Name your second and your weapon."

Someone gasped. Emma had gone very white, but she said nothing. Neither did Gavin. Like Angus, it seemed he would not interfere with the feud.

Jamie bent down and picked up the glove. "Done, Lauder. I'll meet you whenever you choose."

6

Robert sat on a straight-backed chair in the parlor of Mlle. Hébert's Academy for Young Ladies and smiled the smile he had often used to disarm suspicion. The woman seated across from him surveyed him out of calm, appraising eyes. She was a tall woman in her mid-thirties, with light brown hair pulled neatly back from a sensible, intelligent face. Her name was Miss Ramsay, she had told him, and she had taken over the running of the school when Mlle. Hébert died last spring.

Miss Ramsay did not look as though she would deceive easily, but his story was simple enough. "I was visiting recently with some friends in Durham," he began. "They asked me to search for a young woman who was employed by them as a governess. She left them with no warning a little more than a year ago, and all efforts to trace her have failed. But we know she was educated in Edinburgh. She spoke beautiful French, which is why I thought your school . . ."

Miss Ramsay folded her hands, perhaps a sign of impatience. "There are many schools for young ladies in Edinburgh, Captain Melton, and many have competent teachers of the French tongue."

"Sorel. Her name was Lucie Sorel."

Miss Ramsay's eyes widened. She stared at Robert, but

she seemed to be looking beyond him. "Lucie." The name was a bare whisper of sound. In this neat, spare parlor far away from Blair House, he had found the first link to his wife's past.

"Forgive me, Captain Melton. It was not a name I expected to hear." Miss Ramsay unfolded her hands and smoothed the dove-gray skirt of her dress. "Yes, I knew Lucie Sorel. She was a pupil here and later a teacher."

"Can you tell me when she left here and where she went?"

Miss Ramsay took a moment to order her memories. "It was in the autumn of 1803. September. I remember the date because I had been here just a year."

It fit. Robert had met Lucie early in 1804. She said she had been in Paris four months.

"But where she went, or why, I cannot tell you," Miss Ramsay went on. "She left only the briefest of notes to Mlle. Hébert, who was quite overcome by the young woman's want of gratitude."

"They were close then?"

Miss Ramsay hesitated. "There is really no reason I should not tell you. Lucie made no secret of it. She was a foundling, an illegitimate child of someone wealthy enough to pay for her care. Mlle. Hébert took her in at the request of Mr. Logen, a minister of our city. Lucie was only an infant at the time and the arrangement was meant to be temporary, but her guardian, whoever he was, failed to make other provisions for her."

"She was abandoned?"

"I didn't say that. There was always money to pay for her keep and her education, but where it came from I cannot say. Mlle. Hébert never met the girl's father, if he was indeed her father, nor did she know his name. The arrangements were made through Mr. Logen, though I think there was a lawyer involved as well."

"His name?" Robert asked.

"I don't know."

"It's of no importance." He crossed his legs and leaned back in his chair with every show of ease. "Miss Sorel did not become governess to my friend's daughters until three years ago. Could she have left here to take another post?"

Miss Ramsay tightened her lips. "I think it far more likely that she left here with a man." She lifted her hand to her mouth as though she would bite back her words. "Forgive me, I am speculating without reason. But if you had known Lucie as I did . . ."

Robert leaned forward, his voice urging confidence. "If I had known Lucie?"

Miss Ramsay shifted her gaze to the window as though to bring back the image of the departed girl. "She was a young woman of extraordinary beauty. Clever, but impatient and restless. She could have stayed on here as a teacher—indeed, Mlle. Hébert hoped that she would—but she did not have a teacher's temperament." Miss Ramsay turned back to Robert and gave a rueful smile. "I thought marriage would be her passport to freedom, but I fear she saw it as another form of slavery."

Robert winced inwardly. "She had suitors?"

"One. Lucie had little chance of meeting men, but Hubert Cullen was a nephew of Mr. Logen and came here frequently in the company of his uncle. His father was a silk merchant and the boy had good prospects. Lucie thought him tedious, but he was a good-looking lad, and in the end she accepted him."

Sacrebleu. Three years after her death, Lucie could still surprise him. "She ran off to escape the marriage?"

"Perhaps. But not, I swear, to become a dependant in another woman's house. That's why she agreed to have Cullen in the first place, to have her own establishment. Lucie was impulsive, but she had a practical streak. It's likely she would have run off with someone. Or to some-one."

"She had friends?"

"None that I knew of."

"A fellow pupil perhaps?"

"It's possible, Captain Melton, though there was no one she spoke of with any fondness. She was a secretive young woman. With Lucie one never knew what was truth and what was invention."

Lucie to the core. The words brought her back so vividly he could almost smell her jasmine scent and hear her vibrant laugh. "Is it possible she was running away from someone?"

Miss Ramsay's eyes widened. "I'm not sure I understand."

"Was there someone of whom she was frightened? Someone she felt might do her harm?"

Miss Ramsay laughed. "Lucie? No. She was frightened of nothing and no one. Not brave, I think, as much as foolhardy."

Robert looked up and met Miss Ramsay's gaze. Her brows were drawn together as though she were struggling with a particularly knotty problem. He smiled and spread his hands. "Perhaps if I spoke to Mr. Logen . . ."

She shook her head. "Dead these ten years. I fear there is nothing more I can tell you. Mlle. Hébert never spoke of Lucie after she left."

"I see." Robert got to his feet. "I will not take up any more of your time." Then, as though it were an after-thought, he said, "The man to whom she was be-trothed—Cullen, wasn't it—where may he be found?"

"He has an establishment in the Lawnmarket."

When they reached the front door, Robert thought to ask Miss Ramsay if there was a likeness of Lucie Sorel. "But of course," she said after a moment's reflection. She left him standing in the hall and walked to a room at the back of the house from which she emerged a few minutes later carrying a miniature portrait in a thin oval gold frame. She held it out to him. "I'd forgotten about this. It was taken at the request of Mr. Cullen, shortly after they were betrothed. She had no chance to give it to him."

Robert looked down at the delicate wash of color. The enormous blue eyes stared out at him from a long delicately modeled face. Emma's face. The resemblance was not a trick of his memory, it was real. He handed the miniature back to Miss Ramsay. "She was a very beautiful young woman."

"She was that." Miss Ramsay slipped the portrait into the pocket of her dress as though she would put away the uncomfortable memories Robert's visit had brought her. Then she took it out again and pressed it into his hand. "Perhaps this will help you in your search. I have no more need of it." She stared at him a moment, her eyes vaguely troubled. "I wish you luck in your quest, Captain Melton. But if you fail—and I think it likely that you may—you must tell your friends not to be concerned with the fate of their governess. Lucie was not always wise, but she was a survivor."

Emma threaded her way through the maze of outdoor tables in the Lawnmarket. For once she felt no impulse to finger the bolts of silk and velvet and wool. She had accompanied Arabel to the tailor's but was too restless to wait while her cousin was measured for a new riding habit. Images of her brother felled by Matt Lauder's bullet or forced to flee the country had haunted her since last night.

She stepped aside to avoid two black terriers chasing after a ball. A glint of russet hair caught her eye in the crowd up ahead. She shook her head to clear it. Even now, though her mind was preoccupied with Jamie, Captain Melton intruded on her thoughts. Yet that gray coat did look very like the one he had worn to Edinburgh. She moved around a table bearing bolts of tartan, and caught a glimpse of the man's profile as he entered a shop on the opposite side of the Lawnmarket. It *was* Captain Melton. And he had just gone into Mr. Cullen's establishment.

Emma gathered up the skirt of her pelisse, then hesitated. She wouldn't want him to think she was following him. But whatever his business at Mr. Cullen's, it could hardly be private.

The memory of the touch of his hands and the warmth in his eyes last night came back, heating her body, banishing her doubts. She made her way across the street and left the bustle of the Lawnmarket for the more refined precincts of Mr. Cullen's.

A decisive voice rose above the soft-spoken murmur of the clerks, the questioning voices of the customers, the discreet rustle of fabric. "I'm afraid I cannot help you, Captain Melton. I haven't—"

"Captain Melton, this is a surprise." Emma walked toward the counter where Melton and Cullen faced each other, Cullen regarding Melton as though he were a wolf got in among the calves. "How do you do, Mr. Cullen. I see you've met my husband's friend Captain Melton. He's staying with us at Blair House."

Hubert Cullen's manner thawed somewhat. He was a dark-haired man of middle height. He might have had some claim to good looks, before the sense of his responsibilities and position in society had drawn down the lines of his face and prosperity had added flesh to his body. He nodded at Melton in response to Emma's introduction but did not volunteer any more of the information Melton had plainly been seeking.

Emma smiled at Melton, memories of last night dancing in her nerve endings. "I take it it was more than Mr. Cullen's excellent wares which brought you to the shop?"

An echoing smile lit Melton's eyes. "How did you guess? I'm trying to trace the former governess of my friends in Durham. I learned this morning that she was acquainted with Mr. Cullen."

"But how extraordinary." Emma turned back to Cullen with a look intended to remind him of the number of bolts of silk she had purchased over the years. "I'm sure Mr. Cullen will be happy to do so."

Cullen did not look precisely happy about it, but he did suggest they retire to his living quarters. He led them up an outdoor staircase to a fourth-floor flat with cabbage rose wallpaper and well-polished furniture, apologized for his wife's absence, and offered them tea, which they declined.

Emma listened with interest as Melton recounted the story of his friends' governess, Lucie Sorel, and what he had learned about her at Mlle. Hébert's only this morning. "I thought you might have been privy to information unknown to Miss Ramsay," he concluded. "Do you know of anyone Miss Sorel might have consulted for advice? A lawyer perhaps. There must have been matters to arrange in connection with her marriage."

"She made me a laughingstock." Cullen was sitting away from the light of the windows, but there was no mistaking the bitterness in his voice. "She had no cause to leave me. She had no family. She was born on the wrong side of the blanket." He stopped short and cast a glance at Emma.

Emma suppressed a smile. "You needn't fear for my sensibilities, Mr. Cullen. I have heard of such things."

Cullen coughed and fidgeted with his tightly tied neckcloth. "Miss Sorel had no prospects save teaching others what had been taught to her. It didn't matter to me. I made her an honorable proposal."

"It was generous of you," Melton said, "taking on a penniless young girl with no connections."

Cullen's face suffused with color. "Not quite penniless. She had a marriage portion."

Melton raised his brows. "Whoever paid for her schooling was generous as well."

Cullen looked him directly in the eye. "Not that that influenced my decision to wed her."

"Of course not. I understand she was a very beautiful young woman."

Cullen's face softened. "Very beautiful."

"Was it a large sum?"

Cullen's gaze shifted to the daffodils painted on the fire screen. For a moment Emma thought he would not answer. When he did speak, his voice was reduced to a whisper. "A thousand pounds."

A thousand pounds. Emma glanced at Melton and saw her own surprise echoed on his face. A thousand pounds was a substantial dowry for girls far better situated than Lucie Sorel. To a woman in her position, it would have been a fortune. "She abandoned it as well as you?" Melton asked. "Or was she able to claim it on her own account?"

"How could she? The money was contingent on her marriage." Cullen turned to Emma. "It was your cousin's husband who handled the arrangements. Mr. Bramwell Martin."

"Bram?" Emma leaned forward in surprise. What had hitherto been simply an interesting story proved to touch her personally.

Cullen nodded. "He'd worked for the lawyer who first arranged Lucie's care, but the lawyer died shortly before our betrothal. Martin inherited his clients. You might speak to him about the matter, but I doubt he has anything to tell you. I was not to ask any questions. It was a condition of the marriage settlement. Whoever paid for Lucie's upbringing did not want his part known." Cullen turned back to Melton. "Tell your friends to forget Lucie

Sorel. She went her own way, and she cared naught whom she might hurt."

Emma said nothing until she and Melton had left Cullen's flat and descended the outdoor stairs. Then she looked up at him with a smile that was part teasing, part curious. Just as she had begun to think she was wrong to suspect him of being interested in Arabel, here he was pursuing another young woman. "You're a secretive man, Captain Melton. You should have told me of your search earlier. I would have been glad to make inquiries."

"I didn't want to impose on you."

Emma laughed. "After all the times I've imposed on you? Does it violate some code of manly honor to seek help from a woman? For shame, I thought you were above such quibbling."

"I'd like to think so." He offered her his arm. She took it, wishing walking allowed for as much touching as dancing. Yet though her hand, decorously encased in a cream-colored kid, merely rested on the gray kerseymere of his sleeve, she felt a shock of heat as sharp as it was pleasurable.

They moved around three ladies examining a length of merino, and a cart delivering bolts of silk, and with one accord, made for the High Street. "How odd that Bram should be involved in the business," Emma said. "It's a pity he's in Paris. Would you like me to write to him?"

Melton hesitated a moment. "Thank you. I know my friends would be grateful. But I think it would be best if you said nothing to the rest of your family. Talk can spread quickly and a governess's reputation is a fragile thing."

Emma nodded. A gust of wind came up, brushing the moss-green folds of her pelisse against his legs. "If Miss Sorel had stayed in Edinburgh, she'd have been married to Mr. Cullen for more than eleven years now," Emma said. "Poor Mr. Cullen. There's nothing precisely wrong with him, but I cannot imagine eleven years as his wife. Lucie Sorel was quite clever to escape the tedium of his embrace."

"If you'd been in her place, is that what you would have done?"

She looked down at the imprint of her wedding band beneath her glove. "Yes. Yes, I would. Not that I don't understand how difficult the choice must have been. There is more than one kind of drudgery. Yet I would want to preserve at least the illusion of independence."

They had reached the North Bridge, which spanned the valley that divided Old Town from New. "Are you bound for your uncle's?" Melton asked. "Or may I escort you somewhere in recompense for interrupting your morning?"

Emma hesitated. Arabel had said she would find her own way home from the tailor's. But Emma didn't want to go back to Gavin and Eleanor's. She wanted to prolong these precious moments alone with Robert Melton. When she was with him, the world became an enticing labyrinth filled with possibilities she had thought closed to her years before. "If we go back to St. Andrew Square, I'll only lose my temper with Jamie and call him seven kinds of fool. Again. It won't do any more good than it did last night."

Melton's brows drew together. "Have you spoken to Gavin about the duel?"

"First thing this morning." Her free hand curled into a fist. "He said Jamie's a man and we have to let him go his own way. I said I'd be happy to do so, the minute Jamie starts behaving like a man."

Melton smiled. "Apt, if not tactful."

"No, I suppose not." She unclenched her hand. "I'll talk to Angus when we return to Blair House tomorrow. If anyone has the authority to stop Jamie, he does. Whether or not he'll use it is another matter."

Melton's gaze moved over her face. "For all their talk, I don't think your brother and Lauder mean to hurt each other."

"Nor do I. But that doesn't mean they won't." The wind tugged a strand of hair from beneath her bonnet. She pushed it back. "Oh, enough of Jamie. At least he can't do anything about the duel until we return home. Meanwhile, I won't let him spoil our visit. Let me show you Edinburgh as it should be seen. From above." She pointed to the large green conical hill rising above the houses just beyond the end of the bridge. "Calton Hill. We bury our great men there. More important, it's the finest view of the city. And it's a glorious day for a walk."

He laughed. "Meaning that the sky is a shade less gray than usual and the wind a bit less sharp?"

"Exactly. It's enough to make one believe in the possibility of spring."

Melton seemed content to walk in companionable silence. But sweet as the silence was, Emma still had questions about the day's revelations. "Did you know her well?" she asked. "Lucie Sorel, I mean."

"I scarcely knew her at all." A smile pulled at his mouth. "She's not a former mistress, if that's what you're wondering."

Hot color flooded her face. She forced herself to meet his gaze, because to look away would be to take the cowardly way out. "I'm sorry. That was unpardonably rude of me."

His eyes glinted back at her. "Not in the least. It's a very natural question. But while I'm not a paragon of virtue, that's one place I draw the line."

"Seducing governesses?"

"Seducing any woman whose livelihood is dependent upon her respectability."

They were walking along the road that wound up Calton Hill. The sounds of the city receded. The air was sweeter here, cleaner, fragrant with promise. Emma stopped and turned to Melton. The crisp air made her reckless. "And women whose position in life is more secure, Captain Melton?"

The spark that was always banked in his eyes flared to life. "I never claimed to be a saint, Mrs. Blair."

Emma felt a smile playing about her lips, though her chest had gone tight and the braided collar of her pelisse seemed to bite into her throat. "Nor did I, Captain Melton."

His hand closed on her arm. For an exhilarating moment, she was sure he meant to pull her to him. Then she realized he was merely drawing her to the side of the road. A young couple was descending the hill, their heads bent over a volume of poetry.

Melton released her and they resumed their climb. Emma fixed her gaze on the unfinished Nelson monument at the top of the hill, surprised she could feel at once so painfully self-conscious and so gloriously alive.

The wind was sharper at the top of the hill, biting and free. She tugged at the green velvet ribbons on her bonnet and lifted her bared head to the sky. The city was spread before them. To the south lay the jumbled streets and alleys of Old Town, overhung by blue smoke, dominated by the bulk of the Castle. Nearer at hand were the crescents and terraces of New Town, laid out with elegant rationality, glittering in the fitful sunlight. "It's a splendid view, isn't it?" she said, her voice strained, her breathing quick and fast.

"Yes." Melton's voice sounded as strained as hers. He was standing a handspan away. She turned and met his gaze. The city vanished. She was on a windy hill alone with a man she'd been longing to kiss from the moment they met.

"Emma," he said. There was a note of wonder in his voice and something else, something she would almost have called pain. Then she was in his arms, her body pressed to his, her lips parted eagerly beneath his own, and all thought fled.

The heat of his mouth filled her. Her gloved hands clutched the smooth fabric of his coat. His fingers slid into her hair. She felt liberated, cut loose from the world. And at the same time, as though she had gone home.

Then suddenly it was over and she was no longer in his arms. They stood facing each other while scruples and rules and propriety and self-doubt choked the air between them.

"I'm sorry." Emma laughed, a desperate, gasping sound. "No, I'm not sorry at all. I—Thank you, Captain Melton."

He smiled. "At the very least, don't you think it's time you began to call me Robert?"

A genuine laugh escaped her, cutting through the awkwardness. "Robert."

He bent and picked up her bonnet, which had fallen unnoticed in the course of the embrace. She put it on her head, hiding her disordered hair, feeling her sober, responsible self return as she tied the ribbons. She was tempted to pull the thing off again, to tug all the pins from her hair, to run back into his arms.

But she did not, because Kirsty would be wondering where she was and Eleanor would be waiting luncheon for them and she didn't entirely trust Jamie not to ride back to Blair House and plan to fight Matt at dawn. Besides, Robert did not open his arms to her. She had the odd feeling that if she kissed him again, he would pull back.

A host of questions hovered on her lips as they walked down the hill. She knew now that Robert Melton wanted her. The knowledge warmed her, even against the quickening wind. But she could not have said whether what he felt was transitory desire or something deeper. Whether he simply wanted her body or whether he had begun to hunger for her soul.

As she had for his.

David kept his eyes on the miniature of his mother while Robert told him Lucie's story as it had unfolded that day. "Whoever her parents may have been," Robert concluded, "they cared enough for her to see that she was well educated and to give her a generous marriage portion."

David ran his finger around the gold rim of the miniature. "Do you think Mr. Cullen knows more than he told you?"

"I think he guessed Lucie was related to the Blairs— he was uncomfortable talking about her in front of Emma. We aren't the only ones to notice how much she resembles Lucie. I suspect Lucie's relationship to so powerful a family was part of what led Cullen to offer for her. But I don't think he knows anything concrete."

David nodded, started to ask something else, but instead was overcome by a cough.

Robert studied his son. Even in the warm lamplight, David looked paler than usual. "I may be an absentee father, but I don't like the sound of that cough. Shall I get you some hot lemonade?"

"No, I'm all right." David snuggled back into the fluffy pillows and let Robert pull the quilt up around him. But when Robert had climbed into bed beside him, he said, "What about Emma? Do you think she suspects anything?"

"Why should she? My lies are more probable than the truth." Robert turned down the lamp. "It's as well she knows something of your mother's story. She's going to write to Bram Martin. We'd have had to find a way to contact him in any case."

But later, as he stared up at the patterns the moonlight made on the chintz canopy and listened to the even sound of David's breathing, Robert acknowledged the risks he had run in the course of the day. He had had to improvise when Emma discovered him in Cullen's shop. And so, under the guise of taking her into his confidence, he had told her more lies. And then, when she had shown too great an interest in Lucie's story, he had distracted her with a kiss.

No, that wasn't it. Or at least not all of it. If there had been any calculation in his kissing her, there had been none at all during the embrace. In that instant of time he had been happy. It was an unfamiliar emotion, compounded of hope and longing, feelings to which he had long been a stranger.

He rolled onto his side, shutting his eyes against the shimmering moonlight. If he had learned nothing else in his twelve years of soldiering, he had learned that you couldn't let personal feelings interfere with a mission.

Emma Blair could be nothing to him.

7

The sound of the breakfast parlor door slamming shut reverberated through the great hall. Robert paused midway down the stairs. Emma was leaning against the closed door, her breathing hard with anger, her eyes dark with frustration.

"Sir Angus refused to stop the duel?"

"He refused even to discuss it." Emma drew a long breath and walked toward the stairs. "How's David?"

David's cough had developed into a cold by the time they returned from Edinburgh late the previous day. "He says his throat's scratchy. I got him a mug of hot lemonade and told him to spend the day in bed. Kirsty's reading to him."

"Then I can't promise how much rest he'll get, but at least he won't be bored."

Emma stood at the foot of the stairs, her hand resting on the newel post. Robert paused one step above her, his hand on the railing, inches from her own. He looked down into her eyes. The starched white muslin at the neck of her gown framed her face but could not contain her vitality. There was a line between her brows he longed to smooth away, just as he longed to pull the pins from her hair and undo the fastenings on her gown for far more carnal reasons. "You can't always prevent others from committing folly," he said.

"No, but I can try." Her fingers tightened on the newel post. "I'm going to ride over to Lauder Hall and see if Lord Lauder is more willing than Uncle Angus to stop Jamie and Matt from killing each other. I was wondering—"

"If I'd go with you?"

"Yes."

Her gray-green eyes were clear and open, filled with trust. Robert swallowed the self-disgust that welled up in his throat. "We can leave whenever you want."

They looked in on David and Kirsty, who assured their parents they'd be perfectly all right. Downstairs, Emma spoke to Arabel, who wished her good luck and promised to keep an eye on the children.

The air was heavy with damp and there was an ominous line of clouds massed to the north, but the rain would probably hold off for a few hours. Besides, Emma told Robert as he helped her into the saddle, if Scots let the prospect of rain keep them indoors, they'd be housebound nine tenths of the year.

Robert reined in his horse to a comfortable trot. "How long has it been since you've called at Lauder Hall?"

"Over a year. But when I was a girl, we were in and out of each other's houses all the time."

"So the hated Lauders were your childhood friends?"

"The girls were. And Charlie. He and Arabel were playmates. Archie and Matt were always getting into fights with my cousins and Jamie, but even that wasn't as—as virulent as it is now."

She glanced at a herd of cattle grazing in the distance. "Mary Lauder died two years before Aunt Alice. I went on visiting Lauder Hall for a time, but once the Lauder girls married and moved away I no longer had an excuse.

With their wives gone, Uncle Angus and Lord Lauder became more intransigent than ever."

They said little more as they crossed into Lauder land, passed the ruins of the south barn, and at last came within view of the house. Lauder Hall was more elegant and controlled than Blair House, a solid, carefully symmetrical building of tawny stone with a lavish baroque facade. Yet despite the pilasters and horseshoe stairs and elaborate ironwork, there was nothing soft about the house. In its own way it was every bit as powerful and commanding as the untidy stone pile of Blair House.

The groom who took their horses stared at Emma as did the footman who opened the pedimented front door when she rang for admittance.

"Hullo, Ned." Emma gave the young man a sunny, confident smile. "Captain Melton and I have come to see Lord Lauder."

The footman swallowed. He appeared not much more than twenty and looked uncomfortable in his elaborate neckcloth and heavy blue-and-buff coat. "I'll inquire if his lordship is at home, Mrs. Blair."

Robert followed Emma into a high-ceilinged entrance hall lined with dark paneling and embellished with gilt. A cry of recognition came from the gallery above.

"Emma. Melton." Charlie started down the stairs two at a time. "Take their cloaks and tell Father we have guests, Ned. We'll be in the small parlor."

Charlie led Emma and Robert to a handsome, well-proportioned room with pale blue silk covering the walls and classical plasterwork ornamenting the ceiling and mantel. "Sorry about Ned," he said, poking up the fire. "He's a little unsure of himself, and it isn't every day a Blair comes to call."

Emma pulled off her gloves. "I promise we haven't come armed." Her color was high from the ride, her eyes glowing. Robert wondered if he would ever be able to look into them and not be affected.

He turned away and moved toward the windows. His gaze was caught by one of the portraits that hung on the silk-covered wall. Emma's face seemed to be looking down at him. Christ, he was obsessed with her.

He looked again at the portrait. The woman was painted in a kind of grotto whose darkness was illuminated by her glowing skin and the white of her dress. Her eyes were a startling blue, her hair a dusky cloud that broke free of its confining pins. It was not Emma but his wife he looked upon. Lucie's eyes, Lucie's hair, and still more a resemblance born of carriage and expression. Lucie used to stand just so, her weight carried on her left foot, her head tilted so that her gaze was provocative and indirect.

He stepped closer to the painting, vaguely aware of Emma's and Charlie's voices murmuring in the background. The woman's features were not as fine as Lucie's. The nose was too short and the mouth too thin. Yet that she was related to Lucie he could not doubt.

His gaze went to the necklace about the woman's throat. His pulse quickened with the thrill of discovery. The necklace was gold, intricately wrought in clusters of leaves and flowers. Each flower held a pearl. He counted them. There were seven. A large tear-shaped topaz fell from the necklace and nestled between the woman's breasts. He had seen that necklace about Lucie's throat. There was no doubt it was the same.

The voices behind him had grown silent. He turned, schooling his features into an expression of polite interest. "A charming portrait. She has something of the look of Mrs. Blair. Don't tell me portraits of Blairs are to be found at Lauder Hall."

Emma laughed. "Hardly. Or not exactly. You see those things in families that have intermarried."

Robert raised his brows. "Blairs and Lauders? I don't believe it."

"But it's true nonetheless." Emma came to stand beside him. "Now and again they'd try to patch things up and a marriage would be arranged. It never worked. It's a hundred years or more since that was tried, but the blood's been mixed and now and again it shows."

Robert glanced back at the portrait. No, in Lucie's case it was more than that. The resemblance was too strong.

Charlie joined them. "That's my aunt. Lucilla."

Lucilla. *Sacrebleu,* could the evidence be any plainer? Robert turned to Charlie, seeing him as though for the first time. The sable hair. The deep, startlingly blue eyes. The pale skin, healthily tanned in Charlie's case, tended to alabaster perfection in Lucie's. "Your father's sister?"

Charlie nodded. "She died young, on a trip abroad. France. Or Flanders. One of our black sheep."

"I take it there was a man involved?"

"What else? Her parents packed her off to the Continent to get her away from him or else she ran off with him and they pretended she was traveling abroad to cover up the scandal."

"We used to like to speculate about it when we were children," Emma said. "There's nothing like a scandal to stir the imagination."

Robert turned to look at her. "Did you ever meet Lucilla Lauder?"

"Oh, no, she died before I was born." Emma's brows drew together, level, unplucked, so different from Lucie's. "It must have been 1783, because I know it was just after my cousin Neil was born. I remember Aunt Alice telling me Mary Lauder came over to see the baby and told her they'd just had news of Lucilla's death. Aunt Alice said she knew it was selfish of her, but it quite ruined the delight of showing off her firstborn."

Seventeen eighty-three was the year Lucie had been born. "You never learned who the man was?" Robert asked.

Charlie shook his head. "I tried to tease it out of my father once, but he wouldn't talk about it. I'm not sure he knows himself."

But Robert knew or at least suspected. Just as Charlie had had the audacity to fall in love with Arabel Blair, one of the previous generation of Blairs had fallen in love with Lucilla Lauder. No wonder Lucie's birth had been kept such a secret.

The door swung open behind them. "This is an unexpected pleasure." Lord Lauder stood in the doorway, his harsh face composed into a host's formal smile. "I'm sorry Archie and Matt aren't here to greet you. They've ridden out to one of the farms."

Emma took a step toward him. "Lord Lauder—"

Lauder held out his hand. "A moment, Emma. I've asked Ned to bring in tea. Won't you be seated?"

Robert studied the man who must be Lucie's uncle. Lauder's eyes were a blue not unlike Lucie's, but otherwise he did not much resemble his sister Lucilla. He had the same finely drawn features and aquiline nose as his sons, but his face was marked with fifty-some years' experience. Not a man who would have taken kindly to his sister's love affair with a hated Blair.

Emma moved to a small chair upholstered in pale blue satin. "How is Sally Drummond?"

"Recovering." Lauder's voice was composed, but his eyes betrayed the anger he still felt over the fire. "And her young man as well. I had a word with her father, and he's consented to a betrothal."

"I'm so glad. I was worried about them."

Ned brought in a tea tray and a plate of biscuits. Robert took a swallow of tea, longing for a good cup of coffee, and waited. This was Emma's fight.

Emma settled back in her chair and regarded Lauder over the rim of her cup. "Now, can we both admit this isn't an ordinary visit?"

"No?" Lauder returned her gaze, his eyes shrewd. "What is it then?"

"A parley. A plea for an end to four hundred years of madness."

Lauder gave a dry smile. "Only four hundred? Wasn't there a cattle raid in 1382?"

"Don't." Emma set down her cup with such force that tea sloshed into the saucer. "Don't treat me like a child. At least give me a fair hearing. Surely you owe that much to your wife's memory."

A muscle tensed in Lauder's jaw. For a moment Robert saw stark grief in the older man's eyes.

"You must know that Matt has challenged Jamie," Emma said.

Lauder carefully crossed one booted leg over the other. "My sons keep me ill informed of their doings, but I had heard something of the sort."

"And you intend to sit by and let it happen?"

"Short of locking Matt up, I don't see how I can stop it."

"For the love of God." Emma gripped the arms of her chair. "You have more authority than that."

"Do I? Matt's a grown man, a soldier. In this he won't obey me. If I forbid the fight, it will only make him more determined."

"Send him away."

"Jamie will follow, as Matt followed Jamie to Edinburgh." Lauder sipped his tea. "Let them settle this between themselves, lass. At least this time there won't be anyone else involved."

Emma swallowed. "Your son could be killed. Or my brother. I think that involves us both."

"They won't let it come to that."

"Even they can't know what they may let it come to." Emma's knuckles were white where she gripped the chair.

Charlie leaned forward. "Father—"

"Stay out of this, lad." Lauder set down his cup. "You're trying to battle something that's gone on for centuries, Emma."

"Just because it's gone on for centuries doesn't mean it has to go on forever. When Aunt Alice and Lady Lauder were alive—"

"When my wife and Lady Blair were alive, the feud was swept under the carpet." Lauder's gaze was direct and uncompromising. "Now it's erupted again, stronger than ever."

Emma drew a breath. "You can't think—"

"I think what lies between the Blairs and the Lauders goes beyond any one person. My father and your grandfather got on better for a time as well. Then their relationship worsened. I never knew why. I'm not sure it matters. It's been that way for as long as anyone remembers. Lauders steal Blair cattle. Blairs carry off a Lauder daughter in retaliation. Lauders betray Blairs to the English. Blairs set fire to Lauder Hall while the Lauder men are away fighting for Queen Mary. Years later a marriage is arranged to try to patch up differences. The groom's brother stabs the bride's brother at the wedding feast."

"In 1650," Emma said. "I've heard the story. Charles II was among the wedding guests, seeking help to regain his crown. In God's name, sir, those days are past."

"Are they?" Lauder glanced at Robert. "You're a soldier, Melton. You'll understand."

Robert met Lauder's gaze. "I think Lord Lauder means that for all we call ourselves civilized, we fight wars with guns and cannon that take far more lives than were lost in border skirmishes two hundred years ago."

"And that makes it all right?" Emma's voice trembled with fury and disgust.

"We aren't discussing the way the world should be ordered," Lauder said gently. "We're discussing the way it is. The way it's always been."

"No." Emma stood, her back very straight. "If you accept that, then nothing will change, ever."

Lauder got to his feet and faced her. "My dear girl, I long since gave up hope of much of anything changing within my lifetime."

"Then you'll do nothing to stop the duel?"

For a moment, Lauder's polite facade was stripped away. He looked as Lauder men must have looked through the centuries when confronting a Blair. "Your brother and cousin set fire to our barn and nearly killed two of our tenants. No man should be asked to let an insult go unanswered."

"Then God have mercy on us all." Without another word, Emma turned and walked from the room.

8

Emma swept past Ned, pushed open the heavy front door, and hurried blindly down the curving stone stairs. Tears of frustration stung her eyes. A bitter sense of failure rose up in her throat, choking her.

She had reached the courtyard before she heard Robert call her name. "Emma. Emma, don't." His hands closed on her shoulders and he drew her into his arms.

A shuddering sob escaped her lips. She clung to him for a moment, dimly conscious of his warm breath against her face. Then awareness returned and she pulled back, realizing they might be seen from any of the windows that ran along the front of the house.

Robert's eyes smiled into her own. "I brought your cloak and gloves." He set the heavy wool about her shoulders and fastened the ties, then adjusted her hat, brushing his fingers against her cheek. "Ready to face the ride back?"

She nodded, took her gloves from him, and tugged them on with more force than was necessary.

"Ye'll have a wet ride," the stableboy said when he brought out their horses.

The numbing wind carried clear warning of a storm. Though it was little past twelve o'clock, the heavy clouds made it seem more like twilight. But Emma would not spend further time under the Lauder roof. She glanced at Robert. He gave a nod of understanding.

Emma spurred her horse to a gallop as if she could outrun the memory of the scene in the parlor. But the whir of wind and pounding of hoofbeats could not drown out the echo of Lord Lauder's words. *No man should be asked to let an insult go unanswered.* At the crest of the hill above Lauder Hall, she reined in and waited for Robert to catch up, her breath coming quick and hard.

"You can't outrun it," Robert said, drawing up his horse beside her own. "You can only wait for it to pass."

"I don't want it to pass. That would mean I've given up."

He smiled. "I can't imagine you giving up, Emma Blair. But you won't do much good if you take a tumble and break your leg."

They continued at a more moderate pace. As they neared the stone wall that divided Lauder and Blair land, the rain began, not a preliminary shower but a sudden, drenching downpour. The wind whipped up, blowing icy water in their faces. Sturdy pine and rowan trees swayed like saplings. As they jumped the stone wall, a flash of lightning illuminated the dark sky. Moments later thunder roared like a cannon blast. Emma's mare, a sure-footed animal used to traveling in all weather, jumped sideways, tossing her head.

"Easy, girl." Emma pulled up on the reins. A fresh gust of wind cut against her, nearly knocking her from the saddle. This was no ordinary rainstorm, to be ridden through with only the risk of a soaking. They would have to find shelter.

"There's an abandoned cottage beyond those trees," she said, fighting to make herself heard above the noise of the storm.

Robert nodded and turned his horse in the direction she indicated. Emma prayed her memory was not playing tricks on her. She had not visited the cottage since she and the other young Blairs had gone there to play as children. It had been empty as long as she could remember, a remnant of the days before Angus had built larger, more comfortable houses for his tenants. Nestled at the foot of a hill and sheltered by trees, it was difficult to spot even in clear weather.

The lightning came in quicker flashes. The thunder rolled closer, as if it were chasing them. A heavy branch cracked and fell to the ground not four feet away. Emma's fingers were numb with cold and her sodden cloak dragged heavily on her shoulders.

Suddenly the rough gray stone of the cottage rose before them, blessedly solid in the chaos of the storm. They tethered the horses, then ran to the shelter of the cottage, huddled together, Robert's arm around her shoulders.

The hinges creaked in protest as Robert pushed the wooden door open. Inside, the air was stale and musty. The meager light seeping through the shutters revealed the outline of a table and, to Emma's surprise, a lamp. Robert reached in his pocket and struck a spark with a flint. Yellow light flared from the lamp, spilling over the edges of the table and illuminating the cottage's main room.

Emma stared about her in surprise. When she last saw it, the cottage had been empty save for the broken-down table and a quantity of cobwebs and dust that had added to its charm for the children. Now the lamplight revealed that a simple linen cloth had been spread on the table, the floorboards had been swept clean, a basket by the stone fireplace was stacked with peats, and there was a pallet on the floor before the fireplace, covered with a gray blanket.

Her first thought was that someone was living in the cottage, unbeknownst to Angus. But there was no food or clothing or any other sign of a permanent home. A more likely explanation occurred to her. "Some of the tenants must be using the cottage as a trysting place."

Robert grinned. "That would explain why the bed is in the center of the floor."

Emma grinned back, then felt her throat go tight. She looked away and found herself staring at the pallet.

Robert stripped off his wet cloak and coat and knelt by the crude stone hearth. "The trysting lovers have left us a gift." He lifted a flask from the basket of peats, unstopped it, and sniffed. "Not bad, if you'll trust an Englishman's judgment. See what you think."

Emma took the flask and sipped the contents. Smooth, pungent whisky spread its warmth through her body. Her nerves steadied, she tugged off her gloves and removed her drenched hat and cloak. She pulled the gray blanket off the pallet and found a second blanket beneath.

Robert got the fire going. They spread their wet boots and cloaks and Robert's coat on the hearth and sat side by side on the pallet, each wrapped in a blanket, sharing the whisky between them. The smell of peat smoke and damp wool filled the room. Rain beat against the roof. Lightning cut through the cracks in the shutters. The thunderclap that followed shook the walls.

"I'm sorry." Emma pulled the rough wool blanket closer around her. "I should never have tried to go to Lauder Hall with a storm threatening. I seem to have failed at everything today."

Robert turned to look at her. The light of the fire warmed his skin. His wet hair fell over his forehead. He had removed his damp cravat, leaving his shirt to gape open at the neck. "You said everything you could to Lord Lauder." His eyes were kind yet honest.

"Perhaps." Emma began to pull the pins from her hair so it would dry faster. "But I failed nonetheless." She tugged at a pin. "Is that how you felt about the French? Single-minded, uncompromising hatred?"

He was silent for a moment. "It's not quite the same. The French and English may be old enemies, but they don't share as personal a history as the Blairs and the Lauders. And yet—" He stared into the fire. "Hatred is destructive, whatever form it takes."

The remembered horror in his eyes made her shiver. She reached for the flask. It was lighter than it had been. They had already drunk half the contents between them. "I feel a bit guilty," she said. "Highland whisky is too dear for most of the tenants to afford."

"We'll replenish it." Robert's expression lightened. "No, we'll leave double the amount."

Emma took a swallow of the whisky. It flooded through her, easing her anger. Smiling, she held the flask out to Robert. His fingers brushed against her own as he took it from her. A fleeting touch, but it burned stronger than the fire of the whisky. Her pulse raced. As if compelled, she looked into his eyes. His gaze caught and held her own.

A sharp, almost painful tension coiled between her legs and spread upward, forcing her to draw a ragged breath. The pressure of the damp fabric pulling across her breasts suddenly seemed unbearable. A cry escaped her lips, part an answer to the hunger in his eyes, part a plea born of her own longing. She leaned forward and reached out to pull him to her. His muscles tensed beneath her hand as if he was holding himself in check. Then his arm closed hard around her shoulders and his mouth covered her own.

His skin smelled of peat and rainwater. His mouth was hot and demanding. She slid her fingers into his damp hair and parted her lips, meeting the thrust of his tongue, tasting whisky and desire.

Molten longing coursed through her. She tried to

move closer to him, but the blanket was in her way. She lost her balance and felt herself slipping backward onto the pallet. It didn't seem like a bad idea. She pulled him down on top of her.

The weight of his chest on her breasts was an exquisite torment. The hardness of his arousal pressed against her thighs. She strained against him, trying to press even closer, but as she sought his mouth again, he drew back.

"Emma." With a harsh breath he rolled off her and pushed himself up on one elbow. "You make a man forget he ever knew the meaning of honor."

The air stung her skin. Remorse and scruples and common sense should have come flooding back. They didn't. She looked steadily into the eyes that betrayed his desire for her. "I'm not a virgin."

"You don't know me," he said in a flat voice. "You told me once you had no love for soldiers."

"The war's over."

His eyes clouded. "Some things are never over. And I—" He looked away, his features twisting with a bitterness she had never before seen on his face.

She laid her hand on his arm.

He looked her full in the face. His gaze held at once brutal honesty and stark torment. "I can offer you nothing."

The words cut through her. And yet, he would not have spoken them if he did not care for her. She searched his face. "You're saying that this"—she touched him between his legs with deliberate provocation—"is only lust for a woman's body?"

He sucked in his breath. "It's certainly lust."

"And nothing more?"

His eyes blazed with the feelings he would not allow himself to voice. Triumph surged within her. She gripped his shoulders. "I want this. I want you."

"Think, Emma." His voice was rough with strain. "We could make a child."

She laughed, recognizing this as his last resistance, knowing she could sweep it away. "We won't. It's the wrong time of month." She pulled him against her.

His breath left him on a shuddering sigh. She moved her hips beneath his own. With a groan, he sank his fingers into her hair and took her mouth in a raw, scorching kiss. His lips moved over her cheek and the line of her jaw and down her throat to meet the starched frill of her habit shirt.

"We're ahead of ourselves." His voice shaking with laughter and urgency, he pulled her up so he could reach behind and undo the buttons.

His fingers played against the nape of her neck, making her shiver. He unbuttoned her gown, untied the tapes on her habit shirt, ran his fingers over her collarbone, traced the swell of her breasts.

Emma tugged at the buttons on his waistcoat. He shrugged it off, then helped her struggle out of her dress. She yanked his shirt free of his breeches. He pulled it over his head and tossed it after the waistcoat.

Kneeling a foot apart on the pallet, they stared at each other in silence. His eyes glowed with an admiration that made her breath catch and the blood run hot through her veins. The firelight washed over his skin, showing the hardened muscles of a soldier and the dark remembrances of battle. She leaned forward, moved her mouth over the thick hair on his chest, and found one of his nipples while her fingers undid the fastening on his breeches.

He groaned, his hands twisting in her hair. "You're astonishingly practiced, Mrs. Blair."

She raised her head and grinned at him. "We Scots aren't as staid as we appear, Captain Melton."

She pulled down his breeches and he kicked them off.

They collapsed together on the coarse linen sheet that covered the pallet. He pushed down the sleeves of her chemise, stroked the hollows beneath her arms, eased her breasts free of the fabric. Her nipples hardened beneath his touch. When he drew the sensitive flesh into his mouth, she cried out, cradling his head between her hands.

He slid his hands down her back, over the contours of waist and hip, and pushed up the hem of her chemise. Though his breathing was fierce, his touch was gentle as he brushed the inner length of her thighs and closed his fingers over the thatch of hair between her legs.

Her blood pounded louder than the beat of the rain and the crack of the thunder. Her body was alive with sensation, more brilliant than the flash of the lightning. His hand slipped lower, stroking inside her. She pressed up against him.

"Emma?" he asked, his voice hoarse.

"Yes." Her breath was quick and uneven. "Now." She grasped hold of him, feeling him shudder and grow harder still at her touch.

"Dear Christ," he whispered, lifting her hips.

Trembling with joy and desire, she parted her thighs and drew him into her.

She knew he was as desperate as she, but he went suddenly still. He looked down at her with a longing that went beyond the joining of their bodies, and brushed his fingers against her cheek. Her heart constricted. She pulled his head down to her own. "Love me, Robert," she said, wrapping her legs around him and pulling him deeper into her.

The feel of his flesh filling her own was beyond anything that had gone before. A wave of heat swept through her, blotting out all thought of past or future. His breath was warm on her face, his skin slick with sweat, his body hard and sure as it drove her to madness. She clung to him, her fingers digging into his back, until sharp, blinding pleasure sang through her.

A cry was torn from her throat. He shuddered as if relaxing the control he had kept on himself. His movements quickened. He breathed her name, in wonder and need, and then he too found oblivion.

Robert's heart hammered against his ribs. A sense of well-being coursed through his veins. His face was buried in the softness of Emma's hair. Her chest heaved beneath his own. A faint scent of lily of the valley mingled with the smell of sweat and sex. Her thighs were wet where their bodies were still joined. Wet with his seed.

God in heaven. He squeezed his eyes shut. He had done the unforgivable. He had taken Emma, the daughter of a family whose secrets he sought to expose, the widow of a man whose friend he pretended to be, the sister of a man he had opposed in battle. In his years in the Peninsula, he had bedded women who believed him to be English, French, Spanish, and Portuguese, peasant, aristocrat, even priest. He had learned to use sex as both a tool and a weapon. But never had the deceit seemed so blatant or the taint of it so rotten.

His mind drifted back to haylofts and stone cottages, to whitewashed tavern bedchambers and the war-torn luxury of once elegant palaces. He had been more than three years married when he was sent to the Peninsula. It had taken two of those years for him to accept that Lucie was unfaithful and another year before he betrayed his own marriage vows. But surrounded by chaos and death, one learned to take solace in the only sort of beauty that was left in life. He had done his share of betraying and being betrayed, using and being used. But he had also known pleasure and friendship and in some cases deep affection.

None of his lovers had asked questions or demanded commitments. Emma had not done so either. Yet her eyes and the tone of her voice and her very caresses told him she wanted far more than transitory pleasure.

He braced himself on his elbows and looked down at the woman who had shaken his soul and destroyed his sense of honor. Her hair was spread about her, burnished by the fire. Her face looked more contented than he had ever seen it. Her eyes shone with a joy that stabbed him to the core.

She reached up and ran her fingers through his hair. "I've thought about doing that a good deal these past days. But I didn't expect—"

"Nor did I." He seized her hand and brought it to his lips. "Emma—"

"I wanted you." Her mouth curved in a smile. "I all but seduced you." Her eyes grew serious. "You don't owe me anything."

He owed her honesty at the very least, but he couldn't give it to her without destroying all he had come to Scotland to achieve. As he struggled to find adequate words, she pulled him to her and kissed him lightly. "Hold me," she said against his lips.

The rain still thudded against the roof. They could go nowhere for a while yet, he told his conscience. He pulled the blankets over them and cradled her in his arms. She threaded her fingers through his own and relaxed against him as if they had lain thus for years. He stroked her hair, basking in a treacherous contentment.

Eventually contentment gave way to something stronger. His body stirred against her own. Her skin grew warm with desire beneath his touch. She rolled toward him, open and eager.

They were slower this time, courting each other with fingers and lips and soft, whispered caresses. He eased her chemise off and got a proper look at the creamy flesh of her thighs and the tantalizing thatch between them which held the same glints of fire as the hair on her head.

Such patience drove them both to a frenzy. By the time they were joined, his breath was quick and labored and reason had mercifully fled. She clung to him in the throes of release as if he were her last refuge in a world gone mad.

When sanity returned, he was forced to admit that the rain had stopped. Without speaking, they gathered up their clothes and put themselves to rights as best they could. When he helped do up the buttons on her dress, he nearly damned his good intentions and took her again. He turned away quickly and sought refuge in straightening the blankets on the pallet.

"I'll be eternally grateful to whoever furnished the cottage," Emma said.

Robert returned the near-empty flask to the peat basket. He knew one pair of lovers who could afford Highland whisky. The cottage was not far from the stand of trees where he and Arabel had met Charlie Lauder the day they had gone riding. Robert hadn't realized how far their relationship had progressed. Perhaps he had been wrong to further the illicit affair. But thinking of what he had just shared with Emma, he decided he wouldn't deny it to anyone.

He and Emma retrieved their horses and rode in silence through the rain-drenched countryside. Despite the ravages of the storm, it looked much as it had a few hours before. And yet nothing would ever be the same.

By the time they reached Blair House, the shadows of early evening slanted across the courtyard. They entered the house by a side door. As they climbed the steps to the great hall, they heard voices from the sitting room. Raised voices were nothing out of the ordinary at Blair House, but the words that followed brought them both up short.

Shores of Desire

"I came as soon as I heard. I knew you'd want to know."

The voice was Andy Blair's. Something had happened that had made him travel from Edinburgh to Blair House in the midst of the storm. Emma crossed the hall and pushed open the sitting room door. Robert followed a few steps behind her.

Angus was sitting in his favorite chair, an uncharacteristic look of amazement on his face. Will leaned against the mantel, rubbing his temples as if he could not take it all in. Jamie was pacing in front of the fireplace with suppressed excitement. Arabel sat on the sofa, arms folded around her, eyes wide with surprise. Andy stood in the center of the room, his coat drenched, his usually well-combed hair damp and windblown.

"What's happened?" Emma asked.

Andy looked across the room at her. "Napoleon's escaped from Elba. He's landed at Frejus with a thousand men."

9

A host of conflicting emotions welled up in Robert's chest. Admiration for the emperor's audacity. Fear that audacity would not prove enough. Elation at the possibility that the Bourbons would be swept from power. Above all, a burning sense that he should be there, taking part in the struggle that would decide the future of his country.

Emma stared at Andy. "When? How?"

"March first. How isn't very clear. There are a lot of different stories."

"Idiots." Angus scowled. "Can't they even manage to guard one plaguey short fellow who's surrounded by water?"

Emma sank into the nearest chair. "Has there been fighting?"

"Not yet." Andy pushed the wet hair from his eyes. "Though God knows what's happened since the news left France. It's been more than two weeks."

Robert walked forward, into the circle of Blairs. "What else do you know?"

"Very little," Andy said. "The reports are chaotic."

Jamie stopped pacing and turned to Will. "We'll leave at first light. This is no time to be away from our regiments."

"Shouldn't you wait and see if there's going to be a war?" Arabel asked.

Jamie spared her a withering look. "We're not going to stand by and let Boney march all over the Continent again."

"He hasn't even marched into Paris yet," Arabel retorted. "The French may handle this for themselves."

"Fat Louis?" Jamie gave a shout of laughter. "No chance, Bel. The French couldn't cope with Boney the first time. Mark my words, we'll have to do the job again."

Robert swallowed. Hard. "If you'll excuse me, I should see how David's faring."

Arabel looked at him, eyes stricken. "I'm sorry. I should have said something right away. He's complaining now that his throat is sore. I told Kirsty we'd better leave him alone for a bit so he could get some sleep."

"If you've persuaded him to sleep, you've worked wonders." Robert smiled at her, feeling a stab of guilt at having left David alone all afternoon.

His guilt was reflected in Emma's eyes. But her gaze held fear and understanding as well. Jamie and Will could wait to be summoned back to their regiments. Soldiers stationed in the Netherlands, as Robert Melton was supposed to be, would be expected to return to their post immediately. She knew Robert would have to leave Blair House.

And she was right. Robert left the room and made for the stairs. It was twelve years since he had fled home to take part in another war, eager to prove himself. The world had been on fire and the battlefield, he had been convinced, was the place to be, not sitting tamely in Paris, working on his father's newspaper, writing articles that would never be read by the people they were meant for. His own youthful voice sounded in his head, addressing his father with all the confidence of the young and self-righteous: *You can't expect me to stay home and scrib-*

ble pamphlets. We need something stronger than words. And his father's quieter tones: *Words never killed anyone.*

The years that lay between the determined hothead of that exchange and the man he now was were filled with harsh lessons. Ambiguity was as much a part of warfare as the stench of saddle damp. And yet—Robert paused at the head of the stairs, gripping the stair rail—he could not sit on the sidelines. War might be folly, but if folly consumed France, he must play his part.

David's room was quiet and filled with shadows. A single lamp burned on the table beside the bed. Robert stood looking down at his son. Asleep, David always seemed younger, perhaps because his all-too-sharp eyes were veiled. There was something particularly vulnerable about the way he was lying now, with his arm flung over his face and the covers in disarray. He was only ten years old, and the father he was just coming to know was about to take him home to a country on the brink of civil war.

David opened his eyes and pushed himself up on his elbows. "You're back."

"Sorry to be gone so long. We got caught in the storm." Robert pushed aside memories of those wondrous hours in the cottage and sat on the edge of his son's bed. "How are you feeling?"

"All right. My throat's sore."

That wasn't promising. If David had felt remotely better, he would have insisted he was well enough to get out of bed. As his eyes adjusted to the dim light, Robert noted that his son's pale skin had an unhealthy flush. He put a hand on David's forehead and felt the damp heat of fever.

David twisted his head away. "I've been lots sicker. Grandmère doesn't fuss."

"Grandmère has been through this before. You're the only son I've got." And while he had been giving way to wanton indulgence with Emma, his son's health had taken a turn for the worse.

"Where's Emma?" David asked.

"Downstairs with the family." Robert hesitated. "Andy Blair rode out from Edinburgh. There's news from France. Napoleon's escaped from Elba and landed at Frejus."

David stared up at him. "You'll have to go back, won't you?"

"*We'll* have to go back," Robert said, wondering how long it would be before it was safe for David to travel. "I'll take you to Grandmère."

"That'll be awfully dangerous, won't it? If the king is still in Paris."

As usual David had an uncanny ability to put his father's thoughts into words. "We'll manage."

David sat up against the headboard and wrapped his arms around his knees. "Couldn't I stay here?"

"Here?" Robert stared at his son. "At Blair House?"

David nodded. "I could go on finding out about Maman. Besides, I like it here. I like Kirsty. I like Emma too."

Robert's throat tightened. David had become no less entangled with the Blairs than he had himself. "It wouldn't be safe."

"And going back to France is?"

Robert drew a breath. There was no way of knowing the state of affairs they would find in France. The country might even now be plunged into war. He and David could find themselves caught between two opposing armies. Yet to leave David at Blair House was unthinkable. Besides the danger of discovery, he couldn't ask it of Emma. He laid his hand over David's own. "We can't impose on the Blairs that way."

That silenced David. "It will be hard to get a ship, won't it," he said after a moment.

"If we pay enough, we'll find someone who's willing to make the trip and not ask questions. But we won't leave until you're feeling better."

"I'm all right."

"Don't try to fool your father." Robert grinned to mask his concern. The longer they delayed their departure, the riskier their charade became.

A knock at the door put an end to his reflections. Emma came into the room still dressed in the claret-colored gown she had worn to visit the Lauders. The damp fabric clung to her skin. As she walked forward, Robert had a vivid memory of the feel of the soft wool beneath his fingers and of the softer flesh beneath.

She perched on the bed opposite him and looked at David. "Arabel says you've got a sore throat."

"It's not so bad." Now that departure was imminent, David seemed determined to make light of his illness.

"You look as if you might have a fever." Emma felt his forehead.

This time David didn't turn his head away. He looked up at her with trusting eyes. "Papa says you got caught in the storm."

Even in the shadowy light of the single lamp, Robert was sure he saw a hint of color creep into Emma's cheeks. "You'd think we'd have had the sense to not go out on a day like this, wouldn't you?"

"You wanted to see Lord Lauder. About the duel."

"Yes." Emma straightened the tangled sheet and cover-let.

"Is he going to stop them from fighting?"

"No." Anger flashed in her eyes. "But we've had at least a temporary reprieve. Your father told you the news from France?"

David nodded.

"Jamie says he and Matt can't fight each other when they'll both be needed by the army."

David looked steadily at her. "Does he think there's going to be fighting in France?"

"Jamie always thinks there's going to be fighting. I'm not at all sure I agree with him." Emma smoothed David's hair. "Could you manage to go back to sleep?"

"I'll try." David snuggled down into the pillows.

"Good lad." Emma kissed him and pulled the covers up.

"You'll have to tell me how you do it," Robert said when they were outside in the corridor. "I can barely get him to admit he's sick."

Emma smiled, making his heartbeat quicken. "He'll be fine if we can persuade him to rest. Fevers aren't as dangerous in children as in adults."

Robert nodded. "Has Jamie really changed his mind about the duel?"

"That would be too much to hope for. But he's agreed that he and Matt have to fight the French before they can fight each other."

"The British may not have to fight."

"That's what I keep telling myself. It's difficult to take it all in. I was so sure the war was over." They had reached the half landing. Emma turned and looked up at him. The candles in the wall sconces cast flickering yellow light over her face and struck sparks of fire in her hair. "How soon do you have to leave?"

Robert sucked in his breath. If he had the right to call her his own, he would take her in his arms now, to offer comfort and receive it; he would take her to bed tonight and they would seek what solace they could to sustain them through the coming months of separation. But he did not have the right. He couldn't even promise to come back. "As soon as David is well enough to travel."

She nodded. "Come into the sitting room. There's something I want to talk to you about."

The family had dispersed and the sitting room was

now empty. Emma sat in a chair by the fire and looked at Robert with her usual directness. "What are you going to do with David?"

Despite everything else that had happened, she was thinking of David. Robert was humbled. He was also aware that the conversation was headed into difficult waters. He sat in a chair facing her. "I'll take him back to Devon."

"And leave him where? The grandmother who raised him is dead. You told me you have no other close relatives."

Robert leaned back in the chair. He had thought it would be simpler if Captain Melton did not have a living mother in Devon to account for. Now he saw the pitfalls of his decision. "Devon's our home. I'll manage something." As soon as the words were out of his mouth, he realized how inadequate they sounded.

"I have a better idea. Leave David with us."

They were sitting only three or four feet apart. With Emma he needed much more distance to think clearly. The sound of the rain dripping from the eaves and the crackle of the fire filled the silence. "I couldn't impose on you like that," he said at last, repeating the words he had used with David.

"Rubbish. David's no trouble. We've all grown very fond of him."

"As he has of you." Robert chose his words with care. "But I have no notion what the next months will bring or how long I'll be gone. I think it would be best for David to be at home. I'll leave him with friends," he added, thinking to amend his earlier vagueness about who would look after his son.

"I thought we were friends," Emma said.

Robert swallowed. The message in her eyes was clear. *After what passed between us this afternoon, don't you trust me?*

David was in no condition to travel. Paris might be at arms by now. Robert was not even sure where his mother and his cousin Paul were to be found. They had been visiting friends in Provence when he left for Scotland. "I don't know where I'll be posted," he said. "I may be reassigned."

"You mean you'll leave David here?"

He looked into her eyes and nodded slowly. "If there's any problem, if you have to reach me for any reason, write to Adam Durward. Andy's friend. He's in Brussels, an aide to the British ambassador. He'll know where to find me." David would be able to write to Adam, as well, if for any reason he needed to leave Blair House. "And if I don't return—"

Emma's face was suddenly drained of color, but she made no protest. She had been a soldier's wife, and she was a soldier's daughter.

"If I don't return, send my son to Durward. He'll know what to do."

Emma hesitated in the corridor outside Robert's room. The cool night air seeped through the wool of her dressing gown. Her candle made a pool of light on the floorboards, giving the illusion of intimacy. The house was quiet, with only the drip of rainwater from the roof and the faint whisper of wind through gaps around the windows to disturb the stillness. No one would know that she had left her room and brazenly gone to Captain Melton's door. Not that the risk of being discovered bothered her much. Such considerations seemed paltry in the face of today's news. No, what gave her pause was the possibility that Robert might not welcome her company.

The light wavered as her fingers tightened around the candlestick. Since they had left the cottage this afternoon, their world had been turned upside down. Tomorrow Robert would leave Blair House and sail for the Netherlands. It would be understandable if he was in no mood for lovemaking.

But the risk of rejection was nothing beside the prospect that this might be the last night they would spend under the same roof. At the very least, it would be a long time before she saw him again. She needed something more than that dreamlike interlude at the cottage to sustain her during the months ahead. Even more than the solace of his passion, she longed for time alone with him. There had been so much confusion all evening, with David's illness, Robert preparing to leave, Jamie and Will arguing about what they should do, and everyone debating what Bonaparte's escape would mean for the future. She and Robert had exchanged no more than a few words since he had agreed to leave David with her.

Tomorrow he would ride off to war as her father and brother and husband had done. She would have to say good-bye to him in front of her family. She wanted a private farewell. Her pride melting away like the wax of the candle, she lifted her hand and knocked on the door.

The silence in the corridor seemed to intensify as she waited for an answer. She felt herself trembling and gripped the candlestick with both hands to steady it. The sound of footsteps on the other side of the door made her mouth go dry. Then the door opened and she was staring into Robert's eyes.

"I came to say good-bye." Her voice sounded thin and hollow to her own ears. "I won't stay if you don't want me to."

Robert's eyes were as dark and unreadable as a midnight sky. Without speaking he took the candle from her hands and set it down on a table near the door. Then he pulled her into his arms and pushed the door shut behind her.

For a long moment he simply held her, his unshaven

cheek resting on her hair, his heartbeat strong beneath her ear, his arms warm and solid around her. She shuddered and clung close to him, savoring his scent, the feel of his hands, the warmth of his breath.

At last he took her face between his hands and looked down at her. "I didn't let myself think you might come."

His eyes held the pain she had glimpsed that afternoon, a pain she still could not understand. Now perhaps she never would. She closed her eyes and pulled his head down to her own, losing herself in the sweetness of his kiss.

He lifted her in his arms. As he carried her to the bed, she wrapped her arm around his neck and pressed kisses against his face.

He laid her against the Irish linen sheets that had been Aunt Alice's pride. Somehow her dressing gown was discarded. He undid the buttons at the neck of her nightdress. She pulled him close, and his mouth was against the hollow of her throat and the swell of her breasts. He did not speak, but his touch and the look in his eyes told her all she needed to know.

It was different from this afternoon, different even from that second, less frantic time. Then they had still been caught up in the wonder of discovery. Now they sought not to discover but to hold on to memories.

His lips moved over her skin as though he were determined to taste every inch. His hands wooed her. He was so gentle it was almost a torment, but she could not bear for it to end. She gave back caress for caress, knowing she would relive every moment of this encounter on many lonely nights to come.

When they were both finally naked, he looked down at her in the dim glow of the single lamp, as though committing every contour of her body to memory. She knew as surely as if he had spoken that he was wondering if he would ever see her again. She wanted to cry out that he was wrong, they did not even know if there would be fighting. But the words stuck in her throat. She knew the fragility of life all too well. So instead, she pressed her hands against his chest, feeling the beat of his heart, tracing the line of his ribs one by one.

When she touched the hard ridges of his scars, fear stabbed through her. She reached lower and wrapped her hand around him. He was pulsing with life. She wanted to feel that life inside her body. She fell back against the sheets and drew him to her.

He came inside her slowly, carefully, his eyes never leaving her face. Tears of bittersweet joy stung her eyelids. She pulled him against her heated skin. His mouth met hers in a kiss that blended longing and passion. They moved together with care, as though each meeting of their flesh were a moment of precious communion. Her body screamed for release, but she wanted to hold him to her forever.

Need could be denied only so long. The tension within her became unbearable. She felt him tremble. "I'm sorry," he gasped.

The only answer she could make was a sob as she surrendered to brilliant, consuming heat.

Even the oblivion of release could not banish the aching knowledge of what tomorrow would bring. Yet holding him cradled on her breast, Emma knew that whatever the future held she would never doubt that in this moment he had been hers.

Afterward she lay in his arms for a long time. At last he propped himself up on one elbow and looked down at her.

"You should be asleep." She reached up to touch his face. "You have a long journey ahead of you."

The corner of his mouth lifted in a crooked grin. "Sleeping seems a sad waste of time when I have you in my bed."

She smiled into his eyes, hoping that was an invitation. But he lay down on the pillow beside her and turned her face toward his own. "Em."

It was the first time he had called her that. The sound made her absurdly happy. "Yes?" she asked, watching the play of the lamplight over his features.

His thumb stroked her cheek. "If there's a child, promise you'll write to me."

She was suddenly aware of the coolness of the night air. "There won't be a child."

"You can't be certain." He held her gaze with his own. "I want your word you'll let me know."

Emma searched his face. Did he mean he would marry her if she was pregnant? And that he had no intention of doing so if she was not? "I'll write to you in any case. To let you know how David is."

"Thank you." He smoothed her hair back from her face. "I'll write when I can. God knows the state of affairs I'll find in the Netherlands, but Durward can forward letters for me." His hand stilled. He looked at her for a long moment as if searching for the right words. "I don't know what the future may hold."

His eyes seemed to plead for understanding. And she did understand. He wasn't just speaking of the possibility of war. He was saying, as he had in the cottage, that he could make her no promises. That he was not ready to do so bothered her less than the fact that she did not know his reasons. Despite all they had shared, she was barely coming to know him. There were dark places in his soul of which she had had only the briefest glimpse. Now he was returning to a world of which she could not be a part. Though his hand still rested on her face, the distance between them seemed far vaster than a few inches of bed linen. She was shut out of his life, as she had been shut out of Allan's.

But Robert was not Allan. Owing her less, he had

shown her greater consideration. "Don't think of the future," she said. "Let's take what comfort we can from the present." Seeking the one way in which she could reach him, she wrapped her arm around him and placed her lips over his own.

A blanket of morning mist hung over Blair House. The folds of Robert's cloak were already damp, but he was weighed down by far more than wet wool. He had said good-bye to David inside. Now he faced the Blair family, gathered in the courtyard to see him off.

Angus shook his hand warmly. He had no doubt Boney would be quickly dispatched. They counted on seeing Captain Melton back at Blair House soon. Jamie, who had been reluctantly persuaded to wait for a summons before galloping off to his regiment, said he expected they would meet up on the Continent. He didn't sound entirely happy about it. Will was more cordial. Andy, who had spent the night at Blair House, asked Robert to remember him to the Durwards. Kirsty hugged him. So did Arabel, with a whispered "Thank you for everything."

When it came to Emma, Robert wasn't sure what to do. They had said their farewells last night. He couldn't kiss her in front of her family. But neither did he want to leave her with a cold handshake. Finally, impulse winning out over prudence, he took her hand and pressed it to his lips.

Her fingers gripped his own for a moment. "May I ask you to be careful?"

He managed to grin. "I'm too old to run risks."

There was little more to be said. He took his horse from the stableboy and swung up into the saddle. Goodbyes were best ended quickly.

But when he reached the crest of the first hill, he

permitted himself to turn back for one last look. Blair House looked much as it had on his arrival, solid and uncompromising against the Scottish landscape. The family were still in the courtyard. He could see Emma, her hands on Kirsty's shoulders, her hair caught by the morning breeze. As he watched, she lifted her hand and waved. He waved back, thinking it was appropriate that he remember her thus, surrounded by her family.

He gathered up the reins and turned his horse toward Edinburgh and France.

10

Brussels
June 1815

Emma adjusted the folds of her loose white muslin gown and pushed her hair back from her damp forehead. By late afternoon, the heat was stifling, different from anything she had known in Scotland. Even this room, shaded by the trees on the ramparts of the city, felt oppressive, as if the sun had soaked into the yellow silk wall hangings.

Brussels was a hothouse in more ways than one. The social life was a frenetic whirl—balls, picnics, races, military reviews—yet the threat of military engagement hung in the air like the promise of a summer thunderstorm.

Emma looked at the man seated across from her in the salon of the house that had been her home for the past six weeks. "Tell me the truth, Adam. Is there going to be a battle?"

Adam Durward was silent for a moment. With his unruly black hair and penetrating brown eyes, he was not at all the image of an English diplomat. The dark skin of his Hindu mother marked him as an outsider, even before he opened his mouth and voiced his unconventional opinions. There was always an air of suppressed energy about him. Now Emma could feel the tension coiled within him, as if he were preparing himself for what was to come. "There's been an attack on the Prussian outposts," he said, "but Wellington suspects it's a feint. He thinks Bonaparte will attack from the west."

Emma fought back images of her brother and cousin and the man she loved lying torn and bloody on the beautiful fields of rye in which she had ridden and picnicked in the past weeks. "So there *is* going to be an attack?"

"It looks that way." Adam gave an unexpected grin. "I'm under strict orders not to let English civilians panic. Are you panicked?"

It's perfectly safe. That's what Arabel had said when she convinced Emma to make the trip to Brussels. *Wellington's own niece is there. She's about to have a baby. Don't you think Wellington would have insisted she go home if he thought there was any danger?*

During Napoleon's exile, the British had flocked to the Continent, eager to travel for the first time in over ten years. Many had stayed abroad after Napoleon's escape, and others had joined them. If there was to be fighting, surely it would be in France itself, which Britain and her allies were preparing to invade. Brussels, headquarters of the Allied Army, had become a glittering social center for the expatriate English, including Andy's cousins Jack and Lord Sheriton. Andy had accepted an invitation to join them, and Arabel had convinced Emma that they should accompany him.

Emma had longed to visit the Continent ever since she discovered an ancient travel book in the Blair House library at the age of eight. Will and Jamie were stationed with the Allied Army. Jenny and Bram, forced to leave Paris, had taken lodgings in Brussels. And then there was Robert. For all the anguish of saying good-bye to him, Emma hadn't realized the depth of longing she would feel when they were apart. Love made her reckless.

"Should I be panicked?" she said at last in response to Adam's question.

"No." Adam's reply was blunt and, Emma knew, quite honest. "If worse comes to worst and the Allies are defeated, there'll still be time for you to get to Ostend or Antwerp and take ship for Britain."

Emma nodded. She had told herself as much when she decided to come to Brussels. The fear that gripped her was not for herself, or even Kirsty and David, but for the men who would take the field. "Has Wellington issued marching orders?"

"Not yet. He's waiting for a report from his intelligence staff. News from them is damnably slow."

Emma heard a rattling sound and realized she was clenching her teacup and saucer. She set them down. "Have you heard anything from Captain Melton?"

"Not since the letter I brought you." Adam's sharp eyes softened with sympathy. Emma suspected he understood her feelings about Robert all too well. She had called on Adam as soon as she arrived in Brussels, seeking news of Robert. Adam and his wife, Caroline, had greeted her warmly but had not been able to give her Robert's direction. Robert was in intelligence, Adam had told her in confidence. If she raised questions about his whereabouts, she might jeopardize his safety, for there were many Bonapartists among the Bruxellois and even among the Dutch-Belgian troops who were under Wellington's command. Emma had been forced to content herself with the knowledge that at least she and Robert were on the same continent.

Robert had written her only twice, once before she left Scotland, telling her he had reached the Netherlands, and once after she had written to tell him of their arrival in Brussels. Both letters had been brief and guarded. It was folly to have hoped for more. But in her heart, Emma confessed that she had.

Adam was watching her with eyes that saw far more than she wished. To her relief, the door opened and her host, Lord Sheriton, came into the room, accompanied by Caroline Durward, who had taken her six-year-old daughter Emily out to the garden to join Kirsty and David.

"Emily," Caroline said, "is explaining to Kirsty and David that even if the French march into Brussels, they won't clap us in irons, only prevent us from traveling for a time."

Adam moved to his wife's side. "Very true. But as I've been telling Emma, there'll be plenty of time to reach the coast before the French get anywhere near Brussels. If we lose."

Sherry tossed his gloves onto an ormolu side table. "My dear fellow, don't tell me you admit there's a chance we will?"

Adam grinned. "Wellington doesn't, at least not publicly. But I always try to consider every possible outcome. I'm satisfied my wife and child aren't in danger."

"Emily and I aren't going anywhere." Caroline sat on the sofa beside Emma. "This family have been separated enough as it is." She gave Emma's hand a sympathetic squeeze. "I think children find separation from their parents more frightening than anything. I've often berated myself for taking Emily into danger, but looking back, I think it would have been worse to have left her behind."

Sherry dropped down in an armchair. "An old woman stopped me in the street this morning and told me Bonaparte would be back by the end of the week and wasn't that splendid. I told her, begging her pardon, that I didn't think it had quite come to that."

Emma smiled at him. They had been friends since they first met, at the wedding of Sherry's cousin Eleanor to Emma's uncle Gavin. Emma had been a freckled six-year-old, Sherry a gangly towheaded boy of twelve. In the years since, he had grown into a tall, broad-shouldered man and his hair had darkened to straw-color, but his open, friendly face and unfailing good humor remained. Emma had planned to take her own lodgings in Brussels, but when they arrived, she found the city teeming with soldiers and English civilians. There were no accommodations to be had. Bram and Jenny could not take four more people in their rooms, but Sherry, who had arrived earlier, said his house was far too large for him and his brother. He had made several visits to Blair House through the years. They must let him repay their hospitality.

Recalled to her duties, Emma poured tea for Sherry and Caroline. "Adam has to go back to headquarters, but I'm going to take Emily to the park," Caroline said, accepting a cup. "Do you mind if Kirsty and David come as well?"

"I think it's a wonderful idea. All the tension has made them restless. I'd come with you myself, but we're expecting Jamie and Will. They're supposed to come into town for the Duchess of Richmond's ball this evening. Though if the army are about to march—"

"Oh, canceling the ball is the last thing Wellington would want to do," Caroline said. "Imagine the panic that would cause. Could you pass the milk, Adam?"

From his vantage point beneath a cluster of leafy trees in a small hollow, Robert had a clear view of the refreshment pavilion and the smooth glassy sheet of water at the center of the park. He waved his hand, stirring the hot, humid air. Rain seemed imminent, if not tonight, then soon. It could play merry hell with the coming battle. He pulled his watch from the pocket of his very red, very British uniform. Half past four. He had sent a note to

Caroline begging her to bring David to this spot in the park between four and five.

It was a lot to ask of Caroline, but it was the only way to arrange a meeting with David away from the Blairs. Not that he hadn't considered presenting himself at the house in the Rue Ducale where Emma had written him they were staying. He had come to Brussels in the guise of Captain Robert Melton of the 52nd. It would hardly seem suspicious if Captain Melton called to see his son.

Robert glanced toward the iron railing that enclosed the park. The street beyond was lined with rows of elegant houses painted in buff or white or green, gracefully ornamented with Ionic pilasters. Emma lived in such a house. Emma. The image of her face blotted out the shrubbery and rolling lawns before him. The remembrance of the scent of her hair and the taste of her skin stopped his breath. It was three months since he had seen her and the memory had not dimmed. It had stayed with him through his journey to France, through his arrival in Paris, where Napoleon had already resumed power, through the succeeding weeks when the allies declared Napoleon an outlaw and it became clear that, while France would not face civil war, war with the rest of Europe was inevitable.

Robert reminded himself that it would not be safe to call in the Rue Ducale. It was bad enough to have left David in Scotland, playing at the charade of being an Englishman's son. In Brussels, surrounded by the Allied Army, hearing daily talk about the preparations for war, he must find it doubly hard to maintain the pretense. A reunion conducted under the eyes of the Blairs would strain even David's skills at playacting.

A woman in a pink dress and flower-trimmed bonnet came into view. She was partly hidden by the crowd, but her posture and grace of movement told him it was Caroline. She moved closer and he saw that she held two little girls by the hand. One had Caroline's fair hair and heart-shaped face. The other had bright eyes and auburn hair that could not but remind him of Emma.

A boy ran beside them. Robert's heartbeat quickened. Caroline bent over and said something to his son, then guided the girls toward the water. David ran to the trees where Robert was standing. When he reached the rise of ground above the hollow, he stopped, his eyes widening.

For a long moment Robert and his son looked at each other in silence. David wore no coat on this hot day, but his trousers, which had fit perfectly in Scotland, did not reach quite to his ankles. His hair was windblown and his skin darkened by the Brussels sun. His face seemed leaner and more defined, as if the man he would be was beginning to emerge from the boy.

David drew in his breath, hurtled forward, and flung his arms around Robert. His head now reached almost to Robert's shoulders. A lump rose in Robert's throat. He had missed three more precious months of David's childhood.

When he could bring himself to let go, Robert looked down into his son's face. "I'm sorry I couldn't come sooner."

David gave an abashed grin, as if embarrassed at having behaved as if he were still a child of eight or nine. "I wasn't sure you'd be able to come at all." He touched the decoration on Robert's shoulder. "Are you here to get information?"

"I'm here for a number of reasons, but chiefly to see you." Robert placed his hands on David's shoulders. So little time. He couldn't afford to give in to sentiment. "Is it very difficult? I could ask Adam and Caroline to take you. Then at least you wouldn't have to pretend."

David shook his head. "No. It's hard sometimes, pretending to be English, but I like it with the Blairs. And I am part British."

Robert swallowed. "So you are. So am I."

David turned up the ground with the toe of his shoe. "There's going to be a battle, isn't there?"

"Probably."

"And you're going to fight." David looked at the sabre that was part of Robert's British uniform.

Robert managed to smile. "I'm a staff officer. I carry messages."

"But you'll be where there's fighting."

"Yes."

David was silent for a moment. "I don't like to think of you fighting the Blairs."

"Nor do I." Four months ago Robert would not have imagined he could feel this way.

"Emma misses you. She doesn't talk about you a lot, but she gets a funny look in her eyes whenever you're mentioned. I suppose you don't want me to tell her I've seen you."

Robert drew a breath, the memory of Emma's laughter echoing in his ears. "I think it would be best not to." He reminded himself that there were still important things that needed to be said. "Listen, David. I've come through a lot of battles with little more than a scratch. I'll probably spend most of my time behind the lines, carrying messages from one general to another."

He didn't add that staff officers were frequently sent on errands that put them in the thick of battle, an all too easy target for the enemy. He hesitated over his next words, wanting to be honest with David yet not wanting to frighten him before there was cause. "But you should be prepared for whatever happens. If for any reason I don't come back—whichever way the battle turns out— you can go to the Durwards. They'll get you to Grandmère and Uncle Paul when it's safe to travel."

David nodded. Robert felt as if he were watching his son grow up before his eyes. "Adam talked to me after we came to Brussels," David said. "He told me he'd let me know whenever he had news. He's been splendid."

"He's a good friend." It was, Robert knew, a gross understatement.

Silence fell. Robert could hear the sound of voices from the refreshment pavilion and splashing in the water. Emily and Kirsty would be wondering what was keeping David. There was a great deal more he wanted to say and little he could actually put into words. He had said goodbye to David before, but never on the eve of a battle. In the past year he had formed a bond with his son that made the leave-taking all the more painful.

He forced himself to relax his hold on David's shoulders. He searched his son's face, hoping he could make him understand. "I love you, David. And I'm proud of you."

David swallowed. His eyes seemed unusually bright. Robert wondered if it would have been better not to have spoken. Then David smiled. "I'm proud of you, too."

Robert watched David rejoin Caroline and the girls, watched Caroline buy ices for the children, watched until they moved out of sight down one of the winding walks. Then he reminded himself that he had other business in Brussels. It was a friendly city for French agents. With so many foreign soldiers about, wearing such a variety of uniforms, it was easy to blend into the throng. There were even a number of Dutch-Belgian troops who had fought for Bonaparte before his exile and still wore the uniform of the Empire. But there were few French agents who could pass as English, as Robert did. English soldiers were far more open with one of their own than with their foreign allies.

Two hours later, Robert emerged from the dim light of a tavern common room into the hazy shadows of early evening. The party of officers with whom he had been drinking spilled through the doorway. "God's teeth," said a young lieutenant, tugging at his collar, "it's past seven and this place is still an inferno. Sure you won't dine with us, Melton?"

"Thanks, but no." Robert knew the dangers of carrying his masquerade too far.

The lieutenant shrugged. "Suit yourself. But if the rumors are true, it could be our last chance for a decent meal for God knows how long."

One of his companions gave a mordant grin. "Could be our last chance ever."

The others laughed, though there was a sense of unease beneath their bravado. They were all very young. Robert tried not to think how many of them might fall to French bullets. He waved as they set off down the street. Then he turned in the opposite direction, toward the Marché aux Herbes, the great vegetable market. The narrow street was crowded, horse hooves and bootheels resounding against the cobbles, shouts of greeting and snatches of conversation rising to echo off the overhanging gables. One could smell the expectation in the air as surely as the yeasty aroma from a nearby bakeshop. Despite the hour and the lengthening shadows, knots of civilians stood talking in doorways and on street corners. Enlisted men greeted each other with assumed nonchalance. Officers hurried by with preoccupied looks on their faces, several clutching bouquets, gifts perhaps for women attending the Duchess of Richmond's ball this evening.

Robert knew about the ball. Robert knew a great deal about what was happening in Brussels. The officers in the tavern had welcomed him cheerfully and had spoken freely of English fears that when it came to battle the Belgian troops would desert and fight with their former French comrades. The French also suspected as much, for many Belgians considered themselves French and were angry at being made part of the Netherlands. But it was useful to know the feeling was so prevalent among the British.

As he turned a corner, Robert caught sight of a young man in the uniform of a private holding the hands of an even younger girl wearing a blue dress and a white Flemish cap. They stood close to the black stone wall of a house, oblivious to the press of traffic. Robert did not need to hear their conversation to know they were wondering if this would be the last day they would spend together.

"Melton!"

The shout came from across the street. Robert turned to see a soldier dodging his way between two fiacres that had pulled up to let off passengers. He wore a red coat, not the rifleman's green of Robert's companions in the tavern. And his dark hair and blue eyes were unmistakable. It was Charlie Lauder.

"I say, what luck." Charlie came up beside him and held out his hand. "We've been wondering what had become of you. Arabel's been dropping hints about secret missions."

"Believe me, it's not half as interesting as it sounds," Robert said, shaking Charlie's hand. "Emma wrote that you'd joined up. Didn't you once tell me you had no taste for soldiering?"

Charlie grimaced. "I can't say a few weeks in the army have changed my mind. But with so many of our troops in America, I suppose we all have to do our part. Besides—" He glanced away.

Robert studied his face. Charlie was even younger than the soldiers in the tavern. Young and in love and full of promise. "Besides, there's the temptation of prize money," Robert said.

"I have to find a way to support Arabel." Charlie looked at him as if pleading for understanding. "I can't count on either of our fathers to help us."

"Then I wish you luck. But don't try anything fool-hardy."

"Lord no. I expect I shall be too busy trying to remember how to load my musket." Charlie shifted his weight from one foot to the other. "Have you heard anything?"

"I'm afraid I know no more than you." It was almost the truth. Robert could not claim to be privy to Wellington's plans.

Charlie nodded and did not press him further. "I'm on my way back to my billet to change for the ball. Are you going?"

Robert laughed. "I don't move in such exalted circles."

"Nor do I exactly. But the duchess knew my mother when they were girls. She gave me a handful of tickets—they have tickets, you know, because there's such demand for invitations. One of the fellows in my company just cried off so he can spend the evening with his Belgian sweetheart. You can have his ticket."

"Thank you, Charlie, but—"

"Do say you'll come. God knows when we'll have another chance for dancing and champagne."

Robert hesitated. But the part of him that still relished the intricacy of the espionage game could not resist the idea of attending a ball at which the Duke of Wellington and numerous generals, officers, and diplomats would be present. Besides, the chance to see Emma, to dance with her, to hold her—

He thought of Emma's shining eyes and bewitching smile and knew he had no choice. "Do you think you could lend me a pair of knee breeches?" he asked Charlie.

11

"Wellington isn't here yet," Sherry murmured as he led Emma from the dance floor. "It's beginning to cause talk."

Emma glanced around the ballroom. Laughter and light conversation filled the air, but there was a brittle edge to it, as if everyone realized that the fragile cocoon of champagne and candlelight was about to be shattered. She scanned the gleaming multitude of uniforms, hoping, as she always did at a large entertainment, to find Robert. It was silly, of course. If Robert was in Brussels, he would have come to see David.

"I don't think I've ever seen so many uniforms in one room." Arabel joined them, her arm linked through that of her friend Georgiana Lennox, the Duchess of Richmond's daughter.

"It's certainly impressive." Emma smiled at Georgiana. "Your mother is to be congratulated."

Georgiana grinned. "You'd never guess we play battledore and shuttlecock in this room, would you?"

The duchess had draped the ballroom in the royal colors of the Netherlands, crimson, gold, and black, which stood out starkly against the delicate rose-trellis wallpaper. Because of the heat of the evening, the French windows on either side of the room had been flung open.

Shores of Desire

Moonlight spilled onto the parquet floor to blend with the warmer light of the candles in the chandeliers.

"The only trouble is that the uniforms make our dresses look positively faded." Arabel smoothed the skirt of her pale blue crepe gown. Her voice was light, but Emma thought the lightness was forced.

"I know." Georgiana strove to match Arabel's tone. "And the diplomats are quite as bad with all their medals. There are so many dignitaries, from so many countries, that it's quite a chore keeping the precedence straight. Mama has been in a dreadful state." She surveyed the crowd, the social mask she wore as the hostess's daughter slipping to reveal concern. "I do wish Wellington would come. It's not knowing what's happening that's so dreadful."

Arabel squeezed her friend's arm. Sherry stopped a passing footman and procured champagne. Emma considered champagne a wonderfully decadent luxury. But tonight the effervescent liquid could not dispel the knot of fear in her stomach.

A woman in silver net brushed by them, nut-brown hair coming free of its pins, cheeks flushed with exertion and rouge, two cavalry officers in tow. Two more officers ran up to join the crowd around her. "I wonder what her secret is," Arabel said.

Georgiana made a moue of distaste. "That's Lady Rutledge. Mama says she's always seeking sensation. I supposed that's why she came to Brussels."

"It's no more than the rest of us did." Arabel glanced at the doorway. "Oh, good."

"Wellington?" Georgiana turned around.

"No, Adam and Caroline. Thank goodness," Arabel added as the Durwards joined them, "a diplomat without medals."

In truth, Caroline's husband was a more striking figure in a plain black coat than the more splendidly dressed men in the room. "Well?" Emma asked him. "Any fresh news?"

"Wellington's still waiting for intelligence from the west to see if the attacks on the Prussians are a feint or in earnest," Adam said. "But he's ordered the army to be ready to march."

Arabel nodded. "Jamie and Will told us. But officers have permission to attend the ball."

Adam gave an ironic smile. "War should never be allowed to interfere with the business of being a gentleman."

Caroline looked up at her husband. "No one but you, Adam, could make 'gentleman' sound like an insult."

"No offense meant." Adam grinned at Sherry. "Some of my best friends are gentlemen."

Emma turned to Caroline. "Thank you again for taking the children out. It did them a world of good, especially David."

Caroline smiled, though Emma thought her eyes were a little troubled.

"What, not dancing?" Jack Sheriton came up beside them accompanied by Andy. "There's a waltz about to start."

"Surely we can persuade someone to dance with us." Andy smiled at the women. In five more years, Emma thought, her cousin was going to be a dangerous young man.

"I'd be delighted, Mr. Blair." Georgiana took his arm.

Jack turned to Arabel. "I say, isn't this exciting? It's enough to make a fellow want to join up."

"No," Sherry told him, an unusually firm note in his lazy voice.

Jack regarded his brother with a touch of defiance. They looked very much alike, save that Jack's hair was even blonder than his brother's, he was half an inch taller, and his lanky frame still showed his youth. "There are lots of chaps my age in the army. Charlie Lauder's only two years older than I am."

"Just because Charlie's a fool doesn't mean you have to be one too," Arabel said.

Andy touched his friend's shoulder. "Going back to university may not be exciting, but at least we know we *are* going back."

"Oh, Lord," Jack exclaimed. "I wasn't thinking about Will and Jamie. You must be worried—"

"Worrying doesn't do any good." Arabel took his arm in a firm grip. "Do let's dance and stop talking about what can't be helped."

Jack led her onto the dance floor without further comment. Andy and Georgiana followed, and Bram appeared to remind Emma that she was promised to him for the next waltz.

"I think I've heard the same set of rumors at least three times since we arrived," he said as they took their places on the dance floor. "Jenny still refuses to believe there's going to be a battle."

"Perhaps that's just as well."

Bram's mouth twisted in ironic acknowledgment. "True, Jenny's not at her best in a crisis. God knows she isn't you," he added under his breath.

For a moment they looked at each other, unspoken words hanging between them. "I'm sorry," Emma said. "I didn't mean—"

"No, *I'm* sorry." The first notes of the waltz sounded. Bram put his arm around her waist, touching her lightly, holding her a little further distant than was necessary.

And yet, Emma realized as they moved into the dance, she did not find his touch as disturbing as she once had. When she first saw him—she had been fifteen, leaning over the gallery railing to catch a glimpse of Jenny's suitor—she had thought him the handsomest man she had ever seen. Twelve years later he was still every bit as attractive, tall and lean, with gleaming walnut brown hair and the finely chiseled features and full-lipped mouth of his French ancestors. But the attraction seemed pallid and harmless beside the bone-deep hunger she felt for Robert.

"Emma," Bram said.

She looked up at him.

"Guilt is a singularly useless emotion."

Emma bit her lip. She hadn't been feeling guilty, she had been thinking about Robert. Yet when it came to Bram, she knew full well she had cause for guilt.

Robert and Charlie made their way through the crowded hall and paused for a moment just beyond the entrance to the ballroom. Robert drew a breath. The candlelight and the shadows from the open windows lent a fragile beauty to the scene before him. The notes of the waltz seemed to shimmer in the warm, perfumed air. The sight of officers in silk stockings and dancing shoes whirling about the floor with ladies in gauzy pastel frocks seemed wildly incongruous on the night before a battle.

In a few hours, the lilting strains of the waltz would give way to the beat of the drum and the pounding of guns and the cries of men in agony. Fools, didn't they realize what wanton savagery awaited them? War was not a gentleman's game.

Yet Robert could understand the looks of fevered yearning on the faces of the couples before him. He scanned the ballroom with a hunger he could no longer contain. At last he saw her beneath one of the chandeliers, the light making her hair glow like a flame touched by sunlight. She was wearing a filmy sea-green dress, and her hair was pinned high with curls falling about her face. For a moment, Robert was not sure if he could breathe.

Emma did not seem to be aware of him. Her gaze was fixed on the man with whom she was dancing, a dark-haired man in civilian dress in whom she appeared far too interested. Jealousy twisted in Robert's chest with a sharpness he had not known since the early days of his marriage.

"That's Bram Martin," Charlie said. "Jenny's husband."

So the dark-haired man was married and a kinsman. And yet Emma had spoken of Bram Martin all too fondly. Robert watched Martin's head bend closer to Emma's and felt a distinct desire to stride across the dance floor and yank her out of the other man's arms.

"Excuse me," Charlie murmured. He walked forward, his gaze fixed on Arabel, who was on the other side of the room dancing with a tall, blond young man.

Suddenly Robert was unsure of his welcome. So much had happened since that afternoon in the deserted cottage. He followed Emma and Bram Martin with his eyes as they circled the floor.

"Good evening, *mon ami*. I should have known I would find you here."

Robert turned. The man before him wore a Belgian uniform, but the handsome, reckless face belonged to Charles de La Bédoyère, who had taken his regiment over to Bonaparte and was now one of the emperor's aides-de-camp. Robert wondered how many other French officers had managed to attend the ball disguised as Allied soldiers. "Tickets of admission were difficult to obtain," Robert said. "I congratulate you on your enterprise."

La Bédoyère grinned. "I have an ambition to shake Wellington's hand." He glanced around the ballroom, a wistful look in his eyes. "So many lovely women. Yet all I can think is how much I miss my wife."

Robert gripped his friend's arm in sympathy. La

Bédoyère had left a wife and baby son in Paris. "With luck you'll be home soon," Robert said, though home seemed a very long way away.

"Yes. Of course." La Bédoyère gave one of his devil-may-care grins. "I may not see you again tonight, but we will meet tomorrow I expect." He glanced at the insignia of rank on Robert's uniform. "Captain," he added with an ironic smile.

The need to find Emma was becoming unendurable. But La Bédoyère had no sooner moved off than Robert's eye was caught by another familiar figure on the edge of the dance floor. Adam Durward was smiling at Caroline, his face softened by tenderness as it was only when he looked at his wife or daughter.

Robert waited until his friend turned in his direction, then looked full into Adam's face, knowing Adam would understand his unspoken message. *I won't try to hide. Turn me in if you must.*

Adam would not, of course. Just as Robert had not turned Adam in two years ago in Salamanca. Just as neither had turned the other in on a score of similar occasions since their first meeting in Spain, when they had got very drunk while each worked out that the other was a spy for the opposite side. Both had found it useful to have a friend in the enemy camp. But it was more than that. Each had placed his life in the other's hands on more occasions than they could count.

Though he had written to the Durwards, Robert had avoided calling on them since his return to the Continent. He would not put Adam in an awkward position by approaching him at the ball, and he did not think Adam would seek him out. As he expected, Adam turned away, as though Robert were no more than another guest. But just as Robert once more glimpsed Emma and Bram Martin in the throng, he heard a rustle of silk beside him.

"My husband," Caroline Durward said in a low voice,

"says he's doing his best to pretend he hasn't set eyes on you. He's instructed me to ask you what the hell you think you're doing here."

Robert smiled at Adam's wife. She had always been lovely, but it was difficult to reconcile this elegant lady in a clinging rose-colored gown and a stylish mass of ringlets with the malnourished woman he had met in Salamanca two years ago, desperate to find her missing child. He took her hand. "Thank you for bringing David this afternoon."

"You're welcome." Caroline's gray eyes did not waver. "You haven't answered my question."

"An impulse," Robert said. "Probably a mad impulse. But then I've known Adam to be prone to them himself, especially where you're concerned."

Caroline's gaze drifted over the dancers in Emma's direction. "I suspected as much." She looked back at Robert. "I'm very fond of Emma Blair. I haven't liked lying to her, though I understand you have your reasons."

Robert swallowed. "I haven't liked lying to her either. I owe you and Adam a debt I can't possibly repay."

Caroline's eyes softened. "There are debts on both sides. You restored Emily to us. We'll never forget that."

"Tell Adam I won't stay long. And tell him my business here is purely personal."

Caroline smiled with a hint of mischief. "You'd say that in any case, wouldn't you?" She placed her hand on his shoulder and pressed a kiss against his cheek. "Be careful. You'd be hard to replace. Adam doesn't make friends easily. And Emily will never forgive the British army if you come to harm."

By the time Caroline moved off, the dance had come to an end. Emma was talking with Bram Martin on the edge of the dance floor not far from the entrance. Robert started toward them. He did not think Emma had seen him yet. Pearls shimmered at her throat and in her hair and at her ears. He could see her gown more clearly now, blue-green gauze over a satin slip that clung close to her body, outlining one leg that was thrust slightly forward. The gown was drawn in tight beneath her breasts and cut low, more revealing than any of the dresses she had worn in Scotland. Robert felt a rush of heat, reminded of the body beneath that scant covering.

He slipped past a quartet of officers and a woman in silver net, dodged around a couple bent on flirtation, and stopped a half-dozen or so feet from Emma. His heart hammered like the drum of a battle charge. A moment passed and then another. Then she turned in his direction and went suddenly still.

The talk and laughter and music died away. He was conscious of nothing but Emma and his longing to take her in his arms.

Her gaze met his own. Her eyes widened in joy and surprise, more brilliant than he had ever seen them. For a moment he actually thought she would run to him. She hesitated, then walked forward, pulling Bram Martin with her.

"Captain Melton." She held out her hand. Her voice sounded tight, as if from an effort at control. "I'm so glad. We'd begun to despair of ever seeing you in Brussels."

Emma clasped Robert's hand. He was wearing gloves, as was she, but she felt the shock of the contact and saw it reflected in his eyes. She forced her gaze away long enough to introduce Bram.

She scarcely heard the polite words Robert and Bram exchanged, but she drank in the sound of Robert's voice, rougher than Bram's polished accents. Only a few minutes ago, she had been wondering if she would ever hear his voice or look into his eyes again. And now he was here beside her. She wanted to walk into his arms and pull his head down to her own and kiss him until she could no longer think. Yet deep inside she felt another ache, sharp and bittersweet. She couldn't bear the thought that she had found him only to lose him again.

"Emma wrote to me about your search for Lucie Sorel." Bram's words broke through her reverie. "I'm sorry I couldn't be of more help. As I told Emma, the last I saw of Miss Sorel was when we finalized the details of the marriage settlement."

"I suspected you'd say as much. It's of no matter, Martin. Thank you."

Robert truly sounded unconcerned. Any doubts Emma had felt about his feelings for Lucie Sorel vanished in the face of her happiness.

The crowd nearest the door burst into applause. The musicians stopped playing. Even before Emma turned to the doorway, she knew who must have come into the room. She looked at Wellington's sharp profile with its distinctive hook nose. This man, so calmly surveying the crowd, was going to take Robert away from her.

Wellington paused near the entrance to the ballroom, surrounded by a group of blue-coated staff officers. Georgiana Lennox ran up to him, dragging Andy by the hand. "Do put an end to the suspense," she said, her voice carrying clearly. "Are the rumors true?"

Wellington looked down at her. His face softened slightly, but his gaze was direct. "Yes, they are true; we are off tomorrow."

There was a buzz of conversation as the duke's words were repeated throughout the ballroom. Emma's stomach tightened with cold, sickening fear. She looked up at Robert. "It's no more than we suspected. Jamie and Will have orders to join their regiments after the ball."

Jenny appeared beside them, a breathless stir of white tulle and red-blond ringlets. "Have you heard? They're to march tomorrow."

"We already knew that, my love." Bram took his wife's hand.

"Yes, but—" Jenny looked from Bram to Emma as if she did not realize Robert was there. Her blue eyes filled with horror, making her seem even more fragile and petite than usual. "I don't think I really believed it until now," she whispered.

Emma put an arm around her cousin and introduced Robert. Jenny murmured a distracted greeting. Bram steered her toward an anteroom. At last Emma found herself alone with Robert. Or as alone as they could be in a room filled with four hundred people. She looked at him, vividly aware of his uniform, where before she had seen only his face. For an unnerving moment, she felt she was looking at a stranger. It was as if Wellington's brief words had already pulled Robert away from her.

She studied his face, seeking the man she loved. The mouth she had felt soft and warm against her own seemed to have hardened into an uncompromising line. The eyes she had seen lit with tenderness and desire now seemed to hold a steely determination. He was about to march off to engage in the brutal game that had taken the lives of so many Blair men. It seemed incredible that this man who had made her tremble with passion and need would soon be engaged in wholesale slaughter.

Robert watched the emotions flicker across Emma's face. Wellington's announcement had created an unseen barrier between them. He had to find a way to pull her back. He wanted to touch her so badly he ached with it. "Dance with me?" he said. The musicians had resumed playing and couples were circling the floor, though some officers were saying farewells and making for the door.

Emma nodded and stepped into his arms. He could feel the tension in her body. Then she gave a shuddering sigh, as if accepting the inevitable. He held her against him for a moment, breathing in the sweet clean smell of lily of the valley. They moved into the dance without speaking. Robert reminded himself not to hold her too close. He could feel her breath against his throat, above the collar of his coat.

"Thank you for your letters," he said at last, his voice husky. "I'm sorry I couldn't write more often myself."

"You've been busy." It sounded as if her mouth was dry. "Will you come to see David tonight? I know he wouldn't mind if you waked him."

Robert had anticipated such a question and had decided truth would serve him best. "I saw David this afternoon in the park. I was only supposed to be in Brussels for a few hours," he said as her brows drew together in puzzlement. "I didn't know when I'd be sent out again. By sheer luck I ran into Caroline and the children. I knew I wouldn't have time to call at the house, so I asked them not to speak of it."

"Of course." Emma smiled, though the smile was strained. "There was no need to call once you'd seen David."

Though she was still in his arms, he felt her withdraw from him again as surely as if she had moved away. "As it turned out, I stayed in Brussels longer than I expected," he said. "I came to the ball solely to see you."

Her eyes searched his face as though she were trying to discover if he told the truth. She gave a tiny sigh and her mouth curved in a smile. "I don't care whether that's a lie or not. It sounds so lovely I'll believe it."

Robert released his breath and pulled her closer. It scarcely mattered. Many couples were clinging together, propriety abandoned in the face of separation and death.

They danced dance after dance together without question. They spoke of the children and of everyday events in Brussels and of the news from Scotland. Sometimes they didn't speak at all, content just to be together. Robert rested his face against her own, closed his eyes on the color and candlelight, and felt a cold wash of fear. In his years in Spain he had never courted death, but with an unfaithful wife and a son who was a virtual stranger, there had been little to tie him to life. Now, in a world on the brink of madness, he felt an overwhelming longing for a future. A future with Emma. A future that seemed as natural as breathing and as out of reach as the moon.

The thought made him dizzy with hope and despair. He opened his eyes, forcing himself to confront the world, and caught sight of Adam and Caroline among the dancers. He had promised Caroline he would not stay at the ball long. There were limits to how far he could strain the bonds of friendship and honor. But just as he was steeling his courage to take his leave, he and Emma were joined by Charlie and Arabel. "Captain Melton," Arabel said with enthusiasm. "You must have supper with us. I insist."

Robert's good intentions fled. Already the guests were beginning to move toward the hall to form the procession to supper. He gave Emma his arm. As they were caught up in the press of people, he saw Wellington himself standing not far off with two ladies and a thin, sallow-faced young man. From his vantage point, stopped by the crowd, Robert had a clear view of what happened next. There was a stir of movement at the doorway. An officer, dressed for riding, not dancing, and looking as if he had just ridden hard, pushed his way through the crowd and handed a paper to the sallow-faced man. He regarded it without much concern and handed it unopened to Wellington.

"You'd think Slender Billy would want to read the dispatch himself, wouldn't you," Charlie muttered.

So that was who the sallow-faced man was. The Prince of Orange. As heir to the throne of the Netherlands, he had been given command of one of the Allied divisions despite his lack of experience. He certainly looked no older than his twenty-three years.

Wellington opened the dispatch and read it through quickly. His face was unreadable, but Robert saw his shoulders tense. Wellington looked up and barked an order at the officer who had brought the dispatch. "Webster, four horses instantly to the Prince of Orange's carriage."

"Wellington must have been wrong about the real attack coming from the west," Arabel murmured as whispers spread through the ballroom again. "If he's worried about the security of the prince's headquarters—"

"Then Bonaparte must be attacking on our eastern flank," Charlie finished for her, "trying to separate us from the Prussians."

Robert said nothing. Charlie and Arabel were right. If Wellington had only just realized it, the French had gained valuable time.

Wellington issued more low-voiced instructions, then said something to a handsomely dressed lady who must be the Duchess of Richmond. The company made their way across the hall to the dining room. But Robert had barely helped Emma into her chair when the Prince of Orange hurried into the room, pushed his way between the linen-covered tables, and began to whisper to Wellington. The conversation went on for several minutes while an anxious silence fell over the company. Emma's breathing quickened. Arabel darted an anxious glance at Charlie.

"I have no fresh orders to give," Wellington said at last, in a voice meant to carry. "I advise Your Royal Highness to go back to your quarters and to bed."

The prince looked at him in surprise, then nodded and made his way from the room at a more dignified pace. Wellington smiled and said something to Arabel's friend

Georgiana that made her laugh. Supper continued. Wellington, with Georgiana on one side and another pretty young woman on the other, appeared quite at ease. Robert credited him with being a good actor.

The duke was one of the few people in the room still trying to act as if this were a normal social occasion. Troubled glances and anxious frowns replaced polite smiles. Speculation about the Prince of Orange's message took the place of gossip and small talk. Robert said little and contented himself with looking at Emma and reveling in the feel of her shoulder or leg brushing against his own. Some couples were openly holding hands. If Charlie and Arabel hadn't been nearby, he might have reached for Emma's.

As if aware of the pressure of his gaze, Emma turned toward him and smiled. Robert looked into her glowing eyes. Everything he had thought and felt since he had walked into the ballroom seemed to rush together in his head. His throat ached with the words he could not say. He wanted her in every way possible. He wanted to take her to bed, not just tonight but every night, and wake up holding her in his arms in the morning. He wanted a home where he could live with her and David and Kirsty. He wanted to give her more children.

Emma watched him, her gaze questioning. Abandoning his last vestiges of caution, Robert reached for her hand. Her fingers curled tightly around his own as if with a desperation she would not allow herself to voice.

All too soon, supper came to an end. The company seemed to realize that the time to say good-bye had truly come. Soldiers spilled into the entrance hall, calling for their horses and carriages. Some sought out parents and sweethearts to say farewell. A few couples went back to the ballroom, where the musicians were still playing, for one last dance.

Emma turned to Robert, her eyes wide and very dark.

Not trusting himself to speak, Robert helped her to her feet. It was nearly impossible to move in the throng. Through the open door to the hall, he saw Wellington going into another room, accompanied by a small group of men. Adam was among them.

He could feel Emma trembling. As they stood waiting, Charlie and Arabel behind them, Jamie and Will fought their way through the crowd.

"We're off, Em," Jamie said. "We have to ride to Ninove. Melton." He gave Robert a curt nod. Then his brows drew together as he caught sight of Charlie and Arabel. "See here, Lauder, what the devil do you mean hanging about my cousin all evening?"

"Don't be silly, Jamie." Emma laid a hand on her brother's arm. "If you had a particle of sense, you'd be glad to see her with a childhood friend instead of some dashing hussar with questionable intentions."

Jamie stared hard at Charlie. "By God, if you ever think of doing more than dancing with her—"

"He won't," Will said. "Not if he knows what's good for him. Anyway, Bel isn't *that* daft."

Jamie continued to look at Charlie. "If you see your brother, remind him we have business to settle when this is over."

Will held out his hand to Robert. "Glad we saw you, Melton. Best of luck if we don't meet in the field."

Jamie shook Robert's hand as well and muttered good wishes, though in a less cordial tone. Charlie drew back as Jamie and Will kissed the women good-bye. But when the Blair men started to move off, Charlie called after them. "Good luck."

Jamie continued to make his way through the crowd. Will hesitated a moment but did not look back.

Arabel drew in her breath. "I could kill—"

"No." Charlie gripped her arm. "Don't say anything you may regret."

Emma looked at Robert. "You'll need to be going too."

"Yes."

She held his arm very tightly as they made their way to the hall. Charlie murmured something about looking for Matt, and he and Arabel contrived to get lost in the crowd.

It was minutes before Robert and Emma reached the hall, precious last minutes spent picking their way through the crowd. He could hear the quiet sound of a woman sobbing beneath the strains of music and the shouts for horses. Someone had dropped a champagne glass, which lay shattered on the floor near the entrance to the hall. Robert steered Emma around the shards of crystal, nearly bumped into another woman, and realized it was Caroline.

"I was coming to find you," she said. "Adam's just been with Wellington. It seems the French are at Quatre Bras, much closer than we believed."

"That was what the Prince of Orange came back to tell the duke?" Emma asked.

Caroline nodded. "Wellington says Bonaparte has humbugged him." She looked at Robert. "You should be leaving."

"I'm about to do so."

He released Emma's arm and turned her to face him. Caroline moved a little away.

Emma tugged off her long white glove and laid her fingers against his cheek. "I told you once to be careful."

"And thus far I have been." Her hand was warm against his skin. Her eyes shone with trust. He placed his fingers over her own, took her face between his hands, and kissed her full on the mouth, knowing it was a kind of pledge. One day he would come back and tell her the truth.

He drew back, gripping her hand, and looked at Caroline. "I won't ask you to take care of her because she's very good at taking care of herself. But I trust you'll both keep an eye on each other."

Caroline smiled. "Godspeed, Robert."

Emma squeezed his fingers, her eyes on his face as if she could not bear to stop looking until he was gone from sight. He released her at last and strode into the knot of British soldiers at the door, against whom he was shortly to take the field.

12

The sound of troops being called to assemble could be heard in the Rue Ducale. Emma stepped down from Sherry's carriage and entered the house, leaving the others to follow. Only an hour ago she had said good-bye to Robert. She wanted a moment alone.

As she moved into the hall, she looked up and saw Kirsty and David sitting at the top of the stairs. "We were waiting for you," Kirsty said. "We heard the drums. What's happening?"

Her face showed more curiosity than fear. Emma ran up the stairs and sat down beside the children. "The soldiers are summoned to join their regiments. They're marching tonight to their stations."

"There's going to be a battle, isn't there?" David's eyes betrayed his apprehension.

"Probably." Emma tried to be as honest as she could. "There's already been fighting between the Prussians and the French. The French are also at Quatre Bras, and Wellington is sending more troops to meet them. I don't think the 52nd have been ordered there."

David was silent for a while. "When will we know?"

He meant *When will it be over, when will we know who stood and who fell?* but Emma did not want to put his fear into words. "I imagine it will be a day or two before we know anything at all," she said.

"I see." He stood up. "Then I guess there's nothing to do but go to bed."

He looked so forlorn that Emma put her arms around him. He clung to her a moment, then pulled away and gave her a shaky smile. "It's hard to wait."

"The hardest thing of all." She took the children's hands and walked with them to their rooms. David said good night at the door, indicating he did not want her company. Emma stayed with Kirsty until her daughter, tired of asking questions, at last fell asleep. Then she returned to the bedchamber she shared with Arabel.

For herself, sleep was impossible. She stood at the window, the sash thrown up to let in the warm, humid air. All the inchoate fears of the past welled up, a choking mass that turned her dizzy with panic. She took a deep breath, willing herself to calm, but the effort left her throat raw and rasping.

Her father's death. Allan's. Aunt Alice's. The death of her mother at the moment of Jamie's birth, a death she had always blamed on her father's absence. Surrounded by a family that loved and needed her, there had been a core of her self that felt alone. She had always known herself to be abandoned. A betrayal, not understood but deeply felt. She had never been able to believe that God had a plan for allocating loss and pain. It was easier to blame men's penchant for making war. How else to account for the randomness of death?

She knew now, with startling clarity, that she could lose them all. Jamie. Will. And Robert. How quickly he had become as vital to her happiness as the men she had known all her life. Losing Robert would tear her in two. She put her hand to her face, remembering Robert's kiss. It had been both farewell and promise. Surely that would not be the sum of what would be allowed them.

She pressed her hands on the sill and leaned out the window. The night was filled with sound. Trumpets rang out all over the city. Drums beat a call to arms. Soldiers were assembling and beginning to march. She could hear the muffled tread of their feet and cries and shouts too distant to be understood. Horses whinnied and hooves beat a rapid clop-clop on the cobbled streets. There were wagons, too, their iron wheels protesting under their heavy loads.

The predawn darkness was pierced by the flare of torches in the streets and candles burning in the windows. Soldiers were quartered in nearly every house in Brussels. There was a constant banging of doors and calls of farewell. A carriage clattered down the street beneath her window. A moment later two horsemen galloped by. Officers, she supposed, racing to join their regiments.

She was suddenly aware of a presence beside her. "I can't sleep either," Arabel said. She was barefoot, her hair streaming down her back, her white nightdress reflecting the first lightening of the dark sky. "When will it begin?"

"It has begun." Emma thought of the men who had already fallen. The Prussians had been fighting throughout the long, hot day while here in Brussels the idle British thought only of the night's festivities.

"It doesn't seem real, does it?" Arabel folded her arms on the sill and looked down at the empty street. "All these weeks, it seemed like we were on holiday. And all the while . . ." She made a vague gesture in the direction of the distant torches.

Emma grimaced. "I know. And yet . . ."

"It's been so absolutely wonderful."

It *had* been wonderful. Brussels had given Emma an intoxicating sense of freedom, as liberating in its way as crossing the threshold from maid to wife. It was not merely the excitement of change nor the informality of

social intercourse nor the excessive round of engage-
ments, all of which Arabel adored and Emma enjoyed
nearly as much. It was rather a sense of being in a wider
world, a recognition of a lack of boundaries, an awareness of possibilities. Emma had never been able to articu-
late clearly her dissatisfaction with her life. Accepting
that the repeated performance of common tasks was a
part of everyone's life, she still hoped for something
more. And here in Brussels she thought that she had
glimpsed it.

"I knew there might be fighting," Arabel continued,
"that people might be killed. But somehow I never
thought they would be people I knew." She straightened
and in the dim light Emma saw that she was biting her
lip as though to keep the tears at bay.

"Will has been through years of fighting. Jamie too."

"And Captain Melton." Arabel turned her head to look
at Emma. "You worry about him, don't you?"

"Of course I worry about him," Emma said with a
burst of feeling that was stronger than she meant to
show. "He's David's father," she went on in a calmer
voice. "The child has already lost his mother. I don't want
him to lose his father as well."

Arabel looked away, apparently satisfied, though of
what Emma dared not guess. "I'm worried about Charlie," Arabel said after a moment. "It's all new for him. He
barely knows how to load a musket. He's not— He
doesn't really like to fight."

"And bless him for it."

"I couldn't bear it if anything happened to him, Em. I
couldn't." Arabel had turned once more to face Emma.
Her eyes were dark hollows in the indistinct oval of her
face, but Emma did not need to see her features to know
what she had heard. A sharp pain gripped her heart.
You're too young, she thought, then realized she had
been even younger when she married Allan. She put her

arms around her cousin while Arabel clung to her and wept. Oh, unwise, Arabel. Not a Lauder.

"Come to bed." Emma smoothed Arabel's hair. "It will be a long day."

Emma quickly undressed and climbed into bed beside her cousin. Arabel, worn out from the excitement of the day and her bout of weeping, was already asleep. Emma listened to the soft sound of her breathing and wondered how far it had gone between Arabel and Charlie. There was no privacy at Blair House and as little at Lauder Hall. They must have found somewhere else to meet, someplace to talk without the heavy presence of their families, someplace to declare their love.

With a rush of heat that made her grateful for her cousin's oblivion, Emma suddenly knew where that place was. She saw again the cottage in which she and Robert had taken refuge. She relived once more every moment of that rain-driven afternoon. The pallet, the blanket, the flask of whisky. They had thought it had been arranged by a lad from one of the farms, but the whisky should have told them this was unlikely. Arabel had lain there with her lover, the young boy she had known all her life who had become man enough to carry a musket and die for his king.

Man enough to father a child. Emma buried her face in the pillow and prayed that Arabel had remembered the things she had told her. It was bad enough that Arabel should love a Lauder without the complication of an unplanned child. If Charlie survived the coming battle, if he was constant—and he would be; if Arabel was firm in her resolve—and she was a stubborn girl—then how were they going to get Angus to agree to the match?

Robert rode out of Brussels pursued by demons of his own making. He was surrounded by British troops. He noted the marching battalions, the supply wagons, the horse-drawn cannon, scarcely aware that he did so. He would be able to give a detailed report of what he saw, but his observation was automatic, a skill perfected by long practice. His mind was in Brussels, in an overheated ballroom made gaudy with women's finery and men's gold-encrusted uniforms and the brilliant colors of their host country. And his heart, a useless appendage he had grown accustomed to doing without, was possessed by a woman he should never have met.

He knew exactly when it had happened. Not in his first days at Blair House, where he had found a spirited woman with a glowing beauty and come to admire her. Not in the deserted cottage where they had agreed, in all their years of discretion, to take their pleasure from one another. Not even in the moment of madness when he had engaged to leave his son in her care. Not until tonight when he had seen her in the ballroom after three months' absence and known, with a certainty nothing would ever quench, that he was committed to loving her for the rest of his life.

It should have been a joyous feeling. Under the circumstances it was a damnable inconvenience. For a moment, as they had said good-bye, he had thought that love could transcend the truth of what was between them. Now, in the darkness of the night, in the midst of men marching to kill other men with whom they had no quarrel, love seemed a feeble shield against enmity. Emma was a generous woman, but he was twice her enemy. Because he loved her, he owed her the truth. And the truth would make it impossible to declare his love.

He pulled up his horse. An overturned wagon blocked the road, and men were scrambling to right the horses and wagon and retrieve the boxes strewn on either side. A high-ranking officer's goods, judging by the contents of the boxes that had been split open. Only a high-ranking officer—only a damned aristocrat—would go to war with a silver tea service and a set of crystal glasses. The polished teapot shone dully in the light of the torches. The crystal was shattered, its pieces crackling under the feet of heavy-booted men.

The wine had survived the accident. One crate had broken open and the bottles rolled across the road and onto the grassy verge. The men scrambled for them, cursing the darkness. More than one bottle found its way into a soldier's pack.

Robert watched, attracting no particular attention. He was one more officer riding to rejoin his battalion. After a few minutes the sergeant in charge of the wagon escort came up to him, his face glistening with sweat in the torchlight. By way of apology for the delay, he offered Robert a bottle of wine. "A good fino," the sergeant said. "The colonel won't miss it, he'll have other things on his mind in the morning. Can't hold up half the army searching for every bit of finery his lordship drags with him."

Robert had no qualms about accepting the sherry. The night was turning cold and the ride would be long, with few comforts at its end. In war one took what was offered. He thanked the sergeant, wished him fair fighting on the morrow, then let his horse pick his way through the cleared area around the wagon and its still-frightened team.

He had left Brussels far behind. He had been too long a soldier to live in anything but the present. Pain, questions, regrets—even thoughts of the future—had no place in what he was about to do. The pain of losing Emma would become no more than the dull accompaniment of the tasks before him, a faint but ever-present reminder that happiness was not his goal. He had chosen this life, and if he sometimes wondered if the choice had been a mistake, he knew that now he had no choice at all.

He rode due south, through the Forest of Soignies, past the villages of Waterloo and Mont-St. Jean and Genappe. Napoleon was headed straight for Brussels, where he hoped to arouse Belgian support and annex Belgium once more to the French Empire. But to do this he needed to prevent Wellington from joining the Allied forces with the Prussian army under Marshal Blücher. Separately the French outnumbered the two armies. If the Allies and the Prussians fought together . . .

The French could lose, and meantime the Austrians and the Russians were gathering on France's eastern frontier. The emperor had to prevail here, in Belgium, to survive. The Empire was a dream turned sour, but in Robert's eyes still preferable to the return of the monarchy.

The sky was edged with light by the time he reached Quatre Bras, where he learned from a Belgian sentry not eighteen years old that French troops were camped two miles away. The boy was clearly frightened. "Their lancers attacked one of our picquets about five, and then their light cavalry came, but we fought them off and they retreated. They'll be back in the morning. There must be thousands and thousands of them, and they know how to fight." The boy shook his head, and when he spoke again, his voice was despairing. "I don't have any quarrel with the French."

"That's not what war's about." Robert had no quarrel with the British save for their insistence on changing his government. He drew his cloak around him. It would hide his red coat from the French outpost guards who would challenge him when he rode on. In the morning he would change it for the blue of his own uniform.

He had left France less than forty-eight hours ago and since then Napoleon had brought his army across the frontier, engaged the Prussians—who had lost twelve hundred men according to the sentry—and established positions well into Belgium.

"There'll be more fighting today," the boy said. His eyes held the certainty that he would not survive it. "I'm afraid I'll want to run."

"Everyone does. But when it comes to it, you'll stay." Robert was not sure this was true. So much depended on one's fellows and the desire to stand well among them. Morale was poor among the Belgian troops.

Robert remained with the young sentry awhile. He could still remember the gut-wrenching fear of his first battle, and the boy needed reassurance. But he also stayed to learn what he could of the Allied strength near Quatre Bras. The village stood at the crossing of two major roads, one leading north from Charleroi—which the French now held—to Brussels, the other providing the link between Wellington's troops in the west and the Prussians in the east. If the French could take the crossroads, they would have Wellington in their grasp.

Robert said farewell to the boy and rode off. Once out of Quatre Bras he made his way by a side road to Frasnes, a village held by the French. There he learned that the emperor was encamped at Charleroi some ten miles further on. He did not stay to learn more. He would go straight to the emperor. More than an hour's hard riding was before him, and it would be day by the time he arrived.

But when he reached Charleroi, he was informed that the emperor was asleep. The emperor's aide-de-camp, General Flahaut, summoned from his bed, refused to wake him. Face drawn with fatigue and annoyance, Flahaut listened to Robert's message.

"The Allies have only a battery of eight guns at Quatre Bras and no more than four thousand infantry," Robert said. "We can take the crossroads easily if we move at once."

Flahaut threw up his hands. "My God. We've been marching and fighting since two yesterday morning. Fifteen hours without rest or refreshment, and more than that for the forward troops. Our men are scattered from Marchienne to Fleurus and they're exhausted."

"Wellington ordered his troops to march last night. He'll have reinforcements at Quatre Bras by the afternoon. Tired or not—"

"It will be Ney's business, God help him. He's been given command of the left wing. He didn't arrive 'til seven last night, and he doesn't yet know the strength of his regiments or the names of their colonels—even their generals—or the number of men who kept up with the columns by the end of the march. He was closeted with the emperor 'til two this morning. It's their decision, not mine, thank God. All right, all right, I'll deliver the message."

Flahaut turned away to indicate the interview was at an end. Then he looked back at Robert with a grimace of distaste. "Lescaut, get out of that damned British uniform."

An hour later, properly clothed, shaved, and with twenty minutes' of sleep to refresh him, Robert presented himself once more at the emperor's headquarters, where he was informed that he was assigned to Marshal Ney's staff and should await further orders. He did not learn if his message had been delivered nor how it had been received.

13

Emma woke early after a fitful sleep. She slipped out of bed and ran to the window. It was so quiet outside. No trumpets, no drums, no skirling of pipes or marching feet. Brussels was as it had always been, and last night might have been a dream.

But she had to see for herself. Arabel was awake and determined not to be left behind. They dressed hastily and ran downstairs, where they found Kirsty and David waiting for them in the hall. It was not yet eight o'clock when they left the house and ran into the street. The city seemed empty, its inhabitants sleeping off the strong emotions of last night's farewells. They walked to the Place Royale, where many of the troops had gathered before their march. It was deserted. A few heavy baggage wagons were lined up around the square, guarded by weary sentinels, but no other soldiers were to be seen.

Kirsty pointed to the rows of tilted carts, their drivers asleep inside. "What are those for?"

"To bring back the wounded, I expect." David spoke in a matter-of-fact voice, as though war were an everyday occurrence.

Emma shivered. Fear brushed over her as her imagination, always too active, saw them filled with hacked and bleeding men. "Let's go home. There will be things to do."

It was the longest day Emma could remember, though she filled it with activity. She sent messages for Jenny and Caroline and Georgiana Lennox and all of her other friends and acquaintances to join her in the Rue Ducale. Even the children were put to work. There was lint to be scraped and bandages to be torn, pillows and blankets and flasks of water to be collected for the expected influx of the wounded.

About three in the afternoon they heard the distant rumble of cannon. Andy and Jack, who had been fretting about being confined to women's work, set out on horse-back. They would ride as far as Waterloo and see what could be learned.

Emma maintained a facade of normalcy, which the other women adopted as well. There was nothing to be done but to be as cheerful as one could and try not to frighten the children. Though the children seemed calmer than their parents.

Toward evening the women dispersed. Some time after six Andy and Jack returned. "They say Blücher's been badly beaten," Andy said when he met Emma and Arabel in the hall. "The Prussians couldn't stand up to the French troops."

"Depends on who you believe." Jack was eternally optimistic. "I heard a British sergeant say Blücher's trounced Bonaparte. Thirty thousand Frenchies dead."

"Probably the same thirty thousand other people say are marching on Brussels." Andy's voice was caustic. "Some Belgian soldiers who've run back to Brussels say the British are retreating in confusion, but no one really believes them."

Emma had to be satisfied with the conflicting stories. It was clear no one knew anything at all. The cannonade continued. Later in the evening Adam stopped in the Rue

Ducale and they immediately besieged him for fresh news. "I spoke to an officer who was at Quatre Bras as late as five this afternoon," he said. "Our troops are engaging the French, and all was going well when he left. The cavalry hadn't arrived, but the 8th and 9th brigades were in the thick of it."

Arabel made a small sound of dismay. Charlie Lauder was in the 9th. Emma put an arm around her, part in comfort, part in warning. "Will and Jamie will be all right, then," she said with bright determination. And Robert. No one had mentioned the 52nd.

That evening Sherry took them up on the city ramparts where they walked for an endless time, listening to the cannonade. Around ten the sounds grew fainter and then ceased altogether. "It's over," Emma said. "Whatever has happened, it's over. For today."

Arabel shuddered and laid her head on her cousin's shoulder. "Charlie's all right," she said, her voice breaking. "Oh, Em, he has to be all right. I'm going to have his baby."

Emma stared down at Arabel's shining hair, hoping she had not heard right, knowing that she had. Dear God. Death on one hand. New life on the other. Emma put her arms around her cousin, grateful that Sherry and the boys were out of earshot. "It's all right. We'll talk later. I'll see you through this." But for now they had to live one day—one hour—at a time.

It had grown cool. Sherry approached them. "Are you tired? Shall we go back to the house?"

"I couldn't possibly sleep," Arabel said.

He grinned "Nor could I. What do you say to a game of whist? It will pass the time."

But when they returned to the house, Arabel turned away from the card table and retreated to a nearby sofa, where she was soon lost in her own thoughts. Andy and Jack, eager for distraction, entered the game with enthusiasm. Sherry behaved as though nothing were amiss. He had been a sea of calm on this turbulent day.

Some time after midnight they heard the noise of rapidly moving carriages. It seemed to come from the vicinity of the Place Royale, the heart of the city. With a cry of alarm that made a sham of his composure, Sherry threw down his cards and ran downstairs. The rest of them crowded after him.

The street outside the house was filled with people, some angry, some frightened, all shouting at cross-purposes. Emma finally made out the burden of their words. A train of artillery had just passed through the city, the British were retreating as fast as they could, the French were within a half-hour's march of the city, and there were no soldiers to hold them off.

Her control snapped. Jamie wouldn't run away, nor Will. Nor Robert. Nor would their commanders, Picton and Hill and Uxbridge and Wellington himself. She was sick to death of the timid hysterical rabbits who had nothing better to do than spread rumors and raise alarms. She ran into the street and screamed at the milling throng. "Liars! Imbeciles! We'll never retreat. Never!"

"The artillery," someone shouted.

"Idiot, they're going to the front."

The crowd ignored her and swept on. Defeated and inexpressibly weary, Emma turned and climbed the steps to the front door, where the others were clustered. "To hell with the bloody French," she said, pushing her way through them. "I'm going to bed."

Arabel fell into the exhausted sleep that follows a storm of weeping, though she had shed no outward tears. Emma lay beside her, racked with anxiety for Arabel, fear for the men she loved, and fury at the people milling in the street. The night before, she had danced with Robert at the Duchess of Richmond's ball. Today their troops had met the French at Quatre Bras. Who knew what tomorrow would bring.

Toward morning she dozed, only to be awakened by shouting and a pounding on the street door. Arabel was sitting bolt upright beside her.

They ran to the window and flung it open. A man standing in the street looked up at the sound and shouted, *"Les Français sont ici! Les Français sont ici!"* Then he ran off to give his message at the next house.

Emma leaned out the window and looked down the street. Once more it was filled with people, some half dressed, some with their nightcaps on, all running around in a distracted manner. The more enterprising were carrying furniture and pictures and treasured objects down to their cellars.

"What do they expect?" Arabel's voice trembled with indignation. "The French aren't barbarians."

"Of course they aren't. Oh, the devil take these people. We'd better get dressed."

They found Sherry downstairs, calming the servants. "Jack and Andy have gone out to see what's happening," he said when the servants had gone about their duties. "The children seem to have slept through the uproar. There'll be coffee in a quarter hour, and perhaps later we can have a civilized breakfast." He led them to the breakfast room and within a few minutes had them laughing. They vowed they would not be serious again until they knew they had cause.

Adam joined them a short time later. He had been with Sir Charles Stuart, the British ambassador, and had had word from his friend Fitzroy Somerset, Wellington's secretary. "There was a retreat," he said, accepting a cup of coffee from Emma, "but it was Belgian troops. Some of them ran away. Their cavalry galloped through the city this morning as though the hounds of hell were on their heels and it set off a panic. People are leaving the city any way they can. The road to Antwerp is clogged with carriages and wagons and carts and people on foot. Some of them are English. So much for British pluck."

"Some of us are staying, Adam."

"The best never flinch."

Adam left soon after, taking Kirsty and David with him. Caroline had invited the children to spend the day with Emily. He returned at noon to tell them that one of the duke's aides-de-camp had brought information that the Allies, though badly outnumbered, had thrown back the French at Quatre Bras.

"Is it over?" Arabel whispered.

"I fear it's scarcely begun. The French were driven back, but they gave the Prussians a stinging defeat at Ligny."

Alarm filled Arabel's eyes. "Were there many casualties? At Quatre Bras, I mean."

"The Duke of Brunswick is dead, but if you want other names, I fear I can't tell you. The cavalry came up late—apparently some confusion about orders—but the infantry battalions acquitted themselves well. They say the Highlanders were badly hit."

Arabel paled. "The Royals?"

Adam shook his head. "I haven't heard. You have friends among them?"

"Not exactly." Arabel looked down, then raised her eyes. "Yes. Charlie Lauder."

Adam smiled. "And you wouldn't want harm to come to a fellow Scot. Even if he's a Lauder." His smile faded. "I'll make inquiries. I expect they'll be bringing the wounded back before long. Someone will know."

The promise sustained Arabel through the long afternoon, an afternoon filled with horrors the like of which Emma had never seen. They went out into the streets, armed with scissors and lint and bandages and flasks of water and brandy. The wounded lay everywhere. It was more than twenty miles to Quatre Bras and some men had walked the entire way, their uniforms encrusted with blood and dirt. Others too ill to stand were brought in carts and wagons. Now that a crisis was at hand, the people of Brussels responded with compassion and efficiency. As did the English ladies of fashion. Every house was open, but many soldiers were forced to lie in the streets, some on straw pallets, some on the cobbled stones.

Emma was used to dealing with everyday injuries, wounds from fights and falls and accidents. Save when Allan had been invalided home, his wounds already neatly stitched, she had never seen the damage done by musket shot or cannon or sabre. The wounds were filthy and infected. Her heart aching with pity, she cleansed and picked out pieces of cloth and debris and bandaged as best she could. She gave water to men who could ask for nothing more. She promised to send the letters of dying men to wives and sweethearts, and when there was nothing more to be done, she closed their eyes.

Arabel worked beside her with fierce determination, doing what must be done, then asking each man his regiment. Some had fought with the Royals, but only one man knew Charlie by name. He thought Charlie had fallen, but he did not know if he was dead. Arabel bit her lip and worked on.

By midafternoon the sun, which had been oppressively hot, was hidden by clouds. Emma wiped the sweat from her face, grateful for the absence of the glare. There was a sudden flash of brightness and she heard the rumble of thunder. The rain began, drenching wounded and helpers alike. Emma took a young soldier with a gaping wound in his side into the shelter of a nearby house. As she returned to the street, Andy ran up. He was in his shirtsleeves. The rain was washing out the blood and mud with which his clothes were stained. His hair hung lank and dripping about his face.

"You're a mess," she said. He looked as shattered by the events of the day as she was herself.

"So are you." He grinned, then turned serious. "Get home, Em. You can't do more out here. Sherry's turned the house into a damned hospital. We found Charlie and took him there. He won't fight tomorrow, but if he doesn't die of wound fever he'll be all right. Tell Arabel before she frets herself into a decline."

Emma breathed a silent prayer of thanks. "Bless you, Andy. Arabel's been surviving on sheer pluck, but she's torn apart inside. What about you?"

He made a wry grimace. "Splendid, love. I've had my fill of soldiering, and I've not gone near the army. Damn the rain. We're getting men into shelter as fast as we can. Sherry's off arranging billets for the living and graves for the dead. God love us, what a piece of work."

Emma kissed him and went looking for Arabel, who on hearing the message, ran all the way to the Rue Ducale. When Emma reached the house, Arabel was directing the footmen to carry Charlie upstairs. "Where will you put him?" Emma asked. All the bedrooms were occupied.

"I can't leave him here." Arabel gestured wildly around the hall. The floor was covered with pallets and wounded men, the air thick with the smells of blood and putrefaction.

"Put him in Kirsty's room. She'll sleep with us." Emma looked down at the man she had known since he was a boy, the father of Arabel's child. His pale face was distorted with pain, but he was conscious and his eyes were clear. "Hullo, Em," he whispered. "Thanks for taking me in. Sorry I'm not up to walking."

Emma's throat tightened. "I'm glad we found you. Does it hurt much?"

He grimaced. "Like bloody hell."

She looked at the gory mess of his leg, then turned to Arabel. "Shall I come up?"

"No. I'll do it myself."

There was more than enough to occupy Emma on the ground floor. She worked with the servants tending the men who lay there, bandaging wounds, giving comfort and food and drink. By evening they had done all they could. One man was dead. They covered his face but let him remain. It seemed unfeeling to put him outdoors in the pelting rain.

When she was done, she took two bowls of broth upstairs. "One is for you," she told Arabel. "I'll feed Charlie."

He was propped up in bed, looking somewhat better though still in obvious pain. There was an enormous clean bandage around his left thigh. "I took a musket ball," he said in answer to Emma's look. "I wouldn't let them cut my leg off."

"Sensible," Emma said and hoped it was so. If gangrene set in, it would prove a disastrous decision. She wondered how Jamie and Will had fared this day. And Robert. Had they come through unscathed or had they too been wounded? And if so, were they being tended or did they lie abandoned on the field? Striving to keep her face calm, she gave Charlie a spoonful of broth.

He swallowed, then shook his head. "I'm not very hungry."

"You'll eat it. How did the day go?"

His face clouded. "I never thought there'd be so many. The Frenchies came at us in waves. The corn was high, you know, as high as a man's head. We could hardly see them 'til they were on top of us. And their guns kept pounding us all afternoon. The 79th took the worst of it, but we all fought like the devil was after our souls. Bloody French."

He sank back on the pillow and closed his eyes. After a

moment he stirred and was persuaded to take more broth. "That's enough, Em," he said at last, pushing her hand away. "I'll do better tomorrow."

Emma set down the bowl. "We'll get you some laudanum. It will help you get through the night."

As she rose from the bed, Charlie took her hand. "We did well, you know. We started out in line, but later we formed a square with the 28th. The cuirassiers came at us again and again, but they couldn't break us. When one of us fell, we'd pull him inside and close ranks. We stood them off. It took all day, but we stood them off."

Emma's eyes prickled with tears. She squeezed his hand. "I'm sure you did, Charlie." She picked up the bowls and moved toward the door.

Arabel remained seated by the bed. "I'll sit up with him tonight." She looked so fierce that Emma did not dare utter a word of protest.

Downstairs, Emma found that Adam had brought Kirsty and David back. The children were sitting on the floor, talking to the wounded men, seeming undismayed by their groans and injuries. They had spent the day, Kirsty informed her, helping Caroline take care of the sick men who had been brought to her house.

Emma kissed her daughter, gave David a hug, said she was proud of them, and sent them to the kitchen for supper. Then she walked with Adam to the door. When they reached it, he turned and took her hands. "We haven't won, you understand. Nothing more than breathing space. We'll meet the French tomorrow, if the rain lets up. Sunday's hardly a day for a battle, but war doesn't wait on piety. Wellington has picked his spot. A field just south of Waterloo."

Emma thought of the map that hung in the library. "Then he *has* retreated. It must be ten miles at least."

"He had to. The Prussians have fallen back. He wants to keep the armies close together."

"You're sure there will be more fighting?"

"Without question." He squeezed her hands, opened the door, and stepped out into the torrential rain that must even now be turning the field of Waterloo into impassable mud.

14

Robert reined in his horse on the ridge just east of the inn of La Belle Alliance and looked across the valley to the opposing ridge where Wellington had gathered his army. A paved road bisected the fields before him, running north straight to Brussels. It was four o'clock on Sunday morning. Darkness had given way to light and the rain was still falling.

Robert pulled his cloak closer about him and cursed the fate that had sent them storms in the middle of June. Eighteen hours of pelting rain had flattened the high-standing rye and turned the fields into a sea of mud. It had been near midnight before the troops were bivouacked for the night, drenched, tired, hungry, and dispirited. Many of the soldiers had arrived barefoot, their boots and shoes sucked into the mud on the slow march from Quatre Bras. There was no shelter. Officers and staff occupied the few farms and huts that could be found. No fire would burn, no musket would fire. Scarcely a shot had been exchanged the entire day.

And Wellington had had time to retreat and get his army into position.

They should not have had to fight Wellington here. The emperor's strategy was clear enough. The French were outnumbered by the combined strength of the Allies and the Prussians. Separately they could take them, one after the other. And that is what should have happened two days ago. Grouchy, commander of the army's right wing, had been sent to hold off the Prussians while Ney, commander of the left wing, had marched on Quatre Bras.

If Robert's message had been heeded—Ney would have been ordered to attack at once. They would have taken Quatre Bras before it was reinforced by the Allies, and Ney would have marched on Brussels. But Ney delayed, waiting for orders that were unconscionably late and unclear when they finally arrived. It was two in the afternoon before he hurled Reille's corps at Quatre Bras.

Robert still shook with fury at the stupidities of that day. Ney had expected his attack to be reinforced by the emperor's reserves, but Napoleon decided to concentrate his troops on the Prussians and didn't bother to inform Ney. Even worse, General d'Erlon, commander of Ney's own reserve corps, had spent the day marching back and forth under contradictory orders from the emperor and Ney.

Then yesterday again Ney had waited for orders that did not come. It had been afternoon before the emperor appeared. Furious to find Ney's troops at rest, he had ordered them to follow the Allied Army. But it was too late. With a perversity that showed that God—if there was a God—was not on their side, the storm broke, turning the roads to mud and making movement near impossible.

The men lying on the ground around Robert were beginning to stir, cursing the day, lighting fires, firing muskets to make sure the rain had not ruined the powder. A sea of men, many of whom would never leave this field.

Robert turned his horse and made his way back to Chantelet, where Ney had lodged for the night. There was a wrenching pain in his gut. Fear gripped him before every engagement, but this was more than fear. He had no stomach for this battle. Not when his son stood poised between two worlds. Not when the memory of Emma's glowing presence blurred all distinction between friend and foe.

The farmhouse at Chantelet was quiet, men and animals taking what rest they could. Robert stabled his horse and entered the house. A fire was still smoking and the air was humid with the damp from sodden uniforms. A half-dozen men lay on benches and a scarred wooden table, the sound of their snoring breaking the quiet of the room. "Oh, there you are, Lescaut." Colonel Heymes, another of Ney's aides, raised his head. "Wondered what happened to you. Writing a farewell note to a lady?"

Robert smiled and shook his head. There was nothing he could say to Emma. He wrapped his cloak about him, lay down near the hearth, and willed himself to sleep.

At eight he was once more on the ridge near La Belle Alliance. The rain had stopped and the day promised to be clear and hot. With the coming of day and the welcome sun, the men's spirits rose. They were impatient for action, but word came that the battle would be delayed. "The ground's still too wet," Ney told Robert. "The men can't move fast enough and we can't bring the guns into position."

At ten the emperor rode among his troops. A brave sight, a thumb in the eye of the British, though their uniforms were shabby, put together as best they could in the brief weeks since the emperor's return from Elba. Shouts of *"Vive l'empereur!"* rose all along the lines.

Robert watched the man who would command the battle, an unprepossessing figure wearing a thin gray riding coat. A flawed genius, Napoleon Bonaparte could inspire a compelling devotion. Robert was no longer young and naive, but he felt it still.

Robert glanced from the emperor to Ney, wondering

at Napoleon's reasons for giving the red-headed marshal command of the battlefield this day. To Robert's mind Ney was likely suffering from battle fatigue. In action he was often rash, but sometimes too slow and cautious. Yet there was no doubting his bravery under fire. The men would follow him anywhere. And he was not, like many of the emperor's commanders, an aristocrat.

Robert's horse danced from side to side. He controlled the animal, feeling the same need for activity. His world had become the few square miles before him, their quiet broken by the murmurs of men and the neighing of horses and the occasional rat-tat-tat of a drum.

An hour and a half later, new orders were brought to Ney. Within a few minutes the peaceful morning was torn asunder by the sound of guns. The French were on the attack.

Reille's forces moved forward to clear the Allied skirmishers from the wood that stood before the fortified chateau of Hougoumont, which the allies held west of the Brussels road. It was intended as a diversion, for the main French attack would come from d'Erlon's forces on the right of the road, but resistance from the defenders of the chateau proved unexpectedly fierce. Robert soon lost track of the engagement. For the next hour he supervised the placement of a battery of eighty guns—twelve-pounders and eight-pounders and horse artillery—in front of d'Erlon's infantry divisions.

At one o'clock the guns sent out a crashing barrage of fire. The Dutch-Belgian troops stationed in front of the opposing ridge were cut to pieces, but most of Wellington's army escaped, concealed on the reverse slope of the ridge or behind the thick hedges that bordered it. The cannonballs that should have ricocheted over the crest of the ridge and reached the men sheltering behind it were engulfed by the mud.

The guns fired repeatedly and then the French advanced, their infantry deployed in huge columns. "It's a mistake," Robert muttered to Heymes, who had pulled up beside him. "Only the forward men can fire. The columns will be gunned down."

Heymes shrugged. "I'm past understanding the minds of generals, Lescaut."

The French faltered, then drove on. Squadron after squadron of Allied heavy cavalry charged down from the ridge. The French met them in a thundering clash of arms near the farm of La Haye Sainte, which the allies also held. The cuirassiers should have held them, but the Allied horsemen were better mounted. The French cavalry fled before them. Much of the French infantry followed suit, sustaining heavy losses.

From his station at the gun battery, Robert rode forward to try to stem the tide of retreat. His horse took a shell in the chest and dropped. Robert sprang free, took one look at the stallion's wound, then put a pistol shot through its head. The air was thick with smoke and the screams of fallen men. Robert ran forward and seized the reins of a riderless horse, a white mare neighing wildly with fright. He mounted quickly. More Allied cavalry had appeared from the eastern side of the ridge, hacking wildly at men and beasts as they came. Robert rode to the rear, seeking reinforcements.

It was a rout. Formations dissolved, men ran away, others stood their ground and fought fiercely before retreating or falling to the sword. The eagles of the 45th and 105th regiments were captured.

The British cavalry should have rallied and drawn back. But the Scots Greys, drunk with their triumph, rode on across the valley, overrunning the French gunners. Robert stared at them. They were madmen. They would be slaughtered.

The Greys tried to rally, but they were too tired and too scattered. They fell beneath the blows of the cuirassiers and lancers who had been sent up as reinforcements. Those that survived made a frantic and undisciplined retreat, covered by the British light cavalry units that had been sent to their aid.

At three o'clock a sort of quiet came over the battlefield, though there was still fighting at Hougoumont and La Haye Sainte. Robert turned the now docile mare back toward the scene of slaughter to organize the search for the wounded. A straggling group of Allied prisoners was being marched up the slope toward La Belle Alliance. The sound of a bugle pierced the air. On the field soldiers stole from the dead, their own and the enemy, performed small acts of kindness and vicious acts of retribution. Robert scarcely noticed these. It was war.

Stretcher parties carried the wounded up the ridge to makeshift hospitals. Wounded horses were shot to spare them further misery. Riderless horses were rounded up to be returned to service. Robert dismounted and took a ring from a dying young lancer who begged him to send it, with the letter in his coat, to his wife and child. After he left the lancer, he ordered a count of the guns, their condition, and the number of gunners available to man them. He closed the eyes of an infantry sergeant he remembered from Spain. He acted quickly, did what was necessary, and did not allow himself to feel anything at all.

A lieutenant of a lancer regiment was rounding up British prisoners. One man, an officer in the blue coat of a British light dragoon, straggled behind the group, fell to his knees, and collapsed. Swearing, the lieutenant rode back and raised his sword to plunge it into the dragoon's back.

Robert shouted, spoiling the lieutenant's aim but not arresting his thrust. He ran up, pulled the lieutenant from his horse and seized him by the throat. "Your name! Damn your soul to hell, tell me your name!"

The lieutenant's eyes went wide with fright. "Bernays. Sir."

Robert's hands slackened. He threw the lieutenant from him. "Do that again, and I'll kill you."

"Sir." The lieutenant gave a shaky salute, mounted his horse, and rode on, shouting at his prisoners to move.

Robert turned his attention to the enemy dragoon. He was moaning, a high keening sound. Blood bubbled from the sword thrust that he had taken, not in the heart, as intended, but in the side. Robert tugged off his neckcloth and improvised a rough binding around the dragoon's torso, turning him onto his back to fasten it. Damnation, one did not kill prisoners. Robert reached for his water flask, raised the dragoon's shoulders, and looked into the filthy, sweat-drenched face of Will Blair.

A chill swept him, though the sun beat down and the air was hot with smoke and powder. He was back in the Duchess of Richmond's overheated dining room and Will was wishing him good luck. Fifty thousand Allied soldiers, perhaps more, and he had to find a Blair.

Awareness flickered in Will's eyes. "Melton," he whispered, his voice cracking.

Robert found the flask and raised it to Will's lips. Will drank greedily. Then he sank back. "Am I done for?"

Robert owed him honesty, at least in this. Will had taken a shot in his chest as well as the sword in his side. "You'll not fight again today. You need a surgeon." He laid Will down carefully. "I'll get you back to your lines."

He stood and looked down at the man who had offered him the beginning of friendship.

Will returned his regard. His gaze traveled over Robert's coat, not the red faced with buff of the 52nd but a dark blue coat with a sky-blue collar. A puzzled look came into Will's eyes. He frowned. "Damme. You're a Frenchman."

Robert grimaced and turned away. He retrieved his

horse and commandeered another, one of a group being rounded up for return to the French lines. A British horse, he judged, not one of theirs. It was fitting.

Will could not sit the saddle. Robert hoisted him across the horse's back and tied him on, then led the horse across the trampled green fields in the direction of the Allied lines.

The Allied soldiers were doing as their French counterparts, clearing the fields of the wounded, shooting horses, organizing prisoners to march behind the lines. When Robert came in sight of a stretcher party, he raised his voice in a loud halloo. The sergeant in charge of the party whirled round, then raised his musket. Robert put up his hands to indicate his peaceful intent, then gave the horse by his side a great blow on the rump, sending him trotting with his burden toward the waiting men.

The sergeant hesitated, then lowered his gun. Robert spurred his horse to a brisk canter and rode back to his own lines. In the smoke and confusion, his rescue of the British dragoon might not have been noted. But if it had, no matter. He would kill any man who dared to question what he had done.

He found Ney in a fury at the defeat of d'Erlon's troops. "We'll have no help from Grouchy," he told Robert. "He was supposed to turn west, to support our right wing. God knows what orders he's following. There hasn't been a clear command all day. Save this." He waved a paper under Robert's nose. "We're to take La Haye Sainte. Now. See to it."

By the time Robert rounded up two of d'Erlon's brigades and sent them against the farm of La Haye Sainte, Ney had ordered a brigade of cuirassiers to charge the Allied troops on the western half of the ridge. "We can take them now," Ney said. "Wellington is trying to retreat."

Robert thought Ney was wrong. The Allied soldiers

were moving to their rear, but they were doing no more than carrying their wounded and their prisoners to shelter. The ridge would be fully defended. Sensing disaster, Robert watched the cuirassiers thunder up the hill. It was four o'clock.

Within minutes the small French cavalry charge became a massive attack. One after the other the divisions of the heavy and light cavalry raced into battle, some on orders, some on their own initiative. Ney ordered the gun battery moved to the west side of the road. It did no good. The long columns of men and horses made it impossible to cover the advancing troops with fire. No supporting infantry was called up, no horse artillery. The French cavalry were easy targets for the Allied guns, but they continued to come, wave after wave of mounted men, swords and sabres raised. Robert was in their midst, at Ney's side.

The Allied soldiers had formed into a great checkerboard of squares, four men deep, the front line kneeling, bayonets at the ready, the rear lines holding muskets ready to fire. No horse would charge through the bayonets. The French horsemen wheeled and slashed, retreated, re-formed, charged again. And again and again. The squares held.

The piles of dead men and horses grew. Smoke and the smell of blood filled Robert's nostrils. Guns and screams assailed his ears until he could no longer distinguish sound. It was unbearably hot. Thirst was a torment. The sun had disappeared in the pall of smoke.

He heard the sound of cannon in the distance and wondered if the Prussians had at last come to Wellington's assistance. It did not matter. Nothing mattered save what he could see before him. He became a machine, slashing, thrusting, killing, and maiming.

The piles of dead grew higher. Some of the squares dispersed, some were penetrated. They took a half-dozen

Allied colors. They withdrew, then charged again, now properly supported by infantry and guns. It was nearly seven when the cavalry charges ceased, and Robert could not say whether they or the Allies had prevailed. He looked down into the valley and saw that they had finally taken La Haye Sainte. It was a small victory.

They retreated to their own lines and learned that the emperor would at last bring up the Imperial Guard, his old soldiers, the pride of his army. The troops would have to reengage and support the Guard's attack. "General de La Bédoyère brought orders from the emperor," Ney told Robert. "Do you see those columns coming from the east? Tell the troops it's Grouchy, coming to our aid."

Only then did Robert know how close they were to losing the day. "It's the Prussians, isn't it?"

Ney stared through him. "Those are orders, Colonel."

Robert needed no more. He had lost his hat in battle, but he begged one from a fellow officer, raised it on the tip of his sabre, and galloped up and down the lines. *"Vive l'empereur! Soldats, voilà Grouchy!"*

The shout was taken up by the troops and multiplied a thousandfold. Ney took his place at the head of the Guard battalions. Robert fell in beside him. They advanced to the beating of drums and the battle cries of the men. Heymes, who was riding beside Robert, turned his head and grinned. "Thought you were dead, Lescaut. Glad you're not."

Robert kept his eyes on the waiting Allies. "It's not over yet." He'd lost count of the number of his friends who had fallen.

The Allied infantry rose up from behind a bank, fired repeatedly at the advancing troops, then charged them with bayonets. The French fell back, rallied, and advanced once more to the crest of the ridge. More Allied soldiers appeared behind a screen of rye. Robert hastened to turn the chasseurs toward this new attack.

Shores of Desire

The scarlet coats of the British troops were the last thing he saw. A piercing pain went through him. He knew as he fell from his rearing horse that he had taken a musket ball in the chest. Another struck him before he reached the ground. Then the world turned black.

He floated in and out of consciousness. Swords and sabres clashed above him, making music with the drums. *L'empereur*. He had lost. Robert knew that even before he heard the cries announcing the Guard's retreat. The earth trembled with the pounding of running men and horses. A hoof struck him on the back. He felt his bones give beneath it. *"Trahison!"* someone cried. Treason. Poor bastards. They had expected Grouchy. They had believed his shouted lie.

It had grown quieter. The mud was soft beneath his cheek. The pain was a distant discomfort. Robert felt himself floating above it. It was not a bad way to die. Death was an endless sleep, and he was tired, consumed by the need for rest.

But first he would like a drink of water. He saw a face and knew it was his son. He felt the touch of a hand and knew it was Emma's. The pain flared anew. At least, he said, his lips struggling to form the soundless words, at least I gave her back Will.

When he woke again, it was night. He was cold and stiff. Why wasn't he dead? Or was this a mockery of death? He blinked his eyes and realized the blackness had lifted. Dim shapes moved about the battlefield. Soldiers seeking their wounded. And peasants, men and women alike, come to rob the dead. Why not? The armies destroyed their land. They should have something for their pains.

Not satisfied with the dead, the dark, silent figures robbed the living as well. Robert heard muffled and angry speech, then a cry of protest cut short in gurgling sound. Someone had had his throat cut. An unpleasant way to die, Robert thought, aware of his own helplessness. He had not gone through this murderous day to become meat under a scavenger's knife.

When they reached him, they took his pistols and his sabre, then turned him roughly over on his back. With a strength he did not know he possessed, Robert raised his head and bared his teeth. A low growl came from his throat, a howl of fury and anguish at the waste that had taken place this day. The woman above him shrank back. Her hair fell lank about her face. A knife gleamed between her teeth. She rose hastily, stumbled, called off a nearby companion. Robert heard them running and sank back into pain and oblivion. He had won his final battle.

15

In the Rue Ducale they heard the thundering of the guns shortly before noon on Sunday morning. It went on, without ceasing, until darkness fell over the city.

The wounded brought in the day before still commanded their attention. Others arrived throughout the day, some on foot, some in wagons and carts and carriages. Every conveyance in Brussels had been sent to bring them back.

Andy appeared in the early afternoon with a blood-drenched soldier slung over his shoulders. "I found him in the street," he said, laying the man on a straw pallet on the hall floor. "He said he fell at Quatre Bras—God help me, that was two days ago. He crawled out of the field sometime last night and made his way to the city. It must be twenty miles. Look at him, Em." He pointed to the white face contorted into a grimace of suffering. "He was out of his head with pain and thirst."

"Andy. He's dead."

Andy stared at the young soldier, barely older than he was himself. "Why so he is." He closed the soldier's eyes with a gentle hand, then burst into tears.

Emma held him, rocking him back and forth as she had when he was young. Her own tears would not come, though she was filled with them. So much waste, so much senseless, unnecessary waste.

Rumors of a French victory swept the city all day. Emma knew for a fact that some of Brussels' wealthier citizens were preparing a grand supper for the emperor and his officers who were expected to arrive that night. Some had fled in terror of Bonaparte's soldiers. Others went calmly about the business of relieving distress and preparing for the battle's aftermath.

Adam stopped by and told them not to believe everything they heard. "I don't," Emma said. "At the moment I don't believe anything at all."

Sherry repeatedly drove toward Waterloo to bring back what men he could. The day, he said, seemed sometimes to be going with the Allies, sometimes with the French. He was nearly dropping with exhaustion, but he planned to return.

In the evening Emma went into the street, desperate for a breath of air that was not fetid with the stink of death. She was startled by the sudden quiet. It was dark and the guns had ceased. She trembled with fear and fatigue. And hunger. She had taken no food since morning.

"Mama." Kirsty was standing at the door, David beside her. "The guns have stopped."

Suddenly aware of the children's needs, Emma returned to the house. Her daughter's eyes were wide with apprehension. David's face was white. "The fighting's over." Emma put her arms around them. "Have you eaten?" They nodded. "I seem to have forgotten about it. Come to the kitchen with me."

The servants, exhausted by the demands of the day, had gone to bed. Emma searched the dark, cavernous kitchen and found a half loaf of bread and some cheese and apples. She shared them with the children, who were always hungry. A single candle lightened the gloom and made a small haven of safety in a world that seemed too deranged for comprehension.

David was staring at a knife he had picked up to cut his apple as though he had forgotten why he held it. "When will we know?"

"Tomorrow, perhaps. It must be madness out there. There are thousands and thousands of men."

David set down the knife and got to his feet. His face was a mask about to crumble. Emma took him in her arms and held him fast as she had Andy. "We'll find your father. I swear we will. Tomorrow, when it's light."

When they went upstairs, they found the hall in an uproar. Sherry had returned. Jack and Andy were beside him and half a dozen of the wounded men who were well enough to get to their feet. There was a shout of "Old Boney!" followed by excited exclamations and feeble cheers. In a corner a man cried out, "Sweet Jesus! Sweet Jesus!"

"Isn't it wonderful?"

Emma looked up and saw Arabel standing at the head of the stairs, her face flushed, a lamp in her hand. Two of the maidservants, nightcaps on their heads, crowded behind her.

Sherry turned toward Emma, a smile widening his face. "We've won. The French are in retreat."

David burst into tears and flung his arms around Emma's waist. "Do you know anything?" she asked Sherry, stroking David's hair. "Tell us quickly."

"I saw Jamie briefly. He's battered but still in the saddle."

Emma let out her breath. God be thanked. She could not have borne it if she had lost her exasperating brother. "Will?"

"He fell sometime in the afternoon but was carried off the field. I couldn't find out where he was taken." Sherry touched David on the shoulder. David pulled away from

Emma and raised a tear-stained face in inquiry. "I'm sorry," Sherry said, "I wasn't able to learn anything about the 52nd."

Tears welled once more in David's eyes. He looked around the hall, an animal trapped in a cage, desperate to find a way out. He sobbed, then turned and ran up the stairs.

Emma woke after a brief sleep that left her feeling heavy and unrested. Arabel was with Charlie. Kirsty was still deep in sleep, her mouth slightly open, her arm flung across her eyes. Emma touched her daughter's hair, then pulled on fresh clothes and went to David's room. It was empty, the bed neatly made, a note square in the center of the pillow. Dear God, had the boy decided to look for his father himself? She had told him Sherry was taking her to the battlefield in the morning. She picked up the note and read it quickly. David had gone to the Durwards'.

Of course. Adam was his father's friend, and Adam had ways of gathering information. Caroline would know what to do. Even so, Emma sent Andy to the Durwards' to make sure David was all right.

Next she looked in on Arabel and found her curled up asleep in a chair next to the head of Charlie's bed. "Can you manage without me? Sherry is going to take me to the battlefield."

Arabel's eyes widened.

"We don't know where Will is," Emma said.

"And Captain Melton?"

Emma shook her head, not trusting herself to speak. After a moment she said, "David's gone to the Durwards'. Can you keep an eye on Kirsty?"

Arabel, now wide awake, said that she would.

Emma found Sherry in the hall giving instructions to

the servants. The carriage was at the door, but they waited until Andy returned. "I spoke to Caroline," he said, breathless because he had run all the way. "David's all right, but he wants to spend the day there." Emma pressed his hand, then entered the carriage.

If Quatre Bras had put an intolerable burden on the city, Sunday's battle was infinitely worse. Surely the city could not contain such a mass of shattered and bloody men. It was no better when they left the city gates and entered the cool darkness of the massed beech trees in the Forest of Soignies. The road that led south from Brussels was wide, but only its center was paved. The sides were a mass of deep churned mud. The paved section was crowded with vehicles of every kind. Those on foot were forced to trod through the unforgiving mud. Many lay where they had fallen, dead or dying or too badly wounded to crawl farther. Some had been crushed under overturned wagons. Others had found refuge among the trees from which it was unlikely they would ever emerge.

Emma made a small sound of dismay.

"I told you," Sherry said.

"Yes, I know." She swallowed and kept her eyes on the road, searching among the stragglers for a familiar face. Sometimes they got out of the carriage to look among the men lying near the edge of the road, but there were few officers to be seen and none from the right regiments.

When they left the forest they saw before them the brick dome of the church in the village of Waterloo. They stopped again to make inquiries about Will and Robert. They were directed to drive on to the small hamlet of Mont-St. Jean where they learned that Lieutenant William Blair of the 12th Light Dragoons had been brought in the day before with a musket ball in his chest and a sword cut in his side.

"I remember him." The surgeon's face was drawn with

fatigue, but he had a kind of manic energy. "He kept saying that he was done for and then he was saved. A bloody miracle, that's what he called it, a bloody miracle. Is he a religious man?"

Emma laughed from joy and relief. "Yes. No. Where is he now?"

"Sent him back to Brussels last night. You should find him there. He'll take a while to mend, but he'll do."

"Have you had any officers of the 52nd in hospital?"

The surgeon gave her a knowing look. "Another cousin?"

Emma returned his look with what dignity she could muster. "A friend."

"Let me think. A Major Rowan. Others perhaps. I can't remember their names."

"Melton? Captain Robert Melton?"

The surgeon shook his head. "I'm sorry."

Emma bit her lip and thanked him. They returned to the carriage, where Sherry instructed the coachman to stay with the horses lest they be stolen by men fleeing the battlefield. "We walk from here," he told Emma. "This is where the army was bivouacked Saturday night. They sheltered behind this ridge."

"And fought here." Emma looked at the carcasses of horses strewing the trampled grass, the bodies of men still unburied. Some, she saw to her horror, were still alive. She ran and knelt beside one man knowing it couldn't be Robert but hoping someone would do the same for him. His face was covered with flies and half buried in the mud, a gurgling sound issued from his throat. "Here!" she called to a stretcher party passing just beyond her. "This man's alive!"

The sergeant in charge of the party came toward her, rolled the man over roughly, brushed the flies from his face, lifted his eyelids. "Not for long."

"But—"

"He won't make it to hospital, ma'am." The sergeant stood. "There's others need attention more."

It was Sherry who helped her to her feet. She swayed against him. "I know," she said. "I know. You told me."

"Are you going to be sick?"

She straightened, moved away from him. "No," she said as she was seized by a sudden wave of nausea. She bent over and was violently sick. Sherry held her until the heaving stopped, then gave her his handkerchief to wipe her face. "I'm so sorry," she whispered. "I'll be all right now."

They walked up the slope to the crest of the ridge and stopped. The field of yesterday's battle was laid out before them. What Emma had seen already had been nothing. What she saw now would make her ill for the rest of her life.

The field was littered with small dark objects. They were caps, she saw, caps and hats lying abandoned in the bloody grass. The dead were everywhere, men and horses, with wounds too terrible to contemplate. Many of the bodies were naked. "They took their clothes," Emma said in wonder. "They took their lives and then they took their clothes."

"I suspect it was the people hereabout," Sherry said, "though soldiers aren't above plunder."

There seemed to be hundreds of soldiers moving in small groups about the field. Most of them carried stretchers, like the sergeant and men she had seen before. A faint blurred sound rose from the battlefield. Perhaps it was the moaning of the wounded. Perhaps it was the dead, shrieking out to heaven, asking why, why, why? A pistol shot rang through the air. Startled, Emma spun around. Someone had dispatched a horse, too long in dying.

She stumbled over a musket, kicked it aside. "Where did the 52nd stand?"

"They were in General Adam's brigade. They stood on the right, about there, just west of Hougoumont." He pointed to the smoking ruins of the chateau.

"I'm going down."

"No, it's not safe. I'll take you back to the carriage, then I'll look for him. I know Melton's face."

"No!" Emma whirled to face him. "I won't be sick again. I have to look for him myself."

Sherry looked at her and nodded. "Of course. We'll go together." They descended the slope, walking slowly through churned mud and beaten rye, avoiding the bodies of the slain with their hacked limbs and grimacing mouths. Caps, shoes, belts, weapons were scattered everywhere. Books, too, and letters. Sherry collected these. "I'll send them on," he explained. "The dead have a right to speak."

Emma pressed his arm and moved on, searching always for Robert's face. She was stopped by a voice mumbling inarticulate words. She dropped down by the side of a young soldier with hair so fair it was almost white. He made a sound, then fell back in distress. "Water? Is that what you want? Here." Thinking of Jamie now, Emma held out the flask she carried with her. Water was always needed with the wounded. She put her arm beneath the soldier and raised the flask to his lips. The water dribbled out of his mouth. She moistened her fingers and brushed them against his mouth, dry and cracked from the hours he had lain unheeded on the field. He opened his eyes and closed his lips around her fingers, watching her all the while. She fed him thus, remembering how she had given suck to Kirsty. The soldier was no more than an infant now, helpless as her own child had been. When he was able at last to take a sip from the flask, she felt a surge of pure triumph.

"Sherry," she called. "Get help."

Another stretcher party was summoned. This time she

was more successful. "He'll do, this one," the soldier in charge said as the flaxen-haired man was loaded onto a stretcher. "Thank'ee, ma'am."

The success of this small act made the next hour bearable. They walked slowly over the field, back and forth, peering into the faces of red-coated men and those who had been stripped of their coats, turning over men whose faces were hidden in the still-damp ground, doing what they could to ease their pain. As each new face proved not to be Robert, the fear in Emma's gut grew. A numbness came over her, a diminution of the horror she had felt on her first sight of the battlefield. Don't forget, she told herself fiercely, don't ever forget.

Thinking of Allan, she knelt again to close the eyes of a grizzled soldier whose breath had stopped as she tried to succor him. She sat back on her heels and took a deep breath, no longer aware of the stench of blood and putrefaction. The air felt cool against her face.

As she stood and turned around looking for Sherry, her attention was caught by a white mare cropping the grass, a bloody gash in one ear. A soldier lay on the ground nearby. Emma's heart stopped. For a moment she thought it would never beat again. It was Robert, lying not a dozen feet from her, his thick tawny hair clinging damply to his face. She murmured his name, then called it again more loudly. Then she ran and tumbled to her knees and gathered him up into her arms, pressing her lips against his forehead, his eyes, his cheeks, his lips.

His eyes were closed and he gave no answer, but he was warm, God be praised, he was warm. She unbuttoned his coat and slipped her hand inside to feel his heartbeat. It was there, slow, faint, but there. She screamed. "Sherry!"

He came running across the field and stopped beside her. She looked up at him, the tears, dammed for so long, streaming down her face. "He's alive." She kissed his hair. "He's alive."

Sherry dropped down and felt the pulse in Robert's neck. Without a word he lifted him from Emma's arms and hoisted him across his back. The white mare pushed her head against Sherry as though to ask where he was taking her master. Emma gathered up the mare's reins.

They walked in silence up the slope, past the crest, to Mont-St. Jean where the carriage waited. Sherry deposited his burden carefully inside, then turned to Emma. "Do we take him home?"

She stared at him. "Of course we take him home."

"We could find care for him here. Or elsewhere in Brussels."

"Sherry—"

"Look at him, Emma. He's French."

16

Emma walked into the small salon and pulled the door shut behind her with a force that shook the yellow silk walls. Adam was standing in the center of the room, feet planted a little apart, hands clasped behind his back. His black hair tumbled over his forehead as if he had traveled in haste. His dark face was darker than usual, but his eyes—damn his eyes—showed nothing but compassion.

He knew why she had summoned him to the house. In a fury of incoherence and disbelief she had sent him barely two lines, but they had been enough. *We have found the man calling himself Robert Melton. Bring David.*

Emma's hand closed around the dark blue coat she was holding. It was smeared with dried mud and stiff with Robert's blood. She strode across the room and thrust the coat in Adam's face. "Tell me it's not true." Her throat was parched and her voice cracked with the effort to speak. "Tell me there's a reason." When he did not answer at once, she beat on his chest. "Tell me, damn you, tell me the truth."

Adam took the coat from her hand and stepped back. He shook out the bloody, rent garment, then looked at her, alarm written in his face. "How is he?"

"Alive. Barely. He's not conscious. Adam."

"I want to see him."

"Adam!"

He dropped the coat and spread his hands in a gesture of surrender. "His name is Robert Lescaut. Colonel Lescaut."

Emma felt her head grow light. She swayed, no longer certain of her balance. Adam was there, clasping her arms, holding her to the present. The dizziness passed and she stepped away. "And David? Who is he?"

"His son."

His son. Robert had come to them in treachery and deceit. He had used his own son in his game of deception. And Adam had abetted him. "Does Caroline know?"

Adam hesitated just long enough to draw a breath. "Yes."

Emma shook her head. "You lied to me. I thought you were my friends and you lied to me. Why? Why did you let me believe him? Don't you owe anything to friendship?"

Adam's eyes clouded. "Robert is my friend. I owe him more than I can tell you."

She clasped her hands and paced back and forth across the room. "He pretended to be English. Why? What did he want from us? He said he'd known Allan in Spain." She turned on Adam. "That was a lie, wasn't it?"

"Probably."

She remembered Angus's delight in talking to Robert of his dead son. "He *used* me." She swallowed, thinking of just how he had used her. "He used us all. He played on our grief, on our gratitude. He made himself useful. He burrowed into our family like a mole. He took our affection, our trust. He—" She broke off. She could not say, *He invaded my body, he captured my heart.* "A lie," she went on, her voice flat and without expression. "All of it. Allan, the 52nd. Was he even in Spain?"

"That's where we met. He was in intelligence, and in a manner of speaking so was I."

"A spy?" Emma stared at Adam. "Is that why he came? To spy on us? Why, in God's name?" As she spoke she realized the enormity of Adam's admission. "You knew it, didn't you? You knew he was a spy and you kept it secret. We've been at war and you've made a friend of a French spy. You're a traitor, Adam Durward."

"No." The syllable was sharp and short and seemed to contain everything Adam was unwilling to say.

Emma pressed her advantage. "Does Sir Charles know? Does he know what his trusted aide is doing? Have you told him that four nights ago you saw a French spy standing not six feet from the Duke of Wellington and raised no outcry?"

"That's enough, Emma. I have not betrayed my country."

"We're at war. The French are our enemies. You're English. You have to know which side you're on."

"Christ, Emma, do you think it's so simple? I was torn between two countries the day I was born."

Emma had forgotten that Adam's mother had been Hindu and his father an English soldier. But the rage that churned within her would not be stilled. "That's no answer. Why did Robert come to my house? Why did he pretend to be my husband's friend?"

Adam was silent for a moment. "I can't tell you more. If you want answers, you must get them from Robert."

"Answers?" She laughed, and the sound was harsh to her ears. "You mean lies. Other lies, fresh lies, lies newly minted—"

He strode toward her and took her hands. "All right. I'll take him away."

She tore herself loose. "You can't. The doctor says he's not to be moved."

"He can't stay here. If we're careful . . ."

"No. I won't be responsible for his death. I'll kill him myself." She was struck by the absurdity of what she had said. She pressed her hands to her temples, weary beyond belief. "Oh, go away, Adam. Go away. I don't want to see you."

She watched Adam leave the room, lacking the will to move or think. The world had crumbled around her, as it had when she learned of Allan's death. But that had been the random cruelty of war, owing to nothing but man's folly and the path of a bullet's trajectory. It had not diminished her.

But Robert . . . His had been a calculated betrayal. He had used her, for what reason she could not fathom. He had denied her humanity. She would never trust herself again.

The sound of voices in the corridor forced her to confront the demands of the present. Nearly a dozen wounded men were lying on straw pallets in the hall below. Arabel was nursing Charlie Lauder. Sherry had returned to the battlefield. Andy and Jack were searching for Will. And at the back of the house the Frenchman she had thought of as Robert Melton was lying with the smell of death upon him.

So far no one in the house knew Robert's identity save Sherry and herself. And David. The thought of the boy brought Emma up short. Last night she had held him with love and compassion, but he had not wanted to talk about his fears. She understood his silence now. He dared not speak lest he expose his father's lies.

And his own. David had lied as surely as Robert had done. How could Robert have forced his son to take part in such a monstrous deception. It was an intolerable burden for a child.

Emma made her way down the corridor to David's room. Robert lay in his son's bed, white with bandages and pallor, his shallow breathing barely disturbing the bedclothes. David sat on a chair nearby. There were traces of tears on his face. At her entrance he stood up, his eyes wary. "You know, don't you?"

"I know." Emma strove to keep her voice calm. She couldn't bear to see David shrink from her.

David's face crumpled. "Don't tell Kirsty."

Emma put her arms around him as she had last night and stroked his hair while he clung to her and sobbed. "It's all right, David," she said over and over again. It was not all right and never would be, but what had been done was not his fault. "Sherry knows, too, but no one else. I don't want you to speak of it, do you understand? Not to Kirsty nor to anyone else in the house. As far as they know you're still David Melton." She drew back and took him by the shoulders. "Can you manage?"

He nodded and swallowed his tears. "I won't say anything." He looked at the still figure in the bed. "It's bad, isn't it?"

Emma put her arm around his shoulders. "Yes."

"I want to stay with him. Here."

She looked into the boy's face. It would be much harder for him if he were kept from his father. "Very well. We'll make up a pallet on the floor."

Later that afternoon Emma pulled Arabel into the small salon and told her that they had brought Captain Melton, seriously wounded, back from the battlefield. Arabel was momentarily jolted out of her preoccupation with Charlie. She embraced Emma and asked if there was anything she could do. "There's very little anyone can do," Emma said, "save watch and wait."

"Oh, Em. Are you all right? You look quite dreadful."

"Everyone looks dreadful. How is Charlie?"

"Weak. But out of danger, the doctor thinks." Arabel pushed the salon door closed. "Em, I told him. About the baby. I know it was a shock for him, but I couldn't bear his not knowing. He says we must marry as soon as he's up."

"Of course you must marry. But you're underage. You have to have your father's consent."

"He'll never give it. I'll lie about my age."

"Angus will never forgive you if you do." Emma took Arabel's hands in her own. "Wait a few weeks. I'll write to him. He'll be angry, but in the circumstances he can't withhold his permission. And Charlie must write to his father too."

Arabel pulled away from her. "They'll find some way to keep us apart."

"You don't know that. They may surprise you. I'll write today. Let me try."

Arabel sighed. "Oh, Em, you know what Da's like when he's in a temper."

Emma put her arm around her cousin. "You'll marry Charlie, Bel, if I have to lie about your age myself. I swear it."

Arabel grimaced but gave a reluctant nod of acquiescence. They left the salon and moved into the corridor. A commotion at the front entrance sent them flying down the stairs. It was Andy and Jack bearing a stretcher on which lay a wounded man. "Will!" Arabel shrieked. She bent over her brother and clasped his hand.

"Move aside, Bel." Andy's voice was cheerful, but his face was covered with sweat. "The bugger weighs a ton."

Jack grinned. "We'll put him in our room and doss in the library. Found him in hospital, but they were glad enough to get rid of him."

Will swore. Emma bent over him. He was conscious, though his face was contorted with pain. "Almost there," she said, signaling Andy and Jack to start up the stairs. She walked on one side of the stretcher, Arabel on the other.

Will reached for Emma's hand. "Tell them," he whispered, "that I don't weigh more than thirteen stone."

It was several hours before Emma had the leisure to seek ink and paper and begin her letter to Angus. She told him first that Jamie had come through the battle unscathed but that Will was wounded. Not dangerously, but it would be some time before he was on his feet. Then she told him about Arabel and Charlie Lauder. Her words were blunt, for Angus liked plain-speaking. There would be a baby. The young people must marry. They were determined to marry, one way or another, but they wanted his consent, and she urged him to give it. It's time, she said, to put the past to rest. Charlie is a decent young man. Arabel could do far worse.

She wrote a little more in this vein, praising her uncle's tolerance and good sense. Then she sprinkled sand on the letter and sealed it. Despite her words to Arabel, she was not at all certain that Angus would not disown his youngest daughter.

The next few days were filled with frantic activity. Two men died and a third recovered enough to return to his battalion. Sherry brought three more wounded men to take their place, and the chalked scrawl on their door continued to read *Militaires blessés—dix soldats, quatre officiers*. Ten men of the line and four officers—Will, Charlie, Robert, and a Belgian lieutenant who lay dying in the hall.

The white chalk signs indicating the presence of wounded men appeared on every door in Brussels. One could not escape the aftermath of battle. The streets were nearly deserted, but a few men were about, hobbling on crutches, their heads bound up, or their arms in slings. The pale faces of the wounded appeared in nearly every window. A ballad singer passed before their house shouting a newly minted song about the downfall of the monster Bonaparte and the glorious role played by the Belgians. Emma ran into the street and gave him some coins, begging him to move on so he would not disturb her patients. In truth, she feared that David might hear him.

In her concern for the boy, she had lost the center of her resolve. She could hate Robert, but she could not hate his son. She had become a coconspirator. She would allow no one to attend to Robert but herself, fearful that in his fevered state he would say something indiscreet or revert to his native French and give away the secret of his identity.

She was not concerned about the servants. The French wounded were being cared for alongside the British and Belgians and Dutch. But she wanted the truth from Robert before her family learned how they had been gulled.

She said nothing to Sherry about her interview with Adam, and Sherry never referred to their discovery on the battlefield. Robert's telltale coat had been burned.

Will's wounds healed cleanly and he was soon up, shuffling about the house on two canes Andy made for him. Charlie was able to leave his room a day later, and the two men developed a wary companionship. When they had word that Matt Lauder had been killed, Will was the first to throw his arm around Charlie's shoulders.

Jamie was in and out of the house, elated and boastful because the cavalry had acquitted themselves well at Waterloo and he had been promoted to major. When he heard about Matt's death, he groaned. "I knew he'd find a way to get out of meeting me." Then after a moment he added, "Poor bugger."

Will looked uncomfortable when he heard that Robert was in the Rue Ducale, as though he had something to say and was not sure he should do so. Emma was surprised, for Will had been cordial to Robert at the ball, but she had no time to speculate over her cousin's motives.

Robert was sometimes lucid, but the moments were brief. He seemed to dwell in a twilight of consciousness. She thought he recognized David, but she was not sure he was aware of her own presence. He was consumed with fever. The wound in his chest was inflamed and oozing putrid matter. The doctor shook his head and said there was nothing to be done, but Emma cleaned the wound several times a day and bathed it with an infusion of comfrey. She washed him with cool cloths to bring down the fever and sat with him through the night when he took a turn for the worse. She would not let him die, for David's sake but also her own. She was determined to call him to account.

It was a week before she could do so, a week in which she teetered between compassion and loathing. Her fear for Robert mingled with her anger until she knew only that she was torn apart by his presence in the house. She could not forget that she had lain with this man. She could not forget his tenderness nor the passion he had aroused in her nor the way he had seemed to read her innermost thoughts. But then she would remember the service to which he had put these gifts, and her hatred cut deeper. It had all been a sham. He had never cared for her. In moments of honesty she remembered that it was she who had initiated their lovemaking, he who had held off. The memory made her cringe. She despised her own gullibility.

She was on her way to see him when she was intercepted by David who came running down the corridor. He stopped abruptly before they collided. "He's better," he said in a breathless voice. "He spoke to me. He's going to be all right." He looked up at Emma, and the joy was suddenly wiped from his face. "He wants to see you."

"I'm on my way." Emma's voice was calm, but her heart was pounding and a piercing pain split her temples.

"Shall I come with you?"

"No." She put a hand on his shoulder. "This is between your father and me. Kirsty's in the kitchen having breakfast. Why don't you join her?"

David was child enough to be relieved, old enough to feel some guilt. He gave her a twisted smile and ran toward the stairs.

Emma continued down the corridor. As she walked her anger grew. She flung open the door and slammed it shut behind her. There was no more need for quiet. Nor for darkness. She crossed the room and pushed back the heavy gold damask curtains. Daylight flooded the small chamber and overpowered the candle burning on the table near the bed. The smell of sickness filled the room. She would have opened the windows as well, but she knew that voices carry. She would tear Robert's secrets from his throat, but she had no wish to have them spill out into the narrow street below.

Only then did she turn and look fully at the man in the bed. Robert had pulled himself up and lay propped against the pillows. The blankets were tangled about him. She subdued an impulse to straighten them. She walked toward him and stopped at the end of the bed, gripping the footboard. He was pale, as he had been since she had found him, and gaunt, for he had taken little nourishment. A stubble of beard covered his face, the stiff hairs gleaming russet in the bar of sunlight that fell across the bed. His eyes were clear, narrowed against the light. "I have to thank you for saving my life."

His voice was cracked, unused to speech. A glass of water stood on the table by the bed. He reached for it slowly, as though the movement pained him, and took two careful swallows. His gaze stayed on her face, and she wondered what he saw there. Anger, bewilderment, despair? Did he have any idea what he had done? Did he even care?

He drew in his breath. It might have been a sigh. He said her name. "Emma." It was a plea or a question.

She said the only word that mattered. "Why?" It came out as a whisper and she said it again, infusing it with all the pain he had brought her. "Why, in God's name, why?"

"Emma, I—"

"You lied. You betrayed me. You betrayed us all. What were you after, Robert Melton? No, it's not Melton, is it? What did Adam call you? Lescaut, that's it. Robert Lescaut. A good French name. Why didn't you use it? We weren't at war. Why should a Frenchman fear to travel in Scotland?"

"Would you have welcomed him? A man who fought against your kin? A man who might have killed your husband?"

They would not have, of course, but that was not the point. The mention of Allan brought up the most cruel deception of all. Tears stung her eyes. "You didn't know Allan. That was a lie, wasn't it? You used us, Robert Lescaut. You used us barbarously. You even used your son against us."

He winced. "Leave David out of this."

"I can't." Her voice rose with triumph. "*You* brought him to Scotland. *You* brought him to Blair House and told him to live a lie. How could you? How could you do that to a child?"

He put up his hands as though to ward her off. She leaned toward him over the footboard, forcing him to look at her. "Why us, Robert Lescaut? Why the Blairs? What do we have that you wanted? What did you hope to gain?"

His face hardened. He fumbled with the neck of the nightshirt she had begged from Sherry and drew out a ring attached to a leather cord about his neck. "This." He cupped it in the palm of his hand. "This is why. I left it with David when I went back to France. He returned it to me this morning." When she made no move, he yanked the cord off his neck and held the ring out to her. "Take it, Emma. Look at it. Tell me what you see."

Emma hesitated, then walked forward. He had put her on the defensive. This was not the way it was supposed to be. She took the ring from his hand and retreated to the window under the pretext of needing more light to examine it properly. In truth, being near Robert made her skin prickle and her stomach churn.

The ring was made of silver, heavy, a man's ring, its top carefully engraved. Emma brought it closer, refusing to acknowledge what was before her. She did not recognize the ring, but she knew what it represented. A wolf cub, holding a thistle between its teeth. The badge of the Blair family.

She walked slowly back to the bed, dropped the ring on the covers, and stared at Robert, her throat tight with the beginnings of apprehension. She forced herself to speak. "Tell me."

Robert's hand tightened about the ring. "It belonged to my wife." He grimaced, but whether with past or present pain, Emma could not say.

A Blair ring in the hands of a Frenchwoman. There were any number of ways she could have come by it. "She was not French," Robert went on. "She was a Scotswoman, or so she told me."

"The governess." Yet another lie became apparent. "That was a lie, too, wasn't it? It was your wife you were looking for."

"It was a lie."

The admission strengthened Emma's resolve. Nothing was going to excuse what Robert had done.

"But not all of it," he said. "Her name was Lucie Sorel.

She was raised in Mlle. Hébert's school in Candlemaker Row. Someone—I assume it was her father—paid for her keep. Someone intended to give her a marriage portion when she married Cullen. The arrangements were being made by your brother-in-law, Bram Martin."

Fragments of thought whirled through Emma's head. "You think she was a Blair? On the strength of a scrap of silver she could have found in a thousand ways? Even if you believed it possible, why didn't you come to us with the story? What were you after that you had to resort to treachery and deceit?"

Robert closed his eyes and placed a hand on his bandaged chest. The fever had gone down yesterday, but he was scarcely recovered. It must hurt him to talk. Unless this behavior, too, was a sham. "Tell me," she insisted.

He opened his eyes and fixed her with a hard gaze. "Lucie was murdered. She was hacked to death in a small waterfront inn in Ostend. She'd gone there in secret, to meet someone from Britain."

Emma stared at him. The horror of his story was dwarfed by its implications. "And you thought a Blair . . ." She could not bring herself to complete the thought.

"When I found her she was barely alive. I asked her who had done it. She couldn't speak, but she showed me the ring which she wore around her neck. I came to Scotland to find my wife's killer."

"One of us," Emma whispered. "You thought it was one of us." She retreated a few steps, as though distancing herself from something unclean.

Robert stretched out a hand to her. "If I had put the question to Sir Angus, he would have turned me away. I had to be accepted. I had to get to know you." Please, his eyes said. Please try to understand.

She shook her head. "You charmed us, you helped us, you made yourself useful. You set your son to make friends with my daughter. You made love to me. Oh, you're a clever scoundrel."

"Emma, no." Robert tried to push himself up and fell back against the pillows.

"May you rot in the deepest dungeons of hell." Had he not been so helpless, she would have beaten him with her fists. With a cry of anguish, she turned and fled the room.

Robert slipped the leather cord around his neck and tucked the Blair ring under his nightshirt. He had told Emma the truth, or at least as much of it as she was willing to hear. Her words slashed him like a sabre cut. It wasn't like that, he wanted to shout. It wasn't that way at all.

When David returned to the room, Robert called his son to his side. "I saw Emma," David said before Robert could speak.

Robert reached out and caressed the boy's head. "It's not your fault. It was a quest gone wrong."

"Is it over?"

"The quest?" Robert shook his head. "No, though I'm damned if I know how I'm going to pursue it. The Blairs? Yes, I fear that's at an end."

David's eyes welled with tears. "Perhaps someday you can explain it all to Kirsty," Robert said. "Not now. Everything's too raw. Emma's fond of you, but she'll never speak to me again."

David swallowed. "I'm not sorry I came with you."

"Nor am I." Robert reached for David's hand and held it as tightly as he could.

David dashed the tears from his eyes. "Emma's keeping the horse in Sherry's stable."

"What?" Robert wasn't sure he had heard right.

"Your horse from the battle. The white one. Her ear was hurt, but Emma put salve on it and it's better now."

The white mare. Robert gave the ghost of a smile. "Then we'll have to take her with us. She deserves a warm stable after all she's been through." He squeezed David's hand. "Will you do something for me?"

David nodded.

"Go to Adam's house. If he's not there, talk to Caroline. Tell them we need to find another lodging."

The Durwards' maid showed Emma into a white-paneled sitting room, bright with sunlight gleaming off the polished floorboards. Caroline was arranging a vase of geraniums on the mantel, but she turned at the opening of the door. Surprise flared in her eyes then was quickly brought under control. "Emma. I'm so glad. Thank you, Isabelle."

The door clicked shut behind the maid. Emma and Caroline regarded each other in silence. Caroline wore a simple beige muslin gown. Her fair hair was caught back with a clip and flowed loose down her back, but there was something uncharacteristically formal about her manner. Even her smile held a hint of reserve. She did not take Emma's hands or give her a hug as she would have done in Brussels. They hadn't seen each other since Emma confronted Adam about his friendship with Robert Lescaut. All she had heard from the Durwards in the month since was a brief note from Adam telling her that he and Caroline were to accompany the British ambassador, Sir Charles Stuart, to Paris, and that Robert and David would travel with them.

Emma drew a breath. "I came to apologize. Whatever my disagreements with Rob—with Colonel Lescaut"— her throat tightened painfully as she said his name—"I had no call to blame you and Adam. You have your own loyalties."

"You're very generous," Caroline said. "You have every right to be angry at us. We deceived you."

"I understand things better now." Emma swallowed, thinking of what she did and did not understand about Robert Lescaut.

Caroline looked her straight in the eye. "I don't like lying. But there are debts owed to friendship which one must pay."

"Adam and Colonel Lescaut have been friends for a long time." Emma kept her voice level. *We were friends too,* she wanted to cry. *Didn't that mean anything?*

"It goes beyond friendship." Caroline stepped forward then hesitated. "Please sit down." She gestured toward a pair of cane chairs. "I'd like to tell you about it."

Emma sank into one of the chairs. She felt as if she had stumbled late into the pages of a novel. She had a desperate need to make sense of it all. Of how an honorable man like Adam had formed a friendship with the enemy. Of how Caroline, her first real friend since Susan Lauder married and moved away, had lied to her from the day they met. Above all, to make sense of Robert.

Caroline folded her hands in her lap. "Two years ago Adam and Emily and I traveled through French-occupied Spain to Portugal, where the British army were head-quartered."

"I thought Adam was stationed in Lisbon."

"He was, but he spent most of his time in the field, gathering intelligence for the British. Adam's good at languages. He can pass as Spanish or Portuguese. Or French."

"He was a spy." Adam had told Emma as much. She paused, then added, "Like Colonel Lescaut."

Caroline smiled. "Very much like Colonel Lescaut. That's how they met. Adam says it's ironic that one of the few men who sees the world as he does is on the opposite side."

"Colonel Lescaut helped you in your journey across Spain?"

Caroline smoothed the skirt of her figured muslin gown as if disquieted by her memories. "When we were near Salamanca, Emily was kidnapped by Spanish bandits." She looked Emma full in the face. "You must understand what my feelings were."

"Dear God, Caro." Emma recalled her own sickening fears the previous December when Kirsty had got her pony caught in a snowdrift and had been missing for hours.

"It's every mother's nightmare, isn't it?" Caroline's eyes were dark with remembered fear. "Salamanca was controlled by the French. Robert was stationed there and Adam went to him for help." Caroline rubbed her arms. "It was the first time I met Robert. I would have trusted the devil himself if he restored Emily to me, but I was terribly frightened of Robert at first. My experience with French soldiers had not been pleasant, and I knew Adam would be shot if Robert turned him in. But Robert couldn't have been kinder. He immediately dispatched men to search for Emily." She gave a rueful smile. "I was shocked when he told me he had a child of his own. Somehow it had never occurred to me to think of an enemy commander as a parent."

Emma saw again the concern in Robert's eyes as he sat by David's sickbed. "He would understand what it means to fear for a child."

Caroline nodded. "I don't think I've ever lived through a longer day. It was late that night before we found Em-

Shores of Desire

ily. The kidnappers had left her at a foundling hospital in the city while they sent to us for ransom. When I thanked Robert, he told me it isn't often a soldier gets to do an unabashedly good deed."

That sounded so like Robert that Emma nearly smiled. She schooled her features. "You had no trouble getting away from Salamanca?"

"Robert gave us a safe conduct which saw us to Portugal with no further difficulties." Caroline looked at Emma for a moment. "Emily still remembers that Robert helped us find her. I think she'll always have a special feeling for him because of that. I know I will."

Her eyes begged for understanding. And Emma did understand. At least she understood the loyalty and obligation Caroline felt toward Robert. Robert himself remained an enigma. The generosity he had shown the Durwards only threw into harsh relief the way he had manipulated the Blairs.

Emma stretched out her hand. "I have quarrel enough with Colonel Lescaut, Caro. I'm not going to let him spoil our friendship."

Caroline clasped her hand tightly. "I can't tell you how relieved I am to hear that."

They settled back in their chairs. The breeze had come up carrying the scent of an orange tree through the open French windows. "Despite Colonel Lescaut's lies, it seems we too are in his debt," Emma said. "He saved Will's life on the battlefield."

Caroline's eyes widened. "He didn't tell us."

"He didn't tell me either. I got the story from Will when I told the family the truth about 'Robert Melton.' Will said he was waiting for Robert to recover and tell his side of the story. For my cousin, that's a remarkably temperate viewpoint."

Caroline smiled, though her eyes were serious. "It's

difficult to feel indebted and betrayed at the same time. Straightforward anger is much simpler."

"Yes." Emma tugged at a pearl button on one of her gloves. "I told my cousin Bram of Colonel Lescaut's claims about Lucie Sorel. I was sure Bram would say she couldn't have been connected to us. Instead he told me to ask Angus. He refused to say anything further. But since he didn't deny the story—"

"You have to admit there must be some truth to it."

Emma clasped her hands together. "Yes." She could still hear her own shocked voice. *You lied to me, Bram. You said you didn't know anything more about Lucie Sorel.* And Bram's reply, more reserved than he had ever been with her. *It's not my story to tell, Em.*

Emma looked at Caroline. "David may be a Blair. We have a responsibility to him." Besides, David had been in her care too long. Neither she nor Kirsty could forget about him, whatever his father had done.

Caroline leaned forward. "Em, I'm sure—"

Her words were drowned out by the opening of the door and Adam's cheerful voice. "Look who I found on the front steps, Caro."

"Caroline!" David ran past Adam only to come to a skidding halt midway across the room. A wordless cry escaped his lips. He strained forward as though he would run to Emma. Then he drew back and went still.

Emma checked her impulse to embrace the boy. That would put him in an unfair situation. She smiled at David, aware of his father standing in the shadows of the doorway. Her pulse raced and her face grew embarrassingly warm. Like a trapped animal, she wanted to bolt for safety yet was transfixed.

"Emma, how splendid." Adam broke the silence with an ease that proved his skills as a diplomat. "I didn't know you were in Paris."

"We only just arrived." Emma forced the words past

her trembling lips. "David, I'm so glad to see you. Kirsty's been asking about you."

A fleeting smile crossed David's face. He glanced at his father, then looked back at Emma. "Tell her I said hullo." His voice was so carefully controlled it brought a lump to Emma's throat.

Knowing she could not avoid the ordeal, Emma raised her gaze from David to his father. The man who had risked his own position to rescue a four-year-old girl. The man who had lied to Emma from the moment she met him. The man who had saved Will's life. The man to whom she thought she had given her heart. "Colonel Lescaut."

"Mrs. Blair." Robert took a step forward. His skin was pale and there were lines and hollows in his face that she did not remember. But it was his eyes that chilled her. All trace of joy and laughter seemed to have been drained out of them. She could have sworn she saw ghosts lurking in their depths.

Caroline got to her feet and held out her hand to David. "Emily will be wanting to see you. Let's go and find her, shall we?"

Emma was tempted to follow her friend from the room. Every moment she spent in Robert's company was a knife-sharp reminder of all that lay between them. But if she wanted to see David again, there were things she had to say to his father. Besides, he had saved Will and a Blair honored her obligations.

She forced herself to look into the haunted eyes of the man she had loved. "Will told me what you did for him. My family owe you our thanks."

Robert's mouth twisted in a half smile. "If it wasn't for you, I would have died on the field. I'd say all debts are discharged, Mrs. Blair."

Emma gripped her hands together. To have him address her as "Mrs. Blair" made a mockery of the past. She remembered how happy she had been when he had called her "Em." Then only a few inches of bed linen had separated their naked flesh. Formality could not erase what had passed between them.

The two men seated themselves. Robert avoided looking at her, but Emma felt his presence like the heat from a roaring blaze.

"When did you get to Paris?" Adam asked her.

"Just yesterday. Will and Charlie Lauder were well enough to rejoin the army, and we decided to accompany them. We heard Paris is considered safe now."

"Oh, it's safe enough for the English. I'm afraid it may not be so comfortable for French soldiers in the next weeks." Adam glanced at Robert. "The Royalists are out for blood. You'd best be on your guard."

Robert gave a smile that did not reach his eyes. "I'm a civilian now."

"You're an intelligence officer. A number of people may think you know too much."

Emma looked from one man to the other. She had considered the war over three weeks ago when Paris surrendered. Now their words sent an unexpected jolt of fear through her. Not that there was any reason she should feel fear on Robert's account.

"Be careful," Adam insisted. "For David's sake if nothing else."

Robert inclined his head but would say nothing further.

Emma seized the opening she needed. "Kirsty would like to see David." She looked Robert full in the face and felt the air grow taut between them. She considered a number of approaches and abandoned them all. There had been too much pretense already. "I don't want our quarrel to affect the children."

For a moment she thought Robert's eyes lightened. He looked at her in silence for so long that she found it difficult to breathe. "You're very kind," he said at last. "If you would like to bring Kirsty to our house, David and I would be happy to see both of you. Number eleven, the Rue Percée."

Robert ran his fingers over the worn metal of the type resting in the rack before him. Lit by the cool, colorless moonlight seeping through the shutters, the print shop was filled with the specters of memory. Robert breathed in the pungent smell of ink. He could almost believe his father was standing just beyond the curtain of drying news sheets, hurrying to meet some midnight deadline.

"You're up late."

His cousin Paul stood in the doorway, holding a candle that brought an unexpected glow of warmth to the room. "So are you," Robert said.

"I have a paper to get out." Paul lit a lamp on a nearby table, then touched his finger to one of the news sheets to check the dryness of the ink. "What's your excuse?"

"Do I need one?" Robert found the lamplight an invasion. He was in a mood for darkness and shadows.

Paul's gaze went from Robert's face to the tankard in his hand. "How much have you had to drink?"

"Coffee." Robert lifted the tankard in an ironic toast. "I couldn't get a decent cup of it in Scotland."

Paul dropped into a scarred wooden armchair beside the printing press and propped his feet up on a stack of books. "You've been here two weeks. Don't you think it's time you talked about it?"

" 'It'?"

Paul's gaze was steady in the flickering lamplight. "Lucie."

There were dangers in friends who had known you since childhood. Bowing to the inevitable, Robert hooked his foot around the leg of a ladder-back chair and dragged it closer. He'd often perched on this same chair as a boy. He could remember when it had been an effort to clamber onto it. "Lucie was a Blair. I was convinced of that the moment I got to Blair House."

"There's a family resemblance?"

An image of Emma as he had first seen her, auburn hair spilling from the hood of her cloak, sprang to Robert's mind. "Emma Blair, one of the daughters of the house, looks very like Lucie," he told his cousin. Though now it was Emma's face he saw whenever he closed his eyes, while sometimes it was an effort to conjure up the memory of his wife.

Paul settled back in his chair, the chair that had once belonged to Robert's father. Robert still found it odd to see his cousin sitting there, but it was Paul, not he, who had earned the right to do so. "Do you have any idea who her parents were?" Paul asked.

"I think Lucie was the result of a liaison between one of the Blair men and Lucilla Lauder, the daughter of a neighboring family with whom the Blairs have been feuding for as long as anyone can remember. Lucilla probably died in childbirth. Lucie was brought up by a Frenchwoman who ran a girls' school in Edinburgh. Money was paid regularly for her keep."

"By a Blair?"

"I suspect so. Most likely Sir Angus, the head of the family. The details were kept secret. Twelve years ago, Lucie became betrothed to a local tradesman. Her mysterious benefactor arranged to settle money on her, but before the marriage, Lucie disappeared. No one admits to hearing of her again."

Paul shifted his position. "I can't see Lucie settling for life as a tradesman's wife."

"Nor can I." Robert stared down into the tankard. The heat of the pewter warmed his chilled hands. Since Waterloo, his senses had felt dead. Numbness had seemed preferable to facing the ruin of his country and the destruction of whatever he might have known with Emma. But now he felt the faint stirrings, if not of hope, at least of purpose.

"I'd always thought Lucie ran away because she feared her family," he said. "Now I begin to think she ran from the boredom of marriage. The Blairs had been supporting her for years. Why should they drive her away?"

"She may have left Scotland on her own. But she didn't commit suicide."

"No." Robert gripped the tankard more tightly.

"But you no longer think a Blair killed her?"

"I couldn't discover any motive." Emma's face again rose up before Robert's eyes. For a moment he could almost hear Angus's bellowing voice and Kirsty's laughter. "I went to Scotland prepared to think the worst of the Blairs. But they're not an easy family to hate. And now I probably owe them my life."

Paul's head snapped up. "What?"

"Emma Blair found me on the battlefield and brought me back to Brussels."

"Good God." Paul sat forward in his chair. "She was looking for you?"

Robert thought of those last minutes at the Duchess of Richmond's ball, the feel of Emma's fingers against his skin, the way her gaze had clung to his face. "She was looking for Captain Robert Melton of the 52nd."

"I see." Paul surveyed Robert. "She had reason to be fond of him?"

Robert saw Emma again as she had been this afternoon at the Durwards'. The shadows her bonnet cast on her face. The way the sunlight glinted off her hair. The coldness in her eyes when she looked at him. "She thought she had reason."

"Oh, Christ." Paul swung his legs to the floor with a

thud. "You haven't been fool enough to fall in love, have you?"

Robert started to voice a denial and found he could not utter the words. So much had died on the field of Waterloo, but the force of what he felt for Emma could not be destroyed. He leaned back in the chair. His wounds still pained him when he moved too quickly, but that pain would pass. The torment of losing Emma would be with him to the day he died. "We're all capable of madness," he said.

Paul gave a groan of disgust. "I thought you'd learned your lesson with Lucie."

"Emma's nothing like Lucie."

"You said there was a strong resemblance."

"On the surface. But Emma is incapable of duplicity."

Paul laughed. There had been a bitter edge to his laughter ever since he returned less than whole from Austerlitz. "All women are capable of duplicity. All men too." He pushed the tangled hair back from his face. "You of all people should understand that."

"Duplicity is my stock in trade. But not Emma's."

"Nor mine. And yet I bedded my cousin's wife."

Robert met Paul's gaze. "You did a damned poor job of keeping it secret. Drunken confessions aren't considered part of duplicity."

Paul's eyes glinted with self-mockery. "I don't suppose it's ever occurred to you that I killed her. Discarded lovers make good suspects."

Robert started to say that he knew Paul was incapable of murder. Then it occurred to him that that was probably exactly how Emma felt about her family. "You couldn't have killed Lucie," he said instead, his voice mild. "You were still in Paris when I left to look for her. Besides, she showed me the Blair ring before she died."

"Which makes it hard to discount the Blairs as suspects."

"Yes." Robert saw his wife lying on the floorboards of the inn room in Ostend, blood foaming from her mouth, the ring clutched in her hand in a last plea for justice. He knew now that Emma meant more to him than Lucie ever had, but he would never be able to forget what he owed to the woman who had borne his child.

"So what now?" Paul asked after a moment.

"That depends on Emma Blair. I saw her this afternoon at the Durwards'. She's coming here tomorrow."

Paul raised his brows. "She's coming to see you?"

"She's bringing her daughter Kirsty to see David."

Paul gave Robert a speculative look. "She means a great deal to you, doesn't she?"

Pain closed Robert's throat. He took a sip of coffee and found it had gone cold. "No," he said, his voice harsher than he intended. "She can't mean anything to me anymore."

18

Emma reached for Kirsty's hand as the fiacre pulled away, leaving them alone on the narrow cobbled street. Noise and movement buffeted them on all sides. The air held the sharp scent of the nearby river. Fragments of French, too rapid and colloquial for Emma to understand, flew thick and fast. The houses on either side were tall and dark, stained by the grime of centuries, but open windows showed the brightness of flowers and drying laundry. The whole street pulsed with life and exuberance. Even in Edinburgh, Emma had experienced nothing quite like it.

"Is that Robert's house?" Kirsty pointed to No. 11.

Emma nodded, her mouth suddenly dry. For a moment, the chaos of the street seemed safer than what awaited her behind the door. But she was an adult. If she was to do her duty by David, she would have to learn to meet his father with equanimity. Detachment, that was what was called for, and a cool head. Emma led Kirsty to the door and rang the bell.

A few moments later the door was opened by a man in his shirtsleeves. "You must be Mrs. Blair and Kirsty," he said in English as unaccented as Robert's own. "I'm Paul Lescaut, Robert's cousin. Come inside. Robert and David are giving me a hand in the shop."

Emma stepped into the narrow entrance hall and studied Robert's cousin. His hair was lighter than Robert's, glinting gold even in the dimly lit hall, and his eyes were brown not blue, but there was no mistaking the relationship. Paul Lescaut had the rough-hewn features that had become so familiar, and his smile stirred unwelcome memories, though his mouth had a cynical twist that Robert's lacked.

Paul was watching her closely. Emma sensed that she was being judged and that Paul was not predisposed to like her. But he was polite and he grinned at Kirsty with genuine warmth. "Sorry about the chaos," he said, opening a door off the hall. "With Paris in this state, it's harder than ever to keep abreast of the news."

The smell of ink greeted them as they stepped into the room. Strands of clothesline were strung across the ceiling. Manuscript pages littered every available surface. A boy of about fifteen stood at a table near the windows, cutting sheets from a large roll of paper with deft precision. David was carefully taking metal letters from a rack and handing them to his father, who was bent over a machine that Emma realized was a printing press.

As she stopped on the threshold, Robert looked up and met her gaze. Sunlight spilled through the open shutters, streaking his hair with russet and outlining the contours of his body beneath the muslin of his shirt. Like Paul, he was coatless, his shirt open at the neck and rolled up at the sleeves. The memory of the last time she had seen him thus came flooding back. The blood rushed to her face.

Before the adults could speak, Kirsty ran across the room to David. "Are you making words?"

"We're making a newspaper," David said, very much on his dignity.

"Like the *Edinburgh Gazette?*"

"Not quite as big, but it causes more of a commotion."

Kirsty studied him for a moment. "Mama says you might be my cousin."

"Yes," David admitted as if unsure how this piece of information would be treated.

Kirsty smiled. "I'm glad. I have lots of cousins, but none of them are as much fun to play with as you are."

The tension left David's shoulders. He smiled back, looking, to Emma's relief, like a ten-year-old boy again.

Robert reached for a towel and wiped the ink from his fingers. "Come upstairs and meet my mother."

Emma stared at him. "But—"

Robert tossed the towel aside and met her gaze, his mouth twisting with irony. "Robert Melton's mother was dead. Robert Lescaut's is very much alive."

She shouldn't be surprised. She hadn't known Robert had a cousin either. Or that he worked on a newspaper. She hadn't known him at all.

Robert led them to a sunny sitting room on the first floor with faded plaster and cheerful forget-me-not–splashed curtains. "Here they are, Maman."

A slender woman with gray-streaked chestnut hair came toward them. Emma was aware of the scent of lavender as her hands were seized in a firm grasp. "How can I ever thank you, my dear," Madame Lescaut said in English. "I owe you my son's life."

Emma looked at the mother of the man she knew she could never forgive. What could she say? *I wouldn't have done it if I'd known who he really was?* That would be unforgivably cruel. And it would not even be true. "I owe Colonel Lescaut my cousin's life," she murmured.

Madame Lescaut squeezed Emma's hands and stepped back. "I know how you must feel. Robert practiced an unpardonable deception on you." She regarded Emma with blue-gray eyes that were the twin of her son's. "That makes your actions all the more commendable. Now do sit down and have something to eat. I'm sure you don't want to talk any more about it."

Emma had been prepared to see Robert, telling herself the meeting was for the children's sake. She had not bargained on his mother's warmth. As they sat around the table, drinking iced lemonade and eating warm, buttery croissants, it was impossible to maintain the detachment with which she had tried to armor herself.

Kirsty studied Madame Lescaut over the rim of her glass. "You're English."

Emma looked more closely at Robert's mother. There was, she realized, something very British about Madame Lescaut's narrow, finely boned face. And her English was as free of an accent as Robert's own.

"I was born in Devon," Madame Lescaut said. "My maiden name was Melton."

So Robert's lies had been rooted in truth. Not that it made any difference. Emma tore off a piece of croissant with more force than was necessary.

Madame Lescaut kept up a cheerful conversation, managing to make no reference to battles and deceptions and invading armies. It was clear where Robert got his ability to put others at ease. David relaxed and was soon chattering happily with Kirsty. Robert himself said little. Once or twice Emma thought she felt his gaze upon her, but whenever she glanced at him, he was looking away.

Paul, who had joined them, was quieter than his aunt, though his dark eyes seemed constantly watchful. He was patient with Kirsty's endless questions about the printing press and became more animated as he talked. As he gestured, Emma noticed for the first time that the bones of his right hand were bent at an awkward angle, as though it had been smashed and badly set. She wondered if he, too, had been a soldier.

"Can I help you make the newspaper?" Kirsty said

when the last of the lemonade had been drunk and the croissants had been reduced to flaky crumbs.

Paul smiled. "If your mother has no objection."

"Not in the least." Emma subdued a twinge of alarm. She needed to talk to Robert alone, but she was not sure she was ready to do so.

Within a few minutes Madame Lescaut had provided a smock to cover Kirsty's dress, the two children had gone off with Paul, and Madame Lescaut herself had vanished into the kitchen. Emma felt the absence of the others as a physical force, pushing her and Robert closer together. Whatever distance she tried to maintain from him, he had been her lover. That stark fact hung in the air between them. It informed the most casual comment with unintended meaning, turned a simple gesture of courtesy into an unexpected trap.

"How's the white mare?" she managed to say. "Have you kept her?"

"I could hardly abandon her after she'd been so loyal."

"Then you've given her a name?"

"Liberty." The word carried echoes of revolution, of past triumphs and vanquished causes. Robert pushed his chair back from the table. "Why don't we take a walk."

For a moment Emma was genuinely grateful to him. Air and crowds would dissipate the thicket of emotion between them. And though they would walk side by side, at least she would not have to look into his eyes.

Outside the house she hesitated, assaulted by the sheer mass of color and sound. Robert glanced at her. She thought he meant to offer her his arm. Without further hesitation, she stepped forward, gathering her skirt in one hand so it did not brush against his legs. He fell into step beside her, close enough to offer protection but not so close that there was any risk of their touching.

There was no pavement for foot traffic. Pedestrians and carriages alike were forced into the narrow space between the buildings. An open gutter down the center of the street bubbled with a foul-smelling stream of liquid, but the thin strip of sky overhead was clear and bright, with none of the choking smoke she had seen on her one visit to London. For months she had believed Robert had grown up in Devon. She had never been there, but she could imagine the English countryside. Now she realized what very different worlds they had come from.

She fixed her gaze straight ahead. "I didn't know you worked on a newspaper."

"My father ran it. It's Paul's now. I help out when I'm home."

The sound of hooves and wheels rose suddenly above the babble of noise. Robert seized her arm and dragged her against the wall of the nearest house. A cabriolet clattered down the street at a reckless speed, sending pedestrians hurrying to the side and spattering sewage in all directions.

The stone wall was rough against her back, but Emma was more aware of the pressure of Robert's hand and the warmth of his breath. His face was inches from her own. She could see the shadows beneath his eyes. She could not help but look into the eyes themselves, dark and unfathomable. Something leapt hot and bright within her. She wrenched away from him and walked down the street, heedless of the crowd.

Without another word they turned into the Rue de la Harpe, which was wider but even more chaotic. Street vendors strolled by crying their wares, oranges and ribbons and knives. An intense bearded man worked at an easel. A trio of young men of about Jack and Andy's age pushed past, intent on their discussion. Emma caught the name "Descartes."

"The university is nearby." Robert's voice sounded unusually strained.

"Did you—?" Emma broke off, for she was not sure it was wise to ask Robert about his life.

"I spent three years there. And then proceeded to throw it all away by joining the army."

"Who said so?" She looked up at him, curiosity momentarily overcoming her discomfort.

"My father."

There was a note in his voice that made her want to touch him in sympathy. She looked ahead, toward the river. Why couldn't anger be a solid wall barricading one against the treacherous assaults of memory? Instead it was a fragile curtain, with great rents that let in the thoughts and impulses of the past.

They were nearing the river. A gust of cool breeze tugged at the ribbons on her bonnet and whipped her thin muslin skirt tight against her legs. She pulled at the fabric. Then she realized she was being foolish. Robert had seen her far more scantily clad. Robert had seen her with nothing on at all. Robert had touched her— She drew a breath. There were some things she could not let herself think of.

She forced herself to concentrate on her surroundings. She could swear she heard fragments of English. She understood this a few minutes later when they reached the broad, tree-lined quai that ran along the water. It was unexpectedly spacious after the cramped streets. And it was thronged with British hussars and dragoons.

Robert went very still, taking in the scene before him. Emma watched his eyes harden and his mouth go taut and thought of how she would feel at the sight of so many foreign troops milling around Edinburgh.

"Forgive me," he said, his voice stripped of emotion. "I fear I don't find this part of the city as beautiful as I once did. We can talk somewhere else."

They made their way back along the Rue de la Harpe

to a small café with tables spilling out into the street beneath the shade of a green-striped awning. The floor was cleanly swept and there was a pleasant smell of wine and coffee. Most of the customers appeared to be students, but there were women present who looked perfectly respectable. Everyone seemed oblivious of the street traffic. Lively discussions and arguments were under way over newspapers and books or games of dominoes and backgammon. There wasn't a British uniform in sight.

The proprietor greeted Robert as an old friend, showed them to an outdoor table, and brought them two glasses of Bordeaux. Robert took a sip of the wine and managed to smile. "I should grow used to it. I have a feeling there are going to be foreign troops in France for some time."

"I understand," Emma said. And then, feeling she had yielded too much, she added, "I understand that at least."

Robert set his glass down. "Thank you for bringing Kirsty. It means a great deal to David."

She looked full into the eyes that had once seemed to promise such trust and caring. The blue of the cornflowers in the nearby window box intensified their color. "David means a great deal to me. Besides, he may well be a Blair. We have an obligation to him. And to his mother."

Robert's eyes widened, but he said nothing.

"I told Bram your story," she went on, speaking quickly. "He said I'd have to ask Angus about it. But he didn't deny it. If it was untrue, he would have." She forced herself to continue in a level voice. "It seems likely your wife was a Blair. She may have been my cousin. I want to find out what happened to her. But I refuse to believe a Blair had anything to do with her death. She must have shown you the ring because she wanted to tell you who she was before she died."

"I see." He watched her, his gaze appraising. "What now?"

She took a fortifying sip of the wine, which was dry but not harsh. "I'll write to Angus. But I must wait until I hear from him on another matter." Until she received a reply from Angus about Arabel, she had no intention of troubling her uncle with anything else.

"I'd like to talk to Bram Martin myself," Robert said. "Is he in Paris?"

"He and Jenny traveled with us. But he won't tell you any more than he told me."

"Perhaps."

"He won't." If Bram would not confide in her, he would certainly not discuss Lucie with the man who had deceived them all. And if he did, she would never forgive either of them.

"You've done a great deal," Robert said. "I had no right to expect your cooperation."

His smile was sweet and seemingly open. The softness of his voice sent a chill along her nerves. "I told you, I want to know the truth."

"Then there's more you should know." He pushed aside his glass. "I said I wasn't sure of the identity of Lucie's father. But I'm fairly certain her mother was Lucilla Lauder."

She stared at him. Impossible. Or perhaps inevitable. A Blair and a Lauder. Just like Charlie and Arabel. Her stomach gave a sickening lurch. The secrecy surrounding Lucie's birth and upbringing no longer seemed so very strange. "How can you be sure?"

"Lucie had a necklace, her only legacy from her mother, just as the ring was her only legacy from her father. Lucilla's wearing the same necklace in the portrait at Lauder Hall."

Her fingers closed around the stem of her glass. "So that was why you were so interested in the portrait. And that morning in our picture gallery"—when she had poured out her soul to him—"you were looking for Lucie's father."

"Among other things." His gaze was unreadable.

"Who do you think it was?"

"There are a number of possibilities. Starting with Sir Angus's father."

"My grandfather? But he would have been—"

"Young enough to be capable of what is required," Robert said with a faint smile. "Then there are his sons. Angus. Thomas, the eldest, who died young. Gavin." He looked at her for a moment. "Your father."

She felt the blood drain from her face. She was still barely able to accept the fact that she might have a cousin of whom she knew nothing. Now Robert was suggesting she might have a sister who had been raised not twenty miles from Blair House. Words of denial rose to her lips, but she could not speak them. Though she had barely known her father, everyone said Jamie took after him. Impulsive and hotheaded. Just the sort of young man who might tumble into love with a girl his family would never accept and leave it to his elder brother to cope with the consequences.

A snatch of a drinking song came from a nearby table. A barouche rolled down the street. She gripped her legs to still their trembling. Lucie might be her sister. David might be her nephew. And Robert— Robert might be her brother-in-law. She looked up at him, feeling an hysterical desire to laugh. "According to the church it is a sin to—"

"Lie with your wife's sister." He met her gaze steadily. "But there is no way you could have known. If a sin was committed, it is on my head."

Bitterness welled up in her throat. She had accepted Robert's probable connection to the Blairs. She could begin to understand, if not forgive, the reasons for the deception he had practiced on her family. But whenever she remembered their moments of physical intimacy, she felt tainted and unclean. *Was any of it real?* she longed to cry. *Did I mean anything to you? Or was I just one more source of information?* "If a sin was committed, that was hardly the worst one," she said.

His eyes turned bleak. "No," he agreed in a low voice. "I have little use for conventional morality, but I will never forgive myself for hurting you."

She picked up her wineglass for protection. Her throat had gone tight and the view of tables and street turned blurry. Bloody hell. She was not going to let Robert make her cry.

"There's no reason to suspect it was any one of them in particular," he said. "We're only speculating, Mrs. Blair."

She set her glass down with such force that drops of wine spattered on the tabletop. "Don't call me that."

He raised his brows.

She was uncomfortably aware that her outburst had broken her own defenses. She looked down at the spilled wine, dark as blood on the worn table. "We can't pretend the past didn't happen. At least I can't." She looked up and held his gaze with her own. "I haven't had as much practice at deception as you."

His eyes showed her that her shot had hit home, but he merely inclined his head. "Very well then." He picked up his glass and lifted it to her in a silent toast. "Emma."

"Uncle Paul says the newspaper we printed will be all over Paris tomorrow," Kirsty told Emma as they rode home in another fiacre. "He said I could call him Uncle Paul because we're sort of related since David's my cousin. Maybe. Does that mean Robert is maybe related to me too?"

Emma swallowed, wondering if the bitter taste of betrayal would ever leave her. "By marriage I suppose he is."

"And to you?" Kirsty persisted.

Emma was not willing to go that far. "His wife was probably my cousin."

"So he's your cousin, too, the way Uncle Bram is." Kirsty flopped back against the squabs. "Are you still angry at him?"

Emma looked into her daughter's bright, knowing eyes. "Sometimes it's not as simple as being angry or not, Kirsty."

Kirsty folded her arms. "That's not an answer at all."

"No," Emma agreed, "but it's the best answer I can give."

Kirsty nodded. Emma touched her skirt, recalling the moment in the café when Robert had lifted his glass to her. In offering to write to Angus, she had committed herself to an alliance with Robert. She had an obligation to learn the truth, an obligation to David, she told herself, refusing to recall the dangerous look in Robert's eyes.

The fiacre rolled between the high gates of the house Sherry had taken in the Rue de Luxembourg. Emma thought with relief of Sherry's sensible conversation, Andy and Jack's teasing, Arabel's radiant joy. But when she stepped into the cool, marble-tiled entrance hall, she was greeted by a boom of outrage. "Where is the young puppy? By God, when I get my hands on him . . ."

Kirsty gasped. Emma stopped in the doorway, squeezed her eyes shut for a moment, then forced herself to take in the sight before her. Angus stood at the back of the hall, glaring at Sherry. And opposite him, looking equally formidable, was Lord Lauder.

19

Lord Lauder grew very red in the face. "Ye'll not lay
hands on the boy, ye hear me?" In moments of stress he
lost his cultivated manner. "Emma, lass, forgive me.
We're here to do something about the foolish young people."

Emma gave Kirsty a gentle push on the shoulders,
which she knew her daughter would understand. The
grownups were about to discuss something not fit for
children's ears. Kirsty gave her mother a reproachful look
and made for the stairs.

"In here, I think." Emma indicated the small salon
opening off the hall. "Sherry, if you don't mind . . ."

"You'll be all right?" he murmured.

She nodded and followed her uncle and Lord Lauder
into the salon. Only then did she notice that a third man
was with them. "Neil, what are you doing here?" Angus's
eldest son stood just inside the door glowering at her.

"Someone's got to see this right." Neil was big, broad,
and ruddy like his father, though slower in wit and with a
streak of priggishness that had not been his father's legacy. He shook his head. "Emma, Emma, how could you
have let this happen?"

Emma stifled a retort. *Arabel is twenty*, she wanted to
say. *I can't keep her on a leash.* But the words would be

useless, and in any case Emma felt her own measure of responsibility for what had happened.

"Where's the girl?" Angus stood with his feet planted firmly apart, his fists on his hips.

"She's gone out with Andy and Jack Sheriton. She should be back within the hour. Sit down, Uncle. You'll have an apoplexy."

"I'll not sit," Angus announced, "and I'll not stay to see the ungrateful wench. I've come to have my say and there's an end to it."

"We've had this conversation more than once," Lord Lauder said. "We had the misfortune to sail on the same ship, we shared a carriage to Paris, and there's not an hour I haven't tried to get the old fool to see reason. Of course Charlie's got to marry her. I'm not proud of my son. He's been an unholy fool, but he knows what's expected and he'll do right by Arabel."

"Oh, no," Angus roared. "There'll be no marriage between our families. Ye'll see me six feet under before I let her take the name of Lauder."

"It's out of the question," Neil added. "There's not been an alliance between a Blair and a Lauder since our great-great-uncle ran off with a Lauder cousin."

"That doesn't seem to have done us any harm," Emma retorted. She turned on her uncle. "Have you gone mad? Would you see your daughter ruined for the sake of your fribbling quarrel?"

"She'll not be ruined. Who's to know? When it's over, she'll come home like a sensible girl and we'll say no more about it. And if she won't, she's no daughter of mine."

"She'll marry Charlie." Lord Lauder gave Angus a fierce look. "They'll live at Lauder Hall. I like Arabel. I'll be glad to have her about."

Emma saw the pain in his eyes and only then remembered that he would be grieving for Matt. She held out her hand and he clasped it hard.

Angus strode forward until he stood nose to nose with Lauder. "My daughter? At Lauder Hall? I won't have it."

Emma pushed them apart. "Stop it. Stop it the both of you. Have you forgotten Arabel is with child? What would you have her do with it?"

"Get rid of it." Neil had been left out of the quarrel and he'd turned sulky. "It's done all the time," he said when Emma made a sound of protest. "You women know about these things."

"It could kill her."

"Here now. There'll be no talk of killing." Angus's voice diminished to its customary bellow. "If she carries the child—" He gave Emma a hard look. "It happens, you know. Women lose them. If she carries it, she'll have it here, where no one knows her. Then she'll give it away. Ye'll find someplace, Emma. The Frenchies know about bastards. And then ye'll bring her home."

Lord Lauder took a step toward him. "My grandchild? You'd have her give my grandchild away?"

Emma could not believe she had heard Angus right. "It's your grandchild, too, Uncle. God in heaven, this child was conceived in love. And you want to hide it away in shame like Lucie Sorel?"

A sudden quiet came over the room. Angus stared at Emma, his mouth open, his eyes wary. "What do you know about Lucie Sorel?"

All Emma's lingering doubts about Robert's story ended. She chose her words with care. "It's not my story, but I think you should hear it. All of you. Do you remember Captain Melton?" Angus and Lord Lauder nodded. "He duped us. His name isn't Melton. It's Robert Lescaut. He's a Frenchman. He was married to Lucie Sorel."

Angus sat down heavily on a gilded chair that seemed too fragile for his mass of weight and temper. His feel-

Shores of Desire

ings were never far from the surface. Emma could read them easily—the bewilderment, the memory of shared confidences, the awareness of betrayal, the mounting anger. "I know." She tried to forestall the inevitable explosion. "It was an unconscionable deception. He had his reasons. They do not excuse what he did. But you need to hear his story. It concerns our family. And you must hear it, too, Lord Lauder. It concerns your own."

At this last Angus looked up at her. She would have said there was fear in his eyes, save that she had never known her uncle to give way to fear. He pushed himself to his feet. "When?"

"Tonight?" Emma could not wait to have her questions resolved. "I'll send him a message at once. Shall I have him come here?"

"No." The answer was so abrupt that Emma wondered if he feared to see Arabel lest his stand against her weaken. "We're staying with Jenny. Eight o'clock. I'll have Bram there as well."

It was a few minutes past eight o'clock when Emma entered the Rue d'Anjou. It was a quiet street and Bram's house was quieter still, for it lay inside a walled courtyard that muffled the sounds of carriages and the voices of passersby. Emma knew she was late. She had been delayed by Arabel, who had insisted that if Robert Lescaut had something to say about the Blairs, she had every right to hear it.

"It will be better if you don't come," Emma had told her. "Uncle Angus doesn't want to see you."

Arabel's face crumpled at the bald rejection. "Then I don't want to see him. Tell him I'm going to marry Charlie and I don't care if I never see another Blair again."

Her throat tight and her insides knotted from the scene she had just been through and the thought of the one to come, Emma followed the servant up the stairs to the large salon. Jenny was nowhere in sight. Emma suspected that Bram had said they were talking business and sent her away.

The blue-and-gold room was full of angry voices that stopped abruptly at her entrance. Angus was on his feet as was Robert. Lord Lauder looked on from a nearby chair. Neil sulked in a corner of the room. He had always been jealous of Bram, who was far more clever than he. He would be furious that his father had confided part of the story to his son-in-law and had told him nothing.

Bram came forward and led Emma to a low sofa, its classical lines at odds with the raw tension in the room. "We were waiting for you," he murmured as he sat beside her.

"I've told Sir Angus I regret my abuse of his hospitality," Robert said into the silence. "I had reasons I thought sufficient for what I did, but I do not excuse it."

"By God, there's no excuse—"

"That's enough, Uncle," Emma said. "I've railed at Colonel Lescaut enough for both of us. I've called him every name I could think of. You could not have done better yourself. But we're here now to listen, not to cast blame."

Angus made a rumbling sound in his throat. Emma raised her voice. "I should tell you that Will owes his life to Robert Lescaut. Colonel Lescaut fought with the French at Waterloo, but he found Will on the battlefield and brought him to safety. He's paid whatever debt he owes us."

Angus looked at Robert from beneath lowered brows. "Humph." He threw himself into a chair. "Well. Let's get this over with."

Neil came forward to stand behind his father. "All right, Lescaut. What do you want from us?"

"I want nothing," Robert said, "save information."

Crafty, Emma thought. The accusations would come later. Robert intended to call his wife's killer to account, and he expected to find him among the Blairs. But none of this showed at the moment. He looked harmless enough. He was wearing a patched fawn-colored coat, a relic of earlier days, and his hair was in its usual disarray, but he was otherwise neatly habited. His expression was mild but serious.

He put a hand in his pocket, then extended it, palm up, to Angus. "Do you know this ring, sir?"

Angus stared at the circle of engraved silver. He was a huge man, but he seemed to have shrunk within the chair. Neil reached over his shoulder and snatched the ring from Robert's hand, then set it down hastily on the ormolu table at Angus's side. "It's our badge," he said, looking at the ring as though it had burned him. "Where the devil did you get it?"

Robert took the ring back. "It belonged to my wife, Lucie Sorel. She'd been told it was from her father, though she didn't know either of her parents. I saw it last on the night she died. She'd been hacked to death with a knife. I found her on the floor of a shabby room in a small inn near the harbor at Ostend. I asked her who had done it, but she was past speech. She reached for the ring which she wore on a ribbon around her neck and held it out to me. Then she died."

There was a moment of absolute silence. Bram folded his arms and looked at Robert. "I see. You thought she was trying to tell you she was a Blair."

"That isn't what I asked her."

No one spoke. Emma looked at the other men and saw the dawning realization in their eyes.

Robert saw it, too, for he held up his hands as though to ward off an attack. "I accuse no one. I tell you how and why I came to Scotland."

Neil, always slower to respond, came around Angus's

chair, his fists clenched. "Not that way." Bram sprang to his feet and held Neil back.

Neil stiffened. "Very well." He pulled himself from Bram's grip. "Go on with your story."

"Lucie died nearly four years ago. I was home on leave. I did what I could before I had to go back to the Peninsula, but I learned nothing of the ring. It was only when the war was over and I returned to Paris that I could take up the search again. I knew Lucie had come from Scotland. I showed the ring to a soldier who had lived in Edinburgh, and he recognized the badge."

Lord Lauder cleared his throat. "You thought she was a Blair."

"It seemed likely." Robert related the story of his search for Lucie, his interviews with Miss Ramsay and Hubert Cullen, and his discovery that Bram was involved in the arrangements for her marriage. "Someone," he said, "her father or his family, cared enough to see that she did not suffer."

"You're saying—" Neil gulped, unable for the moment to speak. "You're saying that my father . . ."

"Or perhaps one of your uncles. Perhaps even your grandfather."

"By God—"

"Easy, lad," Lauder said.

Neil turned on him. "Keep out of this."

"He can't. He's in it too." Robert turned back to Lauder. "I called on you with Mrs. Blair, if you remember."

"I do."

"While we were waiting in your parlor, my eye was caught by the portrait of a young woman. She wore a necklace of an unusual design, a necklace I had seen on my wife. It was Lucie's favorite piece of jewelry." Robert put his hand in his pocket again and pulled out a small box of worn blue velvet. He opened it and took out a fragile tangle of gold and pearls with a glowing yellow stone that might have been a topaz. He put the necklace in Lord Lauder's hands. "Do you recognize this?"

Lauder held it up, his hands trembling. "I do. It belonged to my grandmother. She gave it to Lucilla. My sister."

"God help me." Angus put his head in his hands.

Emma ran to him, knelt before him, and encircled him with her arms. "It's all right. It's over. But you've got to tell us."

Angus raised his head and looked into her eyes. "Ye must know everything, mustn't ye? Ye can't leave it decently buried."

"No," Emma said, "I can't. Please, Uncle. For all our sakes."

Angus looked hard into her eyes. Then he sighed in a huge exhalation of breath. "It was my brother. Thomas. He'd been on the Continent and settled for a while in Paris. When our father took sick, Thomas came home with an infant daughter he didn't dare keep at Blair House. He couldn't trust the family so he went to the church and told Mr. Logen of his dilemma. Logen found the Frenchwoman, who agreed to take the child in 'til Thomas could decide what to do with her. Then our father died." Angus looked away. "Thomas took his death hard. He brooded and grew careless."

"I know." Emma covered his hand with her own. "There was an accident with a gun."

Angus looked back at her. "I only learned about the girl after Thomas died," he said with sudden vehemence. "The Frenchwoman went to Logen, and Logen came to me. I made arrangements for her keep. What else could I do? Abandon the little bastard?"

"Oh, Uncle." Emma kissed him, then sat back on her heels. "How did Lucie get the ring and the necklace?"

"I don't know." Angus's voice was weary. "Thomas

must have left them with Logen, and Logen must have given them to the Frenchwoman."

"Did you know the child was Lucilla's?" Emma asked.

Angus looked away again. "Not for sure."

He knew, Emma thought. He won't admit it outright. She turned to Lord Lauder, who had sat silent through Angus's recital. A muscle twitched in his cheek, and his face was drained of color. "They told me she was on a visit to the Continent," he said as though talking to himself. "My parents wouldn't speak of her, even when they got the letter telling them she was dead. They thought she'd run off with a man, but they wouldn't have suspected Thomas." He turned to Emma. "I can't credit it myself. I knew my sister. Lucilla wouldn't have looked twice at a Blair."

You can't stop people from loving, Emma wanted to shout. Look at Charlie. Look at Arabel.

Lord Lauder turned to Angus. "Was he with her when she died?"

"He must have been. He brought the bairn home with him."

"Why didn't you tell me?"

"Damme, weren't things bad enough between us? I did what I could. The girl was educated as well as any lady in Scotland. She could have made a respectable marriage, but the ungrateful wench ran off."

"I'm not blaming you, Angus." It was the first time Emma had heard Lord Lauder use her uncle's given name. Shaken by the revelations, he looked up at Robert. "So your Lucie was Lucilla's child. What happened to her?"

"She took ship for France." Robert turned to Bram. "Do you know why, Martin? You must have been nearly the last person to see her before she left Scotland."

Bram shrugged. "I met her two or three times to discuss the marriage settlement, but I can hardly claim to have known her. She never spoke of France nor of any person she might know there. When she disappeared, I was as shocked as Cullen. I tried to find her, but there wasn't a trace of her passing. I'm sorry, Lescaut."

"She may have gone to England and taken ship there." Robert turned back to Lord Lauder. "I don't know how she came to France, but she managed to make her way to Paris. She was clever, she knew the language, and she must have had a little money. When she got to Paris, she became friendly with a young widow with a fashionable house in the Rue Grammont, Henriette Colbert. Henriette took her in. She had the brightest salon in Paris, and her home was always filled with young officers. I met Lucie there and married her."

There were tears in Lord Lauder's eyes. He brushed them away with an angry gesture. "You have a son. Lucilla's grandchild. I'd like to meet him."

Angus was roused by Lauder's words. "The boy's a Blair."

"And has Lauder blood."

"The line is illegitimate," Neil said. "It doesn't count." Then, in a more plaintive voice, "I should have been told. I don't know why I wasn't told."

Angus pushed himself out of his chair. The fire was back in his eyes and once again his presence filled the room. "Are ye satisfied, Melton? Lescaut. Whatever ye call yourself. Ye've got your truth. It's an ugly, sad little story and I'm sorry to tell it. There are ties of blood between your lad and our house, and for his sake I won't tell ye what I think of your vile imposition on our hospitality. Ye did us some service, and we've paid mightily for it. Now leave it be, d'ye hear? I never saw the girl, but it breaks my heart to think on it. I want no more questions." He swung around and pointed a finger at Emma. "And that goes for ye, too, lass."

There was silence in the room. The tide of Angus's

anger washed over them and receded. He had spoken with undue vehemence, even for Angus. For a traitorous moment, Emma thought that her uncle was lying. Or, if not lying, that he was holding something back.

Robert continued to stare at him. "My wife died with Thomas Blair's ring in her hand."

"God's teeth! What cause had I to wish the girl harm?"

None. There was none. Emma looked at Robert, wondering at his obstinacy. A bastard child was no great disgrace. Her uncle had done what he could for Thomas's daughter. It was not his fault that Lucie had chosen to run away.

Yet she could not escape the image Robert had evoked: a blood-drenched woman, unable to speak, offering the Blair ring as a clue to her grisly death. "Uncle," she said. "There has to be a reason—"

He turned on her before she could complete the thought. "There is no reason, d'ye hear? None save what lies in yon Frenchman's head." He stalked across the room to face Robert. "Give it up, Lescaut. The lass is dead. I'm sorry for it, but it's long since over. I have no more to tell ye and I won't twist the knife in my guts by talking about it."

Robert's face seemed wiped clean of passion. He's angry, Emma thought. He's furious because he's come so far and now he's at an impasse. But Robert said nothing. He made Angus a slight bow, thanked them all for their time, and took his leave.

The gathering broke up quickly. Angus and Lord Lauder would not look at each other. Bram was thoughtful. Neil continued to sulk. Emma knew that Robert had not finished with them. His unspoken accusations hung like a pall over the room and threatened them all. Angus had not told them the whole story. She was convinced of that now.

She hurried from the room in time to see Robert in

the hall below, accepting his hat from the footman. "Robert," she called, leaning over the balustrade.

Her voice stopped him. He looked up, his gaze unreadable.

Emma picked up her skirt and ran down the stairs, urgency breaking through the constraint between them. "Henriette Colbert. Does she still live in Paris?"

"As far as I know." Robert nodded to the footman to withdraw. "I haven't seen her in years."

"I want you to take me to meet her."

His brows drew together. "If you think Henriette can unlock the mystery of Lucie, you're liable to be disappointed. I talked to her extensively at the time of Lucie's death."

"You were convinced the answers lay in Scotland. I think they may be in France. Madame Colbert must have seen Lucie almost daily. You were hundreds of miles away."

"So I was."

His voice was even, but the light from the brace of candles on the hall table caught the flare of pain in his eyes. "I'm sorry." Emma took a step forward, then checked herself. "I didn't mean—"

"It doesn't matter." He turned his beaver hat over in his hands. "I think it's a fool's errand, but you have a right to discover what you can about Lucie. If you're determined to meet Henriette Colbert, I'll call for you at half past ten tomorrow."

20

Morning sun lit the Rue Grammont as the fiacre pulled up before No. 31. Robert helped Emma from the carriage and went to pay off the driver. Emma stared up at the building before them. Its once ornate white plasterwork was crumbling and gray with grime. Not the sort of place one would expect to house the brightest salon in the city. But Emma had learned that in Paris a shabby exterior could hide well-proportioned rooms furnished with taste and opulence.

Robert joined her and they approached the door together. The concierge told them Madame Colbert still lived on the third floor. A dour-faced maid dressed in black answered their ring at the door of the flat. Her eyes went wide at the sight of Robert. "Captain Lescaut."

"Colonel now." Robert gave one of his incandescent smiles. "Hullo, Berthe. You're looking as lovely as ever. Is Madame Colbert in?"

A spot of color stole into the maid's cheeks. The dour expression gave way to a smile that was almost pretty. She twitched at her starched skirt. "Madame does not usually receive visitors before noon."

"See if she'll make an exception."

Berthe nodded, then glanced past him to Emma as if

seeing her for the first time. Surprise flickered in her eyes.

"My wife's cousin, Madame Blair," Robert said. "We'll find our own way to the salon."

He led Emma to a light, airy room with soft apple-green walls and white-painted moldings. Lace curtains diffused the sunlight that poured through the high windows. Peach-colored roses, their scent spilling into the room, filled a wide crystal bowl set on a walnut table in front of one of the windows. An ornate clock stood beside the vase. Emma glanced at the time. Just past eleven.

"Don't tell me you forgot Madame Colbert doesn't receive callers early. We could have waited an hour."

Robert ran his fingers along the back of a gilt-trimmed sofa. "Trick of the trade. It's always best to catch people with their guard down."

Emma looked into his eyes. "Is that what you did with us?"

He didn't flinch from her gaze. "Not quite. It was a stroke of luck we found you in the midst of rescuing Charlie."

She looked away, her throat raw with hurt. "You said you didn't think Madame Colbert had anything to tell us."

"I don't. But I could be wrong."

The door opened with well-oiled ease. A small woman with a mass of golden hair pinned hastily on top of her head swept into the room. "Robert. It's too dreadful of you to call before I've had time to dress my hair," she said in musical French. "I understand—" She looked at Emma and went suddenly still.

"I know," Robert said. "The resemblance is pronounced, isn't it?"

"I look like Lucie?" In her surprise, Emma blurted out the question in English.

"Very much so." Madame Colbert switched to English,

accented but clear. She waved them to chairs, then settled herself in the center of the sofa. She was wearing a dressing gown of a thin rose-colored silk whose voluminous folds spread out on either side of her, emphasizing the fragility of her appearance. Her color was delicate. Emma thought that her face was rouged, but if so it had been done with a light hand. Her perfume was heavy, a luxuriant rose scent that overpowered the fragrance of the flowers by the window. She had no particular beauty. Her figure was slight, her features angular, and her nose a trifle large, but her eyes, of a deep blue, were compelling. Emma thought men would find her unforgettable.

Henriette Colbert surveyed Emma with frank interest. "I understand you are Lucie's cousin, Madame Blair?"

"So Colonel Lescaut has recently informed me."

"I see." Madame Colbert glanced at Robert. "So you found Lucie's family."

"But not her killer. Yet."

"Colonel Lescaut is convinced the answer lies with my family," Emma said. "I am equally convinced it does not. Lucie's life was here. She had left Scotland behind her."

"I see." Henriette adjusted the folds of her dressing gown. "You would prove Robert wrong. And Robert, being nothing if not fair-minded, brought you to see me." She glanced at Robert with a lift of her finely arched eyebrows.

Robert leaned back in his chair and crossed his legs. "Go ahead. I'm as interested as Madame Blair in anything you may have to say."

"As generous as ever." Madame Colbert managed to make the word a faint double entendre. She turned to Emma. "What would you like to know?"

"Everything. How you met. Did Lucie make enemies? Was there anyone who could have wished her harm?"

Madame Colbert laughed. "You ask a great deal, madame. It has been eleven, twelve years since I first knew

her, and we were friends up until the time of her death."
She looked down at her hands as though the memories
would be found in the jewels she wore on her slender
fingers. "I met Lucie at an inn outside of Paris. I found
her at once amusing and terrifying. She was an innocent,
you understand, but entranced with the possibilities of
life. She had no idea what would be in store for her, and I
could not leave her to the mercies of the street. In pity I
took her in. She was an engaging companion, she spoke
French without the trace of an accent, and she made
herself useful. She said nothing of her life in Scotland
and I did not press her."

"Was she silent out of fear of what had happened
there?"

"I do not think Lucie was afraid of anything but boredom and confinement."

It was the image Emma had formed of Lucie when she
and Robert talked with Mr. Cullen. She glanced at Robert. She had been right. Lucie had not fled Scotland for
fear of the Blairs. Robert inclined his head in acknowledgment.

"She was a girl who lived in the moment," Madame
Colbert went on. "She was beautiful and young and
much admired."

And here, perhaps in this very room, she had met and
captivated Robert Lescaut. Emma's stomach clenched
with something disgustingly akin to jealousy. "Then she
married."

Madame Colbert glanced at Robert, brows raised
again.

Robert looked at Emma. "Lucie was pregnant.
Shocked?"

Emma returned his gaze. "You're past shocking me,
Colonel Lescaut." Yet the image the story evoked—of
Robert giving way to youthful passion with this unknown

cousin who looked like her and yet apparently had been so different—did uncomfortable things to her insides.

"I urged the marriage as well," Madame Colbert said. "Lucie might have made a more advantageous match—forgive me, Robert—but under the circumstances, she was wise to follow my advice. Marriage gives a woman a freedom she can never know in the unmarried state."

"You think little of marriage," Emma said.

"I am a realist."

Robert uncrossed his legs. "What Henriette is trying to say, with her usual exquisite tact, is that my marriage was doomed from the start. It might have been different if I wasn't a soldier, but as you well know, military orders play merry hell with domestic bliss. A few months after we were married, I was sent abroad. I rarely got leave. Lucie had little taste for motherhood. She gave David to a wet nurse and began to frequent Henriette's salon."

Madame Colbert pushed back a strand of hair that had escaped its pins. "I was glad to have her back."

"It's a sad story," Emma said.

Madame Colbert made a gesture of dismissal. "Everyone's life is a sad story. Lucie was not unhappy. Dissatisfied perhaps, but she knew how to wring pleasure from the moment."

"Did she—" Emma looked from Robert to Madame Colbert, unsure how to phrase her inquiry.

"Take lovers?" Robert's mouth curled with cynical humor. "You could hardly expect her to feel great loyalty to the husband who got her with child then left her alone for months on end."

Emma gripped her hands together. She couldn't censure Lucie. Images of her own transgression were far too vivid. "If Lucie was beautiful, as you say, and if she had lovers, then surely she must have given cause for jealousy."

Robert raised a brow. "You're suggesting I killed her?"

Emma looked steadily at him. "If you had, you wouldn't be inquiring about her death."

"Unless I was extremely devious."

"Even your mind isn't so twisted."

"A spurned lover, is that what you think?" Madame Colbert asked, a note of mockery in her voice. "Or a current lover driven mad by jealousy?"

"Why not? Surely that is more likely than that a member of my family sought to do away with her." Emma did not look at Robert, but she framed the words for his benefit as much as Madame Colbert's. "We paid for her fostering, we were prepared to settle money on her at her marriage. We had no cause to wish her harm. She died in France, madame. She died a violent death. She had lived here for years. You knew her, you knew her friends, her lovers. There must be one of them she angered, one of them she roused to passion."

Madame Colbert shook her head. "Perhaps you are right. But I can think of no one who might have acted so."

"Her lovers. You must know their names where Colonel Lescaut would not."

"You go too far, madame."

"Her last lover . . ."

"Ah, that I can tell you. A young aristocrat whose family had been discreet enough to avoid the Terror. Philippe de Rivaud. Lucie was wildly in love with him. He was knifed and robbed in the street a month or two before her death. She was distraught when he was killed." Madame Colbert stood and shook out the folds of rose-colored silk that billowed around her. "Philippe was not responsible for Lucie's death. I wish you good fortune in your search, Madame Blair. I have told you all I can. Robert, it is always a pleasure to see you, even when you stir unwelcome memories."

Robert went to her side and pressed her hand. "Thank you, Henriette."

Madame Colbert regarded him for a moment, her eyes troubled. "It's a fool's quest, *mon cher.*"

Robert smiled with reckless brilliance. "Very likely. But when have you ever known that to stop me?"

Emma waited until she and Robert were settled in another fiacre before she spoke. "Thank you. That can't have been easy for you."

He turned his head against the dark leather squabs. "None of this is easy for anyone."

Damnation. What was it about his gaze that made her skin go tight and her blood run hot? Emma stared down at her hands. Her defenses against him were as thin as her net gloves. She had told him the story of her marriage the day after they met, but it had taken Henriette Colbert for her to get a glimpse of his marriage. "You must have loved her very much."

"Must I?"

Her fingers curled inward. "What else could drive such a desperate search?"

"Guilt. The need for a sense of purpose. The thrill of the chase." He was silent for a moment. "I loved Lucie," he said, a raw note in his voice that she had never heard before. "But I could never forget that I'd trapped her. So I never felt I could demand anything of her."

Emma looked up at him. "Including fidelity?"

He went still. His gaze shifted out the window. "Fidelity can't be demanded. It has to be given freely."

Her mouth went dry. She had vowed to give Allan her fidelity, but she had broken faith with him.

Robert had directed the fiacre to the Tuileries Gardens where Caroline had taken the children for the morning. They had agreed to meet by the large marble basin at the far end of the grounds. Kirsty, David, and Emily were leaning over the edge of the basin, so close that the fountain sent sprays of water into their faces as they fed bread to a pair of swans. Caroline sat on a nearby bench, but she rose and came forward when she caught sight of Robert and Emma.

"A successful trip?" she asked.

"You could say so," Robert said.

Caroline nodded and asked nothing further. Instead she turned to Emma. "David wants to talk to you. I think he wants to apologize."

Emma glanced at David. He had drawn away from Kirsty and Emily and was looking at the adults, taut with anxiety. "I'll go to him," she said.

"Let me send him over. You should have some privacy."

Emma looked at Robert. "Best for him to get it off his chest," he said. "I'll stay with Caroline and the girls."

Emma watched as Robert and Caroline joined the children. David listened to something his father said, nodded, and walked toward Emma. He slowed and looked at her for a moment, then walked forward with obvious resolution.

Emma smiled at him. "Why don't we talk over there?" She gestured toward a grove of orange trees, away from the crowds who filled the walkways around the basin with chatter and laughter and shouts.

David said nothing as they approached the grove. When they reached a bench shielded by orange trees set in wooden boxes, he stopped, clasped his hands behind his back, and looked Emma straight in the eye. "I'm sorry I lied to you."

Emma returned his gaze with equal directness. "I'm sorry you were forced to do so. Your father should never have brought you, knowing what he was going to do."

"I begged him to take me with him." David looked at

the ground and scraped the gravel with his foot. "I wanted to know about my mother."

He could have been no more than six when Lucie was killed. He was still a child. Emma sat on the bench and drew him down beside her. "I'm not angry. I was never angry at you, only at your father, and I understand now why he came to Scotland as he did. I want to know about your mother, too. She was my cousin."

David's face brightened. "And Kirsty is mine."

"Yes. She's very pleased to have you for her kinsman."

David looked up at her. "You remind me of my mother. Here." He brought out a miniature from his pocket and put it in her hand. "I thought you might like to see this. My father gave it to me. It was taken before she left Scotland. See, she has dark hair, but your face is the same." He looked from the portrait to Emma. "Not exactly, but there is a resemblance."

There was. Henriette Colbert had said she looked like Lucie, but Emma had not dreamed how strong the resemblance was. The shape of the face, the nose, the mouth. Robert must have known from the moment he met her in the streambed that his wife was a Blair.

The girl in the portrait had a striking beauty. In this, Emma thought, Lucie was different from herself. There was a touch of haughtiness in her face, as though she knew she had a quality that set her apart. There was something elusive too. One would find it hard to know the real Lucie Sorel. That must have been part of her allure. Robert must have been captivated by that enchanting girl.

A sickening suspicion washed over her. Did that account, at least on Robert's side, for the sparks that had flared so quickly between them? When he lay with her, had he seen not Emma Blair but an echo of his dead wife?

Emma handed the portrait to David. "She's very lovely."

He slipped the portrait into his pocket without looking at it. "She was pretty," he answered with the simplicity of the young. "I liked her clothes and the way she smelled. She let me sit in her room sometimes when she was getting ready to go out, but she didn't like me to touch her things. She'd get angry and then sometimes she'd be loving and sometimes she didn't pay attention to me at all."

"Perhaps she was unhappy."

David considered this. "I don't think so. She had lots of secrets, and she didn't like people to know them. Sometimes she took me walking with her in the Bois de Boulogne. But when we'd meet one of her friends, she'd send me away. I used to wonder why. Then I decided that was just the way she was."

However hard her life had been, Lucie Sorel had a lot to answer for. No one should treat a child that way. "That must have been hard for you," Emma said.

"Not really. I had Grandmère and Uncle Paul and Papa when he was home." David swung his foot back and forth, making half circles in the gravel. "My grandfather—my other grandfather—he was your uncle?"

"Yes, my uncle Thomas."

"And my grandmother was Charlie Lauder's aunt." He smiled, pleased to have worked it out. "They came to France, didn't they? And my mother was born here."

"I think so," Emma said. "I don't know all the story."

David's level brows drew together. For a moment, Emma caught an echo of Charlie Lauder. "My mother was pregnant before my parents got married." He looked at Emma. "Papa told me. He doesn't believe in keeping secrets about things like that. But they got married before I was born. I wonder why my grandparents didn't get married."

What could she say? That her uncle Thomas had not

been as honorable a man as Robert Lescaut? "I don't know," Emma said.

David nodded and seemed ready enough to drop their conversation. As they returned to the basin he gave a shout and ran off to join Kirsty and Emily. Emma sat on a bench beside Robert and Caroline.

"Thank you," Robert said, his eyes on his son. "He hasn't looked so carefree since Brussels."

"I never wanted David to feel guilty."

There was a moment of silence, heavy with the past. Robert continued to look at the children, but his gaze had hardened. Caroline politely pretended to be invisible. Emma forged on. "David asked me why Thomas and Lucilla didn't get married."

Robert shrugged. "It would have cut them off irrevocably from their families."

"More than giving birth to the baby did? If Thomas had wanted to put the whole episode behind him, he'd have left Lucie in Paris, not brought her back to Scotland with him." Emma looked at the children, now racing leaf boats in the basin, then back at Robert. She framed the suspicion she had not completely formulated in her own mind until now. "We've all assumed Lucie was illegitimate. Suppose we were wrong." She looked from Robert to Caroline. "Where would a Protestant couple get married in Paris?"

21

Adam glanced from Robert and Emma to the man standing beside him. "John Doyle, who serves as chaplain at the embassy." He gestured for his guests to be seated. "Mrs. Blair and Mr. Lescaut are in need of some information, John."

Emma looked across the Durwards' salon at Mr. Doyle. He was a man of no more than thirty, slight and not overly tall, with light brown hair combed back from his face. A pair of spectacles framed brown eyes that looked both kind and intelligent.

"What can I do for you?" Doyle asked. If he knew Robert had fought for the French, he gave no sign that it bothered him.

Robert glanced at Emma. She gave a slight nod. Lucie had been his wife. It was up to him to speak, though she was pleased that he had acknowledged her interest in the matter. "I believe my wife's parents were married in Paris some thirty-three years ago," Robert told Doyle. "But as Protestants in a Catholic country they would have had difficulty finding a minister. Might they have gone to the embassy?"

"Oh, certainly," Doyle said. "I've already had several requests to perform marriages in the few weeks I've been here."

"And records are kept of these marriages?"

Doyle grinned. "Clergymen are trained to keep records of everything. But in the last twenty years diplomatic relations with France have been suspended more often than not. I'm not sure anyone knows what happened to the records from that far back—what would it be? Seventeen eighty-two?"

Robert nodded as though this was what he had expected. "My wife's parents would have wished to keep their marriage secret. They may not have gone to the embassy at all. Where else in Paris might they have found a minister?"

Doyle frowned and pushed his spectacles back up on his nose. "The Protestant religion wasn't precisely welcome in France before the Revolution. No offense meant, Lescaut."

"None taken," Robert assured him. "My mother is a clergyman's daughter, but my father took little interest in religion of any kind."

"There are some of us who minister to English expatriates, of course," Doyle continued, "though most of those I know would be too young. No, wait a minute. There's Christopher Barnes. A friend of my uncle's," he explained. "They corresponded for years, though I never met Barnes myself. He came over to Paris in the seventies to live with his daughter who had married an English merchant with a business here. Barnes stayed right through the Revolution. If he didn't marry your wife's parents, he may have known who did."

"He's still alive?" Emma asked.

"I'm afraid not. He died nearly ten years ago. But his daughter, Mrs. Mercer, still lives in the Boulevard Saint Martin. I called on her only last week to pay my family's respects. A very pleasant woman. Would you like me to give you a letter of introduction?"

A quarter hour later the letter of introduction had

been written and Doyle had departed for the embassy, assuring them that it was no trouble at all and he hoped he had been of help. Emma and Robert followed Adam into the garden where David, Kirsty, and Emily were helping Caroline plant a pair of white rosebushes.

David scrambled to his feet, his hands covered with damp earth. "What did you find out?"

"We have the address of a woman who may know about the marriage," Robert said.

"Would it be all right if we left the children here for a few hours?" Emma asked Caroline.

"Of course." Caroline laid down her trowel and brushed the dirt from her smock. "With this much help the garden will be transformed in no time."

Emma ruffled Kirsty's hair and smiled at David and Emily. It was only when she turned back to Robert that she realized how easily the word "we" had come to her lips.

"Do you mind walking?" Robert asked as they left the Durwards'. "The boulevards are so congested a carriage wouldn't be much faster."

Emma nodded and they set out on foot down the Rue du Faubourg Saint Honoré. The boulevards were a series of streets that ran in a rough circle around the older part of Paris, separating it from the faubourgs. Though Emma had driven briefly along the boulevards with Sherry and Arabel, she had had no chance to explore them. She had been eager to view Paris, but she seemed fated to see it only when her mind was absorbed by other matters.

They turned up the Rue Royale and crossed the Place de la Madeleine to the boulevard of the same name. Despite her preoccupation, Emma could not help but note her surroundings. On foot the boulevards were even more impressive than they had been in a carriage. In most Paris streets sunlight was crammed into a narrow sliver between tall buildings. Here it spilled freely onto the wide cobbled avenue. The road was clogged with fiacres, cabriolets, rough wooden carts, and handsome private carriages, but there was a walkway to the side for foot traffic. Fashionably dressed people strolled by or lounged in chairs that could be hired out from elderly, shabbily dressed men and women.

As in the rest of Paris, soldiers were visible everywhere: fair-haired Prussians in coats of blue or brown or green; Cossacks in short red jackets and immense trousers; dark-moustached Hungarian grenadiers in fur caps; Belgians in orange-faced blue; and of course red-coated Englishmen, here and there relieved by the blue of a dragon, the green of a rifleman, or the kilt of a Highland regiment. Emma glanced at Robert as a particularly boisterous pair of cavalrymen brushed past them, flirting with two French ladies. Robert stared straight ahead and said nothing.

The foot traffic suddenly came to a standstill. Emma was jostled as two ladies walking in front of them drew back in alarm. Up ahead she heard an exclamation in French. It was not a word she knew, but judging by the tone it was anything but polite.

"Bloody French dog," an English voice said in response.

The sounds of hand and boot connecting with flesh and bone followed. "Stay here," Robert said and pushed his way forward.

Ignoring him, Emma slipped through the crowd and emerged in time to see a dark-haired young man still wearing imperial blue grappling with an English hussar who was reaching for his sword.

Robert grasped the Frenchman from behind, as he had once grasped Emma's brother, and pushed him against the wall of the nearest house. "You forget yourself, *mon ami*," he said in a quiet voice informed by steel. "The English are our guests."

"Guests!" The Frenchman spat the word, struggling to no avail against Robert's hold.

"Uninvited guests, but guests nonetheless." Robert glanced at the hussar who was looking on in surprise. "One does not repay rudeness with rudeness."

"If you'd been on the battlefield—" the Frenchman said.

Robert's eyes turned icy. "I am Colonel Lescaut," he said, the words as distinct as rifle shots. "If you honor the uniform you still wear, you will honor the orders of your superior officer."

Robert had no proof of his rank save the unmistakable note of command in his voice and the unyielding force of his gaze, but the French officer gave a curt nod. Robert released him. The Frenchman straightened his coat and walked away, ignoring the hussar.

"Is it wise to advertise your rank?" Emma said as they moved on. "Adam said the Royalists—"

"The Royalists will find me if they want to. I can't hide what I am."

Emma stole a glance at his set profile. For a moment he had been the man who had restrained Jamie and rescued Geordie from the fire. And fought against Englishmen. Now he had retreated behind a contained facade. He was intent on finding answers to the mystery of his wife's death, but some inner fire had been quenched at Waterloo. Emma knew she shouldn't care. But she could not deny that she did.

In silence they moved into the livelier bustle of the Boulevard des Italiens. Sparkling glass shop windows displayed expensive goods. Savory smells of roast meat and fresh bread spilled into the street from elegant restaurants and cafés. The husky voice of a street singer was drowned out by shouts of *"Dix sols pour chacun!"* *"Sept sols seulement, madame!"* from open-air tables offering bottles of scent, carved wooden toys, gaudy glass jewelry, and all manner of other trifles. At another time, Emma would have stopped at each table. Now it all moved past her in a blur.

As they threaded their way through the crowd, Emma willed herself to patience. For David's sake, she wanted Thomas and Lucilla to have been married. But if the marriage had taken place, what had happened to the papers? Why hadn't Angus found them among Thomas's possessions? Even more troubling, if he had found them, why had he kept them secret?

As Thomas's legitimate daughter, Lucie would have been raised in Blair House. After Thomas's death the land would have gone to Angus in any case, but surely there was some money that would have gone to her. Could Angus have begrudged her that inheritance? It seemed very unlike her uncle. Whatever his faults, she had never thought of him as greedy.

But Angus was vehemently opposed to Charlie and Arabel's marriage. Could he have felt the same anger over his brother's marriage to a Lauder? Unable to prevent the marriage from taking place, could he have tried to destroy all evidence of it? Despite the warmth of the sun, Emma shivered, recalling the look on Angus's face when he told them about Lucie. He did not have Robert's talent for deception. Emma would stake her life that her uncle was holding something back.

"Tired?" Robert turned to look at her.

Emma shook her head. She could not bring herself to voice her fears. "I was thinking about Thomas and Lucilla. It must have been difficult for them. As difficult as it is for—"

She hesitated. Robert would not judge Arabel. He had been fond of her. Too fond, Emma had once feared, though at the time Arabel must have had thoughts for no one but Charlie. "Arabel is going to have Charlie

Lauder's baby. They want to marry, but Uncle Angus won't hear of it."

"Damnation," Robert said softly. "I was afraid of this."

"Afraid?" Emma asked, torn between anger and despair. Was there any family secret Robert did not know?

"I came upon them embracing on the stairs."

"I see." So that explained the understanding between Robert and Arabel. Robert had been helping Arabel meet Charlie. But at least in this he had not been motivated by his desire to solve the mystery of his wife's birth or to prove the Blairs guilty of murder. "Lord Lauder says they can live at Lauder Hall," Emma said. "But Uncle Angus will cast Arabel off. It's a beastly way to start out married life."

"And marriage is difficult enough in any case."

She glanced up at him, thinking of their visit to Henriette Colbert yesterday and their talk in the fiacre afterward. "Yes. At least I found it so."

The walkway was again blocked, this time by a crowd that had formed around a man tending sausages hissing in a pan. Emma glanced into the window of a milliner's shop, her eye caught by a white lace bonnet. She had worn a white bonnet at her own wedding. For a moment she caught the scent of the heather in her bouquet, felt the pressure of Allan's hand when he slid the ring onto her finger and the feeling of hope that had suffused her. "I thought my life would be transformed," she said, still looking at the bonnet.

"I was sure mine already had been."

Emma started at the sound of Robert's voice, for she had been speaking half to herself. She turned around and met his gaze. "I wasn't much of a wife." She had never admitted it to anyone. Putting her failure so baldly into words lifted a weight from around her heart. "I wanted Allan to be different than he was."

"I wasn't much of a husband. I never knew the real Lucie at all."

They moved around the crowd and slipped past a boy polishing boots and an earnest young man discoursing on the rival merits of Rousseau and Voltaire. A thin-faced girl who looked no older than David darted through the crowd and ran up to Robert. *"Que voulez-vous, monsieur?"* she said, reaching into the basket on her arm and holding up a handful of toothpicks. *"Deux sols, monsieur. Mon pauvre père, il est malade."*

Robert fished some coins out of his pocket. "Get yourself a decent meal," he said in French, pressing them into the girl's hand.

"Do you think her father is really sick?" Emma asked as the girl ran off.

"Probably not, but she looks underfed. Do you have any use for toothpicks?"

Their moment of confidences was gone. For a few minutes, Robert hadn't been the man who had been her lover or the man who had deceived her but simply someone who understood the disappointment of a marriage gone wrong. After everything that had passed between them, how could he still have the power to draw such intimate confessions from her?

They passed beneath the Porte Saint Denis, an ornate arch built in honor of the triumphs of Louis XIV, and then reached a second arch, the Porte Saint Martin. Emma studied it for a moment. It was simpler than the first. Someone had recently tried to scrape an inscription from the stone, but she could make out the words *"Liberté"* and *"Egalité."* The sight of those powerful words obliterated brought home what Bonaparte's defeat had meant to France. Emma glanced at Robert. "How old were you when the Bastille fell?"

"Six." Robert's gaze was on the arch. "I can still remember. People flooding the streets. My parents' excitement. I never saw my father so giddy."

Emma thought of Bram's stories of the Terror. "And later?"

"Later we lived in fear that my father would be arrested. So many of our friends were killed. Marat stabbed in his bath. Camille Desmoulins sent to the guillotine by his own people." Robert's eyes darkened with the memories. "His wife followed him a few days later. I used to think she was the most beautiful woman in the world."

He would have been David's age. Emma put out her hand, wanting to comfort the boy he had been. But he was no longer a boy. She let her hand fall to her side. "It must have been terrifying."

Robert's gaze moved over the remains of the inscription on the arch. "Marat and Desmoulins were journalists like my father. It seemed to me that the written word was a feeble shield against injustice."

"So you decided to join the army?"

He looked at her as though it was important he make her understand. "I still believed in the Revolution. I thought we had to fight to protect it."

"Small wonder, after growing up in such a bloody time."

"Perhaps. Changing the world isn't as easy as it sounds." He grimaced. "We were trying to do some good in Spain. Joseph Bonaparte isn't a bad man. But the Spaniards wanted us the hell out of their country." He glanced at the arch again. "I can't say I blame them."

Emma laid her hand on his arm.

Robert sucked in his breath. The muscles in his arm went taut beneath her fingers. "I don't think that's a good idea."

Emma snatched her hand back. She had been a fool to let herself be lulled by a few tranquil moments. She had taken Robert into her body and let him glimpse her soul.

Friendship between them was impossible. And after what he had done, anything more was unthinkable.

She fixed her gaze on a nearby stall. It contained engravings, but not the views of Paris and copies of the old masters she had seen elsewhere. These pictures showed men and women in a variety of positions. Some roused disquieting memories. Others seemed physically impossible. She had heard of such pictures, but she had never seen them, let alone seen them boldly displayed in broad daylight.

She was acutely aware of Robert. Though she could not bring herself to look at him, she was sure he had noticed the pictures as well. Her thin, light dress felt hot and tight against her skin. Her hands turned clammy and her face burned, not because of the pictures but because of the memories they evoked: the light of the peat fire flickering against Robert's sweat-drenched skin; the feel of his lips against her hair as he carried her to his bed; the look in his eyes when he entered her body.

He lied to you, she reminded herself. He used you. But her anger was a poor defense against the heat raging through her. She heard a ragged breath and was not sure if the sound came from Robert or herself.

"We French take great pride in being frank about these matters." Robert's voice was thick, yet it held a trace of the familiar humor.

If he could do it, so could she. "At least now when I'm asked how Paris differs from Edinburgh, I shall know what to say."

They moved beneath the arch into the Boulevard Saint Martin. They did not speak or even look at each other until Robert stopped abruptly. "Here we are."

They had at last reached Mrs. Mercer's. Mr. Mercer proved to be a linen draper with a smart establishment. As in Edinburgh, the family quarters were above the shop. After a few inquiries of a young man who proved to be the Mercers' grandson, they were led upstairs to a sitting room filled with floral chintz and earthenware figurines. Mrs. Mercer, a plump, well-dressed lady, greeted them warmly, saying she was delighted to meet any friends of John's and that it was a great treat to have another Englishwoman to talk to. Scottish, was she? Well, that was very nearly the same. She insisted on serving them tea. "For I know how hard it is to get a really good cup of tea in Paris," she said, hovering over what was plainly her best china.

It was some minutes before they could explain the reason for their visit. "But what a romantic story," Mrs. Mercer exclaimed. "And how kind of you to take an interest, my dear," she said to Emma. "Most young women would wish to hear nothing at all of a first wife."

Emma choked on the tea. Robert set down his cup. "I fear you are mistaken. Mrs. Blair is my wife's cousin. That is the extent of our relationship."

"Oh, dear." Mrs. Mercer twitched her skirt into place. "How silly of me. But naturally I assumed— That is, you seemed so—" She reached up to pat her cap. "Not that it's any business of mine, of course. I do run on so." She tucked a curl into place. "You'll be wanting to look at my father's trunks. I was afraid it was sentimental of me to keep all his things, but now I'm very glad I did."

Mr. Barnes's belongings were neatly stacked in a low-ceilinged attic room with dormer windows looking out on the building opposite. Apologizing profusely for the dust, Mrs. Mercer glanced around the room and at last indicated a trunk resting beneath several boxes and crates.

When Robert had freed the trunk and opened its rusting lock, Mrs. Mercer was proved right. The trunk contained her father's papers. With a tact that surprised Emma, she said she would leave them to go through the records in private. "But are you sure you don't want to leave this to Mr. Lescaut, dear?" she asked Emma.

"You're sure to dirty that lovely white dress. If only the attics were kept cleaner. But it's hard enough seeing that the servants do a decent job downstairs."

Emma assured Mrs. Mercer that they would do very well. Her dress was the least of her worries. When the door closed behind their hostess, Emma knelt beside Robert. The trunk had the musty smell of the past. They lifted out bundles of yellowed letters tied up with buff-colored ribbon, an account book, a Bible. Emma opened this last. On the inside cover she found records of marriages and births for Barnes's own family but not for anyone else.

"Emma." There was an odd note in Robert's voice.

Emma closed the Bible and looked up at him. He held out a book bound in faded brown kid. On the inside cover, in the same neat hand Emma had seen in the Bible, was written *Record of ceremonies performed by Christopher Barnes during his residence in Paris.*

"It's your family." Robert offered her the book. "You look."

Emma shook her head. "She was your wife."

A moment of silent acknowledgment passed between them. Emma leaned forward, straining to see but trying not to brush against him. The dates in the book started in the 1770s. Robert flipped through the neatly ruled pages until he reached 1782.

The Blair name leapt off the page and knocked the breath from Emma's lungs. *July 20, 1782, married, Thomas Blair of Blair House, Midlothian, Scotland, to Lucilla Lauder of Lauder Hall, Midlothian, Scotland.*

"David was right," Robert said.

Emma swallowed. "We should go to Angus at once. If he didn't know of the marriage, he should be the first to learn the truth. And if he did know—" Her fingers clenched with fury on behalf of the cousin who had been robbed of her heritage. "God help me, if he did know, I'll never forgive him."

Angus stared down at the page that recorded the marriage of his elder brother. His eyes were dark with pain, his mouth set in a grim line. But nothing in his expression told of surprise. Fear knotted Emma's stomach. All the suspicions she had not allowed herself to voice rose in her throat in a burst of fury. "How could you?" She stared at her uncle across the ebony-inlaid table in Jenny's salon where the book was laid out. "How could you see your brother's daughter branded a bastard?"

"I didn't know," Angus whispered, still staring at the page.

Emma leaned across the table and seized the lapels of his coat. "Don't lie to me, Uncle. There's been too much of that already."

Angus's bushy brows drew together. His chin jutted out. "Are ye calling me a liar, Niece?"

"You knew." Emma's fingers tightened on the wool of his coat. "It's written in your face. Couldn't you bear to have a child with Lauder blood in your house? In God's name, she was all that was left of your brother. Would you have done the same to me if my mother had been a Lauder? Would you—"

"Emma, no." Robert grasped her by the shoulders and pulled her back.

Emma whirled around in his grasp. "You believe him?"

"I think we must let him have his say."

"There's nothing more *to* say. I've told ye. I didn't know." Angus's voice had risen, but there was a hollow sound to it, as though he spoke loudly to hide his lack of conviction. "What the devil is this, Emma? Would ye take Lescaut's side over mine?"

Emma was trembling. She glanced at Robert, then

looked back at the man who had raised her. "Yes." Her breath came quick and hard. "In this case I would."

"God's blood, ye're as bad as Arabel. I don't know what's happened to the women in this family."

"Barnes must have given your brother and Lucilla marriage lines, sir," Robert said. "Do you have any idea what became of them?"

Angus looked at Robert as though seeing him for the first time. "None. Perhaps Thomas destroyed them."

"And bastardized his only child? No." Emma stared at her uncle. "I think he was waiting until his father's illness was over to break the news to the family. The papers would have been among his things. You would have found them after his death."

"And I tell ye I didn't. What does a man have to do to be believed?"

"Tell the truth."

"Oh, for the love of God." Angus took an impatient turn about the room. "My brother was married to Lucilla. Ye've shown me the proof. I don't argue with it. I won't deny David what's due him as my brother's legitimate grandson. That should be the end of the matter."

"I'm afraid not." Robert was standing very still, his eyes on Angus. "There's the question of my wife's murder."

Angus's eyes hardened. "I said I wouldn't deny David what's due him. I can make a braw settlement on the lad. But not if this meddling continues."

Emma felt Mrs. Mercer's tea rise up in her throat. She gripped the back of a chair to keep her legs from buckling under her. "You'd stop us from learning who killed Lucie?"

"I'd have ye not stir up matters that are best left alone." Angus sounded as defensive as a wounded animal. And as dangerous.

"Why?" Emma took a step forward. "What are you

afraid of, Uncle? Do you know who killed her?" Her voice rose to a sob. "Did you do it yourself?"

The color drained from Angus's face. He sank into a giltwood chair and stared at Emma as though he had been dealt a mortal blow.

Emma rushed forward and dropped down on the floor beside him. "I don't want to believe it." She gripped his hands. "I can't believe it of the man I've loved as a father all my life. But you have to tell us the truth."

"It has to stop." Angus sounded like a man pushed to the breaking point.

"Yes," Emma said. "No more lies."

"The questions have to stop. Ye don't know—" Angus pulled his hands away and pressed them to his temples. Emma had never seen such a look of torment on her uncle's face.

Robert's firm steps sounded against the parquet floor as he crossed the room to stand beside them. "Whatever it is, it would be better for Emma and me to know."

Angus looked at him in silence for a moment. "I could never bring myself to see her. What did she look like?"

"Very much like Emma." Robert's voice was surprisingly gentle. How strange, Emma thought, that she should be the one roused to fury, while Robert was able to feel compassion for her uncle.

Angus nodded his head slowly. "If ye knew the truth, ye wouldn't want it to go beyond the walls of this room."

"Tell us," Emma said, "and let us judge."

Angus looked down at her, then turned to Robert as if seeking confirmation that this was his only way out. Robert said nothing.

"All right," Angus said. "If this is what it takes, so be it. But I want your word the story will go no further."

"You can't—" Emma began.

"Very well," Robert said.

Angus stared down at his hands. Emma felt the weight

of the silence in the small room. The ticking of the porcelain clock on the mantel grated against her raw nerves.

"What I told ye two days ago was true, as far as it went," Angus said. "I suspected there'd been something between Thomas and Lucilla, but when Thomas came home I didn't know they'd been married. I certainly didn't know anything of a bairn. Our father was failing fast by that time. One day he called Thomas and me in to see him. Not James or Gavin or Mother, just his two eldest sons. He said he had something to tell us. He said someone in the family had to know."

Angus stared at the windows on the other side of the room as though he could see the past through the pale blue silk of the curtains. "Never understood *Romeo and Juliet* myself. But the forbidden is fair bewitching to some. Arabel and Charlie. Thomas and Lucilla. It must have been the same for my father and Lady Lauder."

Emma drew back, swallowing the implication of his words. "Your father. You mean—"

"They were lovers." Angus looked down at her, back to his usual blunt speaking. "Or they had been, some twenty years before, while old Lord Lauder was fishing in the Highlands. That's what Father wanted to tell us. Lucilla Lauder was his daughter."

It was a moment before Emma understood. She could not speak. For all her fears, nothing had prepared her for this. She turned to Robert as though he could make sense of it. Robert gripped her shoulder, but he was looking at Angus.

Angus met Robert's gaze. "Ye ken now, don't ye? Lucie was legitimate, aye. In a monstrous way. Her parents were brother and sister."

22

Incest. The word conjured images of something dark and shameful, the unimaginable, the unforgivable. "They couldn't have known," Emma murmured, pushing away the horror of what her uncle had said. "It wasn't their fault."

"That doesn't matter." Angus's voice took on a bitter tone. "In the sight of God and man . . ."

"An abomination." Fragments of sermons heard in childhood flooded her memory. Transgression. Unrighteousness. Sin and redemption. "Thomas," she whispered, remembering the stories of his death. "It wasn't an accident."

"He killed himself. He was my brother, but God forgive him, he was a weak man. He couldn't bear the knowledge of what he had done. See here, lass, ye've got to know it all. The fault may lie with me. I suspected he'd been hankering after Lucilla, but when we heard what Father told us I said nothing and neither did he. I thought perhaps I'd been wrong, but then Thomas took his life and I knew there'd been something between him and Lucilla. I didn't know about the marriage, not 'til I'd gone through his papers. When I found the record I burned it. It was another month before I heard about the bairn."

And knowing she was Thomas's daughter, Angus had denied her her rightful place in the family. Emma could not forgive him that. "It was a cruel thing you did, Uncle."

"Was it?" The color flooded back into Angus's face. "Get up, lass. Don't stay on your knees before me." He stood and gave Emma his hand to help her rise. "Let me tell you how it was—you too, Lescaut—and then damn me if ye will."

Emma stepped back and found herself standing near Robert. She looked from one man to the other, torn by divided loyalties and a sense of outraged justice.

"I did what I could for the child," Angus went on, his tone both angry and pleading. "She was innocent enough, but I couldn't take her into our house. She would have been a curse upon us, Em. Old Lord Lauder knew that Lucilla wasn't his child, and he knew who her father was. That's why things got so bad between our families."

Emma remembered the present Lord Lauder saying he didn't know why relations between his father and Angus's had worsened. She wondered if her grandfather had seduced Lauder's wife out of passion or a desire to settle accounts with his old rival.

Angus began once more to pace the floor. "Lauder never liked Lucilla much. He didn't try very hard to find her when she ran off. Lady Lauder was distraught, but he wouldn't let her say a word about the girl. He suspected Lucilla had gone away with a man, and that put her beyond the pale."

"You didn't dare bring Lucie up in your house." Robert spoke for the first time since Angus had told his story. "You thought old Lord Lauder would guess the truth, that sooner or later he'd see the resemblance, that he'd know Lucilla had lain with her brother." He paused and looked at Angus. "Lord Lauder might have been angry or shocked enough to make the incest public. Is that what you feared?"

"But Lucie was innocent," Emma cried. "She was a child."

Angus took a step toward her. "Think, lass. There would have been blood for sure, and we'd had enough blood between our families. I did what I had to and kept the peace as best I could." He fixed them with a fierce stare. "And I'll keep it still, d'ye hear? I've told ye what I swore to tell no other living person, and I'll not have it go a mite further."

"I gave you my word," Robert said. "It won't go beyond this room."

"No," Emma said, surprised by the certainty of her conviction. "No, Uncle, there's one person who deserves to know. You must tell Lord Lauder."

"Before God I will not. Not Matthew Lauder. Not him above all."

"Yes, above all. He's Lucilla's brother, he has a right to know. You've tried to keep the peace, but now you must make peace in earnest. Face the past together. Put it behind you. The secrets have only festered."

"No." Angus shook his head like an animal at bay. "No," he said again, his tone less certain. He turned away and stumbled to the window. He spread his hands against the frame as though to support his weight, and pressed his head against the glass. Emma would have gone to him, but Robert drew her back. Angus did not seem to notice when they left the room.

They walked to the Rue du Faubourg Saint Honoré to collect Kirsty and David. So much had happened since they had left the children with Caroline that morning. Emma felt bruised by what she had learned: her grandfather's criminal folly; Lucilla's wasteful death; Thomas's tragic end; Angus's pain and deceit. She was grateful for Robert's silence.

She had been convinced that Lucie posed no threat to the Blairs. But Lucie had been a danger, at least to Angus, who had sworn to keep her parentage a secret. It was unlikely that Lucie had learned of her parents' marriage, but it would have been easy enough for her to trace her connection to the Blairs, as Robert had done. Suppose she had written Angus, wanting to be acknowledged. What would he have done?

He might have come to France to meet her. Or he might have sent Gavin. Or he might have turned to one of the younger members of the family. He would not have intended to kill her. He would have wanted only to buy her off. But there might have been a quarrel, and in that quarrel . . .

"Robert," Emma said, "when did Lucie die?"

"Four years ago this October. The twenty-seventh." He did not seem surprised by her question. He must have guessed the direction of her thoughts.

Emma forced herself to put her fears into words. "I can't believe that's the answer, but you have to know where they were. Angus and the others. You have to know who could have come to France in October of 1811."

She waited for him to speak. He said nothing. She glanced at him. His face was austere, his eyes preoccupied. She turned away, struggling with her memories. "I remember that time. Allan had been home for three months, convalescing from his wounds. He went back to the Peninsula on All Hallows Eve. He'd been away from home the week before. Neil had business in Dundee and Allan went with him." She did not add that she'd been furious with her husband for leaving her in the last few days they had together. Nor did she say that she'd always suspected the trip was an excuse for something else Allan wanted to do.

"Emma," Robert said, "you don't have to—"

"Oh, but I do."

They were nearing the Durwards' house. Emma looked about her, surprised that they had come so far. She had not been conscious of her surroundings. Grateful that they were walking and she did not have to look at Robert, she forced herself to continue. "If Lucie sent a letter to the Blairs, it would have gone to Angus. He was away the last week in October too. He went to Yorkshire, to see about selling some sheep, and returned just before Allan left."

"It doesn't have to be Angus."

"No, he could have sent someone. Allan or Neil. Or both of them. Or Jamie, he was stationed in London at the time. Not Will, he was in the Peninsula. Nor Andy, he would have been too young. Angus could have sent Bram. Bram traveled a lot, but I don't know where he was at that time. Or he could have sent Gavin. I don't know where he was either."

"Lucie could have written to Lord Lauder," Robert said. "Lucilla's brother."

He was offering her a smoke screen of comfort. She wouldn't take that way out. "I think not. Lucie might have learned her father was a Blair. The ring has the Blair badge. I don't think she could have guessed that her mother was a Lauder." She stopped and turned to face him, her words both demand and accusation. "You have to know about us, Robert. You have to know where we were, what we might have done. You have to turn us inside out. And then . . ." *Then,* she wanted to say, *you'll know that a Blair could never have committed that brutal act of passion.* But she could not speak the words because she was no longer certain they were true.

She turned away and stared at the houses on the other side of the street. She did not know what Robert would do when he found his wife's assassin, what vengeance he would exact. It could be someone she loved. She had to prove that it was not, but even if it was she had to know. Only she could not bear what would follow.

She turned back to Robert and tightened the ribbons on her bonnet. "I'll do what I can. Bram's gone to visit some property that once belonged to his family, but he'll be home the day after tomorrow. I'll see him then. There may be something he can tell us."

Emma set her book down for the third time. She could not force her mind to focus on the words. She looked across the small salon at Arabel, who sat at the clavichord, picking at the keys. "Perhaps we should have gone to the theater with Sherry and the boys."

"No." Arabel looked up from the clavichord. "I wanted to stay here." She got to her feet and moved about the room, straightening a stack of periodicals, adjusting a vase of roses.

Emma swung her feet down from the sofa and picked up her coffee, which had grown cold. She could say nothing of the scene with Angus to Arabel. And so she could say nothing of her hopes that it would smooth the way for Arabel and Charlie's marriage.

The silence was broken by the opening of the door. The one footman Sherry employed stepped into the room. "Lieutenant Lauder and Colonel Lescaut."

"Oh, thank goodness, I thought you'd never get here." Arabel ran to the door and pulled both men past the footman, who discreetly withdrew. She kissed Charlie full on the mouth and hugged Robert, then turned to Emma, one arm around each man. "I asked Charlie to bring Robert here tonight. I haven't had a chance to thank him for what he did for Will. Or to tell him how glad I am that he's part of the family."

Robert looked across the salon at Emma, his eyes holding memories of the afternoon. "I'll go if you like."

"Nonsense." Emma got to her feet. She had kicked off her slippers when she stretched out on the sofa. Rather than go through the undignified business of hunting for them, she stood there in her stocking feet. "Please sit down."

Arabel dragged Charlie to a settee and looked pointedly at the empty space next to Emma on the sofa. Instead Robert moved to a chair separated from the sofa by a low table. It didn't matter. She was as aware of him as if his flesh were pressed against her own.

"Father told me about Aunt Lucilla." Charlie sat on the settee, his fingers entwined with Arabel's. "It's the only civilized conversation we've had since he came to Paris. I was daft not to notice that young David has the Lauder coloring."

Robert crossed his legs. "We've all been daft one way or another, Charlie."

The words were barely out of his mouth when the door opened again. Angus strode into the room, Lord Lauder close on his heels.

Arabel and Charlie sprang to their feet, hands locked.

Angus stopped and ran his gaze over Charlie. "Might have known we'd find you here. No need to look so fierce, Bel. I won't lay hands on the lad. Much as he may deserve it. Lescaut, what are you doing here?"

"Arabel asked him to call." Emma gave Robert a look indicating she didn't want him to leave. Once again he was her ally in the face of family chaos. "Will you take coffee, Uncle? Lord Lauder?"

Angus swung toward her. His blustery manner did not conceal his drawn face and the pain in his eyes. "A dram of whisky wouldn't go amiss."

Emma moved to the bell rope and gave it a tug. "You'll have to make do with good French brandy."

"Ah, well." Angus threw himself into the largest chair

in the room and gestured Lauder to another. "I daresay it warms the belly."

Emma gave the footman instructions, then returned to the sofa. She met Robert's gaze. His eyes glinted with acknowledgment. For a moment they were friends again, sharing an appreciation of the absurd, unpredictable tangle of Blairs and Lauders.

They sat in silence while the footman came and the brandy was poured. Angus passed the glass beneath his nose, inhaling deeply, and took a long swallow. He sighed and the color came back into his face. When the footman closed the door behind him, he raised his glass again and looked at Arabel and Charlie. "May your bairn bring peace to our houses."

Arabel stared at him, her armor shattered. Then she sprang to her feet and threw her arms around her father, laughing and sobbing at once. "Here now," Angus said, "ye've gone and spilled the brandy."

The smell permeated the room. Angus brushed his hand over his coat. Arabel pushed his hand aside and scrubbed the damp out with her handkerchief. "I'll pour you another glass, Da. And if it's a boy, I'll name him after you." She jumped off his lap and ran to get the decanter.

Emma found herself looking at Robert. He smiled back at her. The unexpected dimple appeared in his cheek. His gaze echoed her joy for Arabel and Charlie. But his eyes glowed with something more, something she would almost have called yearning. She drew a breath, clenched and unclenched her hands, and moved to a chair by Lord Lauder. His face was drawn, like her uncle's, and he had the same pained and puzzled expression in his eyes. "We have you to thank for this," she said.

"And your uncle's own good sense. He told me everything, and I doubt there was a harder thing the man ever did in his life. God help us all, he's lived with the tale over thirty years. I heard it an hour ago, and I think I'll never be the same again."

"Are matters then mended between you?"

Lauder gave her a sad, sweet smile. "Ah, well, we've been set to sail in the same boat. We're together in this, he and I, both in the telling and in keeping the secret." He gave a sudden frown. "It is a secret, is it not? My mother's folly."

"What folly?" Emma looked him square in the eye. "I know of none."

"Ah, you're a good lass, Emma Blair." His gaze moved to Robert.

Robert got to his feet and walked over to Lauder. "I heard as little as Mrs. Blair."

"Thank you, Lescaut." Lauder set his glass down on a nearby table. "We acknowledge the marriage, of course." His lips curved in what might pass for a smile. "Angus was shocked that he had never known about it. It's better that we say so, don't you think? Angus is grateful to you both for finding the record."

Emma glanced across the room. Charlie was shaking Angus's hand. "How did you persuade him to agree to this marriage?"

"Our families have tangled with each other in all the wrong ways. It's time we were properly connected."

"Then the feud is over?"

He looked from her to Robert with a wry expression and shook his head. "Now that would be too much to expect, wouldn't it, lass? But I daresay we've damped it down for a while."

"Arabel's already planning the wedding," Emma told Robert and his mother the next morning. She had brought Kirsty to visit David. While the children helped

Paul in the shop below, Emma sat above with Robert and Anne Lescaut.

Anne poured Emma a fresh cup of coffee. "You must be very happy for your cousin. When will the marriage take place?"

"In a week's time, when Charlie can get two or three days' leave. It will be very quiet. The family and a few friends." Emma turned to Robert. "We hope you can come."

"A generous invitation. Charlie's asked me to be his groomsman. I told him I didn't think that would be wise."

For in Robert's eyes the Blairs still stood accused. Emma pulled her shawl closer about her shoulders, chilled despite the warmth of the sun spilling through the windows. She kept her voice bright. "But you must. Arabel depends on it, and on her wedding day she will have her own way."

Robert smiled and threw his hands wide in a gesture of surrender. At the same moment the door opened and Adam Durward came into the room. Anne kissed him on the cheek and poured him a cup of coffee.

Adam stared down into the cup, then looked up at Robert. "I think you should leave Paris."

Beyond a slight narrowing of his eyes, Robert showed no particular concern. Nor did his mother, who returned the enameled coffeepot to the table and said, "You'd better tell us about it, Adam."

"The king has just issued a set of Royal Ordinances listing persons who are to be proscribed. Banishment for some. Execution for others." Adam set down his cup. "General de La Bédoyère is on the list for execution. So is General Lavalette. The list is headed by Marshal Ney."

Anne Lescaut gave a gasp of outrage. Robert's mouth tightened, but he said nothing at all. "Is Robert on the list?" Emma asked.

"No," Adam said, acknowledging the fear she had not

troubled to keep from her voice. "But this may be only the beginning. Robert was high enough placed in the army to catch the government's attention." He turned to Robert and Anne. "It should be no surprise. The Royalists want their revenge. They think the king has been too soft on his enemies and they're furious because none of them has been named to the cabinet."

"We've heard," Anne said. "There've been riots in the south."

"Worse than that. There are bands of Royalists attacking and killing anyone they suspect of Bonapartist sympathies. They're even going after Protestants. The Comte d'Artois and his followers are demanding a purge of traitors in the army and the civil administration. The king has been forced to act. Wellington is urging moderation, but Liverpool has sent him word that the British government want a severe example to be made of the conspirators who brought Bonaparte out of exile. Fouché, to his credit, has already warned many of the men who have been accused."

Emma shook her head in bewilderment. Too much had happened since she arrived in Paris. She had scarcely read the newspapers. She could not understand what Robert had to do with the Comte d'Artois, the king's brother, or with Fouché, the Minister of Police.

Robert blew on the steam from his coffee. "They'll get at the generals. I'm a lowly colonel."

Adam leaned forward, his hands clasped loosely between his knees. "You were an intelligence officer. You were on Ney's staff and Ney is going to be brought down. The Ultra Royalists want victims and anyone will do. King Louis is more temperate and he's surrounded himself with moderate men, but he has no choice. You're a brave man, Robert. You're not a stupid one. The situation is fluid. People are irrational. My God, you grew up during the Terror, you know that well enough. You should leave Paris before you find yourself in the Conciergerie."

Emma stared at Adam. "They'd put him in prison? For fighting on the losing side?"

"For being a traitor."

"I took no oath to Louis," Robert said.

Adam shrugged. "They could shoot you anyway."

Emma looked from Adam to Robert. They might be discussing racing results or the stakes in a prizefight. How could Adam? It was Robert's life that was at stake. She turned to Anne Lescaut, who sat white-faced and composed, staring at her son. "Say something," Emma said.

Anne continued to look at her son. "I've always trusted Robert's judgment."

"I'll leave when I must." Robert turned to Adam and gave a twisted smile. "But not yet. I have things to do. And a wedding to attend."

Emma beat her fists on her lap while Robert walked to the door with Adam and closed it behind them. When they were gone, she ran to the window and looked out into the street below. After a moment Robert and Adam emerged from the print shop and made their way down the street, their heads together in earnest conversation. When she could see them no longer, she turned back to Robert's mother. "How can you be so calm?"

Anne Lescaut looked as though she had shed all the tears in the world and could cry no more. "We're used to danger in this house. Robert learned long ago how to judge risks."

"But you could lose him."

Anne gave her a long searching look. "And so could you. Is that the problem?"

Emma could not trust herself to speak. A sob rose in her throat and she thrust it back. She turned away, afraid to see the understanding in the other woman's eyes.

"I've lost one son," Anne went on.

Emma swung around. She saw the residue of despair on Anne's face. She returned to her chair and clasped Anne's hands in her own.

"It's all right," Anne said. "It's been nearly ten years and I can talk about it." She was silent for a moment, her gaze on the peeling plaster on the cornice, though she seemed to be seeing beyond it. But when she spoke, her voice held its customary calm. "Edouard was my youngest. He was just eighteen when he joined the army. Robert and Paul were going, and he couldn't bear to be left behind. The three of them intended to transform the world. Gerard—my husband—was furious. He had no use for war. He believed in reason, in the power of the word. The young men wouldn't listen. There'd been too much talk, they said, it was time to act." She paused. "Perhaps they were right. Youth is a time for action. Yet I think part of what they longed for was adventure."

Emma understood. Jamie and Will had thrived in the army. Allan had found it a refuge from domestic life. "Did they stay together?"

"Until Austerlitz. Edouard was killed there. Paul was wounded badly and left the army. He came home and went to work for Gerard."

Emma thought of the carnage on the battlefield near Waterloo, of the senseless waste war made of men's lives. "And Robert?"

"He was already an intelligence officer. Paul and Edouard were fighting in the lines. Robert found them on the field after the battle." Anne's fingers clenched convulsively around Emma's own. "Paul had flung himself over Edouard to protect him and nearly lost his own life in the process. I don't think Robert's ever forgiven himself for coming through unscathed."

His brother and then his wife. It was a heavy burden to carry. "Is that why he won't leave Paris?" Emma said.

Anne had no trouble following her thoughts. "He can't give it up. He couldn't protect Lucie any more than he could protect Edouard. But Lucie at least can be avenged." She hesitated, searching Emma's face. "Do you care so much?"

"It's my family he has accused."

"Yet you love him."

Emma looked at the well-scarred wood of the sitting room door. "I thought I did."

They sat in silence for a time while Emma thought how restful it was in Anne Lescaut's company and how quickly she had opened her heart to a woman she scarcely knew. Anne Lescaut had the same ability to elicit confidences as her son. Emma wondered how a woman could leave her country and give herself to a man and a way of life that was foreign to everything she had known, how she could stay with him when her own country and his were at war. "It must have been difficult, living here in France," she said.

"We weren't at war when I first came here. Not that it would have mattered. A woman does things for love she would never dream were possible in the cold light of reason." Anne smiled. "All too often she finds she has been chasing an illusion. But not in my case. Gerard Lescaut was a giant of a man. I've never regretted my choice."

It was too simple, this calm certainty. "Don't you miss your home?" Emma asked. "Don't you ever think of going back to England?"

Anne shook her head. "I have no family in England anymore. My life is here. This is my son's country, and my grandson's, and it has long been my own."

Emma studied the other woman. Surely there was more to it than that. Anne Lescaut, née Anne Melton, had left her Devon home and followed her heart, never once turning back. Emma wondered why it was so important that she understand. Their situations were different.

She was bound to her family by ties too strong to break. Even if she were not, Robert had told her too many lies. There could be nothing between them. "I should go," she said, standing abruptly.

Anne held out her hands. "Whatever happens, my dear, I wish you well."

Emma pressed Anne's hands, left the room, and ran down the stairs. When she reached the ground floor, she paused and drew a breath to compose herself before she faced her daughter and David.

She found them bent over a table at the rear of the print shop. The boy who helped in the shop was hanging news sheets on lines to dry. He smiled at her. Kirsty looked up in dismay. "Please, Mama, just a few minutes more."

Emma did not have the heart to tear her away. She walked back to the front of the shop and saw Robert and Paul standing near the door in earnest conversation. She moved aside. "Don't go," Robert said. "Paul has a story you'll want to hear."

Emma walked toward the two men, adjusting her shawl to armor herself against Robert's smile and Paul's barbs. Paul was patient and gentle with the children. His bitter tongue, she suspected, hid a world of pain, but he did not even try to mask the censure in his eyes when he looked at her and Robert.

At this moment, however, he was wholly intent on his disclosure. "Not a story," he said. "A rumor. The town's full of them. This one's about Philippe de Rivaud."

Lucie's lover. Emma glanced at Robert. His gaze was troubled, but whether because of the mention of Rivaud's name or something else, she could not tell.

"He lived quietly enough, he and his family," Paul went on. "He called himself Citizen Rivaud, and he was always respectful of the government, though he took no particular interest in politics. Now it's being said that quiet little Philippe was something of a hero. He was a courier for the dissident Royalist groups. It's also said his death was not the result of a simple robbery."

Emma started. "He was killed for his Royalist sympathies?"

"He was a spy." Paul was always blunt. "These things tend to get known, but no one suspected Rivaud. If he wasn't killed because he was too well dressed in a city where too many people are poor, someone betrayed him." Paul turned to Robert. "Who could have done it? Who would have known Rivaud well enough to guess his secret?"

Robert leaned against the doorjamb and folded his arms across his chest. "Philippe may not have been betrayed to the government." He turned to Emma. "Contrary to what you may think, we weren't barbarous enough to knife our enemies in the street. They weren't that important." He turned back to Paul. "Philippe might have been killed by someone he thought of as a friend. At a guess, I'd say Georges Demaire."

Paul snorted. "Demaire hasn't the courage to attack another man."

"But money enough to pay someone to do it for him."

"Demaire?" Emma looked from one cousin to the other, unwilling to be ignored.

Paul turned to her as though he had forgotten her presence. "A disaffected aristo. He came of age during the Terror. His family were killed, but he was left alone. Like Rivaud, he lived quietly. When Napoleon was exiled, Demaire attached himself to the Comte d'Artois. Now that the king is back Demaire has hopes of getting a government post. He's got d'Artois's patronage and the Royalists see him as a great patriot." Paul cocked a brow at Robert. "I don't know why. The man's an ambitious toadeater with no convictions of his own. What do they owe him?"

Robert gave a bitter smile. "Gratitude for past favors. Demaire was a Royalist spy."

Paul's brown eyes narrowed. "You're sure of that?"

"Oh, yes. Demaire had links with most of the dissident groups outside the capital, and he provided them with information about what went on in government circles in Paris. But he also sold information on Royalist activities to the Bonaparte government. He liked to hedge his bets."

Paul let out a low whistle. "How the devil did you hear that?"

"I got drunk with a lieutenant of grenadiers in Salamanca who'd worked in the Ministry of Police. They'd known Demaire was a Royalist agent for years and considered him at best a nuisance. Then the fool came to them and offered his services, claiming it was his duty as a loyal citizen. You're right, Paul, Demaire's sick with ambition. He doesn't care who prevails. He wants to stand well with the winning side."

Emma shivered, chilled by the amorality Robert seemed to take as a matter of course. Spying might be necessary if it served a cause one believed in, but to betray one's fellows was despicable. "You think Philippe de Rivaud knew about Demaire's activities and threatened to expose him?"

Robert gave her an appraising look, no longer her opponent or her former lover but a fellow conspirator. "It's a possibility. They knew each other. They both frequented Henriette Colbert's salon."

"Then they both knew Lucie," Emma said. She saw in Robert's eyes that she had startled him. He did not want to admit to what was blindingly obvious to her. "It's important," she insisted. "If Rivaud suspected Demaire was betraying the Royalists, he would have told Lucie." *They were intimate,* she wanted to say, *lovers tell these things to each other,* but he could work that out as well as she, and she did not want to wound him further. "And if Lucie knew, she would have been as great a threat to Demaire as Rivaud was. Demaire could have arranged for her death as well."

She did not say, *See, it was not the Blairs,* but that thought, triumphant, was uppermost in her mind. It could not be one of her own family. Please God, let Robert see it too.

"You have a devious mind, Mrs. Blair." Paul's eyes had softened with what she would almost call appreciation. "It's a quality we value in this family."

Emma stepped into the entrance hall of Bram's house in the Rue d'Anjou. Despite yesterday's revelations about Philippe Rivaud, she still had to learn what she could of her family's whereabouts on the day Lucie was killed.

"Emma, how splendid." Jenny looked over the banister to the hall below. "The children have been driving me to distraction. Thank goodness we left the older boys at school or I never could have stood it. I don't know how you manage to be so clever with them. I'm longing for real company."

"I came to see Bram." Emma climbed the stairs, feeling the familiar bite of shame as she faced her cousin.

"He's out. So are Papa and Neil. But Bram will be back soon. Is it business?"

"In a way."

Jenny made a little grimace of distaste. "Come in, come in, I have so much to tell you."

They entered a small salon at the back of the house that Jenny had appropriated as her own. The windows were thrown open, the muslin curtains fluttering in a soft breeze that carried the scent of heliotrope from the garden below. Jenny pulled Emma to the sofa. Her eyes were bright, her cheeks flushed with excitement. "It's happened, Em. The government said it couldn't be done, but they've done it anyway. They've promised to give back Bram's father's estates. Most of them, at least. Some gifts of land were made which can't be rescinded."

Emma hugged her cousin. "I'm so glad for you, Jenny. Both of you." Bram had been petitioning the Bourbon government for the past year to recover the estates that had been confiscated during the Terror.

"And Bram can resume his title. The Comte de Martin. How does that sound?"

Emma laughed. "A little grand for Edinburgh."

"Oh, we won't use the title at home. But I think it's rather agreeable all the same. It means we'll come here often." Jenny paused for breath. "It *is* nice to have a bit of property."

"Bram is fortunate to have succeeded when so many other exiled aristocrats failed. Whatever made the government change their collective minds?"

"They had to acknowledge what he'd done for them." Jenny pushed back one of the red-blond ringlets falling in an elegant cascade about her face. "It was only fair."

"Done for them?"

"Oh!" Jenny clapped her hands over her mouth. "I didn't mean to tell you. I promised I wouldn't say anything about it. But you're family and it's all over now and I don't know why I should keep silent. I'm quite proud of Bram."

Emma pulled off her gloves. She needed a moment to absorb this new glimpse into the life of her cousin's husband. She had once thought she knew Bram better than anyone. "I'm sure you are, but why? Was he connected with the Royalist groups here?"

"Oh, yes, all those families know one another." Jenny waved a careless, well-manicured hand. "When it was clear the Peace of Amiens wouldn't last, Bram volunteered his services to the British government. He traveled to France many times, in great secrecy of course, and carried messages between the British and the aristos. But most of the time he tried to pick up information about what the Bonapartists were doing. I fear it was very dangerous, though he always assured me it was not."

"And you kept quiet all this time." Emma did not know if she was more startled by the revelation of Bram's activities or by the fact that Jenny had managed to keep them secret. In her youth Jenny had blurted out every passing thought.

Jenny gave a smile of pure satisfaction. "Oh, I've learned how to keep secrets."

Emma drew back against the sofa cushions, trying to make sense of this new image of Bram. "Did he come to Paris?" She wondered if Bram, who had met Lucie in Edinburgh, had ever seen her in the French capital.

"I think so, though he didn't tell me much. Sometimes he'd only go to the coast."

Lucie had gone to the coast to meet someone from across the Channel. Emma saw again the image she had carried with her ever since Robert had told her the story—the dingy room in a waterfront inn, the blood-drenched woman lying on the floor. Not Bram. It could not be Bram.

But Bram provided a link between Edinburgh and Paris. Bram had known Lucie in her last days in Scotland. Could she have turned to him for help? Could he have brought her to Paris? Or—Emma drew a sharp breath—could he have done more? "Jenny," Emma said. "Did Bram have people working for him in Paris?"

"I don't know." Jenny looked as though the question had never occurred to her. "I suppose he must. Someone must have been supplying him with information."

Emma forced herself to follow her thoughts to their logical conclusion. She remembered what David had said about his mother. *She had lots of secrets, and she didn't like people to know them.* Suppose Lucie had been working for Bram.

Suppose Robert's wife had been a British agent.

23

"Emma." Bram paused in the doorway, his face brightening.

"Oh, there you are, darling." Jenny got to her feet and shook out her flounced skirt. "Emma has something to talk to you about and I really must consult with Cook about dinner." She turned to Emma with a mock sigh. "Father and Neil are so fussy. We serve the best French food and they pine for boiled mutton and cock-a-leekie soup."

The door closed behind Jenny. Emma studied Bram. She felt as if she were looking at a stranger. "I understand I should congratulate you."

Bram smiled. "It's amazing what a well-placed bribe will do. Though God knows why I've been fortunate when so many other are still petitioning in vain."

"Not all the petitioners can claim the government are in their debt."

Bram's smile faded. He watched her closely but said nothing.

"Jenny told me," Emma said. "About your work for the British government."

"Ah." Bram seated himself in a chair near her own. "I should have known she wouldn't be able to keep it to herself. Believe me, it wasn't as exciting as it sounds."

Emma did not believe him. His work must have been dangerous, but it was like Bram to make light of the danger. She wondered that it had never occurred to her that he might be working for the British. He would not remain on the sidelines while his country was plunged into conflict. Any more than Robert had after Bonaparte escaped. "You made a great many trips to France," she said, twisting her gloves between her fingers.

"A number of them over the years, yes."

Her hands stilled. She looked at Bram. "Did you bring Lucie Sorel to France?"

There was a slight pause. Emma felt tension creep into the lazy heat of the day. "Why would I have done that?" Bram asked.

"Because she was unhappy and begged you to help her escape." Emma hesitated, watching him. "Because she spoke French like a native and you saw that she could help you in your work."

Bram raised his brows. "A girl of twenty?"

"Who better to charm young officers into betraying their secrets?"

Bram released his breath very slowly. His mouth curved in a faint smile. "Remarkable. If we'd had your assistance, Emma, Bonaparte would have fallen years sooner."

"That's it, isn't it?" Emma leaned forward. "Was Henriette Colbert working for you as well?"

Bram's eyes narrowed. "I didn't know you'd heard of Henriette."

"Colonel Lescaut took me to call on her three days ago."

"What did she tell you?"

"A great deal about Lucie. Nothing about spying."

"No, she wouldn't." Bram gave another faint smile. "Henriette has always been discreet." He shook his head. "It's no good lying to you, Em. You've guessed it almost exactly. Lucie couldn't bear the thought of marriage to Cullen. I was one of the few people she saw outside the school. She begged for my help. I thought of going to Angus, but he'd made it clear he never wanted to lay eyes on her. He viewed the marriage as a convenient way to see her settled. I was sure it would be a disaster."

"So you offered to take her to Paris."

Bram met her gaze. "I made it clear that there was some risk involved. Lucie was young but not a child. She decided for herself."

Emma could easily understand her cousin's choice. The lure of the foreign capital, the intoxicating promise of freedom, the sense that one was doing something useful with one's life. "Madame Colbert said she met Lucie at an inn outside Paris. But that isn't how it happened, is it? You took Lucie to her."

"I was already working with Henriette. She wanted to see the monarchy restored as much as I did, but she'd managed to keep her Royalist sympathies secret. Her salon was always full of young army officers and government officials. She conveyed the information she gathered to me and I took it back to Britain. I carried messages from our government, which Henriette passed along to Royalist contacts."

Bram paused. He had spoken of Henriette dispassionately, but Emma wondered if she was more to him than a fellow spy. She had always suspected there were other women in his life. He lived by his own code. Jenny, he had once told Emma, would not be hurt by what she did not know. Emma dug her nails into her palms, discomfited by the memory.

A carriage clattered by on the street outside, breaking the momentary quiet. "Fortunately, Henriette and Lucie took to each other at once," Bram went on. "Lucie was clever and she could draw out young men. Her information was invaluable to us."

Emma thought of Robert, no older than Charlie Lauder, captivated by her beautiful cousin. An enemy agent. "And after she married Colonel Lescaut? She still worked for you?"

"Of course. Lucie may have appeared flighty, but she was very dedicated."

"Then—" Emma swallowed, aware of an unpleasant taste in her mouth. "Their marriage was part of the deception?"

"I didn't ask Lucie to arrange it."

"She was expecting Colonel Lescaut's child."

"Yes, Henriette told me. I offered to help provide for the child, but marriage seemed the more sensible choice."

"A sensible choice? Bram, Colonel Lescaut loved her."

"And I believe she genuinely cared for him. But this wasn't a fairy tale, Em. Lucie knew that."

Emma stared at him. His eyes were as dark and hard as the black marble tiles in the entrance hall.

"Shocked?" Bram said. "Believe me, Lescaut would talk the same way were our situations reversed."

She knew this was true. She had seen how ruthless Robert could be. Somehow she had not expected the same from Bram.

Bram leaned back in his chair. "You're very fond of Lescaut, aren't you?"

Emma's face grew warm. She stared down at her cream-colored half boots, then forced herself to meet Bram's gaze. "His wife was my cousin. I want to know what happened to her."

"Don't lie to me, Em, I know you too well. I won't deny I'm jealous, but I know I have no claim on you."

Guilt rose up in her throat. "We have no claim on each other. We never could have."

"You have a Presbyterian conscience, my sweet." Bram crossed one leg over the other, elegant and controlled in his well-cut dark blue coat, his immaculate cravat, his tight-fitting breeches. He could not be more different from Robert's rough, raw energy. "Call me a blackguard, but I'm not sorry it happened. Can you say you are?"

"We committed a wrong. Against Jenny, against Allan. Against our own sense of honor."

Bram laughed. "You're a romantic, Em."

"No. I can't afford to be anymore." She had been when she met Bram. When she was fifteen and he was first courting Jenny, she had thought he was the most exciting man she had ever met. She had married Allan thinking he would grow to be like Bram. Or that she could turn him into such a man.

"We married the wrong people," Bram said. "What happened between us was inevitable."

"Perhaps. But a sin nonetheless." Emma still felt hot shame when she thought of those frenzied moments before the library fire. Yet she knew now that her single encounter with Bram had been as much an act of rebellion as of desire, rebellion against Allan and the restrictions of her life at Blair House. She and Bram had both been outsiders in the Blair family. Perhaps that was what had drawn them together.

Bram stood and looked down at her. "Well? Aren't you going to ask if I killed her?"

Emma flinched as though she had been struck. "Dear God, what's happening to us?"

"Not pretty, is it?" Bram bent over her, his arms on the chair, making her a prisoner. She had a sudden memory of the strength in those arms when they gripped her own as he drove into her body.

Bram looked straight into her eyes. "When it was too dangerous to travel to Paris, Lucie would meet me on the coast. We often met in Ostend, it was a convenient port for me to reach from Scotland. We may well have met at the same inn where she was murdered. But I didn't meet her that night. I didn't kill her."

Emma wound her gloves tight around her fingers. "I promised Colonel Lescaut I'd ask you where you were on the twenty-seventh of October in 1811."

"Good God, that's nearly four years ago." Bram stepped back. "Eighteen eleven . . . That was just before Allan went back to the Peninsula, wasn't it? I was in Scotland all that autumn."

"In Edinburgh?"

"Yes. No." He walked to the windows. "I spent the last two weeks of October visiting a client in Aberdeen. It was damned cold."

Emma released her breath. She did not know she'd been holding it. *I couldn't think it of you,* she wanted to say, but the words would be a lie. For a fleeting moment she had wondered, just as she had with Angus. "Lucie's last lover was a man named Philippe de Rivaud. He was working for the Royalists. Did you know him?"

"Oh, yes." Bram put up a hand to straighten his cravat. "Another tragic loss. He died shortly before Lucie."

"There are rumors that his death may not have been an accident."

"It's possible." Bram's voice was grim. "Philippe was something of a hothead. He may have grown careless."

"Lucie met a violent death less than two months after he died."

"You think there's a connection?"

"You've never wondered?"

"Of course I've wondered. Someone in the government could have learned of Lucie and Philippe's activities and arranged to get rid of both of them. But there was never any proof. Believe me, Philippe's friends tried to find it."

"Just as Robert did." Emma didn't realize she had used his given name until the words were out of her mouth.

She looked at Bram. "If I hadn't guessed, would you ever have told us the truth?"

"I don't know." Bram's gaze was direct and uncompromising. "I thought of it when Lescaut told us his story. But would it have eased his mind to know his wife was working for the enemy? Would it have helped David to know his parents were on opposite sides?"

Emma tugged on her gloves. "I don't know. But Robert will have to learn the truth now. I'll have to tell him."

Robert set down the pen and flexed his cramped fingers. The sunlight on the floorboards beyond his desk was tinged with afternoon shadows. He must have been writing longer than he realized. Strange how easy it had been once he forced himself to begin. He'd agreed at first only because Paul claimed he didn't have time to write the column for tomorrow's paper. But when he'd put pen to paper, Robert had found that something of his impassioned twenty-year-old self had survived the years of war and disillusionment and defeat.

He tugged at the collar of his shirt, unfastened in the afternoon heat, and stared down at the pages strewn in front of him. *Words,* he had once called them in contemptuous tones. Yet words remained a weapon when the Army of the Republic, which had become the Army of the Empire, was broken and scattered. He and Paul had joined the army together, full of the same hopes and ideals. But injury had sent Paul home and forced him to put his convictions down on paper, while Robert spent years in Spain, fighting a war in which morality was ground down to shifting sand.

He pushed his chair back from the desk and glanced around the study. It had been his father's and by rights should be Paul's now, but Paul had taken another room for his own use and carefully preserved this one for Robert's rare visits home. The room had changed little since his father's day. Worn bookcases filled with books that were even more worn lined the walls. Framed prints hung in the gaps between bookcases, classical reproductions and scenes from plays, not the sort he and Emma had seen near the Porte Saint Martin. His breathing quickened at the memory of what had passed between them in those moments. A gentleman and a man of honor would want Emma to be free of her feelings for him. But when he had realized Emma was as affected as he, he had felt a moment of fierce, exultant joy.

Forcing his thoughts in another direction, Robert looked from the prints to the sofa. It was covered in a velvet that had once been dark green. Now it was a mossy color that stirred memories of the Scottish countryside and Emma's eyes. Some years ago his mother had thrown a blanket over the sofa back to minimize the damage from the sun. Where the blanket had slipped, the older color was visible, dark against light, the past beside the present.

"Robert?"

It was Emma's voice, clear and vibrant. For a moment he thought he had imagined it. She called his name again and he sprang to his feet. He reached for his coat, then dropped it on the back of the chair. After everything that had passed between them, formality was ridiculous.

Emma had crossed the sitting room and was standing in the open doorway of the study. Robert felt an absurd rush of joy. She was wearing a dress the color of old parchment with a delicate pattern woven into the material. In the sunlight, the unlined fabric at the neck and sleeve turned to gauze, affording a tantalizing glimpse of the flesh beneath. A broad amber-colored sash was drawn tight beneath her breasts, hinting at their fullness. Amber ribbons trimmed her straw hat and fell softly against her throat.

"I'm sorry." She stepped toward him. "The boy in the shop told me I could find you upstairs."

"Come in, please." He gestured to the sofa and turned the chair at his desk around so he could sit facing her. "Paul's meeting with one of his writers and Maman's gone to market with David."

Emma settled her skirt with unusual care. At last she looked up and met his gaze. Her face was pale and her eyes dark with worry. "What is it?" He subdued the impulse to go to her and take her hands.

"I've just learned that Bram has been making secret trips to France for years and bringing information back to the British."

"I see. I can't say I'm surprised." It was easy to understand how a man like Martin, with the memory of his family's losses in the Revolution, could have been recruited into the espionage game. "It wouldn't have been safe for him to tell you until now," Robert said, thinking Emma was upset at discovering the secret life of another man she trusted.

"I understand that. But there's more." Emma swallowed, looked away, then looked back at him. "On one of those trips he brought Lucie to France with him. She was working for him, Robert."

Robert's fingers closed on the chair arms. Emma's words, as sharp and deadly as a rifle shot, blasted to bits his image of his wife. Even as he struggled to make sense of the accusation, the fragments re-formed themselves into a sickening picture. *Working for him.* Working for Bram Martin, who was working for the British. The enemy. He should say it couldn't possibly be true. *Not Lucie. Whatever else she was, she was my wife. I knew her better than that.* But instead the unspoken cry that rose in his throat was *How could I have been such a fool?*

"Martin told you so?" he asked at last, surprised to find his voice so free of emotion.

"I guessed and he admitted it." Emma's gaze was soft yet determined. "There was no reason for him to lie, Robert."

"No." Even as his mind searched for explanations and excuses, his gut told him it was fruitless. He felt drained and pummeled. An inner voice assaulted him with a relentless bombardment. *Of course, of course, you fool.* The mystery of her arrival in France. Her refusal to talk about the past. The secrecy and subterfuge that he had put down to her love affairs.

He dragged his hands over his face and pushed his fingers into his hair. Had he ever told her anything of military importance? Had any lives been lost because he had been too blind to see through his wife's deception? "I suppose Henriette was working for Martin as well." He felt strangely detached, as though he were speaking of people he barely knew.

"She gathered information from the men who frequented her salon and gave it to Bram, who took it to Britain. Lucie helped her."

"Of course. Who better? All the young officers were mad for her." But none more so than Robert Lescaut. The full extent of Emma's revelation burst upon him, shattering his shell of detachment. He remembered Lucie as he had first seen her, a laughing girl in a white dress. Through all the years of bitterness and disillusionment, the memory of their first days together had remained pure and untarnished. Now he knew that Lucie had betrayed him long before she took another man to her bed.

His stomach clenched with grief and disgust. For a moment he thought he was going to vomit. Instead he gave a shout of laughter. "Fitting retribution, don't you think?" He flung himself back in his chair. "I spent years deceiving people. And all the time I was being deceived by the woman I called wife."

"Robert—"

"Was it Martin's idea that Lucie become pregnant and marry me?"

"Bram wouldn't have done such a thing. He told me Lucie genuinely cared for you."

"Kind of him." *Cared for you.* Sweet Jesus. He closed his eyes and saw Lucie's tremulous smile the day they had first made love in the salon of Henriette's house. *I love you, Robert.* She had said it over and over as he touched her, scarcely able to believe she was allowing him to do so. Whatever passed between them later, he had never doubted that at the time she had meant it. Now he would never know.

His shoulders began to shake. He pushed himself to his feet and strode across the room.

He heard the rustle of Emma's dress as she moved toward him, so close he could smell her lily of the valley scent and feel her breath on his skin. "Stop torturing yourself." Her voice was soft and gentle. "You can't know. You can't know where expediency stopped and love began. You can't know whether she was drawn to your soul or to the information you could give her. You'll have to accept that. You'll drive yourself mad if you go on wondering."

Her voice trembled on this last. Robert turned and saw his own pain reflected in her eyes. He had known he had done her a great wrong, but it was only in this moment that he understood how grievously he had hurt her. "What happened between us had nothing to do with expediency," he said. "Believe what else of me you will, but never doubt that."

Tears glistened in Emma's eyes. She started to speak, then bit her lip and turned her head away. In the shadows cast by the brim of her hat, the bones of her face looked fragile and finely drawn. Robert put up his hand and turned her face toward his own. Her skin was as soft as he remembered. He could feel the pulse beating just below her jaw.

Emma's brows drew together as though she were trying to make sense out of the confusion. "It's all gone so horribly wrong, hasn't it?" she whispered.

Because there was no other answer he could make, Robert drew her into his arms. He felt her breath shudder through her. Her head fell forward onto his shoulder, and her arms closed around him. For a long time they stood together in the still warmth of the late afternoon, sharing a comfort that neither dared put into words.

But the moment could not last. Not when her shoulder brushed the naked skin at the open neck of his shirt. Not when her soft breasts were pressed so close to his chest. Not when the fragrance of her skin assaulted his senses. With weary disgust, Robert felt his body hardening against her own. He could not even offer her simple comfort without sparking the flame of lust. He drew back, knowing he had to put her from him.

But Emma would not let him go. She gripped his arms and looked up at him. Her breathing had quickened and her eyes, still brilliant with tears, held at once an invitation and a plea.

He could deny himself, but not her. The sun-warmed air pressed against them. The lengthening shadows promised intimacy. With an impatience born of denial, he tugged at the ribbons on her hat. It fell to the floor. He slid his fingers into her hair, sending a hail of pins after the hat. Her lips parted. Unable to contain himself any longer, he lowered his head to her own.

He had thought he would never again taste the sweet warmth of her mouth, never again feel her lips melting against his own, her fingers twining in his hair, her arm stealing around his neck to pull him closer. The world receded until nothing was left but the magic that was

Emma. He was drowning in it and knew himself willingly lost.

Eyes shut, arms close around her, he brushed his lips against the corner of her mouth, her temple, the hair curling back from her forehead.

"Robert." Her arm tightened around his neck. Her voice held a note of desperation. "Don't stop. Don't let me go."

As if of their own volition, his fingers found the buttons on the back of her gown. The light material slipped easily over her shoulders. He eased down her chemise and grazed his knuckles against the exposed curves of her breasts.

She drew in her breath and tilted her head back. He kissed the pulse beating in her throat, his own heart pounding, then buried his head in the cleft between her breasts. Her hands slipped to his waist. She tugged his shirt free of his trousers and touched the naked skin of his back.

Her touch felt strangely smooth and cool. Through the haze of passion, he realized she was still wearing her gloves. He stepped back and gathered her hands in his own. Dress and chemise falling from her shoulders, Emma looked up at him, then down at the decorous white net gloves. A strangled sound somewhere between a laugh and a sob escaped her lips.

Very carefully Robert pulled the gloves from her hands. He lifted each hand to his lips, feeling the warmth of the blood flowing beneath her skin. Then he threaded his fingers through her own and drew her to the sofa.

He fell back against the worn softness of the velvet and the scratchy wool of the blanket and pulled her down on top of him. Her breasts were pillowed on his chest. Her hips rested against his swollen rod. But he willed himself to patience. What Emma needed from him now, more than anything, was tenderness.

She raised her head and looked down at him. Her eyes were dark and vulnerable. He could see himself reflected in their shining depths. Her hair spilled over them both, glowing like autumn leaves where it caught the sunlight. He let his fingers drift through the heavy strands, skim across the bare skin of her shoulders, brush the soft underside of her breasts.

She shut her eyes for a moment, a look on her face that was part desire, part despair. She touched his face as though to make sure he was really there, then pressed her mouth where his shirt gaped open at the neck. Every muscle in his body tensed with longing.

The fabric of her dress rippled beneath his hands as he traced the line of her back and the tempting curve of her bottom. Impatience getting the better of him, he bunched the skirt in his hands and pulled it up. He felt her quick intake of breath as he stroked her downy cleft. He reached inside her damp warmth and knew a moment's triumph at the intensity of her arousal.

With a sob of need, Emma pushed herself to a sitting position. Straddling him, she reached for the buttons on his trousers.

When her hand closed around him, a shudder tore through his body. "Emma." Her name came out in a harsh gasp. "A man has his limits."

She laughed, a sweet, piercing sound as potent as her touch. Then she pushed herself onto her knees. He grasped her hips, feeling her tremble, feeling the tremors in his own hands. With soul-shattering care he sheathed himself inside her.

Her inner flesh throbbed around him. She eased up and down along his length, slowly at first, then with the quickening urgency of a need that will not be denied. Burning, his own body beyond his control, he caressed her at the place of their joining. She went suddenly still, her mouth opening in a silent cry. Then her head fell back, her hair cascading in a rich waterfall over her shoulders, her body shuddering with the tremors of release.

She slumped forward, her breath warm and ragged on his shoulder, her heart hammering close to his own. He held her to him, feeling something that went beyond the needs of his body, something that drove him over the edge. He gripped her tightly, as though she might be torn from his arms, and exploded deep inside her.

Emma turned her head and pressed a kiss into the hollow of Robert's throat. Peace and joy washed over her. She stretched, savoring the scent of him, the feel of his sweat-dampened skin beneath her cheek, the pressure of his body still buried inside her own.

She pushed herself up on her elbows and smiled down at him. An answering smile crossed his face, a smile so sweet it made the breath catch in her throat. Then, in the same heart-wrenching moment, reality rushed in upon both of them.

The smile faded from Robert's face. Though his arms were still around her, she felt cold and alone. Nothing had changed. Or rather, everything had. She had told herself she couldn't possibly love him after what he had done. Now she knew that she loved him more desperately than ever. The knowledge was like a knife twisting in her heart.

Suddenly aware of the brightness of the sun and the chance that Paul or Anne or David could return at any moment, she sat back and disentangled her body from his. "I'm sorry," she murmured, pushing down her skirt, conscious of the dampness between her thighs. "Your family—I didn't mean—"

"Em." He sat up. His hand closed warm and firm

around her own. "Scream if you must, but don't turn away."

She looked at him, wanting nothing more than to go back into his arms, knowing that if she did so, she would lose all sense of what she owed to her family. "We have to know," she said. "We have to know the truth. There'll be no peace for either of us until we do."

He did not pretend to misunderstand her. He released her hand and stroked his fingers against her cheek. "I'll do up your dress."

As he worked at the buttons, Emma seized hold of the one explanation that might give them a future. "When Paul told us about Philippe de Rivaud, I wondered if Lucie was killed because she knew something about his work for the Royalists. Now it seems more likely than ever."

"It's a possibility." Robert did up the last button.

She turned and searched his face. "But?"

"She was holding the ring." His voice was soft, but it held an undertone of grim determination.

Fear and frustration tore through her. She could say nothing. The question of the ring remained, a tiny, insidious kernel of doubt that made it impossible for her to be sure of the innocence even of those closest to her. She stared at the door to the sitting room, where she had sat only the day before with Robert and his mother. And Adam.

"Can't you at least leave Paris?" she asked, recalling Adam's warning. The thought of Robert in prison filled her with cold terror. "I'll let you know the minute I discover something."

Robert gave a ghost of a smile. "I'll leave when I've done all I can to learn the truth about Lucie."

"We may never know the truth." Emma looked into his eyes, steady and implacable, and realized the extent of the net in which they were ensnared. "And if we don't know, you'll never stop wondering if it's a Blair, will you?" she whispered, her throat raw with anguish.

Robert could give her no answer.

24

Robert stepped into the green-and-white salon where he had first seen Lucie on a sunny day eleven years ago, surrounded by a crowd of officers. The scent of roses was the same, as was the sunlight, but the room held only two people. Henriette Colbert was seated on the sofa, the light from the windows falling at a flattering angle across her face, the skirts of a pale blue gown draped artfully around her. And behind the sofa, hands braced on its back as if to protect Henriette, stood the tall figure of Bram Martin.

"Robert." There was a wary look in Henriette's eyes, as though she was not sure which way Robert would jump, but she greeted him with a smile. "I've been telling Bram you were sure to call."

Robert met the gaze of the man who had turned Lucie into a spy. "Martin. A fortunate meeting. I planned to call on you after I left here."

To his credit, Bram did not flinch from Robert's re-gard. "I expect you'd like nothing better than to thrash me. That's how I'd feel if I learned you'd recruited Jenny to spy for the French."

"But your wife isn't a Frenchwoman." Robert gazed steadily at the other man. "I can hardly blame you and

Lucie for spying for your country. It's no more than I've done myself."

"You can forgive her?" Bram asked on a note of surprise.

"I can understand why she became a spy. Can I forgive the lies she told me? Can I forgive myself for being witless enough to believe them? I fear I'm not such a saint."

"Yet you're still determined to find her killer?"

"If you found your wife brutally knifed, would the fact that she'd been spying for the enemy lessen your anger?"

A moment of silent acknowledgment passed between them. "No," Bram said. "Of course not."

"Revenge." Henriette shook her head, stirring tendrils of blond hair about her face. "It is a man's game. I'm as sorry as anyone for Lucie's death, but nothing you can do will bring her back."

"The living need justice as well as the dead."

"You want to ease your conscience? For the death of a woman who betrayed you in every way possible?" Henriette regarded him with puzzlement and a touch of pity. "You always took things too hard, Robert. But if that is why you have come, you had best sit down and ask us what you will."

Robert dropped into the nearest chair. On his visit with Emma, he had noted that the furniture had been reupholstered since the old days. But he recognized the gilding on the sofa. It was there that he and Lucie had first made love. The thought brought more recent images of another sofa and Emma's body moving urgently over his own. To his surprise the memory was strangely liberating, as though the bond he had established with Emma, however fragile, freed him from what he had known with Lucie.

But not from what he owed her. He had questioned Henriette at the time of Lucie's death and again with Emma only four days ago, but the revelation that Lucie had been a spy changed everything. He clasped his hands between his legs and looked from Henriette to Bram, who was now seated in a chair beside her. "Did Lucie tell either of you she thought Philippe de Rivaud's death wasn't an accident?"

Bram shook his head. "The last time I saw her was some weeks before Philippe was killed."

Henriette smoothed her skirt, her rings catching the sunlight. "Lucie was devastated when Philippe died. She told me he was the love of her life. She'd said so of others, of course, but I think Philippe meant more to her than anyone else. She even talked of seeking a divorce so they could marry."

Robert sat back in his chair. Even in death Lucie could surprise him. "But the manner of Rivaud's death?" he said after a moment. "Was she suspicious?"

"As far as I can recall, she said nothing so coherent in those last weeks."

"But she knew Philippe was working for the Royalists?"

Henriette smiled. "If we did not confide in fellow spies, how would we pass information along?"

"How many others knew of Lucie's activities?"

Henriette glanced at Bram, then looked back at Robert. "You can hardly expect me to give you names."

"Did Georges Demaire know?"

Bram looked at Robert through narrowed eyes. "What does Demaire have to do with this?"

Robert raised his brows. "I would think that was obvious. Demaire visited Henriette's salon. And he was working for the Royalists. He makes no secret of that now." Demaire had also been passing information to the government, but Robert saw no need to play all his cards just yet.

"Georges Demaire is an old friend," Henriette said.

"Naturally he knew Lucie was working with me. He was distressed by her death. And by Philippe's."

"Did he connect her death with Philippe's? Did you?"

"I wondered about it," Bram said. "How could I not? Philippe was besotted with Lucie. He might have mentioned her name to the wrong person."

Robert grimaced. He should have killed Lucie's lover himself. Espionage was not a game to be played by foolish boys. He looked at Henriette. "Whom did Lucie go to meet at Ostend?"

"I don't know." Henriette's eyes were troubled. "She didn't tell me. The first I knew of the trip was when I learned of her death."

"She'd met you there, Martin."

"I wasn't anywhere near France at the time," Bram said with a burst of impatience. "I was with a client in Aberdeen."

"A long journey. No doubt your client will remember the occasion."

Bram stared at him. "Damn it, I don't have to—"

"No. You don't have to do anything."

Their gazes locked. Bram slumped back in his chair. "You aren't going to give up, are you?"

"No." The single word contained all of Robert's determination.

"I could stick to the story," Bram said. "God knows when you'd have a chance to visit Aberdeen and prove it isn't true. But I have no doubt that eventually you would. And when you did—"

"Bram—" Henriette's delicate brows drew together.

"No." Bram put up a hand to silence her. "It's better this way." He looked at Robert. "You're right to be suspicious. I wasn't in Aberdeen. I wasn't even in Scotland. I was here, in Paris. In this house. With Henriette."

"Oh, Bram." Henriette laid her hand over his. "That was foolish, my dear."

"But necessary, I think." Bram continued to look at Robert. "I don't have to justify myself to you, Lescaut. But for my wife's sake I'd prefer that you say nothing of this."

"I want to know who killed Lucie," Robert said. "I'm not interested in anything which is not related to her murder. Why did Lucie go to Ostend?"

"She didn't go to meet me. I was in Paris, but what I said earlier is true. The last time I saw her was weeks before her death." Bram gave a sardonic smile. "I don't expect you to believe me. I wouldn't in your shoes."

"She might have thought she was going to meet you," Robert said.

"You think she was lured to the coast with a false message?"

"It's possible. How did you communicate with her?"

Bram shifted in his chair. Even now, Robert recognized, he was reluctant to reveal such secrets to a man who had been his opponent. "We had a courier service."

"Others in your circle knew of it?"

"Yes." Bram leaned toward Robert. "I tried at the time to discover if anyone had betrayed Philippe and Lucie. I wasn't able to learn anything."

"That doesn't mean there was nothing to be learned." Robert got to his feet. "You've both been helpful. You have my thanks."

Henriette held out her hand. "I was always fond of you, Robert. I never thought Lucie appreciated you enough."

"Rank flattery, Henriette." Robert bent over her hand and brushed it with his lips. "No wonder so many officers poured out their hearts to you."

Henriette looked up at him, brows raised. "I'll never understand you. How can you laugh about what we did?"

"How can I do anything else?"

Robert turned to Bram. "I shall see you at the wedding, I expect. Charlie's asked me to stand up with him. I hope you won't find it awkward."

"On the contrary." Bram regarded him for a moment. "We're more alike than you realize, Lescaut. You called me British, but like you I belong to both countries. My mother was a Scotswoman. My father was as French as yours. I was fighting for the France I believe in. As were you."

Robert thought of the British soldiers crowding the quai in obscene numbers. "And France, I fear, has been the loser."

"Lescaut," Bram said as Robert turned to the door.

Robert looked at the other man in inquiry.

"Do these questions about Philippe mean you've given up suspecting the Blairs?"

Robert turned the door handle with precision. "Oh, I haven't given up anything."

"Damn it, Em, I can't believe you let that fellow in the house." Jamie stared at Robert in the crowd of wedding guests filling the large white-and-gold salon on the first floor of Sherry's house.

Emma pulled her brother into a corner. It might have been easier if Jamie had not been able to get leave to come to the wedding. Standing at Arabel's side during the ceremony, Emma had been aware of the murderous gaze her brother had fixed on Robert. Perhaps she should be thankful that he had not said anything until they left the British Embassy, where the marriage had been performed, and returned to Sherry's house for the wedding breakfast.

"Colonel Lescaut was the husband of our cousin," she said under cover of the quiet accompaniment of Mozart Adam was providing at the piano. "His son is Angus's great-nephew."

Jamie looked down at her, brows drawn low, face dark with scorn. "Next you'll be saying we should take him into the bosom of the family."

"He and David *are* part of the family."

"God almighty. You're still infatuated with the fellow."

Despite the betraying heat in her face, Emma looked steadily at her brother. "Arabel and Charlie wanted them here."

"That's another thing. Why Uncle Angus ever consented to this marriage—"

"Jamie." Emma gripped his arm more tightly. "If you do anything to disrupt Arabel's wedding day, I will personally flay you alive."

It was the voice she had used with her brother in the nursery. She held his gaze with her own, willing him to capitulate.

"Good God, Em." Jamie looked at her as though seeing her for the first time. "You're as bad as Arabel. Worse. At least Charlie never lied to us. Don't expect me to come to *your* wedding if you find yourself pregnant."

If they had been alone, Emma would have slapped him. As it was, all she could do was stand by and compose her features as best she could while Jamie pulled away from her. She waited a moment for her pulse to quiet, then went to rejoin the guests.

Arabel looked radiant. Her hair tumbled with bright abandon from beneath the brim of a white silk hat trimmed with plaited tulle. Her skin glowed against a gown of Brussels lace and sprigged white muslin. She had refused to wear gloves and was holding her left hand so that the simple gold of her wedding band shone in the sunlight. Her right hand was clasped tightly in Charlie's. They hadn't stopped touching since John Doyle pronounced them husband and wife.

Emma smiled at the young couple. Robert's voice came to her out of the murmur of conversation. She could not stop herself from looking for him in the crowd. He was talking to Sherry and John Doyle, but he glanced toward her as if aware of her gaze. For a moment, their eyes met. Emma's breath quickened and her skin felt tight. They had not spoken privately since she left his house six days ago, her body still warm from their love-making. She felt stripped raw by what had passed be-tween them. It was not the memory of her physical nakedness that bothered her—she had never known that kind of shame—but the dismantling of every barrier she had raised against him. She no longer knew on what terms they could meet.

Robert looked away first, as though to spare her pain. Emma summoned up her best hostess smile and began to move about the room. She made sure the children were occupied, asked one of the footmen to bring in more champagne, spoke to Charlie's commanding officer and to the British ambassador, Sir Charles Stuart, an affable man who paid her an extravagant compliment. All the time she kept a wary eye on her own family. At one point she saw Angus, who had consumed several glasses of champagne, throw an expansive arm around Lord Lauder's shoulders. The sight warmed her heart. But it was not the feud that concerned her now. It was the tension between the Blairs and Robert.

Both Angus and Lauder had made their liking for David plain. But unlike Lauder, who seemed to have de-veloped respect for David's father, Angus treated Robert with wary caution. Emma knew her uncle felt a debt to Robert as Lucie's husband, but she suspected he did not trust Robert with the secret of Lucie's parentage. And while Angus did not know the full extent of Robert's sus-picions, he must realize Robert still had questions to ask.

Will, bless him, had gone out of his way to talk to Robert, as had Bram, though Bram seemed unusually quiet this afternoon. Neil, frustrated at not knowing everything that had gone on between his father and Lord Lauder, seemed to have decided Robert was to blame for it. Jamie was talking with some of Charlie's fellow officers, but every so often he glanced in Robert's direction with an expression that made Emma's stomach lurch.

"Here." Caroline appeared at Emma's side and offered her a glass of champagne. "You look as if you could use this."

Emma accepted the chilled glass and gave her friend a rueful smile. "And I thought I was acting as if I hadn't a care in the world."

"You were. But I've moved in diplomatic circles long enough to read beneath the surface. Come outside for a few minutes. The air will do you good."

Emma glanced at the French windows leading to the balcony, then looked back at her brother.

"They won't come to blows in the salon," Caroline said. "Sherry will see to that."

The prospect of a few moments of quiet away from both Robert and her family was too tempting. Emma followed Caroline onto the balcony that overlooked the courtyard around which the house was built. She leaned against the sun-warmed wrought metal railing and looked down at the graceful branches of the lemon tree, the vivid mass of rose-colored geraniums, the soft pink of the carnations. The tension in her head began to ease. "You were right," she told Caroline. "I was coming down with a headache. Silly of me. I suppose I'm not used to entertaining."

"Today is enough to try anyone." Caroline paused for a moment. "When did you realize you were still in love with Robert?"

Emma spun around.

"You've kept out of his way all afternoon," Caroline said. "During the wedding you wouldn't even look at him, though you were standing only a few feet apart."

"Oh, God." Emma put her hand to her face. In all the months of love and longing, of anger and betrayal and the beginnings of forgiveness, she hadn't been able to talk about Robert with anyone. "I was so sure I couldn't love him. Not after I knew how he had lied to me. If that didn't kill my feelings for him, I suppose nothing will."

Caroline smiled. "It's miraculous how resilient love is."

"It's damnable." The words burst from Emma with sudden passion.

"And yet it gives one hope for the future."

Emma shook her head and looked away, feeling the pressure of tears behind her eyelids. "Even if we could forget everything else, Lucie would always be between us. I don't think—" She broke off and glanced through the windows at the crowd in the salon. "It's madness to be talking about it."

"You'll go mad if you don't talk about it." Caroline studied her for a moment. "Robert came to see us the night before last. He told us Lucie was working for the British."

"It was a great shock to him."

"Yes. But it raises the possibility that Lucie was killed for her work in France, not her past in Scotland."

Emma turned her head to look at Caroline. "Did Robert tell you he believes that?"

Caroline returned her gaze steadily. "He said it may have happened that way."

"But he can't forget that Lucie died clutching the Blair ring." Emma took a sip of champagne, trying to wash away her bitterness.

"Robert has always believed the ring is a clue to her death." Caroline's gray eyes were direct and honest. "He's not going to let go of that possibility as easily as you can."

Emma gripped the rail. "Even I can't deny the possibility," she said in a low voice. It was a relief to voice her darkest fear.

Caroline laid her hand over Emma's. "That's a great admission."

"I'm not saying I believe it. Only that I can't be certain it didn't happen that way. I can't be certain of much of anything anymore." Emma twisted the stem of the glass between her fingers, watching the play of the sunlight on the crystal and the bubbling pale gold liquid. "I thought it would be over when we learned the truth. But if one of my family killed Lucie—" Her voice trembled. She controlled it with an effort. Lucie's death had been horrible, but to imagine Robert turning on Angus or Jamie or Gavin or Bram, whatever their crimes— "Then God help me, I know I won't be able to stand by while Robert exacts his revenge. No matter how justified."

"No one could expect you to."

"But how would I be able to live with him afterward? How would he be able to live with me if he learned the truth and did nothing?" Emma drew in her breath, realizing she had confessed to hopes for the future that she had hardly dared admit to herself.

Caroline squeezed Emma's hand. "I can't believe you think a member of your family is Lucie's murderer."

"No. But unless we can prove beyond a doubt that someone else killed her, Robert will always suspect the Blairs."

"Then we must find proof that someone else did."

"If proof exists." Emma would not allow herself to think further. If they could prove Demaire or someone else in France was responsible for Lucie's death, the future would lie clear before her and Robert. And that was a prospect at once too wondrous and too terrifying for her to consider.

* * *

Robert looked at David and smiled. His son was sitting with Kirsty and Emily on a corner of the rose-and-gold Aubusson carpet, amusing Jenny and Bram's small son and daughter. Whatever the Blairs' reservations about Robert, David had been accepted into the family. But then, David had Blair blood in his veins. That counted for a lot.

"Bearing up all right?" Lord Sheriton appeared at Robert's side, a friendly smile on his face.

"How could I not be? It's a splendid party."

"Yes, it's come off rather well. Bit difficult for you though." Sherry glanced about the room, his eyes resting on Angus, then on Jamie. "Family ties can be a fearful burden. I suppose I'm fortunate that my immediate family is limited to Jack and our widowed mother. Though I suppose one day I'll have to bow to the inevitable and take a wife."

Sherry looked at the balcony. Robert followed the direction of his gaze. Through the French windows, Emma and Caroline could be seen standing by the railing. The white damask curtains framed them like a painting. Caroline, in a soft blush-colored dress and matching hat, was as lovely and delicate as ever, but Robert could not take his eyes off Emma. She was wearing a gown with a bodice of cream-colored lace that hugged her skin and a peach-colored skirt that swirled around her legs. Beneath a hat of peach-colored satin her hair glowed in the sunlight and stirred provocatively in the breeze. It had been torture standing so close to her during the wedding, knowing he dared not touch her, dared not even look into her eyes. All that time he had been listening to Charlie and Arabel repeat the vows he longed to exchange with her.

"When you find the right woman, don't let her slip through your fingers," Sherry said, almost as though he were speaking to himself.

Jealousy tightened Robert's throat. Then he realized Sherry was looking at Caroline.

"Not that I had any chance." Sherry turned to Robert, his eyes and voice unusually serious. "Some people are meant to be together."

Robert thought of Adam and Caroline. "Yes," he agreed. And then, thinking of himself and Emma, he added, "And some people are destined not to be together, no matter how strong the feeling between them."

Sherry regarded him for a moment. "Emma's fond of you. More than fond, if I'm any judge of such matters. The day we found you on the battlefield—" He hesitated. "Perhaps I haven't any right to speak of it. But I think you should know. She was desperate to find you. And when she did, she didn't even notice the color of your uniform. I had to point it out to her."

"But it's a sight she'll never forget."

"Forgetting isn't the question, Lescaut. It's getting on with life that is."

Robert was silent for a moment, aware of the sound of the piano. Adam had changed from Mozart to Bach, a piece filled with a piercing, aching quality that accorded well with Robert's mood. He looked at the balcony again. Getting on with life meant learning the truth about Lucie. That search threatened to destroy any chance he and Emma had of a future—assuming Emma could forget the past. Despite Sherry's words, Robert was not at all sure she could.

Before Robert was forced to make an answer, Andy and Jack joined them. "Poor Charlie," Andy said with a grin. "He's always seemed like a sensible chap, but he's been staring at Bel with the most idiotic grin all day."

"Wait a few years." Sherry shook off his serious mood. "You'll understand."

"I suppose we all have to fall sooner or later." Andy turned to Robert. Suddenly he looked older than his nineteen years. "On behalf of my family, I'd like to offer my apologies. In general, we pride ourselves on our hospitality."

Robert smiled at the younger man. "I've been treated most hospitably."

"No, you haven't." There was a grim note in Andy's voice. "It's no use pretending otherwise. Uncle Angus is a good sort underneath, but he can be damned prickly. I don't know what's got into him. Your wife was his niece. My cousin. And I want to know—"

"He means we want to help you," Jack said. "Find out the truth about—"

"My wife's death." Robert looked at Andy. "It's kind of you. But you must realize the questions about Lucie's death are part of the problem with your uncle and the others."

Andy returned his gaze calmly. "You think a Blair may have killed her. I don't. But if that's what happened, we ought to find out."

"By God, Andy." Jamie strode over to them with the force of an avenging angel. "I always knew it was a mistake to send you to school in England. You're a damn sight too tolerant."

Andy looked at Jamie without alarm. "I was assuring Colonel Lescaut that we're as eager to learn the truth about his wife's death as he is."

"Oh, Christ." Jamie glared at Robert. "Have you been filling his head with that nonsense, Lescaut?"

"My wife's death can be called a number of things," Robert said, "but I wouldn't number nonsense among them."

"Never could give a straight answer, could you?" Jamie took a step forward. His eyes were bright, his color high. "A gentleman would have had the tact to refuse the invitation to the wedding. I suppose I should have known you'd accept."

Robert smiled at Emma's brother. "You'll have to do better than that if you hope to insult me, Jamie. I've never considered myself a gentleman."

With an exclamation of pure, blinding fury Jamie lunged at Robert. Robert stepped out of the way.

Sherry put out his arm to stop Jamie's attack. "It's no business of mine if you choose to behave like a fool. But you're not going to do it in my house."

Jamie's eyes blazed with unvented rage. Quiet fell over the salon. There was a moment of taut silence. Then the French windows opened with a soft stir. Robert looked across the room at Emma. Her eyes were dark with worry. He wanted to go to her, to apologize, to free her from the burden of discord. But in an instant her look of worry was gone, replaced by a serene smile. "I think breakfast must be ready. Shall we go down to the dining room?"

The image of her brother's angry face haunted Emma through the wedding breakfast and overwhelmed the revelations she had made to Caroline. Those she could dwell on when she had privacy and leisure. Now her chief concern was to get through the afternoon without a scene.

But when the last of the cake had been eaten and they returned to the salon for coffee, it was not Jamie who caught her attention but Neil. He had been drinking more than usual, perhaps because he felt shut out from family secrets, perhaps simply because of the freedom of being in Paris. She saw him slip from the room, his hand to his mouth, a greenish cast to his skin. She asked Jenny to take her place at the coffee urn and went in search of her eldest cousin.

She found Neil in the small antechamber across the hall, being very sick into a large Sèvres vase. "Oh, Lord, I'm sorry, Em." He looked up at her entrance. His skin was ashen, but it was an improvement over green. "I don't know what came over me. Bloody champagne. Whisky never takes me this way."

"It's all right, Neil." Emma handed him the coffee she had brought with her. Mercifully there weren't any spots on the carpet.

"Damn strange day." Neil took a gulp of coffee. "Bel marrying a Lauder and that Lescaut fellow— First Father railed against him, and now we're expected to shake his hand and treat him like one of the family."

"His wife was—"

"Our cousin, I know." Neil stared into the blue-and-gold cup. "But Father's still got an odd look in his eye when he sees Lescaut. And Lescaut's going around asking some deuced odd questions."

Emma swallowed. A traitorous thought came to her. *If you're ever going to get him to talk about where he and Allan were when Lucie was killed, now's the time. All his defenses are down.* "Neil." Emma gripped her hands together and studied her cousin.

"Mmm?" Neil looked at her, his eyes not quite focused.

"Just before Allan returned to the Peninsula he went with you to Dundee on business. Do you remember?"

Despite the effects of the alcohol, Neil's gaze turned wary. "What the devil's that got to do with anything?"

"That's when Colonel Lescaut's wife was killed."

Indignation flared in Neil's eyes. He set down the coffee cup, his hand shaking. "And you think—"

"I don't think anything," Emma said in as steady a voice as she could manage. "I just want to know— Were you and Allan together the whole time?"

"Of course we were. We told you—"

"You told me a story that was as full of holes as a blanket the moths had got into."

"Are you calling me a liar?" Neil demanded, enunciating the words carefully.

"Oh, for God's sake, Neil. I suspected from the first that Allan was with another woman. If that was it, just say so and be done with it."

Neil stepped back, his brows drawing together as if he were trying to puzzle out a situation that was too complex for his present state. "Em—"

"Neil."

Neil picked up the coffee, then glanced at the vase and set it down again. "There was a—a woman Allan knew—or had known. He wanted to look her up and—uh—see how she was doing."

"You needn't elaborate. I understand." If Allan had betrayed her, it was no more than she had done with Bram. A fine mess they had made of their marriage.

It was a moment before the greater significance of Neil's words hit her. "Then you weren't together the whole time?"

Neil shook his head. "Allan traveled part of the way with me. We met up on my way home."

Emma smoothed a crease from her glove. There was no one, at least no one now in Paris, to account for Allan's whereabouts at that crucial time. It was just possible that he had not been with an old mistress at all. It was just possible that he had gone to France on his father's orders to negotiate with the secret cousin who had been making difficult demands. And if Allan had lost his temper—

With sudden clarity, Emma remembered the one time Allan had struck her. She had been frighteningly aware of how strong he was. He had apologized profusely and it had never happened again. But she could not forget that in anger Allan had lost control and done something of which she would have thought him incapable. The memory was enough to make her sick with doubt.

* * *

"So you're the man who saved Durward's life." Sir Charles Stuart held his hand out to Robert. "I must say I'm grateful to you. Durward's an impudent fellow, but I don't know how I'd manage without him."

Robert shook the ambassador's hand. Stuart was a young man, no more than thirty-five or -six, with a cheerfully informal manner. By report, Robert knew he was an extremely able diplomat. "If I ever got Durward out of trouble, it's no more than he's done for me." Robert smiled at Adam who was standing beside Stuart.

Adam returned the smile. "Anglo-French cooperation. Our government are for it now."

"Mmm," Stuart said. "Just as long as we cooperate with the right French."

"I'll understand if you prefer not to be seen talking to a former soldier of the Empire," Robert told him, only part in jest.

"Oh, nonsense." Stuart waved a careless hand. "The war's over. Anyway, it's up to diplomats to build fences, not tear them down. At the moment, our government have decided Bonaparte's old friends Talleyrand and Fouché are preferable to the Ultra Royalists like the Comte d'Artois." His brows drew together. "A colonel, aren't you?"

"I was. I resigned my commission when Napoleon abdicated."

"That won't make any difference to d'Artois and his followers. They're bent on vengeance. Adam must have told you."

"Tried to tell him," Adam said.

Robert ignored Adam's comment. "I wasn't on the proscribed list."

"Then you're more fortunate than many." Stuart took a sip of champagne. "But I'd still have a care. If you're

arrested, even Adam won't be able to help you. The Royalists dislike the British nearly as much as they dislike the
Bonapartists."

"I don't intend to be arrested."

"That would seem to be the most prudent course."
Stuart glanced around the salon. "Devilish number of
pretty women about, aren't there? The bride's enchanting, though for my money Mrs. Blair is even more taking."

Robert bit back a retort. Stuart was known for his flir-
tations, but he was speaking idly.

"Then there's Caroline, of course," Stuart continued.
"But Adam will strangle me if I so much as notice her."

Adam raised his brows. "No, sir. Only if you do anything about it."

Sherry joined the men in the midst of the laughter
that followed. "Sorry to interrupt." He touched Robert on
the shoulder. "Could I have a word with you?"

When Robert followed him to the windows that overlooked the back of the house, Sherry's expression became
grave. "There are two *gens d'armes* downstairs. They have
a warrant for your arrest."

Robert stared at his host. He'd known arrest was a
risk, but he hadn't expected anything so soon. And for
them to have gone to the lengths of tracking him down
here—"It seems I miscalculated."

"That's one way of putting it." Sherry glanced around
the room. "I can distract them for a time. Do you want to
slip out the back?"

Robert looked out the window at the street below. Two
more *gens d'armes* stood by the area steps at the back of
the house. *Mon dieu,* they were taking precautions. What
had he done to warrant such attention?

"It's a generous offer," Robert said. "But I'm afraid it's
too late."

25

Emma returned to the salon, remembering to smile as she entered. She would have to tell Robert about Neil's revelations. But she would not tell him yet, not while Arabel and Charlie were still basking in the joy of their union. Perhaps later, when the young couple had gone off on their brief honeymoon. She would ask Robert to stay on after the other guests had left.

She moved slowly through the room, stopping to exchange words with some of Charlie's fellow officers, resplendent in their white breeches and brilliant red coats. While she talked and laughed with the officers, she scanned the room, searching for Robert. She saw him standing with Sherry by the windows at the far end of the room. Then he left Sherry and made his way to Adam. No words passed between them. A touch on the shoulder, a look, and both men left the room. Adam's face was drawn. Robert's face held no expression at all. Emma knew something was wrong.

She excused herself and went to Sherry, who was still standing where Robert had left him. "What's happened?"

Sherry took her arm and turned her toward the window as though he wanted to show her something outside. It gave them some privacy. "Robert's been arrested," he said in a low voice. As she pulled away, ready to run from the room, he clamped his hand on her arm. "Don't, Em. You can't help him. Not that way."

Emma quieted and he released her arm. She looked out the window and stifled a start of surprise. Two *gens d'armes* were standing at attention at the back of the house.

"They knew he was here," Sherry said. "He must have been followed."

"Why couldn't he—"

"Hide? I suggested it. He said he'd do better going over the roofs, but he was afraid there'd be a search and it would disrupt the festivities." He looked across the room at Arabel and Charlie, hands clasped, laughing with Caroline and Sir Charles. Their happiness radiated throughout the room.

Emma's throat was tight with panic. She wielded her fan vigorously, hoping it would hide the distress that must be visible on her face. "We can't do nothing."

"But we can be discreet." He took her arm. "Let's find Adam. He'll know what's possible."

They left the room, taking care to seem in no particular hurry. Once outside, Emma walked quickly down the corridor and looked over the gilded metal to the hall below. It was empty save for Adam, who was standing near the door, his head bent, his hands clasped behind his back. She and Sherry ran down the stairs. Adam looked up, then strode forward to meet them. "In here, I think," Sherry said, shepherding them into the small room he used as a study.

Emma could not wait. "Where have they taken him?" she asked as Sherry closed the door behind them.

"To the Conciergerie," Adam told her.

"For how long?"

"Until his trial, if it comes to that."

Emma seized on this glimmer of hope. "You mean it may not?"

"I mean he may meet with an accident before the trial takes place."

"God in heaven." Her voice was a bare whisper.

"You'd better sit down." Sherry took her arm as though to lead her to a chair.

She threw him off. "Adam, what can we do? We can't leave him there."

"No. We'll have to devise something."

"Can Sir Charles pressure the government?"

"It would do more harm than good."

"Bram. I'll talk to Bram. He's—" She was about to say that he'd been a link between the Royalists and the British for years and the Royalists ought to owe him some favors, but it was not her story to tell. "He has friends among the Royalists. He may know the Comte d'Artois."

Adam looked at her from beneath lowered brows. "Would Martin help? Knowing who Robert is?"

Bram had always granted her any favor she requested, but he might be reluctant to jeopardize his own position for a man he scarcely knew. "I don't know," she was forced to admit. "Adam, I want to see Robert. Is it possible?"

"I think they would allow visitors." He was silent for a moment. "Yes, it might be a very good idea. You could bring him food, clothes, any small comforts. Visit him every day. Establish a pattern."

"Let me come with you," Sherry said. "I can protect you from any indignities."

Adam ran his gaze over Sherry as though measuring him. "And the guards can get used to seeing Emma come and go with a man."

The two men were looking at each other in perfect accord. Emma stared at them, puzzled, and then understood. The tightness in her chest vanished and she was able to breathe freely once more. "An escape."

Adam smiled. "Let me tell you what I have in mind."

* * *

Emma listened to the rythmic clanging of the wheels as Sherry's carriage clattered over the Pont Neuf and turned onto the Quai de l'Horloge. She thought of what Adam had told her when he called on her that morning and what it might mean for Robert's safety. To her right rose the stone walls of the Palais de Justice, the immense Gothic palace that had once been home to the French kings. She named the towers as they passed, trying to calm herself by remembering what Andy had told her on one of their first rambles through the city. The Tour Bonbec—the babbling tower, where prisoners held for torture learned to speak. The Tour d'Argent, which had held the royal treasure. Its twin, the Tour de César, where the public prosecutor had sent hundreds of Royalists to their deaths during the Terror. The Tour de l'Horloge, which bore the first public clock in Paris. The towers marked the portion of the palace called the Conciergerie. It had served as a prison for over five hundred years.

"It's a hideous place," Emma said as their carriage turned the corner and pulled up in a vast courtyard.

"It was once. But that was twenty or more years ago." Sherry sprang out of the carriage and gave her his hand. "Wait for us here," he told the coachman, who had handed him the food-filled wicker hamper that was the ostensible reason for their visit. "We'll be out in under an hour."

Sherry's broad-brimmed hat shadowed his face. He carried a silver-mounted ebony walking stick, and his long black cloak, which he wore in defiance of the heat, swirled around him as he walked. "It's what they'll remember," he had told Emma when they left the house. "An eccentric Englishman who dresses oddly and accompanies a beautiful woman. It's you they'll notice. With any luck they won't remember my face at all."

They stopped at the registry office and asked to see the prisoner Robert Lescaut. "My cousin's husband," Emma said. "We've brought him some food."

The clerk harrumphed, looked at them with a scowl, then gradually melted under Emma's smile and her assurance that he was a man who could sympathize with her distress. When a handsome bribe had been offered and accepted, he was eager to be of help. He led them personally through a maze of corridors, their vaulted ceilings rising to darkness above, past dark cells in which movement could be dimly seen behind the iron bars, to a corridor in which the doors were of wood and the floors cleaner than those they had traversed.

Halfway down the corridor a uniformed gaoler sat disconsolate on a wooden crate, his legs crossed, his arm resting on a barrel that bore a battered metal pitcher filled with water or perhaps something stronger. He jumped to his feet at the clerk's approach. "Visitors for the prisoner Lescaut," the clerk told him. Then he turned to Emma. "Tatin, the undergaoler. He'll give you what help you require. You may have half an hour."

Emma made a sound of dismay.

"Well, perhaps a little longer. See me on the way out."

Tatin sported a drooping black moustache, but he had no pretense to smartness. His coat was shabby and stained with use, his shoulders sagged, and his breath told how he relieved the tedium of his days. "Another one," he muttered, shuffling down the corridor and stopping at the second door on the right. He peered in the barred window set high in the door and called out, "Lescaut. Visitors." He selected a key from the large ring that he carried and inserted it in the lock. Then he pushed open the door to let them enter.

Sherry stopped and turned to Tatin. "The lady would

like coffee. Is there a café nearby where you could procure some?" He reached beneath his cloak, drew out a lavish handful of coins, and dropped them into Tatin's waiting hand. The gaoler's face brightened. He sketched a salute, allowed them to pass through the door, and locked it behind them.

Emma's gaze went at once to Robert. He was standing in a narrow shaft of light. He had managed to shave and he looked much as he had at the wedding, though he was not wearing his coat. His face was shadowed with fatigue, but God be thanked, he did not seem to have been mistreated.

He went very still as he took in her presence. Then a light flared in his eyes, singeing her with its heat. Never, not even when they made love, had he looked at her with such hunger. She took a step forward and then another and then her arms were around him and he was kissing her as though he'd been afraid he would never touch her again.

She clung to him, desperate with longing and fear and relief. It was Robert who drew back first. He took her by the shoulders and looked beyond her. "I'm sorry, Sheriton. I forgot myself."

"We both did." Emma turned to smile at her childhood friend. "But I think Sherry understands."

"Don't mind me." Sherry leaned against the closed door. "Pity I didn't bring the morning paper."

"No, we'll be sensible. We have to be." Emma set her reticule on the table and took off her hat, making her movements deliberate. Besides the table, the room contained only a chair and a narrow bed. A shelf along one wall held a covered basket and a few articles of clothing. A high barred window, its panes encrusted with grime, let in a dim shaft of light. Aside from the window, the room was clean, though the air was damp and fetid.

"It could be worse," Robert said, noting her survey of

the room. "I haven't much experience with prisons, unless you call a filthy mud-floored Spanish gaol by that name. Here at least I have a bed and it's reasonably free of vermin."

"That's something to be thankful for." Emma matched his tone.

Sherry set the basket on the table. "We've brought you something to eat. And drink." He glanced at the basket on the shelf. "Though I take it we aren't the first."

"My mother was here this morning. But this is welcome all the same. I'll dine in splendor tonight."

Sherry removed a bottle of wine and a cloth-covered dish from the basket. "We should have brought two bottles. If I were you, I'd get roaring drunk." He reached into the basket once more. "And some books."

Robert's face lit up. "Bless you, Sheriton."

"And pen and ink and paper," Emma added. "When a man can't act, he has to fall back on words." Sherry had thought of the books, but the writing materials had been her idea, sparked by her conversation with Anne Lescaut.

"Bless you both." Robert's eyes smiled into her own. "Have you seen Adam?"

"This morning." Emma glanced at the grille in the door. They were speaking English, but she knew there was danger in their talk.

Sherry went to the door and peered through the barred window. "All clear."

Robert grimaced. "How much did you give Tatin?"

"Enough to keep him happy." Sherry hesitated. "I know everything costs here. Do you need any blunt?"

"I've enough." Robert pulled out a chair for Emma, gestured Sherry to the bed, and sat beside him. "I'm told I'm being charged with murder. Is that a new name for treason or is it something particular?"

"Particular, I'm afraid," Sherry said. He paused as

though reluctant to put the accusation into words. "Encompassing the death of Philippe de Rivaud."

Emma leaned forward across the table. "Georges Demaire was the man who laid information against you. You were right, Robert. It must have been Demaire who informed against Rivaud. Adam says Rivaud's family hadn't been aware of their son's activities, but now that they know, they're raising a hue and cry about his death."

Robert had gone very still. "Clever. Philippe's family would want to believe he was killed because he was a Royalist spy. They'd be hunting for an informer. But how much simpler to convince them he was killed because he was my wife's lover." He had been staring at the table but now he looked straight at Emma. "I wasn't in Paris at the time."

"Can you prove it?" Sherry asked.

"Probably," Robert said, "but it won't matter. They can claim I hired someone to do it for me."

"They'll say—" Emma stopped because the charge was so absurd it was difficult to voice it. "They'll say you not only killed Rivaud—that you had him killed—but that you killed your wife as well."

Robert's smile was bleak. "In a jealous rage. Of course. Lucie's death confirms Demaire's accusation. They never charged me in her death, you know. A husband is the obvious suspect and the police take these things seriously, but in this case they found no cause. The proprietor of the inn was with me when we opened the door and discovered her."

"They'll say you were her first visitor and that you returned to give yourself an alibi."

"It's possible."

"That you did it? No," Emma said with a certainty she could not have mustered when she first learned of Robert's treachery. No, even then she could not have believed it.

She saw her conviction register in Robert's eyes. They looked at each other in a moment of silent acknowledgment.

Sherry leaned forward. "From what I know of the story, they'd have a hard time proving that's what occurred. But from what I gather of the temper of Paris, the rules of evidence don't count for much at the moment."

"We're getting you out." Emma glanced again at the door. "It's not only Demaire. There's been pressure from other quarters as well. Adam hasn't learned its source, but it doesn't matter. Demaire is bad enough. Adam will have papers that will let you leave the country."

"Are you safe, Lescaut?" Sherry asked. "For a few days?"

Robert nodded. "Even Demaire doesn't have that power."

Emma couldn't bear not to touch him. She clasped his hands in her own. He felt warm, strong, an anchor in a shifting world. "Adam's plan," she began.

"I can guess it." He glanced at Sherry.

"We're much of a size," Sherry said.

"Are you sure? It will be troublesome for you."

Sherry smiled. "I'm an English civilian, and a rather stupid one at that. Besides I have a title. I doubt they'll hold me, and if they do it won't be for long. I'm doing it for Emma, Lescaut. If you aren't worth it, she is."

Emma cast an anxious glance at Sherry. She had not intended to save one man at the risk of another's freedom. But Robert's life was at stake, and Sherry—Adam had assured her it was so—was in little danger.

Sherry seemed to read her thoughts. "At the worst they'll ask me to leave the country. And it's time I was going anyway. I need to get Jack and Andy back to their studies."

Emma knew she would have to return to Scotland as well. Arabel had no more need of her and Angus would expect it. She would have to leave Robert behind, not knowing if she would ever see him again. She looked down at their clasped hands. Her fingers tightened around his own. She wondered where he would go but did not feel she had the right to ask. "David." She looked up at Robert. "What will happen to David?"

"He'll stay with Paul and my mother. At least 'til this is settled."

He wouldn't let go of his search for Lucie's killer. If Demaire had anything to do with Lucie's death—and Emma firmly believed that he did—Robert would settle accounts with him, no matter the risk to himself.

But if Demaire did not . . . Emma realized that she had not told Robert of her conversation with Neil. His arrest had driven it from her mind. She disengaged her hands from Robert's. What she was about to say should not be colored by emotion. "Sherry. Could you . . ."

He rose at once and walked to the door, turning his back on the room. He might be able to hear her words, but he could pretend later that he had not. Speaking rapidly and in a low voice, Emma told Robert what she had learned about Neil's and Allan's whereabouts at the time Lucie was killed. Or rather, what she had not learned. "They could have been anywhere," she said. "Not Neil perhaps. He can't tell a convincing lie, and I'd swear he'd never heard of Lucie 'til Angus brought him to Paris. But Allan . . . He left Neil before they reached Dundee. Neil said he was with a woman."

"That doesn't mean it was true." Robert's voice was gentle.

Emma forced herself to meet his eyes. "No. At least not this time. Allan could have gone to Ostend. If it was a Blair Lucie met. Or it could have been Bram or Angus or Gavin. Or Jamie. I know he was in London, but he won't talk to me about it." She shut her mind to images of Jamie's anger. "But if Demaire was behind Rivaud's death, he must have been behind Lucie's death as well. When she showed you the ring, she wasn't trying to name her killer. She wanted you to know who she was. Who David was. The ring was her only link to the past."

Robert pressed her hand briefly. Emma saw compassion and acceptance in his face, but though she had been in his arms not half an hour since, there was something in him she could not reach. She could not tell whether he believed her or not.

When Emma and Sherry left, Robert paced the brief length of his cell, unable to cage his thoughts. His position was more dangerous than he had realized. Demaire could not have known that Robert had linked him with the death of Philippe de Rivaud, but he could know that Robert had been asking questions about Lucie. Demaire's accusations against Robert suggested that Demaire had been involved in Lucie's death and feared his involvement would come to light. He wasn't trying to curry favor with the government. He was trying to save his own skin.

Robert leaned his hands against the table and looked up at the thin oblong of light that was his only link to the outside world. Perhaps Emma had been right. Perhaps he had made too much of the Blair ring and what Lucie had tried to convey. Lucie had known Demaire. She might have suspected he was not a man to be trusted. She might have frightened him by her questions about Philippe. She might even have accused him.

Then what had been the point of his masquerade as Robert Melton, his deception of Emma and all the pain that had followed. He need never have gone to Scotland. True, David would not have learned his mother's history—and a sordid one it was—but he would have been no less content. Angus would have kept his secret and perhaps been happier for it. Emma might be happier as well, as he might himself. And yet . . . Robert smiled at his own folly. Though her nearness was a torment, he would not give up their few hours together for all the treasure in the world.

Besides—Robert straightened up. If a Blair was not behind Lucie's death, then perhaps there was a way for him and Emma to navigate the treacherous mines that lay between them. He sucked in his breath. The possibility was so dizzying he could scarcely allow himself to consider it.

He glanced once more at the high window, then with sudden decision lifted the mattress where he had hidden the writing materials Emma had brought lest they be confiscated by the gaoler. He would set down what he knew and what he conjectured about Philippe and Lucie, about Demaire, and the unknown others who might have played a part in their tragic deaths. The record would clear his thoughts. It might also help to have it in other hands.

"General de La Bédoyère was arrested yesterday," Sherry said when he and Emma arrived the next afternoon.

"Oh, Christ." Robert saw again La Bédoyère's laughing face at the Duchess of Richmond's ball. "I thought he'd left Paris."

Emma touched his arm with sympathy. "He came back in disguise to see his wife and son. He was arrested at the house of a friend."

"There's more," Sherry added. "We heard talk that Ney has been arrested as well."

Robert groaned. The spilling of blood had not ended at Waterloo.

"No one's talking about you yet," Sherry went on. "Not

a word in the papers. The guess is your arrest is being kept quiet until they're sure they have a case. Your cousin Paul considered kicking up a row in print, but decided it would do more harm than good."

Robert gave a wry smile. "Let's give thanks for cool heads." He withdrew a sheaf of papers from beneath the mattress and laid them on the table. "There it is. An account of my history with Demaire. Would you see that Adam gets it?"

Emma picked up the sheets, folded them twice, and stuffed them in her reticule. "I'll see Caroline this afternoon."

"One thing more." Robert handed a single folded sheet to Sherry. "Would you get this to Georges Demaire first thing tomorrow by a messenger who can't be traced."

Sherry raised his brows and tucked the paper inside his coat.

"A drink?" Robert asked.

"I'll wait for coffee." Tatin, again lavishly tipped, had been sent off to the café for refreshments.

Robert looked at Emma. "Then I have one more request."

Andy dropped down on the bed in Robert's cell. "Emma said you wanted Jack and me to stop by. But she didn't say why."

Robert looked at the boys' eager faces. They were young to be involved in such a business, but he had been little older when he first rode off to war. "I'm expecting a man," he told them. "I want to know where he goes when he leaves. He'll be preoccupied, but he's not stupid. Don't let him see you."

Andy stared thoughtfully at the toes of his boots, but Jack said it was a bang-up assignment. "Meanwhile we can have a game." He fished a pair of dice out of his pocket. "Do you mind if we don't play for real money, Lescaut?"

Robert did not, and they spent the next two hours at the table, finishing a bottle of wine and broaching a second. When the door opened and Tatin announced in a bored voice that the prisoner Lescaut had another visitor, Jack pocketed his dice and he and Andy said hasty farewells. Jack made a show of seeming well in his cups. Andy grabbed the bottle from the table and pressed it with fervent thanks into Tatin's hands. They brushed by the visitor, giving him only a cursory glance. Andy shouted in execrable French that they would return tomorrow and seek their revenge.

Tatin disappeared, locking the door behind him, and Georges Demaire stepped into the small room. He was a tall man and might be accounted an ugly one save that his features were striking enough to command attention. His nose was large and misshapen, his lips well-formed and somewhat thick, his cheeks sunken, and his chin prominent. He had thick black brows that met above his nose, giving the impression that he was scowling. His hair was also black and thick, one lock falling over his forehead. He flicked it back without apparent thought, a mannerism Robert remembered from years past.

Robert indicated the chair with a careless gesture. He had remained seated on the bed, his hair disheveled, his shirt unbuttoned. When Demaire was seated and had placed his hat and stick on the floor, Robert leaned forward and rested his arms on the table. "It's been a long time."

Demaire sat very straight, one hand on his thigh, the other playing with a watch chain. "For me it could well be longer. I have no wish to see you."

"You came."

"You said you had information of use to me."

"Did I?" Robert ran a hand through his hair. "I'm

sorry, I've had too much wine. I don't remember what I said."

Demaire reached for his hat. "In that case I will go."

"No." The word was sharp and caused Demaire to relinquish his hat. "I remember well enough what I have to say to you. Georges Demaire. You're doing well for yourself, aren't you, Georges? I applaud you. A man must learn to seize his chances."

Demaire's look of contempt deepened, but he said nothing.

"I don't care what you've done. Do you understand me? I know the games you've played. I have proof. I won't use it if . . ." Robert let the words trail off and smiled at the man sitting across the table.

"You're threatening me."

"Why, so I am."

"Who would believe you? A man who killed his wife's lover and then murdered his wife to make his revenge complete. A Bonapartist spy. A traitor to the crown. You'd say anything to save your paltry life."

Robert knew the first knife had found its mark. "As would you. Who knows which of us would be believed."

"There's no question. No question at all." A faint sheen of sweat appeared on Demaire's forehead.

"Well. Perhaps you're right. But a small seed of doubt will be planted. *There wasn't actually any proof, but perhaps Demaire isn't quite sound.* Not enough to damn you, Georges. Just enough to keep you from advancement."

Demaire brushed back the lock of hair and leaned forward. "What do you want?"

"Lucie. I don't care about Philippe. The whelp was rutting between my wife's legs. He can rot in hell. But someone sent Lucie a message that caused her to run off to Ostend. Someone met her at the inn and twisted a knife in her gut."

Demaire folded his arms. "I wasn't in Ostend that night. I have a half-dozen witnesses to prove it."

"I don't doubt that you have. But then, I never supposed you did the deed yourself, any more than you struck down Philippe in the street. I want the name of the man who met my wife. I want to find the piece of filth and take his life as he took Lucie's."

"Why should I know anything about Lucie's death?"

"Because she knew you, Georges. She knew you spied for the Royalists and betrayed them to the government at the same time. Philippe knew. That's why you had him killed. Lucie blamed you for it. She was going to expose you."

Demaire reached for his hat and stick and stood up, his face white, his voice trembling. "Conjecture. The conjectures of a sick mind."

"She left me a letter, Georges." Robert hoped the lie would have a ring of truth. "It's in a very safe place."

Demaire drew himself up to his full height. He was an imposing figure. "And all for a pretty lying woman who fouled your bed and is four years dead. I don't believe you."

"You can't afford not to believe me."

"What can you do? You're in prison. You won't get out alive. So much for your revenge."

Robert stood, forcing Demaire to meet his gaze. "I don't need to stay here. It was your charge that brought me here. You can withdraw it."

Demaire clapped his hat on his head. "It's too late. It's not up to me."

"Think on it, Georges. Remember what's at stake."

Demaire strode to the door and beat on the grille with his stick. Tatin called out that he was coming, he only had two feet, what did the gentleman expect. Demaire waited, his back rigid, until the door was unlocked. Then he strode out without a word to the gaoler. Tatin looked at his empty palm and shook his head, then locked the door again.

Robert looked after him, feeling the stirring of excitement that comes when the enemy is finally within view. "It was Demaire," he told Emma when she and Sherry came that afternoon. "I'm sure of it now."

Emma stared at him as though not sure she had heard him right. "You have proof?"

"A strong certainty. Demaire was here this morning. The man's afraid. He had something to hide."

Emma gave a great sigh, as though releasing the pent-up tension of the past weeks. "Then it wasn't a Blair."

"No." He forced himself to meet her gaze. "I was wrong, Emma." It was a bald admission, the only one he could make. It was pitifully inadequate.

She rested her hand briefly on his own. "You would have known earlier if we hadn't lied to you. You couldn't have known about Demaire until you learned that Lucie was working for Bram."

Her words were a kind of absolution, as sweet and healing as the touch of her hand. For the first time, Lucie did not stand between them. An insurmountable wall had been breached. He looked into her eyes and saw the same lightening of spirit. God help him, he had to kiss her. "Emma—"

She stepped toward him as though she would go into his arms.

Sherry coughed. "It's dangerous to bait a man like Demaire. Don't take chances now, Lescaut. The escape is set for tomorrow."

Emma stepped back and fiddled with her lawn neckerchief.

Robert turned to Sherry. "But I must. I'm so close to learning the truth. Adam said someone besides Demaire was behind my arrest, and Demaire as good as admitted it today. He's afraid of the man, whoever he is, but he'll want to tell him about my threats."

Comprehension lit Sherry's face. "Jack and Andy."

"I set them to follow Demaire when he left the prison."

26

The following day Emma and Sherry came again to sit with him at their customary hour. Emma went right to him and took his hands. She was wearing a filmy dress the color of champagne, her skin glowed, and tantalizing tendrils of hair fell about her face. Robert pushed a curl behind her ear. In another hour he would be a free man. He would deal with Demaire and his accomplice and at last put Lucie behind him. And then he would ask Emma to marry him. For the first time, he let himself frame the thought. His fingers trembled against her skin with the wonder of it.

"Robert," Emma said when Tatin had left to fetch the coffee he now procured without question, "I have news."

Sherry grinned. "The boys are bursting with pride at their own cleverness."

Robert was still looking at Emma. "They had no trouble following Demaire?"

"None." Emma moved to the table, pulling Robert with her. "He went straight to the Rue Grammont." She sat and clasped her hands. "The house of Henriette Colbert."

Robert started. He was not surprised that Demaire still visited Henriette, but he had not expected she would be the person to whom he would turn. Perhaps she was his mistress and he had gone to her for solace. Or to ask her to deliver a message.

"He stayed perhaps twenty minutes," Emma continued. "Then he returned to his own apartments and did not stir 'til at least eleven o'clock, when Andy and Jack gave up the watch. They sat all that time in a small café across the street, eating their dinner and drinking far more than was good for them. They were quite jug-bitten when they got back." She looked down at her hands. "There's one thing more," she said, her face pale beneath the unbleached straw of her hat. "When Demaire left Madame Colbert's, Bram was with him."

"Bram?" Robert said, more sharply than he intended.

She met his gaze without flinching. "Madame Colbert worked for Bram. It's not surprising that he would call on her. They wouldn't have expected Demaire."

Nor would Demaire have expected to find Bram in the Rue Grammont. But their meeting was an odd coincidence, and Robert was suspicious of oddity.

Emma frowned. "Perhaps Madame Colbert found Demaire troublesome and asked Bram to see him out of the house. She and Bram are friends. It's natural she would ask him for help." She was silent for a moment. "Or are they more than friends?"

Robert looked into the gray-green eyes that had already been dealt such hurt. "Are you sure you want to know?"

"I'm not afraid of the truth. They were lovers, weren't they? Are they still?"

"I don't know. I'm sure it has nothing to do with Jenny."

"It would hurt her nonetheless." Emma's voice had a bitter edge. She drew back in the chair, fingers twisting in the gauzy rose fabric of her shawl. The wall was between them once more. Yesterday he had told her he believed the Blairs were innocent. Today another Blair thrust himself into the puzzle. No matter how he stepped, he hurt her.

Sherry, with characteristic tact, took over the burden of conversation. Tatin returned with the coffee. Sherry offered him one of the bottles of wine he had brought. The gaoler grinned and scurried back to his post in the corridor.

They drank the coffee in silence. When a quarter hour had passed, Sherry rose and removed his cloak. "Time, I think." He stripped off his coat and handed it to Robert. "It should fit well enough. Don't worry about returning it. I have more clothes than I can wear." He took up a position near the bed. "Ready when you are, Lescaut."

Robert threw the coat on the table and stepped in front of Sherry. "You're sure of this?"

Sherry smiled. "It's necessary. Do what you must."

Robert planted his feet well apart. "Emma," he said without turning around, "do you mind moving back."

He heard her gasp. Apparently she had not been clear about this part of the plan. Robert looked at Sherry's jaw, selecting the exact point of impact. He drew his arm back and slammed his fist into the other man's face. Sherry crumpled and fell back on the bed. Emma made a sound of dismay. Robert turned to look at her. "Sorry."

She was breathing hard. "It's all right. Is he . . ."

Robert leaned over the bed and took Sherry's chin in his hand. "Out like a snuffed candle. I should rough him up a bit more, but he'll feel rotten enough as it is." He ripped the neck of Sherry's shirt, then exchanged the shoes he had worn to the wedding for Sherry's boots. The tan breeches could stay. They were near enough to his own. He rolled Sherry toward the wall, put his arm over his face, and arranged the pillow to obscure most of his hair.

"Deep in his cups," he murmured. He uncorked the wine bottle they had not touched and poured most of its contents into the chamber pot. The room reeked with the sour smell. Then he put the near-empty bottle into Sherry's hand. A trickle of wine spilled out on the bed, leaving a thin trail of red.

"It will work," Emma said, her calm restored. She held Sherry's coat for Robert to slip on. He added the long black cloak and the broad-brimmed hat, then picked up Sherry's silver-handled walking stick. Emma took the tray Tatin had brought and set it near the door. "Gaoler," she called through the grille. Robert stood close behind her, his face turned away from the door. It was important that Emma be able to claim later that she had been acting under duress, that he had threatened her with a knife.

Tatin came toward them, his gait slow and unsteady. He unlocked the door with elaborate care, then bent down to pick up the tray. As he straightened he looked into the cell. His gaze went straight to the bed. "Drunk," Robert said. Tatin sniffed the air and grinned. Robert dropped some coins into Tatin's hand, then took Emma by the arm and guided her out of the cell.

Tatin's wheezing laughter and the sound of the key scraping in the lock followed them down the corridor. They had more corridors and stairways to traverse, other guards to encounter, and the clerk who stood at the entrance to pass. Difficult, but Robert had negotiated far worse.

They turned a corner and nearly collided with a guard escorting a black-garbed man who clutched a sheaf of papers under his arm. "Visitors to the prisoner Lescaut," the guard explained to his companion. "They always leave at this hour. He'll be alone now, ready enough for your questions."

Robert stopped and turned round, holding Emma firmly beside him. He could feel the rapid beating of her heart. "If you want to speak to Lescaut, you're wasting your time," he called after them, adopting Sherry's drawling accents. "He's drunk. Ask Tatin."

The two men stopped and looked back. The black-garbed man swore. "You'd think they could keep them sober." He turned to the guard. "We'd better see. I suppose the interrogation will have to wait."

Robert and Emma did not stay to hear more. They quickened their pace through the lower reaches of the prison. Then they were at the entrance with only the officious clerk and the guards at the door to pass. With freedom in sight, the clerk called out in a peremptory voice, "Monsieur de Sheriton."

Emma moaned and fell against Robert. "The lady is unwell," Robert said, "I must get her home." He repeated the words in French and added that they would return the following day. A protective arm around Emma, he hurried toward the entrance, past the guards, and out into the blessed light and air of the courtyard.

Now it was Emma who led the way. The courtyard was thronged with people, all bent on their own business. Sherry's carriage stood just outside the courtyard in the Place du Palais de Justice. The coachman sprang down and opened the door, and in a moment the carriage had turned the corner and was clattering down the Rue de l'Horloge.

"Andy," Robert said, acknowledging the young man who sat across from them in the carriage. "And if I'm not mistaken, that's Jack playing coachman. I wouldn't have known him."

Andy grinned. "I wouldn't have known you. I thought something had gone wrong. I would have sworn it was Sherry coming across the courtyard. You've got his very gait and air."

"And voice." Emma fell back against the squabs as though allowing herself to breathe for the first time in the past quarter hour. "Sherry hasn't much head for languages. His French has an atrocious accent, and Robert caught it exactly."

"I have to thank you," Robert said. "I have to thank you all. I owe you more than I can ever repay."

Andy's eyes brightened. "It's been a great lark." He pulled out a handful of papers. "Adam says these will see you out of Paris."

"Tell him I'm grateful." Robert tucked the papers inside Sherry's borrowed coat. "Now, tell me about Demaire. How did he look when he went into the house in the Rue Grammont?"

"He was preoccupied," Andy said after a moment. "Worried, I'd say. His brows were drawn, his body stiff and tight as though he had trouble holding himself together. Jack said he looked like a horse ready to bolt. But he knew where he was going. The concierge greeted him as though he had been there before."

"And when he left?"

"Much the same. If he hoped for something when he entered the building, I don't think he found it there." Andy smiled. "I couldn't believe it when he walked out of the house with Bram."

"How did they behave towards each other?" Robert asked.

Andy frowned. "I hadn't thought about it. But I see what you mean. Was he afraid of Bram? No. Bram looked grim, too, as well he might if he were escorting an unwelcome visitor out of the house. But—I don't know why—they didn't seem to be strangers."

Emma cast an anxious glance at Robert. "They weren't. That is, they could have known each other. Demaire visited Madame Colbert, and Bram knew her well."

"How did they part?" Robert asked.

"They spoke a few minutes—Demaire seemed tense

and angry—and then he turned on his heel and stalked away."

"Perhaps Madame Colbert was Demaire's mistress too," Emma said, looking at Robert.

Andy stared at her, then gave a low whistle.

Emma swung her head toward him. "Andy, you didn't hear that. And if you did, that's not what I meant. We're talking about Demaire. If he went to see his mistress because Robert upset him, he'd be angry to find her with another man."

Robert rapped on the roof of the carriage with Sherry's stick, signaling Jack to stop. They drew up in the Rue de Rivoli, which was crowded with pedestrians, sedan chairs, and carriages of all descriptions. "Andy," he said. "Find Emma a fiacre. Then send her home."

Emma fixed him with a hard stare. "You *are* leaving Paris."

"I am. But first I need to speak to Martin."

"No." She leaned forward on the carriage seat. "You can't afford to delay. I'm going to ask Bram about his meeting with Demaire. There just hasn't been time. I'll speak to him after you leave and tell Adam what he says. It's too dangerous for you to stay."

Robert touched her hand. "It's my life I risk, Emma."

"And you're bloody ungrateful to risk it after we've been at such pains to rescue you."

He sat back on the seat. "I'm sorry, Em. I have to do this."

She watched him, her gaze so unwavering that her pearl-and-gold earrings hung motionless beside her face. "Very well. We'll both call on Bram."

"No." The word echoed off the silk-lined walls of the carriage. He moderated his voice. "It's one thing for me to run risks. I won't let you do the same."

"What risk can there be to me in calling at my cousin's house? Besides, Jamie and Will are spending their leave

with Jenny. You may need my help if you run into them."
She pulled down the window and called up to Jack.
"We're going to the Rue d'Anjou."

Emma willed herself to silence until they reached
Bram's house. When they pulled up in the Rue d'Anjou,
Robert sprang out of the carriage, let down the steps, and
gave her his hand to help her descend. Andy, who had
been watching them in bewildered silence, leaned out of
the carriage door. "Emma, shall I . . ."

"No," she said, though she would have welcomed his
support. Robert, to whom she had been so close these
last few days, now seemed a vast distance away. "Stay
with the carriage."

She squeezed Andy's hand, then walked to the walled
courtyard that fronted the house. She stopped just inside
the entrance. She heard Robert telling Jack to drive
around the corner and wait. It was late afternoon. Slant-
ing rays of sun made bars of light across the cobblestones. Geraniums, blood red, lined the top of the
courtyard wall and spilled down its sides. Their entry
seemed an intrusion into this quiet place, but when Robert joined her, she walked toward the house without hesitation.

But as they reached the door, it was thrown open and
Jamie emerged. He was freshly shaved, with pristine
white breeches and highly polished boots. "Em," he said
in surprise. He took a step toward her and became aware
that the man standing at her side was not Sherry. "Lescaut. What the devil?" His eyes hardened. "See here.
You're supposed to be in prison. How did you get out?
What have you involved my sister in? By God, if you
bring any more harm to my family—"

Emma stepped between them. "Robert, go."

Jamie thrust her aside and grasped Robert by the arms. "You'll go nowhere. Will," he called, "I need help."

Will, who had followed Jamie out of the house, stood uncertainly on the doorstep.

"Jamie, stop!" Emma pulled at his arm, trying to loosen his grip.

"Are you out of your mind, Em?" Jamie swung his head toward her. "The man's been accused of murder. Will, you bloody fool, come here. He'll get away."

But Robert had not been struggling, though his breathing had deepened and his eyes were dark with anger. "I'm going nowhere. I have no quarrel with you, Jamie Blair. Nor with you, Will. I've come to see Bram Martin." With a quick twist of his body he freed himself from Jamie's grasp. Jamie stumbled in an effort to keep his balance.

Emma once more put herself between them. "Go, I beg you. For the love of God, go."

Robert put her aside. His touch was gentle, but his eyes were hard. He moved toward the house. Jamie pulled his sabre from its scabbard and barred the way. "No. We're going to settle this now, Lescaut. You deceived us and cheated us and accused us of the vilest of crimes. You debauched my sister. Don't deny it, I can see it in her face. The world will be well rid of you. Emma, don't come near or I'll run him through. Draw, you French devil. Draw your sword."

Robert flung wide the long cloak he still wore, making a semicircle of black around him. "I'm unarmed."

"But Will isn't." Jamie stripped off his coat. "Will, give him your sabre. Do it, I say."

Robert unfastened the cloak and threw it aside. "Do as he asks, Will. Can't you see this is an affair of honor? None of us will go anywhere until he's satisfied." His voice was light, amused, but there was a bitter smile on his face. He took off his coat. "You'd better shut the door. We don't want to disturb the servants with our play."

Will stared at him, then slowly drew his sabre.

"Robert, no!" Emma had not done all she had to keep Robert safe only to have her brother injured. Robert had the edge in experience and judgment. Jamie, despite his strength and agility, was a hothead who could not think beyond the moment.

"I'm sorry," Robert said. "He insists on the quarrel." He drew back and raised the borrowed sabre in salute.

Jamie dealt in no such niceties. He lunged at Robert, aiming straight for his heart.

"In a hurry, Blair?" Robert parried the thrust and re-treated. Jamie lunged again. Emma started forward.

"There's nothing you can do, Em." Will pulled her into the shelter of the adjoining stable.

He was right, damn him. If she interfered, she would break their concentration and one of them might be hurt. She stood in the shadows of the stable, eyes trained on her brother and the man she loved.

The fighting was quick, too quick for her to follow. The blades met, clanged, scraped, disengaged, then met again. The men's booted feet scuffed and slithered over the cobblestones. The sunlight gleamed against their white shirts, bounced blindingly off the polished steel of the blades.

Jamie pressed Robert across the courtyard, toward the brick wall. Robert parried each thrust but never moved to the attack. At the last minute, he ducked sideways before Jamie could imprison him against the wall.

Emma released her breath, then gasped. Jenny's in-nocuous, terra-cotta birdbath created an unforeseen trap at Robert's back.

Victory leapt in Jamie's eyes. He lunged forward, his arm extended to its furthest length. Robert dropped to the ground and rolled beneath the overhanging lip of the birdbath. Jamie's sabre crashed into the terra-cotta.

"A palpable hit, Blair." Robert sprang to his feet. "But the wrong target."

"Tricks won't save you, Lescaut." Jamie's sabre flashed as he flung himself at Robert.

Jamie was a far better swordsman than he had been when he and Will practiced in the courtyard of Blair House. Time and again he drove Robert toward the wall. Each time, by some miracle of movement, a twist of his body, a flick of his wrist, Robert evaded him and appeared once more in the center of the courtyard.

"My God, they're good," Will said. "Both of them."

Emma would have glared at him, but she could not take her eyes from the fight.

Jamie redoubled his attack, quick and ferocious. This time, when Robert would have darted aside, Jamie caught Robert's blade with the flat of his own. Steel grated against steel. Jamie forced Robert's blade up until he had Robert pinned to the courtyard wall, their sabres locked overhead, gleaming against the mellow brick. For a moment, they looked into each other's eyes, Jamie's gaze wild with anger, Robert's cool and controlled. Then Robert threw his weight forward. Jamie stumbled back. Robert edged away from the wall but did not press his attack.

Jamie stared at him, his breathing harsh with effort. "Fight, damn you."

"Why should I?" Robert moved sideways so that Jamie had to look into the sun to face him. "It's not my quarrel."

"Christ," Will murmured. "The fool."

Jamie made a blind lunge into the sunlight. Robert stepped out of the way. Emma sucked in her breath. Robert would defend himself, but he would not hurt her brother. Love for him welled up inside her. Fear for him closed her throat.

Jamie had begun to tire. His thrusts grew wide and slashing and he panted with exertion. And he was angry, shouting and grunting and cursing his opponent for not giving him a proper fight. Robert was tiring, too, though he never lost the center of his attention.

Sweat drenched both men's faces, plastered their shirts to their arms, soaked through their waistcoats. "Give it up, Blair." Robert was breathing hard. "It proves nothing."

"Never!" Jamie renewed the attack.

Robert parried the deadly sabre and retreated once more. Then, perhaps because he was tired, he lifted his guard. Emma's blood went cold. She started to cry out a warning, then bit back the words. She did not dare distract him.

Jamie saw the opening. With a great cry of triumph, he lunged forward. Robert's arm moved, faster than Emma could see. The next instant Jamie's sabre flew across the courtyard and clattered to the cobblestones. Robert threw his own sabre aside.

Jamie stared, dismayed, at his empty hand. The door opened and Bram appeared on the doorstep. Jamie picked up the sabre Robert had discarded and hurled himself at Robert.

"You bloody fool." Bram spun Jamie around, knocked the sabre from his hand, and slammed his fist into Jamie's face. With a memory of Sherry falling beneath Robert's blow, Emma watched her brother crumple to the ground and lie still.

Will stirred beside her. She held him back and motioned him to silence. Bram was not aware of their presence, and maybe it was better so. Robert believed Bram was linked with Demaire, and he was bent on confrontation, whether or not she was at his side. Bram would talk more freely in her absence. She had to know what he would say. She could not believe he was touched with guilt, and yet he might know more than he had claimed. He had been a spy, as had Demaire and Madame Colbert and Lucie. They moved in a world she could scarcely comprehend.

While these thoughts raced through her head, Emma held herself still, clutching Will's arm. Bram was on his knees beside Jamie. He raised Jamie's head and listened to his breathing, then set him down with care. "He'll do," Bram said to Robert. "I can't have him running a man through on my doorstep." He stood up, frowning. Despite the lightness of his words, Emma thought he was angry. "What the devil do you think you're doing, Lescaut? You're supposed to be in prison. Don't you know they'll hunt you down?"

"I came to see you, Martin. We have things to settle between us."

"We have nothing to settle." Bram regarded Robert with wariness tinged with what might have been compassion. "I know what you've been through. Any man would be deranged at losing his wife in that way. But you've learned everything there is to know. I've admitted Lucie's connection with my family. Angus has admitted it. He's offered money to your son. Let that be enough for you. Turn around and walk out the gate and don't come back. I'll give you a quarter hour's grace, but then I'll have to call the authorities."

Robert did not seem to hear him. He picked up his coat and shrugged back into it, smoothing the fabric with care. "Georges Demaire sought you out yesterday. Why?"

Even with the distance between them, Emma could read the surprise on Bram's face. "Demaire called on Henriette."

"Knowing Henriette could bring you there within the hour. He must have been pleased you were there already.

You knew what he was, didn't you? You knew he worked for your cause and betrayed it at the same time. And you kept silent. Philippe did not. He learned about Demaire and threatened to expose him."

Bram's eyes softened with what Emma could swear was genuine sympathy. "You're mad with grief, Lescaut. If Demaire was what you say, I of all people would not protect him."

"Demaire didn't work alone. Was it you he came to for help when Philippe threatened him? Did you tell him there was only one way to be safe, that Philippe had to die?"

Bram shook his head. "I don't understand what you're after. Why should you care about Philippe? The man dishonored your bed."

"Is that why Lucie had to die?" Robert continued as though Bram had not spoken. "Because she knew of Demaire's treachery too?" He paused, his gaze sharp as the blade of the sabre. "Or because she knew of your own? It wasn't only Demaire who served two masters, was it? You did so as well."

Bram laughed, a full relaxed sound that dispelled the horror of Robert's accusation. He threw his arms wide. "If that's what you believe, Lescaut, pick up your sabre and run me through."

Emma caught her breath. Did Robert's dark and twisted sense of honor blind him to what was so obvious? Bram was innocent. His laughter confirmed it. She watched Robert tense. If he took one step toward the sabre, she would cry out, distract him, put a stop to this deadly farce they were playing.

But Robert did not look at the sabre. His gaze remained on Bram. "No. There's been too much killing. And Emma would never forgive me."

Will let out his breath in a soft explosion of sound. Emma stood motionless, scarcely able to believe what she had heard. As surely as he had tossed aside the sabre, Robert had abandoned the quest for vengeance that had driven him for so long. Whatever he believed, he would not destroy someone she cared for. It was the greatest gift he could have given her.

The men were silent. Emma could not tell what passed between them. Then Robert spoke again. "But you can't believe I'll be quiet about this. I have to know the truth. You and Demaire. You weren't sure there was any hope for the Royalist cause, so you took care to stand well with the Bonaparte government too. Demaire hoped for advancement. What did you do it for, Martin? Your estates? Did Lucie and Philippe die so you could reclaim your inheritance?"

Bram's face tightened. He stared at Robert for a long moment, his contempt for the man before him written in every feature. "You're not an aristo. You'd never understand."

"Perhaps I wouldn't. It doesn't matter. Lucie went to Ostend to meet you. Why did she take the ring? To remind you that she had family that would protect her?"

"Give it up, Lescaut. Lucie wasn't worth it."

"Damn your lying tongue, she was my wife." Robert sprang at Bram and pushed him against the wall of the house. "Did you have to kill a woman?"

In that moment Emma did not recognize Bram. His cultivated manner was gone. His face was contorted with fury. "Lucie was playing the game, too. She was as dangerous as any man." Bram twisted away and struck at Robert. Robert ducked and the blow grazed his cheek. Bram seized him. They fought with fists and hands and knees and feet, struggling back and forth across the courtyard.

Bram was as strong as Robert, but Robert had had twelve years in the field. Within a few moments Bram was lying on his back with Robert kneeling astride him, his hands at Bram's throat. "It was you at Ostend, wasn't it? You weren't in Paris with Henriette. Lucie sent you a message and you came to meet her. It was you who plunged the knife in her body. Tell me, damn you."

Bram tore at Robert's hands and twisted beneath him. "What if it was. She was a whore."

Robert removed his hands from Bram's throat. He sat back, his shoulders sagging in weariness or defeat. "I should kill you, Martin. I would have killed you once. Get up." He rose and walked to Jamie, who was beginning to stir.

Something died within Emma. She watched Bram get to his feet. And then she saw him draw a pistol from his pocket and aim it at Robert.

"No." She ran to Bram and pulled at his arm, tears running down her face. "Tell me he's wrong. Tell me it isn't true."

Bram's eyes were dazed, his face distorted. "True? What are you thinking of?" His voice was no more than a harsh whisper.

Emma stared at the man who had been her first, if not her greatest, love. "Bram, you tried to kill him."

He looked at her, then glanced at Will, who had left the shelter of the stable and was standing nearby. "Lescaut is dangerous." The composed mask fell back in place over his features. "He's dangerous to all of us."

"No, he's our friend," Emma said. "His son is a Blair."

Bram's eyes narrowed. "He's an escaped prisoner. Go in the house, Em. Jenny will need you. I'll take care of him."

"No!" Emma seized his arms, only dimly aware that he still held the pistol in his hand. "I have to know the truth."

Bram looked into her eyes, his own dark and compelling. "You think I killed Lescaut's wife?" His voice grew soft. "You can ask me that? You've known me half your life. You've known this man less than five months. How can you believe him? How can you take his word over mine?" He reached out a hand and cupped her face. "It's me, Em. Christ, after what we've been to each other, how can you doubt me? You know what you mean to me."

Her skin crawled at his touch. She jerked away from the hand that had once caressed her. "I know what Henriette Colbert means to you."

He laughed. "Oh, Em. Still an innocent."

It was over. From her youthful idolatry to the love she freely gave him, Bram had been her ideal of manhood. That man was gone. He had never been there at all. Worse, Robert knew her folly and deceit and degradation. She had been criminally stupid and she had been a wanton.

Anger threatened to suffocate her. "How could you, Bram? How could you betray the country that took you in? How could you betray your own people in France? You knew which side you were working for. Why in God's name would you serve Bonaparte?"

Bram went very still. "Imagine if you lost Blair House and everything that makes you what you are. I was thirteen years old. Suddenly it was all gone. And my father's pride with it. We had to live on the charity of my mother's family. Do you know what Angus said when I asked him for Jenny's hand? That he would have preferred that his daughter make a more splendid match." Bram's eyes went onyx hard. "Don't talk to me about sides, Em. There are no sides. There's only my family. They claim all my loyalties. You of all people should know that. Don't the Blairs feel the same?"

Emma felt as though he had struck her. The war, Robert's treachery, the secrets her family had kept hidden, all these had shaken the foundations of her being. She had lost her moorings. Now Bram had cast her totally adrift.

Bram raised his hand and leveled the pistol at her. "Will, take her into the house."

Emma stared at the pistol, gleaming in the last rays of the afternoon sun.

"Go, Emma," Robert said. She did not turn around, but she could feel his absolute stillness.

Will took a step forward. "For God's sake, Bram—"

"Get her out of here, Will." Robert's voice was crisp, a commanding officer issuing an order. "Now."

Silence gripped the courtyard. Emma looked from the gun to Bram's unyielding gaze. She picked up her skirt, taking care that her fingers appeared to tremble, though there was little need for pretense. "We have to go in, Will."

"Em—"

"There's nothing more we can do." She gave a sob and took a step forward. Her skirt slipped from her seemingly nerveless fingers. She stumbled as though she had caught her foot in the folds of her gown, and lunged at Bram.

Bram gave a grunt of surprise. He pushed her away. She grabbed for the pistol. For a moment they clung together in a sickening echo of the embraces they had once shared. She had never known his hands could be so brutal. She got a purchase on his arm and tried to pry his fingers from the gun. The folds of her shawl tangled about her arms. Bram's grip on the gun tightened.

There was a sharp report. The impact sent her stumbling backward. Bram stared at her. The pistol slipped from his fingers. His hand went to the spreading stain on his chest. "*Nom de Dieu.* You of all people, Em." His gaze clung to her face. "I meant it, you know. My greatest mistake was not to marry you."

He took a step forward, stretched out his hand to her, then collapsed on the ground at her feet.

27

Emma dropped to her knees and felt for Bram's pulse.
"He's dead." She looked up at Robert, who was kneeling
beside her.

Robert scanned her face. "Are you hurt?"

She shook her head. "There was only one shot."

He took her by the shoulders. "Breathe. Deeply. You're
a mad enough fool for the battlefield, Emma Blair."

The door was flung open with a crash. "Bram? I heard
a shot." Jenny ran into the courtyard, clutching a lace
shawl over her pale blue dress. She came to an abrupt
halt, taking in the scene before her. *"Bram?"* she said
again. The name was a scream of horror.

"Jenny." Emma sprang to her feet and put her arms
around Jenny before she could go any closer. "There's
been an accident. Bram's dead."

"No." The word was torn from Jenny's throat. She
wrenched herself from Emma's grasp and collapsed on
the cobblestones beside her husband. "Bram, oh God,
Bram." She looked about in desperation. "Why doesn't
someone send for a doctor?"

"Madame Martin," Robert said gently. "Your husband
is dead."

Jenny stared down at Bram, her fingers moving against
his face, seeking signs of life. Then she looked at Robert

as though aware of him for the first time. Her body tensed. "You killed him." The words were a cold, flat statement. With a sob of fury she flung herself on Robert and beat her fists against his chest.

"Jenny, no." Emma dropped down between her cousin and Robert and pulled Jenny back. "It was an accident."

"An accident?" Jenny's voice rose to a note of shrill hysteria. "He's a murderer. He went to prison for murdering his wife's lover. How could you bring him into my house? How could you?" She brought up her hand and struck Emma hard across the cheek.

The force of the blow knocked Emma backward. Robert caught her. Will rushed forward as though the sound had released him from his paralysis. "Jenny, don't."

Jenny didn't seem to hear him. She fell onto her husband's bloodstained chest, her body racked with sobs.

Emma twisted around and looked at Robert. "You can't do any more here. Go while there's still time."

Robert hesitated, his eyes dark with feelings there was no time to put into words.

A groan came from the other side of the courtyard. "Em?" Jamie said in a thick voice. "Will? What the devil's going on? Bram *hit* me."

Emma brushed her fingers against Robert's face. *"Go."*

Robert looked at her a moment longer, then gave a quick nod. He got to his feet but stood looking down at Bram and the sobbing Jenny. "Let her believe I did it," he said in a quiet voice. "It will be easier that way."

Emma did not allow herself the luxury of watching Robert leave the courtyard. Will was helping Jamie to his feet and speaking to him in a low voice. Emma tried to pull Jenny away, but Jenny refused to leave Bram. The soft thud of the gate closing told Emma that Robert was gone. She would not let herself look around.

"We'll take him inside, Em," Will said, coming to stand

beside her. Jamie was at his side, fully conscious but for once bereft of speech.

Emma half coaxed, half dragged Jenny away from Bram so that Will and Jamie could lift his body. Jenny struggled, then seemed to go numb as Emma led her into the house.

The footman and two of the maids were huddled in the entrance hall. "There's been an accident," Will told them. "We're taking Monsieur Martin into the library."

The footman hurried to open the library door. "Shall I send for a doctor, m'sieur?"

Will glanced at Jenny. "Yes. Perhaps you should."

Emma asked the maids to make tea and keep the rest of the household quiet. Then she shepherded Jenny into the library after the men.

At the sight of Bram laid out on the sofa, Jenny roused herself. She knelt beside him and pressed his hand to her cheek as though she could still not believe he was really dead.

"By God." Jamie's low, angry voice broke the silence in the room. "Lescaut's going to pay. How could you let him leave after he did a thing like this?"

"He didn't do it," Emma said.

"Damnation, Em—"

"I did."

"*What?*" Jamie seized her arm.

Emma looked him full in the face. "Bram had a gun. He was threatening me. He was threatening all of us. I tried to take the gun away from him. It went off. If anyone killed him, I did."

"Why the devil would Bram threaten you?"

Emma looked at Bram's still figure and the sobbing Jenny. "I think that had better wait until we can talk to someone who knows the whole story."

"Who?" Jamie asked. "Lescaut?"

"No. Henriette Colbert."

* * *

"So your quest is at an end." Adam looked across his study at Robert. "Lucie's death has been avenged, even if not by your hand."

Robert pushed his fingers into his hair. He felt drained and numb. He shouldn't be surprised. The battlefield had taught him that victory was often hollow. "I'd be grateful if you could help hush up any difficulty for the Blairs."

"Of course. Is there anything you'd like me to tell Emma?"

Emma. The sound of her name was a sharp, stinging blow. Robert gripped the arms of his chair. "No."

Adam leaned forward. "It's not my place to interfere, but—"

"Her last words to me were 'You can't do any more here.' She didn't say 'any more harm,' but she may as well have done." Robert stared at his hands, feeling the weight of his failure. "I would have let Martin go. I wanted to spare her this. I couldn't protect my brother or my wife. I thought I could at least protect Emma from pain. But in the end I couldn't even do that."

"You didn't kill Bram Martin," Adam said.

Robert gave a shout of bitter laughter. "No, I got Emma to do it for me."

"He murdered your wife. He was responsible for Philippe de Rivaud's death."

"He was the husband of Emma's cousin. I saw Jenny Martin sobbing over his body, Adam. *Nom de Dieu,* as if I haven't made enough widows on the battlefield." He pressed his hands to his eyes, recalling that last moment when Emma had brushed her fingers against his face. He wondered if she would ever touch him again. "Emma cared for Martin. When she was a girl, I think she was half in love with him." He could say no more to Adam, but he knew now just how much Bram had once meant to Emma. "I betrayed her. Then I forced her to face his betrayal."

"You wish he was still alive?"

"A woman is widowed and four children are fatherless. Sir Angus has lost the son-in-law he relied upon. Emma has lost a friend. Whatever his crimes, the Blairs will never forget I set in motion the events that brought about his death. Emma will never forget that because of me she knows what it is to kill."

"Perhaps you underestimate her."

"On the contrary. I know what loyalty means to her."

There was a light knock at the door. Caroline slipped into the room. Her gray eyes were warm with sympathy, but she merely said, "I've fed Andy and Jack. They're ready to leave whenever you are."

"Then we'd best be off." Robert pushed himself to his feet, relieved at the call to action. As long as there was something to do, it was not necessary to think.

Adam got to his feet as well. "Where will you go?"

"Somewhere that had best remain my secret. The fewer lies you have to tell on my account the better."

Adam raised his brows. "You think I'm not equal to the task?"

"Or do you think we'll tell Emma?" Caroline said.

There would be time, Robert told himself, to think about Emma when he was away from Paris. Time to feel the pain he must now hold at bay. Time to relive each precious moment they had spent together. "You won't be able to tell her, if you don't know where I am."

He turned to go, then looked back at Adam and Caroline. "In a day or so, it will sink in with Emma that she's killed a man. She'll need friends."

"She'll need you," Caroline said.

Robert shook his head. "I'm the last person Emma needs now."

* * *

Henriette Colbert sat on a delicate chair upholstered in ivory satin. Her face was skillfully rouged, her hair carefully dressed beneath a hat trimmed with pale gray feathers. But Emma suspected that the news of Bram's death had affected Henriette as much as it had Jenny, now sleeping upstairs after a dose of laudanum.

The Blair men were gathered with Emma in the main salon of the Martins' house: Angus and Neil, who had returned home in the midst of the confusion, Will and Jamie. Angus's ruddy face was white with shock. Neil's eyes were wide with confusion. Jamie still wore an expression of belligerence. Will's face was a set mask. Bram had been dead less than three hours.

"Thank you for writing to me, Madame Blair," Henriette said. "It is a greater courtesy than most women could expect from their lover's family."

Angus, who had been staring at his hands, looked up and fixed Henriette with a hard gaze. "You were Martin's mistress?"

Henriette returned his stare with composure, though her mouth trembled slightly. "I was more than his mistress, Sir Angus. You know that your son-in-law gathered information for the British. Much of that information came from me."

"But you worked for the French government as well, didn't you? You and Bram and Georges Demaire." Emma was determined to wring a confession from Henriette.

Jamie sprang to his feet. "That's a filthy accusation."

"But it is true, Major Blair," Henriette said.

"You expect us to believe—"

"Be quiet." Will pulled Jamie back into his chair.

"Bram was a Royalist at heart," Henriette continued, "but his first loyalty was to his name. Whoever ruled France, he wanted his title and estates restored to him."

She glanced at each of the Blairs in turn. "Surely you can understand such feelings."

"Is that how Bram justified murder?" Emma said. "In the name of family feeling?"

Henriette folded her hands together. The dove-colored fabric of her gloves was pulled tight against her knuckles. "Demaire was a fool. He drank too much and let something slip to Philippe. Philippe began to suspect Demaire and Bram were working for the Bonapartists."

"So they arranged an accident for him."

"It's a brutal game," Henriette said. "Ask your friend Colonel Lescaut."

"Robert would never kill an innocent person," Emma said with absolute conviction.

"Innocent?" Henriette shook her head. "Philippe was a spy himself. He was prepared to betray Bram to the British."

"And Lucie?"

Henriette's color faded beneath the layer of rouge. "Philippe must have said something to Lucie. I was sure she suspected his death wasn't an accident, but she wouldn't talk to me about it. She sent word to Bram and arranged to meet him at Ostend."

"Where she confronted him with her suspicions and he killed her." Emma held Henriette's gaze with her own.

"I never asked him what happened that night," Henriette said in a low voice.

"But you knew."

Henriette did not flinch from Emma's stare. "I knew. I loved him," she said as if it were explanation enough.

Angus had listened to Henriette's recital in brooding silence. Now he stared at her again. "You expect us to take your word for all of this, madam? Your word against the honor of my daughter's husband?"

Emma turned to Angus. "I heard him admit it, Uncle. He had a gun. He was going to kill Colonel Lescaut."

"You'd believe anything to defend Lescaut," Jamie said. "You're fair bewitched by the fellow."

"But you can't claim I am," Will said before Emma could protest. "And I heard it too."

Angus looked at his son, for once rendered helpless by conflicting loyalties.

Neil rubbed his eyes. "Bram always was damned secretive. Of course Lescaut's French," he added, as though that cast doubt on anything Robert did.

"Oh, for God's sake, Neil," Will said. "He saved my life."

Angus seemed struck by this remark. He looked at Henriette. "Say this *is* true. Why admit it to us now?"

Henriette gave a trace of a smile. "Perhaps it is foolish. But Bram no longer needs my protection. And I have my own sins to expiate. Robert has suffered enough." She unclasped her reticule and drew out a sealed paper. "I can at least prove that Robert had nothing to do with Philippe's death. This is a letter signed by Bram denouncing Demaire as the man responsible for Philippe's murder."

Jamie regarded the paper as though it might bite. "Why would Bram write that down? You claim he and Demaire were friends."

"I said they worked together, Major Blair, not that they were friends. Neither of them trusted the other. This was Bram's insurance in case Demaire ever tried to blame him for Philippe's death."

Angus took the paper from her, slit it open, and stared down at it.

"Bram was clever," Emma said. "But none of us knew him. We're going to have to accept that."

Her uncle looked up from the paper and met her gaze. There was a moment of silence, heavy with the treachery of the past and the pain of the future. Then, with a shuddering sigh, Angus nodded.

* * *

"Henriette wrote down everything she told me and signed it." Emma handed the papers to Adam along with Bram's denunciation of Demaire. "Will it be enough to clear Robert?"

Adam glanced through the papers. "It should. Of complicity in Philippe's murder. Robert is still cursed with having fought on the losing side."

"That's why I didn't take the papers to the French authorities. I was afraid someone who had little liking for Robert might arrange for them to disappear."

"You were right to be cautious. I'll see the papers go through safe channels." Adam set them down on his desk and looked at her, his brows drawing together. "How much sleep have you had since yesterday?"

"I can't remember." The clock above the mantel showed half past ten. Less than twenty-four hours since a pistol shot had shattered her world. Morning sun spilled through the windows, lightening the dark paneling in Adam's study. But it would take more than sunlight to dispel the cloud that had been thrown over the Blair family.

Caroline, who was in the room with them, put her arm around Emma and drew her to the sofa. "It's like Brussels during the battle. One does what one can from minute to minute and scarcely thinks beyond it."

Emma sank into the soft leather of the sofa. She suddenly felt as if her limbs would no longer support her. "The doctor gave Jenny laudanum, but she was still restless. I was up with her half the night. Then there were the authorities to deal with. And the children. Jenny's and—Bram's. They're too young to understand what's happened, but they know something is amiss. Jenny's in no state to comfort them, and their nurse is scarcely more than a child herself."

Caroline squeezed Emma's hand. "I can't imagine anything worse than what your cousin must be going through."

Emma thought of Jenny's ravaged, hollow-eyed face. In the face of tragedy, she had become a girl again, turning to Emma as she once would have turned to her mother. The least Emma could do was care for her cousin in her grief over the man with whom Emma had betrayed her. "She'll have to face the truth about Bram eventually. In time it may make his death easier to bear. But it would be too much for her now."

Adam pushed aside the papers and perched on the edge of his desk. "The rest of your family have accepted the truth?"

"Angus has. It's been a horrible blow for him. He thought of Bram like a son and relied on him a great deal. Neil's taken it the best. He was always jealous of Bram. Even Jamie's starting to come around."

"Have you told Kirsty?" Caroline asked.

"No, but I'll have to soon." Emma gave a ghost of a smile. "I can never manage to keep secrets from her." She thought of her return to the Rue de Luxembourg early this morning. "Sherry got home safely. He says the gaolers may not have believed his claim that Robert knocked him out, but they didn't call him a liar to his face."

"Thank goodness," Caroline said. "Have you been questioned about leaving the prison with Robert?"

"Two *gens d'armes* came by the house this morning." With everything else that had happened, the incident seemed almost trivial. "I told them Robert forced me to go with him at knifepoint. I don't know that they believed me any more than they did Sherry, but they didn't accuse me of lying either. Sherry made a great fuss about being a viscount—it's the first time I've ever heard him do it—

and he made sure they knew I was a British officer's sister."

Caroline glanced at her husband, then looked at Emma. "Andy and Jack should be back by tomorrow night."

Emma's heartbeat quickened. "Do you know where Robert is going?"

Caroline shook her head. "Andy and Jack are only taking him part of the way. He wouldn't tell us his destination."

"He wouldn't want you to be forced to lie for him." Emma swallowed her disappointment.

"That's part of it. But I think he was also suffering a rare moment of cowardice."

"He has every reason to be cautious. His name hasn't been cleared yet."

"Oh, it would take more than the threat of prison to frighten Robert. He's afraid of seeing you."

The air in the room suddenly seemed close and still. Emma drew an uneven breath.

"Robert knows what he's done to your family," Adam said. "He thinks it will be easier for you not to see him at present."

The anguishing pull of divided loyalties tightened Emma's throat and tore at her chest. "It's not that I don't want to see him," she said, pain welling to the surface.

"But he's dealt your family a blow, however justified, and they won't easily forget it," Adam said.

Emma pressed her fist against her mouth. Adam had put it exactly right. Her family were beginning to accept what Bram had been. But though none of them would put it into words, she knew that her uncle and brother and cousins secretly wished they had never learned the truth. And they had learned the truth because of Robert.

"I know how close you and Bram were," Caroline said. Emma looked at her friend through eyes that were suddenly blurred. Caroline was the first person to realize what Bram's death meant to her. But even Caroline couldn't know how deep the hurt went. Emma shivered. She felt unclean. She had let Bram touch her. She had let him inside her. The man who had hacked her cousin to death. She had been so afraid that Robert would hurt her family, but it was Bram who had killed a Blair.

Adam was watching her as though looking for signs of injury. "In all my years on the Peninsula, I never killed a man," he said. "But I doubt it's an easy experience, however justified the death."

"I can't claim to have been clever or brave enough to have killed Bram. The gun went off." And yet she could still feel the impact of the shot, still see the look in his eyes as he staggered back, still hear his final words. They had had the ring of truth. In his own way, Bram had actually cared for her. Somehow, that made his betrayal even worse.

Emma tugged her handkerchief from her sleeve and blew her nose. If she let herself think about Bram or Robert or anything but the needs of the moment, she would never be able to do what was required of her in the next weeks. "I have to go back to Scotland. Jenny wants to go home, and she's in no state to care for herself or the children. We know the truth about Lucie. Arabel's settled, and in any case Charlie hopes to sell out and bring her back to Scotland soon. There's nothing to keep me here."

"Including Robert?" Caroline asked.

Emma clutched the handkerchief. "He would have spared Bram for me. I'll never forget that. But there was no clean way out of this for any of us. Robert understood that." She turned to Adam. "When you hear that he's all right, let me know."

"Of course."

Emma realized she had forgotten the part Adam had

played in Robert's escape. "You won't get into trouble over this, will you? For helping him, I mean."

"I'll manage." Adam smiled. "The Foreign Secretary owes me a favor."

"I'll come see you again before we leave," Emma said. "Kirsty will want to say good-bye to Emily."

Adam nodded, but Caroline was frowning. "This is wrong, Emma. You love each other."

Wrong? So much between her and Robert had been wrong from the very first. That their feelings for each other had survived at all was a miracle. But Robert had never said he loved her. And even if he had— Emma thought back to those last minutes before Bram's death. If she felt tainted by her liaison with Bram, how would Robert feel, knowing she had given her body to the man who had killed his wife. "I'm not sure love is enough," she told Caroline.

"Not enough?" Caroline's eyes went wide with shock. "Don't be a fool, Em. It's the people we care about that matter in the end. How do you think we've managed to stay friends with Robert all these years? If you can't keep faith with those close to you, then other loyalties are meaningless."

Emma twisted the handkerchief around her fingers. Caroline made it sound so easy. But Emma had her loyalty to Jenny and Angus, and Robert his to Lucie.

In the silence, Caroline turned to her husband. "Say something, Adam."

"It's not our place to interfere, Caro. We wouldn't have thanked Robert for trying to arrange our lives."

Caroline looked back at Emma. "I know you have to go to Scotland now. But in the future—"

Emma felt a bleak chill. "I can't afford to think about the future. I only know my family need me now."

* * *

"We aren't going to see them again after today, are we?" Kirsty said as they approached the Lescaut house.

"You'll see David." Emma was determined that David not be denied his place in the Blair family. "But perhaps not for a while."

Kirsty nodded, her face solemn. Emma gave her a quick hug. She had been hugging Kirsty a lot in the past few days. It was the only reassurance she could offer.

Emma had written the Lescauts that they would call this afternoon. David pulled open the door in answer to her ring, an eager look on his face, and led them up to the sitting room where Anne Lescaut was waiting.

"We came to say good-bye," Emma said when they were seated. "We're leaving for Scotland tomorrow."

"When will you come back?" David asked.

"I don't know." Emma found it difficult to think beyond the next few weeks. "But we hope you can visit us in Scotland again. Blair House should have been your mother's home. You'll always be welcome there."

"Perhaps my father can bring me," David said.

Emma swallowed, her throat tight. "Perhaps."

"Uncle Paul says my father may be able to come home soon. He says you found papers that prove he's innocent and gave them to Adam." David traced a flower in the well-worn carpet with the toe of his shoe. "He says it was Monsieur Martin who killed my mother."

"Yes." Emma met Anne's gaze, feeling the anguish of uncertainty. She was not sure how to handle the situation.

"It was because Uncle Bram was a spy," Kirsty said. "For both the British and the French. He didn't want anyone to know about it."

"And my mother found out." David looked at Emma. "She was a spy too. For the British."

Dear God, what a burden they had put on David's shoulders. Both she and Robert had wanted to learn the truth for the boy's sake. Perhaps it would have been better if he had never known. "Your mother was very brave," she told him.

David's brows drew together as though he were still trying to puzzle it out. "She lied to my father. But then my father and I lied to all of you when we came to Blair House. Adam came to see me yesterday. He said he had to tell a lot of lies, too, when he was in the Peninsula. I'm glad I know what my mother's secrets were."

Emma released her breath. So many things had been broken the night Bram died, but David at least would mend.

They stayed half an hour longer, talking about more cheerful matters. Emma had the satisfaction of seeing both David's and Kirsty's faces lighten. Anne said little, but when Emma and Kirsty rose to leave, she took Emma's hand and clasped it tightly. "I'm glad to have met you, my dear. I hope I will see you again."

Emma studied Anne's face, wondering if her words were mere politeness or if she hoped that they might be more closely related in the future. But Anne's expression was as difficult to read as her son's.

There was the sound of quick footsteps on the stairs and Paul came into the room. "Good, I'm not too late. I wanted to say good-bye."

Kirsty ran over to him and gave him a hug. Paul bent to speak to her, then walked toward Emma. "Durward's told me all you've done for Robert. We owe you our thanks."

"Robert suffered a great deal at the hands of my family."

"At the hands of one member of your family." Paul's gaze flickered toward Kirsty and David, who had retreated to the windowseat to snatch a few more minutes of conversation. "Is that the only reason you helped Robert?" he asked softly.

Emma met Paul's gaze. She knew he had mistrusted her from the first. She sensed that the mistrust had to do with Robert's feelings for her. But there was no censure or harshness in his expression now. "No," she said, aware of a tremor in her voice. "I did what I did for Robert because I care for him."

Paul smiled, not the cynical twist of his mouth to which she was accustomed, but a sweet smile that reminded her painfully of his cousin. "Robert told me you were incapable of duplicity," he said. "I told him he was a fool. I think perhaps I was wrong."

Emma knew a moment of bittersweet joy. Robert had told his cousin that he had faith in her. But not that he loved her. Before she broke down completely, Emma called Kirsty to her side and left the Lescaut house for the last time before her return to Scotland.

Robert reined in Liberty on the crest of the hill. The trees
that had been leafless six months ago were now thick
with foliage, the oak still green, the beech just beginning
to show a hint of golden red. The house and courtyard
were almost hidden from view behind the leafy curtain.
The hills beyond were free of snow, and if the air was not
warm, it did not have the brisk chill of March.

David pulled up his own horse. "Do the Blairs still
blame you for Monsieur Martin's death?"

Robert turned from the view below to look at his son.
This was the first time David had referred to Bram Martin since they had left France. "It's not a question of
blame." He ran his fingers through Liberty's mane.
"Sometimes it's hard to separate the events of the past
from the people who were caught up in them. Sometimes
in order to forget the past you want to forget the people
as well."

"You think the Blairs want to forget about us?"

"Not about you."

David frowned. "I don't see how Emma could forget
about you. Could you forget about her?"

Memories at once sweet and painful assaulted him. The joy and laughter that lit her face. The furrow between her brows when she was puzzling something out. The way her eyes met his own in shared understanding. Forget her? It would be easier to forget to breathe. "No," he told David. Then, because he knew he could not bear to wait another moment, he gathered up the reins and touched his heels to his horse.

The longing he had tried to hold in check for the past six weeks broke free of restraint. The image of her face, the scent of her skin, the taste of her mouth were as vivid as if he had seen her yesterday. Yet he ached in mind and body as though they had been parted for years.

But he could not be sure of his welcome. Yesterday he had sought out Andy at the University of Edinburgh. Andy had greeted him with enthusiasm and encouraged him to go to Blair House. But it was clear that the last weeks had been as difficult for the Blairs as Robert had feared. "The news about Bram broke Uncle Angus," Andy said. "Everything's fallen on Emma. As usual."

Robert had forgotten how deceptively close the house seemed from the crest of the hill. Even at a gallop, their descent took a maddeningly long time. They were nearly upon the house before they cleared the trees and got their first good view of the courtyard. It was empty save for a girl with unmistakable auburn hair who was throwing a stick for a small brown-and-white puppy.

Kirsty shrieked and ran to meet them. "You came back."

"Yes." David looked down at her, his face serious.

The puppy nuzzled Kirsty's skirt. "This is Pauline," Kirsty said. "Mama gave her to me for my very own. She sleeps in my room." She picked up the puppy, who licked her face. "Come inside. Mama will want to see you."

They took the horses to the stable, where the groom addressed Robert as Captain Melton. For a moment Robert could almost believe nothing had changed. But he had not yet faced any of the adult Blairs.

Kirsty led them through the side door through which Robert had first entered Blair House. The day he had met Emma. It was difficult to believe it had been little more than six months ago. He could hear voices from the great hall. The words were indistinguishable, but he would have known Emma's voice anywhere. His heart hammered against his ribs. Every nerve in his body felt exposed.

Down the corridor a few more paces, up the short flight of steps to the hall, and he saw her. She was standing near the base of the stairs, holding Jenny Martin's two-year-old son in her arms, surrounded by two housemaids who were in the midst of an argument, and the cook, who looked pained.

"Mama!" Kirsty ran forward, the puppy frisking beside her. "Look who's here."

Emma turned toward her daughter. She was wearing a pale gray dress and some of her hair had escaped its pins. In the dimly lit hall, her eyes were dark and smoky, but Robert could see the utter shock in their depths. He wanted to take her in his arms and kiss her with the hunger raging through him, but the children and the cook and the maids stood quite literally between them.

"Colonel Lescaut. David." Emma smiled, not at Robert but at his son. "I'm so glad to see you again."

"Aunty Emma." The little boy in Emma's arms tugged at her sleeve.

"Yes, darling, we'll get your knee bandaged in a minute. Mrs. Cameron, we'll have to talk about dinner later. Jean, Morag, it doesn't matter who broke the vase. It was a hideous thing anyway."

Mrs. Cameron started for the back of the hall. The maids exchanged spiteful looks and followed. Emma drew a breath and turned back to Robert and David, but

Shores of Desire

before she could speak there was a horrified cry from the staircase. *"Emma."*

Robert looked up to see Jenny Martin standing on the half landing, one hand gripping the stair rail. She wore black, which emphasized her delicate appearance and the gold in her hair. Her face had gone pale, but her eyes were bright with fury.

"Mrs. Martin." Robert walked toward the stairs. "I know nothing I can say will make up for your husband's death."

Jenny would not return his gaze. "Who let him into the house?"

"I did, Aunt Jenny." Kirsty spoke in a firm voice that reminded Robert of Emma. "He and David are my cousins."

"Colonel Lescaut has brought David to see us." Emma moved toward the stairs as though to cut off the growing conflict.

"And you let him walk right into the house? The man who—" Jenny's voice broke off in a sob.

David shrank closer to Robert. The puppy barked. The child in Emma's arms started to whimper. The heavy front door swung open. "God's teeth," Angus exclaimed. "Lescaut."

"Robert. David. How splendid." Arabel ran down the hall and hugged them both at once. Her pregnancy was now visible, but it did not seem to have diminished her energy.

"Father—" Jenny said on a note of appeal.

"Now, now, lass, no time for scenes."

With a sharp, horrified breath, Jenny turned and ran up the stairs.

"I'm sorry." Emma's face showed the strain of the last weeks. "Jenny doesn't—"

"Jenny can't face the truth, so she insists on finding someone to blame," Arabel said. "It's no sense trying to reason with her." She looked from Robert to David. "You'll stay to dinner, won't you? Charlie's gone to Lauder Hall, but he'll be back by then and I know he'll want to see you."

Emma met Robert's gaze for a moment that brought all his longings and fears welling to the surface. "Please do," she said. "I—"

The little boy let out another wail. Emma stroked the child's hair. "I have to get him upstairs. Uncle Angus—"

"Aye, you see to the wean. I'll take care of the visitors." Angus put a hand on David's head. "I'm glad you're here, Lescaut. There are things we should discuss. Come into the library and drink a dram with me."

Emma was gone up the stairs, out of Robert's reach. Robert left David with Kirsty and Arabel, who promised to find the children something to eat, and followed Angus down the hall to the library.

Angus waved Robert to a high-backed chair upholstered in red velvet and went to a side table to pour out two large glasses of whisky. In the light from the windows, Robert could see the scars of the past weeks on Angus's face. But he moved with a sense of purpose. Robert thought he was beginning to mend.

"It's been difficult." Angus gave one of the glasses to Robert and sank into a chair opposite him. "For Emma especially. We've all been leaning on her. Myself included." He took a swallow of whisky as though uncomfortable with this last admission. "Bram was like a son to me."

"I know," Robert said. "I'm sorry."

"Can't blame ye for showing us what he really was." Angus stared into his glass. "When I think— But there's no sense dwelling on it, is there?" He took another drink of whisky and set the glass down on the table next to him with an air of finality. "I said I'd do right by David and I intend to."

"I didn't come here for your money, sir."

"Don't turn proud on me, lad. And don't pretend David couldn't do with the money."

Robert bit back a protest. "I'm through with pretending." He smiled and settled back in his chair.

"That's more like it." Angus gave a nod of approval. "No sense in quibbling. Whatever would have gone to Thomas in his own right should be David's." He coughed. "It'll take a wee bit of time to sort it out, I'm afraid. We've had to take on a new lawyer. How long do you plan to stay in Scotland?"

As long as Emma wants me to if she says yes? As long as I can bear it if she says no? Robert sipped the whisky. It wasn't brandy, but he had come to like it almost as well. There were a number of things he had come to like in Scotland. And some he had come to love. "I may settle in Edinburgh for a time." He watched Angus closely to see what his reaction would be. "The climate in France isn't very comfortable for me just now."

"I see." A smile broke across Angus's weathered face. "Have some more whisky, Lescaut. We'll make a Scotsman of ye yet."

Emma emerged from the nursery, having bandaged her nephew's scraped knee, kissed it better, and left him in the care of his nurse. Arabel was waiting for her on the bench near the stair head.

"You're a fool, Em," Arabel said, springing to her feet.

"Quite possibly. But why now in particular?"

"You're going to tell Robert no."

Hope and uncertainty drove the breath from Emma's lungs. When she left Paris, she had refused to let herself think of the future. It was the only way she could manage to survive from day to day. But Robert could not be banished from her thoughts. Even when her every waking moment was occupied, at night, in the solace of her bed-chamber, she dreamt of the day she might see him again. Such thoughts were the sweetest form of torture. As the days went by, her dreams grew more and more vivid. She had even imagined him coming to Blair House. She had not dared hope it would happen so soon.

But the reality had been different from her fantasies. She had not pictured herself wearing her old gray dress, holding a crying child, surrounded by quarreling servants and angry family. Nor had she expected the sickening uncertainty that followed the burst of joy she felt when she first saw Robert standing in the hall.

"He hasn't asked me anything," she told Arabel.

"He's going to."

Arabel sounded so certain. Emma did not share her cousin's confidence. In the past months, she had learned that not only Robert but nearly everyone in her family harbored secrets. Arabel slipped off to meet Charlie. Neil covered up Allan's infidelity. Angus supported Lucie for twenty years. Even artless Jenny concealed Bram's work in France. And Bram himself—

Emma shivered. She was no longer sure she could judge how anyone felt, let alone Robert. Fear cut through her like a blast of wind from the north. "Then I'll think about it when—if—he does."

"There hasn't been a day these past weeks when you *haven't* thought about it."

"All right, I've thought about it." Emma drew back. She had come to fear hope, for hope could burn so hot it scalded.

"Then when Robert asks you to marry him, you'll say yes?"

Emma's body felt tight and strained, as if she were being pulled in a thousand different directions at once. She thought of her nephew's scraped knee and the maids' quarrel and the dozens of other domestic crises that sprang up every day. "It's not that easy, Bel. If I left now—"

"If you left now, Jenny might grow up. It's the best thing that could happen to her."

Emma stared at Arabel. "But Jenny's never—"

"Jenny's never had to be responsible for anything. It's high time she was."

Emma shook her head. Arabel had always been quick to criticize her elder sister. "Jenny's in no state—"

"No, she isn't. And she'll go on moping about as long as you're here to run the house and look after her children. She doesn't need to be cosseted. She needs something to do."

"But—" Emma broke off, thinking of her own fevered need for activity when Allan died. She had always tried to be sure Kirsty was given plenty of responsibility. In her guilt, had she tried too hard to shield her cousin from the realities of life?

Emma remembered Jenny's burst of fury at Robert. Though she had been told the truth of Bram's death, Jenny continued to blame Robert. It would take more than responsibility to put an end to such anger. Emma was not even sure how Angus felt about Robert. She thought back to her painful visit to Jenny and Bram's elder sons at school to tell them of their father's death. It would be harder for the boys when they grew older and learned the full truth about Bram. The shadow of the events in Paris would hang over the Blair family for years to come. "It's not just the household," she said. "There's—"

"Em, listen." Arabel seized her hands and held them in a firm grasp. "I think Da likes Robert better than you realize. But even if he doesn't, you can't let it stand in your way. Do you think I don't know how difficult it is? I thought if I married Charlie, Da might not speak to me for years. Perhaps not ever."

"I know, Bel. But it's not—"

"It's exactly the same. That night in Paris when you told me Da didn't want to see me, I wasn't sure I could bear it. But I realized that if I gave up Charlie for my family, in the end I'd come to hate my family for it." Arabel glanced down at her swollen stomach, then looked back at Emma. "There must have been times you've thought that if it wasn't for Da and Jenny and her children, you could have stayed in Paris and waited for Robert."

More than thought it. Sometimes Emma wished passionately that she had only herself to think of. But she didn't. And yet Arabel had guessed the truth. In the past weeks Emma had felt flashes of anger, so strong they frightened her, at the responsibilities that kept her at Blair House.

"I'll go sit with Jenny's children," Arabel said. "Kirsty and David have gone to the stables. I think Robert's still in the library with Da." She released Emma's hands and gave her a hug. "You deserve to be happy, Em. Don't throw it away. That's what Mama would tell you if she were here."

Emma walked down the stairs to the first floor, dazed by possibilities. Arabel was right. Emma could almost hear Aunt Alice's voice telling her not to turn her back on happiness.

But even in the guise of Robert Melton, Robert had never said he loved her, let alone that he wanted to spend the rest of his life with her. Emma paused, her fingers trailing over the smooth wood of the stair rail. Was that why she was reluctant to imagine a future with Robert? It was easier to remind herself of the responsibilities that bound her to Blair House than to face the prospect that, even if she was free to go to him, Robert might not want her. Not now that he knew of her intimacy with the man who had killed his wife.

But if he did want her— There was only one way to be sure. She had to speak with Robert alone.

When she reached the first floor, Emma went into her room and cast a quick, despairing glance in the mirror. Her hair was falling down, her dress was creased, and there were black smudges under her eyes. She could do nothing about the smudges, but she pinned up her loose hair, ran a brush over the top, and wrapped a moss-green silk shawl that she had bought in Paris about her shoulders. Heart beating quickly, she walked down the stairs and opened the library door.

Angus and Robert were sitting opposite each other in chairs by the windows. Perhaps it was the mellow quality of the September sunlight, but there was something very tranquil about the scene. A stranger might have taken the two men for friends. For the first time, Emma let herself hope that one day they would be.

"I've come to see if Colonel Lescaut would like to go for a walk." She smiled at Angus. "You've had him to yourself long enough, Uncle."

"True enough," Angus said, "and we've settled what we need to."

Robert got to his feet, but the light was at his back and she could not read his expression.

They left the house without speaking. Fear squeezed Emma's chest and stripped her throat raw. Her body trembled with the longing to touch him, but he had not even offered her his arm.

Outside, the air was clear and fresh, filled with the scent of the pines that lined the avenue leading away from the house. Emma adjusted the folds of her shawl. Her fingers felt numb and awkward. "Are you staying in Edinburgh?" She wanted to say, *How long are you staying?* but she was afraid that would be too blatant a plea.

"We've taken lodgings in Old Fishmarket Close. My mother's with us."

"You should have brought her with you today." Emma looked up at him and felt a shock of heat as their eyes met.

"She'd like to see you, I know." Robert's voice was so gentle it made her shiver. "But I wasn't sure—"

"You thought we might refuse you the house?"

He smiled, though his eyes remained serious. "Hardly that. Your sense of honor is too great. But I wasn't sure you wanted to be reminded of the past." His gaze moved over her face as though seeking signs of injury. "I know how much Martin meant to you."

Emma swallowed, a sharp, bitter taste in her throat. "I was infatuated with him once. I—desired him. Then I thought we were friends. Now I can't believe I ever let him touch me."

Robert stopped and looked down at her. "You didn't really know him. Any more than you knew me."

They were only a few inches apart. She could see herself reflected in his eyes, a clear blue in the sunlight. Whatever deceptions he had practiced, she knew he could never use people as Bram had done. "I didn't know your name, but I think I always knew you."

For a moment she thought Robert meant to kiss her. She could almost feel his lips against her own. Instead he turned and started walking again. The only sound was the pine needles crunching beneath their feet.

"Adam and Caroline send their love," Robert said. "So does Emily. They hope to be able to visit me when Adam gets leave."

Emma nodded. Then she looked at him in puzzlement. "Visit you where?"

"In Edinburgh." Robert's eyes were on the path ahead. "I'm going to stay here for a time. I'm thinking of starting a newspaper."

Emma felt the world tilt crazily. Would Robert ever be

predictable? If he planned to stay in Edinburgh— Hope flared within her, singeing her with its heat.

"I'm not exactly welcome in France just now," Robert went on. "I have to earn my keep. It won't be a large newspaper, but I find that I have a good deal to say. Paul promises to send me news from home. I'll do the same for him."

They had reached the end of the avenue and moved onto the mossy stone bridge over which they had ridden the day Robert first came to Blair House. Blair land stretched before them, splashed with purple heather and golden gorse and bramble hedges thick with berries. "Then," Emma said as carefully as if she were moving through a bank of fog, "that's why you've come to Scotland."

Robert grasped her by the shoulders and turned her to face him so suddenly that she nearly lost her balance. "I came to Scotland to tell you that I love you."

The purple and gold and green of the hills blurred before her eyes. She was aware of nothing but Robert. The blood pounded in her head. The intensity in his face made her dizzy. "I loved you from the first," she whispered. "I loved you all the time." A choking sound between laughter and tears rose in her throat. "Even when I hated you."

Robert released his breath as though he had been holding it for an eternity. His arms closed tight around her. She slid her fingers into his hair and pulled his head down to her own. His mouth tasted of hot longing and aching need and the unspoken promise of the future. For the first time, she went into his arms knowing she would never have to leave.

At last he drew back to look at her. The corner of his mouth lifted in a smile. He touched her face. "Do you think you could bring yourself to live in Edinburgh?"

A joyous laugh burst from her lips. "I think I could live anywhere with you. But Edinburgh will do."

Robert pulled her to him again. The gulf between them had been crossed. Desperation and longing were replaced by frank, earthy lust. She wrapped her arms more tightly around him and found herself wondering if there were still blankets in the abandoned cottage.

But there was something else they had to do. When she could speak again, Emma said, "We should tell the children."

Though his eyes held the same desire that flared within her, Robert nodded.

As they walked back toward the house, Emma turned her face into Robert's shoulder. "I think you and David should stay the night."

He laughed, a warm sound that enveloped her as closely as the arm he had wrapped around her shoulders. "Are you sure that's wise?"

"I'm tired of being wise." She raised her head to look at him. "Would you deny me then?"

He pressed a kiss against her cheek. "I could deny you nothing, madam."

They found Kirsty and David in the stable, feeding carrots to Liberty, the white mare who had survived the battle of Waterloo and traveled all the way to Scotland. The children turned around at their parents' entrance. Pauline, in the straw beside them, thunked her tail on the floor. Liberty pricked up her ears.

Emma realized she was still standing within the circle of Robert's arm. It seemed the most natural thing in the world.

Kirsty and David exchanged glances. "Oh, good," Kirsty said, "you've finally settled it. David's told me all about the house in Old Fishmarket Close. May I have the room with the rose wallpaper?"

HISTORICAL NOTE

Much of the description of Waterloo and Brussels during the battle and Paris afterward comes from contemporary accounts, in particular *The Journal of the Waterloo Campaign* by General Cavailié Mercer (Edinburgh and London: Blackwood, 1870, reprinted by Greenhill Books and Presidio Press, 1985, 1989) and *The Battle of Waterloo* (Manchester: J. Gleave, 1816). *A Sketch of the Life of Georgiana, Lady de Ros* (born Georgiana Lennox) by Mrs. J. R. Swinton (London: John Murray, 1893) contains Georgiana's account of her mother's ball on June 15. Georgiana reports the words Wellington spoke to her when he entered the ballroom.

With the exception of the major characters, the military and political figures mentioned in the book are real people. Charles de La Bédoyère is said to have attended the Duchess of Richmond's ball disguised as a Belgian officer and shaken Wellington's hand. Both La Bédoyère and Marshal Ney were executed by the French in the period after Waterloo known as the White Terror, but General Lavalette escaped from prison with the help of his wife. Robert's escape is loosely modeled on Lavalette's.

Readers of *Shadows of the Heart* may wonder why in that book Emma does not mention that she saw Sophie

Rutledge at the Duchess of Richmond's ball. It is possible that Emma forgot her brief glimpse of Sophie, but I suspect Emma felt it was tactful not to bring up the matter, since Georgiana's words about Sophie were not quite kind.